THE DESOLATIONS OF DEVIL'S ACRE

THE DESOLATIONS OF DEVIL'S ACRE

THE SIXTH NOVEL OF

MISS PEREGRINE'S

PECULIAR CHILDREN

BY RANSOM RIGGS

DUTTON BOOKS

DUTTON BOOKS
An imprint of Penguin Random House LLC, New York

First published in the United States of America by Dutton Books,
an imprint of Penguin Random House LLC, 2021

Copyright © 2021 by Ransom Riggs

Ministry of Peculiar Affairs stamp on pages 317, 323, 356, and case cover © 2018 by
    Chad Michael Studio
Photo of man using computer on page 30 © 2021 by Steve Ciarcia
Bear and antelope heads on pages 268 and 269 © EVGENY LASHCHENOV / 123RF.com
Ram heads on pages 268 and 269 © acceptphoto / 123RF.com
Poster art on page 394 © Natalia Chernyshova / 123RF.com

Dutton is a registered trademark of Penguin Random House LLC.

Visit us online at penguinrandomhouse.com.

Library of Congress Cataloging-in-Publication Data is available.

Printed in the United States of America
ISBN 9780735231535

10 9 8 7 6 5 4 3 2 1

Edited by Julie Strauss-Gabel
Design by Anna Booth
Text set in Sabon LT Pro

For Jodi Reamer, slayer of beasts.

Sometimes an old photograph, an old friend,
an old letter will remind you that you are not who you once were,
for the person who dwelt among them, valued this, chose that,
wrote thus, no longer exists. Without noticing it you have traversed
a great distance; the strange has become familiar and the familiar
if not strange at least awkward or uncomfortable.

—Rebecca Solnit
"The Blue of Distance"
A Field Guide to Getting Lost

CHAPTER ONE

*F*or a long time there is only darkness and the sound of distant thunder and the hazy sensation of falling. Beyond that I have no self, no name. No memory. I am aware, dimly, that I used to have these things, but now they are gone and I am nearly nothing. A single photon of failing light circling a hungry void.

It won't be long now.

I've lost my soul, I'm afraid, but I can't remember how. All I can recall are slow, churning cracks of thunder, and within them the syllables of my name, whatever it used to be, drawn out until unrecognizable. That and the dark are all there is, for a long time, until another sound joins the thunder: wind. Then rain, too. There is wind, and thunder, and rain, and falling.

Something is coming into being, one sensation at a time. I am rising from the trench, escaping the void. My single photon becomes a flashing cluster.

I feel something rough against my face. I hear the creaking of ropes. The flap of something caught in the wind. Perhaps I am on a boat. Trapped in the lightless belly of some storm-tossed ship.

One eye blinks open. Forms thrash dimly above me. A row of swinging pendulums. Overwound clocks all out of sync, groaning, gears about to break.

I blink and the pendulums become bodies dropped from a gallows, kicking and twisting.

I find I can turn my head. Blurred shapes begin to resolve. Rough green fabric against my face. Above me, the tick-tocking bodies have become a row of storm-blown plants swinging from the rafters in creaky wicker baskets. Behind them, a wall of insect screens shudders and flaps.

I am lying on a porch. On the rough green floor of a porch.

I know this porch

I know this floor

Farther away, a rain-whipped lawn terminates at a dark wall of genuflecting palms.

I know that lawn

I know those palms

How long have I been here? How many years?

time is playing tricks again

I try to move my body, but can only rotate my head. My eyes flick to a card table and two folding chairs. I'm suddenly certain that, if I could persuade my body to rise, I would find a pair of reading glasses on the table. A half-finished game of Monopoly. A mug of steaming, still-hot coffee.

Someone has just been here. Words have just been spoken. They hang in the air still, returning to me in echoes.

"What *kind* of bird?"

A boy's voice. *My* voice.

"A big hawk who smoked a pipe." This one gravelly, accented. An old man's voice.

"You must think I'm pretty dumb," the boy replies.

"I would never think that about you."

The boy again: "But why did the monsters want to hurt you?"

A scrape as the old man pushes back his chair and rises. He's going to get something he wants to show me, he says. Some pictures.

how long ago was that

a minute

an hour

I have to get up or he'll worry. He'll think I'm playing a trick on him, and he doesn't like tricks. Once, as a game, I hid from him in the woods, and when he couldn't find me he got so angry he turned red and yelled bad words. Later, he said it was because he was scared, but he wouldn't tell me what had scared him.

It is raining ferociously. This storm is an angry, living thing, and it's already torn a gash in the screen, which thrashes like a flag in a gale.

something is wrong with me

I push up onto my elbow, but that is all I can manage. I notice a strange black mark on the floor. A burned line that tracks around me, tracing the outline of my body.

I try to push myself up fully to sitting. Dark orbs swim in my vision.

Then a giant crash. Everything goes blinding white.

so bright   so close   so loud

It sounded like an explosion but it wasn't; it's lightning, the strike just outside, so near that the flash and the thunderclap are simultaneous.

And now I am sitting upright, heart hammering. I hold a trembling hand before my eyes.

The hand looks weird. It's too big. The fingers are too long. Black hairs sprout between the knuckles.

where is the boy   am I not the boy?   I don't like tricks

Tender red lines encircle the wrist.

handcuffs   latched to a porch rail   in a storm

I can see the tabletop and it's empty.

There is no coffee cup. There are no glasses.

he isn't coming back

But then, impossibly, he does. He is there, outside, at the edge of the woods. My grandfather. Walking in the tall grass, back bent against the wind, his yellow raincoat vivid against the dark palms and his hood pulled low to shield his eyes from the stinging rain.

what's he doing out there   why isn't he coming in

He stops. Peers down at something in the too-tall grass.

I raise my hand. Call his name.

His back straightens, and only then do I realize: He's all wrong. His frame too narrow. His walk too smooth for an old man with arthritic hips.

because it isn't him

He jogs toward me, toward the house, to the torn and flapping screen.

the storm didn't do that

what kind of monsters?

hunched and awful with rotting skin and black eyes and squirming

I am on my feet as he throws open the screen door and fills the threshold.

"Who are you?" he asks.

His voice is flat, tense. He pulls back the hood of his raincoat. He is middle-aged, his sharp chin accentuated by a trim red beard, eyes masked behind sunglasses.

It's such a foreign experience to be in the presence of another person and standing on two feet that I hardly register the strangeness of his wearing sunglasses in a rainstorm.

Automatically, I answer.

"Yakob," I say, and only after hearing it aloud does it sound wrong.

"I'm the realtor," he says, but I know it's a lie. "I came to board up the windows for the storm."

"You're a little late for that," I say.

He enters slowly, as if approaching a skittish animal. The screen door hisses closed. He glances at the burn mark on the floor, then returns his cold gaze to me.

"You're him," he says, fingers grazing the card table as he clomps toward me in heavy black boots. "Jacob Portman."

My name. My actual name. Something bubbles up from the trench, from the dark.

a horrible mouth formed in spiraling clouds, thundering my name

a girl, raven-haired and beautiful   next to me   screaming

"I believe you were acquainted with a friend of mine," the man says. There is venom in his smile. "He went by many names, but you knew him as Dr. Golan."

the horrible cloud-mouth

a woman writhing in the grass

The images surge into my mind with sudden blunt force. I shuffle backward until I hit a sliding glass door. The man is removing something from his pocket as he comes forward. A small black box with metal fangs.

"Turn around," he commands.

I am suddenly aware that there is a great deal at risk, and that I need to defend myself. So I make myself docile, raise my hands as if in surrender, and when he comes close I bring my fists down on his face.

He shouts as his glasses fly off. The eyes behind them are shining blank eggs burrowed into his skull, and they have murder in them. There's a loud snap as blue light arcs between the fangs in his black box.

He throws himself at me.

I feel a shock, a singe as he tasers me through my shirt, and I fly back against the glass door. Somehow it doesn't shatter.

He is on top of me. I hear the whine of the taser recycling. I try to fling him off, but I am still recharging, too, and still weak. Pain rockets through my shoulder, my head.

And then he jerks and lets out a scream and goes limp, and I feel something warm running down my neck.

I am bleeding. (Am I bleeding?)

The man grasps at something and falls away from me. The something has a bronze hilt and protrudes six inches from his neck.

And now there is a strange new darkness behind him, a living shadow, and out of it flashes a hand that picks up my grandfather's heavy ashtray and smashes the man in the head with it.

He groans and collapses. A girl steps out of the shadow.

The girl—the one from Before—long black hair tangled and wet with rain, long black coat smeared with earth, deep black eyes wide and fearful, searching my face and then sparking with recognition. And though all the pieces haven't surfaced yet, and though my mind is reeling, I know that what's happening is a miracle: that we are alive, and we are here, and not in the other place.

my God

such horrors I can hardly name them

The girl is on the floor with me now, kneeling, embracing me. My arms encircle her neck like a life preserver. Her body is so cold, and I can feel her trembling as we hold on to one another.

Without slackening she says my name. Repeats it again and again, and with each reprise the Now gains an ounce more weight, grows more solid.

"Jacob, Jacob. Can you remember me?"

The man on the floor groans. The aluminum bones of the porch screen groan, and the storm, the angry weather we seem to have brought with us from the other place, groans, too.

And I begin to remember.

"Noor," I say. "Noor. You're Noor."

◆ ◆ ◆

In a flash, it all came to me. We had survived. Had escaped V's collapsing loop. And now we were in Florida, on the green Astroturf of my grandfather's porch, in the present.

Shock. I think I was still in shock.

We huddled together on the floor, gripping one another as the storm raged, until the tremors racking our bodies began to subside.

The man in the yellow raincoat lay unmoving, save the diminishing rise and fall of his chest. Blood soaked the Astroturf around him in a sticky pool. The bronze handle of the weapon Noor had stabbed him with protruded from his neck.

"That was my grandfather's letter opener," I said. "And this was his house."

"Your grandfather." She pulled away, just far enough to look at me. "Who lived in Florida?"

I nodded. Thunder cracked, rattled the walls. Noor was looking around, shaking her head doubtfully. *This can't be real.* I knew just how she felt.

"How?" she said.

I gestured to the burned outline on the floor. "I woke up there. No idea how long I was out for. Or what day it is, even."

Noor rubbed her eyes. "My head's all fuzzy. Everything's out of order."

"What's the last thing you remember?"

She frowned, concentrating. "We went to my old apartment. And then we were driving . . ." She spoke slowly, as if piecing together a dream. "And we were in a loop . . . we found V's loop! And we were running from a storm. No, a tornado."

"Two tornadoes, wasn't it?"

"And then we found her! Didn't we? We found her!" Her hands grabbed mine and squeezed. "And then . . ."

Her hands went slack, her face blank. Her lips parted, but no words came. The horrors were returning, crashing over her.

Over me, too.

Murnau. Knife in hand, crouched above V in the grass. His arm raised in triumph as he ran toward the whirling maelstrom.

Heat flooded my chest, blocked my breathing for a moment. Noor buried her face between her knees and began to rock. "Oh my God," she moaned. "Oh God, oh God, oh God." I thought she might dissolve before my eyes, or burst into flame, or suck the light from the room.

But after a moment she jerked her head up. "Why aren't we dead?"

A shudder rattled through me, involuntary.

Maybe we are.

For all I knew, we'd been crushed by V's collapsing loop, just as Caul had intended. Noor herself seemed the only concrete evidence that what I was experiencing now was more than just some purgatorial memory hole, the last-gasp fireworks of a dying brain.

No—I chased away the thought—we were here, and we were alive.

"She got us out somehow," I said. "Got us here."

"Through some kind of emergency exit. An eject button." Noor was nodding and kneading her hands. "It's the only explanation."

To my grandfather's house—the home of her mentor, her boss. He trained her, worked side by side with her. It made enough sense. What made no sense was that there wasn't a loop here. So how had she done it?

"If she got us out," Noor said, "maybe she got herself out, too." There was hope in her voice, but it was manic, balanced on a knife's edge. "She could be here. And she could still be . . ."

She couldn't quite bring herself to say it. *Alive.*

"He took her heart," I said quietly.

"You can live without a heart. For a little while, anyway . . ." She waved her hand. The hand was shaking.

We had only just regained our grip on reality, and already she was losing it again.

"Come on, come on, we have to *look*," she was saying, already on her feet, words coming rapid-fire. "If there's any chance at all, then we have to—"

"Wait a second, we don't know what's—"

In there, I meant to say. *Waiting for us.*

But she had already run into the darkened house.

◆   ◆   ◆

I planted a hand against the wall and wobbled up to standing. Noor was fraying, and I couldn't let her out of my sight. She had used this wild hope that V might be alive to shore herself up, to shove away the despair that threatened to crush her. But I worried it would only be doubly crushing when she was inevitably disappointed. And I could not let Noor Pradesh break.

If Murnau's vile task had succeeded, if what I had seen materialize in that tornado was real—Caul's face in the whirling clouds, his voice splitting the air—if he was well and truly *back*, then the prophecy's most terrifying predictions had started coming true. Which meant that all peculiardom was about to be buried. God only knew what Caul was capable of now that he had consumed one of the most powerful jars from the Library of Souls, then been crushed in its collapse, and resurrected.

Born again.

I am become Death, destroyer of worlds.

However bad it was or would be, I knew one thing: The world needed Noor Pradesh. She was one of the seven. One of the peculiars whose coming was foretold, who could emancipate peculiarkind—from Caul?—who could *seal the door*—to what? Hell?—and as bizarre as it all sounded, it was no more bizarre than the parts of the Revelator's prophecy that had already come to pass. I was finished doubting it. Finished doubting my own eyes, too.

This was no dream nor the last reverie of a dying mind. I was even more certain of it as I tripped over the track of the sliding door into the living room. The house was just as my friends and I had left it the last time I'd been here, a few weeks ago: hastily neatened and mostly empty, the books my father hadn't thrown away placed back onto shelves, trash that had littered the floor stuffed into black plastic bags. The air was stale and suffocating.

Noor pinballed from corner to corner looking for V. She tore a dust sheet off the couch, then flung herself over the back to look behind it. I caught her at the window—started to say, "Noor, wait"—when a crack of thunder cut me off and made us both jump. We looked out through the rain-blurred glass. The yard was strewn with trash. The houses across the cul-de-sac were shuttered and dark. A dead neighborhood.

And still.

"That wight probably had friends," I said. "More could come any minute."

"Let them come." Her eyes were shards of ice. "I'm not leaving until we search every room. Every broom closet."

I nodded. "Me neither."

There was no one in the bedroom. No one under the bed. It felt silly to get down on our knees and look, like kids checking for the boogeyman, but I did it anyway. There was a rectangular impression in the carpet where my grandfather had kept his old cigar box, the one I'd found after he died, filled with the snapshots that would forever change the course of my life. But there was no V, dead or alive. Not in the closet. Not in the bathroom, where Noor tore back the shower curtain to find only a bar of withered soap.

There was nothing in the guest bedroom but a stack of unused moving boxes and spots of blackening mildew on the carpet. I could feel Noor's desperation mounting. By the time we came to the garage she was calling out for V, which was killing me, splitting my heart by the seams. I flipped on the lights.

Our eyes scanned a jumble of discarded junk and fix-it projects my grandfather never finished: two ladders, each missing a step. A boxy old television with a cracked screen. Coils of wire and rope. My grandfather's workbench, piled with tools and woodworking magazines. I saw my ghost and his there, shoulder to shoulder under the pooled light of a gooseneck lamp, stringing red yarn across a map with pushpins. The boy thinking all the while it was only a game, a story.

The storm's shifting pressure rattled the garage door, jolting me back into the present. I saw my grandfather's gun cabinet, the only thing in the garage large enough to conceal a person. Noor moved first, got there before me, and yanked the handles. The doors popped open an inch and then a chain pulled taut. Someone, almost certainly my dad, had padlocked the cabinet. Through the crack we could see a row of oiled rifle barrels. The weapons that might've saved my grandfather, had I not taken the key.

Noor drew her head back in surprise, then turned without speaking and ran into the house. I chased her to my grandfather's office, the only room we hadn't searched yet. The room where Olive had stomped her feet to find a hollow-sounding spot, then rolled back the rug to discover a door in the floor and a bunker below it. A bunker that V probably knew about—and might've even known the code to enter.

I tried to tell Noor, to shout above the storm's rising roar and Noor's own shouts—*Are you here? Mama, where are you?*—but she couldn't hear me and wasn't looking, was shoving aside Abe's empty desk and running to bang open the tiny closet, so I gave up and wrestled back the heavy carpet on my own and tried to remember where the hinged floor panel was, but I was too frantic and couldn't seem to find it.

There was no V in the room. I decided there was no V down in the bunker, either. I couldn't imagine her escaping here only to shelter in the bunker and shut us out. So when Noor ran out of the room I stood up and chased after her.

I found her still as a statue in the middle of the living room, breathing hard but focused. She beckoned me closer.

"What if we all came through together?" she said quietly, her eyes locked on a point in space at the edge of the room. "And we were the same distances apart that we'd been on V's porch." She raised her arm. "There. That's where I woke up." She was pointing at the corner where my grandfather's worn recliner sat. On the floor beside it was a burned outline, vaguely Noor-shaped. "And you woke up there." She pointed through the door to the screened porch, where my burned outline was disappearing under a spreading pool of the wight's blood. "That's exactly how far apart we were on V's porch. You were handcuffed to the rail over there and I was over here."

I felt a spark, a quickening. "And V was out in the grass."

We both looked up at once, our eyes darting to the flapping porch screen, the overgrown yard, the tall grass by the woods where the man in the yellow raincoat had paused and looked down.

"Right there," I whispered.

Our bodies unlocked. Together we bolted out into the storm.

CHAPTER TWO

V's body looked like it had been swallowed by the earth and spat out again. She lay twisted in the grass like a tossed-away doll, arms splayed cartoonishly and legs tangled beneath her. Her gray hair was knotted and clotted with mud, her red cardigan and black dress soaked with blood and rain. She'd lost a boot, and the patched woolen sock on her unshod foot made me think, incongruously, of the wicked witch in *The Wizard of Oz,* the one who gets pancaked under Dorothy's house. I locked my focus there, on what I remembered of that old acid trip of a movie, on the worn toe of V's striped sock, so it wouldn't wander north . . .

how many times had she patched that sock

. . . to the dark hole in V's chest . . .

a thing

she is just a thing now

. . . to an open mouth pooling with rain . . .

there's no place like home

Noor was crying. Her head was bent forward, hair covering her face, but I could see her chest heaving. I tried to put my arms around her but she wrenched away suddenly.

"*I did this,*" she whispered, "*it's my fault, it's my fault, it's my fault.*"

"It's not," I said. I tried again to wrap my arms around her and this time she let me. "It isn't."

"*Yes, yes, it is,*" she whispered. I held her tighter, tighter. Her body shook. "She was safe in that loop for so many years. And then I led that man to her. Let him in, led him right past all her defenses."

"You didn't know. There's no way you could've known."

"And now she's dead. Because of me she's dead."

Because of us, I thought, though I would never have said it. I had to kill this poisonous idea before it took root, or it would destroy her. I knew it from experience; a similar poison had infected me.

"You can't think that way. It's not true." I tried to sound calm, reasonable. But it was hard when V's body lay a few feet away in the grass.

"I only just found her. God. I only just found her again." Her voice was cracking.

"It wasn't your fault!"

"STOP SAYING THAT." She pushed away suddenly, shoved me back to an arm's length. Then, softer: "It makes me want to die."

Suddenly bereft of words, I nodded. *Okay.*

Rain stung our faces, dripped off our chins. The house had started to groan.

"I need a minute," she said.

"We should get her inside."

"I need a minute," she said again.

I gave it to her. Got up and walked to the edge of the trees, bent forward against the gale, trying not to think about how stupid it was to be standing outside in a hurricane. Thought instead of my grandfather, of how he had died and where—just through these woods. The strange mirroring of his body and his protégé's. I had only seen my grandfather cry once, but I knew this would have made him weep. Heat flared through my chest, my bones. I could almost see his ghost now, gleaming through the black and shuddering trees, could almost hear him moaning, *Velya, Velya, not you, too.*

I turned back to look. Noor was kneeling beside the body, wiping mud from V's face, straightening her twisted limbs. Noor, who had found V only to lose her again. Who would surely and forever blame herself, no matter how I reasoned with her. But if it was her fault, it was equally mine. We had been fooled, had let ourselves be tricked. V had surely missed her adopted daughter, but she had never, for the sake of Noor's own safety, tried to see her again. I remembered her greeting when we found her. *What the hell are you doing here?*

Our mistake had cost V her life. And I feared it had resurrected a demon. We had much to atone for, and little time to grieve.

A gust of wind nearly knocked me over. There was a screech and then a sharp crack from the next yard, and I swung my head around to see part of the neighbor's roof peel away.

When I looked back at Noor she was still kneeling, head tilted as if in prayer.

Just one minute, I told myself. *Just give her one minute more.* It might be her only chance to say goodbye. Or *I'm sorry*. I didn't know what the future held. Whether we'd have a chance to bury V, to hold a funeral. Just one minute more, and maybe Noor would be able to make some measure of peace with this, or at least keep herself from drowning in poison. And then we'd be able to—what? I had been so consumed with the terrors and tragedies of the present moment that I had not yet thought beyond them. We had to cover V's body. Bring her inside. Had to warn our friends and allies, had to reach them—if Caul had not already. There were a thousand terrors clawing at the edge of my mind, but I couldn't afford to let them in yet.

Noor had gone still. The storm was worsening. I couldn't wait any longer.

I'd only taken a few steps toward her when it felt like something punched me in the stomach, and I staggered and fell to my knees. Struggling to draw breath, I searched the grass for the object that had struck me, but there was nothing. And then I gasped as fresh pain bloomed in my midsection and raced down both legs.

I know this pain.

"What happened? Are you hurt?" Noor was bending over me,

tilting my head up. I tried to speak, but it came out as a mumble. My mind was on the thing that had hit me, which wasn't a thing at all, I realized, but a feeling. And now some dynamo in my gut that had been still was spinning again, and it compelled me to turn and look into the woods.

"What is it?" Noor said.

I got a sudden flash: rotting, black-eyed, built like a monstrous spider, crashing through the bracken toward us.

"The man in yellow," I said hoarsely, my heart thudding as my eyes searched the trees.

"What about him?"

It had felt him go. Felt its master die.

"He wasn't alone."

*   *   *

My mind went to the gun safe in the garage, but it was locked, chained tight, just as useless to us now as it had been to my grand-father on the night he died. There was only one option left, other than running, which was useless, or facing it here in the yard with no weapons, which was idiotic.

"My grandfather had a bunker," I said, already on my feet and pulling Noor toward the porch. "In the office, under the floor."

Halfway to the porch she planted her feet and pulled us to a stop.

"Not without her."

She meant V.

"There's a hollowgast in the woods." I realized I hadn't actually said the word, named the threat. I tried to pull her onward, but she would not be moved.

"I've seen what they do to people like us, especially dead ones. They already took her heart. I won't let them take her eyes, too."

She wasn't shaking, wasn't manic. I could see there would be no arguing.

Noor took V's arms and I took her legs. V was not a large woman, but her sodden body felt weighted down with stones. We struggled to the porch and hefted her past the unmoving wight into the house, leaving a drip-trail of mud behind us. We set her down by the pulled-back rug in the office. I could feel my inner compass ticking back and forth, trying hard to pinpoint the location of a hollow I hadn't yet seen with my eyes. All I knew for certain was that it was coming, and it was angry. I could feel that anger like pricks from a hot knife.

I dropped to my knees and pounded the floorboards until an echo answered my fists, then asked Noor to find me something to pry the hatch door with while I ran my palms across the boards. I found the disguised hinge just as she returned holding the bloody, bronze-handled letter opener, which only moments ago had been buried in the neck of a dead wight. I could almost hear Miss Peregrine's voice say *What an endlessly useful little doodah* as I stuck it into the thin gap and pried up a three-foot section of floorboards. Underneath was the armored bunker door.

Noor expressed no surprise at any of it. V had her own secret time loop; compared to that, an underground bunker must have seemed like a foregone conclusion.

The bunker door was locked with an alphanumeric keypad. I started to punch in the code, but just like that, my mind went blank.

"You're not typing," Noor pointed out.

I stared at the pad. "It's not a birthday. It's a word . . ."

Noor raked a hand down the side of her face.

I shut my eyes, tapped my head. "It's a word. A word I *know*."

The compass needle wobbled, then steadied. I could feel the hollow tearing through the woods, nearly out of them now. I stared until the keypad began to blur. *It was in Polish. Little something.*

"Please, for God's sake, hurry," Noor said through her teeth. "I'll be right back."

She left and came back a moment later with the dark brown comforter from my grandfather's bed. She settled it over V's body.

Tiger! Little tiger. That's what he used to call me. But what's the word in Polish?

Noor rolled V over, wrapped her in the blanket. A mummy in a microfiber shroud. And then it came to me, and my finger stabbed the keys.

T-y-g-r-y-s-k-u

The lock tumbled open. I could breathe again. I swung back the heavy door and it banged like a gunshot against the floor.

"Thank God." Noor sighed.

A ladder descended into darkness. We slid V's shrouded body to the edge. I climbed down three rungs, one arm wrapped around her calves, but she was too heavy to carry down by myself, and there was no time to lower her gently into the bunker tunnel, with the two of us inching downward rung by rung.

A loud metallic groan came from the porch, which might have been the wind tearing the screens away—or a hollow.

"We've just got to drop her," I said. "I'm sorry."

Noor didn't reply, just nodded. She drew a deep breath. I silently apologized to V for what was about to happen, then let her slip from my arms into the dark. There was a loud crack of bones breaking as she landed. Noor winced and I suppressed a shudder, and then we climbed down after her.

Noor pulled the hatch door closed above us. It shut with a reverberating clang and locked automatically, and we were engulfed in dark. Crashes echoed from the other side, and we heard a howl that was definitely not the wind. I climbed the rest of the way down the ladder, stumbled over V's body, and ran my hands along the rough concrete wall until I found a light switch.

Green fluorescents built into the walls flickered on. Thankfully, we still had power despite the storm. Knowing my grandfather, the bunker was connected to a backup generator somewhere.

A crash from inside the house echoed off the tunnel walls.

"So, this place is hollow-proof?" Noor asked, looking up at the hatch.

"Supposed to be."

"Was that ever tested?"

The hollow started pounding on the hatch, the sound like a bell ringing dully.

"I'm sure it was."

A lie. If the wights had ever found out where Grandpa Portman lived—before last year, that is—he'd have had to move his family, go into hiding, and never come back. Which meant the integrity of this forty-year-old bunker was being tested for the first time, right now.

"But let's get away from that door," I said. "Just in case."

◆   ◆   ◆

The command center at the heart of the bunker was as I remembered it. Twenty feet from end to end. Bunk bed against one wall, military-issue supply locker against the other. A chemical toilet. A hulking old teleprinter machine atop a hulking wooden desk. The room's most obvious feature was a periscope that hung down by a cylindrical tube from the ceiling, identical to the one in V's house.

Even through the thick hatch door and down the long concrete tunnel to this underground room, sounds of destruction from above echoed vividly. The hollow was on a rampage. I tried not to think about what it was doing to the house—or what it would do to us, if given the chance. I didn't have a lot of faith in my hollow-taming abilities at present. Our best chance at survival was to stay away from it. I felt strangely superstitious, too, about trying to fight a hollowgast here, in the very place my grandfather had been killed by one. Like it would be tempting fate.

"All I see is tall grass." Noor had put her face to the periscope and was turning a slow circle. "Your grandfather's surveillance system doesn't work because nobody bothered to mow the lawn." She pulled her face away and looked at me. "We can't stay down here."

"Well, we can't go up there," I replied. "That hollow will turn us inside out."

"Not if we find something to kill it with." She went to the supply locker and opened the door, revealing shelves of neatly stacked survival gear. Food and medical supplies. Nothing deadly.

"There aren't any weapons down here. I've looked."

She was excavating the locker anyway, raking a shelf of tinned food onto the floor with a clatter. "There was an NRA convention's worth of guns in the garage. How can there be none in your grandpa's *survival bunker*?"

"I don't know, but there aren't."

I went to help her, though I knew it was pointless. I shoved aside a stack of mission logs, procedural manuals, and other books to look behind them.

"What the *hell*." Having searched every corner of the locker, she turned her back on it and threw a can of beans across the floor. "Whatever. We still can't stay down here." She had remained remarkably composed ever since we'd come in from the yard, but now panic was creeping back into her voice.

"Just give me a minute," I said. "I need to think."

I plopped down in the swivel chair. There was another way out, of course: through the second tunnel, up into the dummy house on the other side of the cul-de-sac, where my grandfather's white Chevrolet Caprice sat waiting in the garage. Then again, maybe the hollow would run outside the moment it heard the Caprice's motor and murder us before we could even back out of the driveway. More to the point, maybe I was not yet ready for the blind rush and perfect execution such an escape would require.

It sounded like someone was jackhammering in the house.

"Maybe he'll get bored and leave," I said, half joking.

"He's not going anywhere, except to get reinforcements." She started pacing the narrow floor. "He's probably calling for backup right now."

"I don't think hollows carry phones. Or need reinforcements."

"What's it *doing* here? Why are a wight and a hollowgast at your grandfather's house?"

"Clearly, they were expecting us," I said. "Or expecting *someone*."

She leaned against the bunk bed, frowning and frustrated. "I thought Murnau was the last uncaptured wight. And almost all the hollows were dead."

"The ymbrynes said there were still some in hiding. Maybe there were more than they thought."

"Well, they're not in hiding anymore. At least, these two weren't. Which means someone called them into service. Which means—"

"We don't know that," I said, reluctant to follow that line of reasoning. "We don't know anything."

She squared her shoulders to me. "Caul's back, isn't he? Murnau succeeded. Brought him back from . . . wherever he was."

I shook my head. Couldn't meet her eyes. "I don't know. Maybe."

Her back slid down the bed post until she was sitting on the floor, knees hugged to her chest. "I felt him," she said. "Right before I blacked out. It was like . . . like a blanket of ice covering me."

And I saw him. Saw his face in the heart of the storm. But still I said, "We just don't know," because I couldn't be certain, and because I didn't want to admit that such an awful thing was true until the truth of it was inescapable.

She tipped her head to one side, like something had just occurred to her, then jumped up and dug in her pocket. "I found this in V's hand when I was wrapping her. She must have been holding it when she died."

I stood up and she extended her hand. She held what appeared to be a damaged stopwatch. It had no hands and no numbers. Around the dial were strange symbols and what might have been runic letters, and the glass face was cracked and partially smoked over, as if it had been dropped into a fire. I took it from her and was surprised by its weight. On the back, in English, was stamped:

SINGLE USE ONLY. 5 MIN COUNTDOWN.

MADE IN EAST GERMANY.

"An eject button," I said quietly, awe stealing over me.

"She must have had it in her pocket when we showed up," said Noor. "Maybe she knew something was coming for her."

I was nodding. "Or maybe she always carried it with her. So she could be ready to escape at a moment's notice."

Like a fugitive, I thought sadly.

"But it didn't work quickly enough. It says right here, five minute countdown. So even if she'd hit the button the second Murnau came in . . ."

Noor looked past me, at the wall, at nothing.

"Fast enough to save us," I said. "But too slow to save herself." I handed back the stopwatch. "I'm sorry."

She drew a shuddering breath, steadied herself, then shook her head. "It doesn't make sense. She was a preparer. A planner. And she'd had years to plan for an invasion. She had that ejector watch. A house full of weapons. Yeah, she got taken by surprise—thanks to me—but I bet she had a plan for that, too."

"Noor, Murnau shot her in the chest. How do you plan for that?"

"She *let* it happen. I'm telling you. If she'd managed to dive out a window or something, his next move would have been to kill one of us, then use the other as a hostage. So instead she let him shoot her."

"But her own *heart* was on Bentham's list of resurrection ingredients. She must have known that. I think it's the whole reason she locked herself in that loop—to keep the wights from stealing her heart. Letting Murnau kill her in order to save us would've endangered *everyone*."

"We were supposed to stop him." She wiped a smudge from the stopwatch with her thumb. "But we failed."

I started to object, but she cut me off. "Look, this is pointless. There's nothing to do but warn the others. We've got to get back to Devil's Acre and tell them what's happened. And soon."

Finally. Something we could agree on.

"I think I know how," I said. "There's a pocket loop in the backyard of my parents' house. It connects directly to the Panlooticon, inside the Acre. It's on the other side of town."

"Then we've got to go. Now."

"*If* it's still operational," I added.

"I guess we'll find out."

There was a loud metal creak from the periscope. It spun suddenly on its tube, then raced upward and smashed against the ceiling. We dove out of the way as broken glass sprayed across the floor.

"So much for our surveillance system," Noor said.

"He's pissed. And he's not going anywhere."

"We'll just have to take our chances."

"We can afford to take chances with *my* life," I said. "But if Caul really is back, we can't take any chances with yours."

"Oh, come *on*—"

"No, hear me out. If there's any truth to that prophecy—and by now I think we've got to believe there is—then you're the best hope we've got. Maybe the only hope."

"You mean the seven thing." She frowned. "Me and six others. Which, who knows if they're even—"

"You're safe now, and I've got to keep you safe. V didn't sacrifice herself just so you could end up in a hollowgast's stomach. I don't know how long we were unconscious. Hours, at least—maybe longer. So please, just wait another couple of minutes, and let's see whether this asshole gets bored of chewing on sod. *Then* we'll make our move."

She crossed her arms. "Fine. But there's got to be *some* way to warn the others while we're waiting. Is there a phone? A radio?" She scanned the room. "What's that thing behind you?"

She was talking about the teleprinter. "It's obsolete," I said. "Belongs in a museum."

"Can it talk to the outside world?"

"Not anymore, I don't think. They used to use them to talk to other loops, but they weren't secure enough—"

"It's worth a shot." Noor sat in the swivel chair and bellied up to the keyboard, which looked like it had been sawed off an old fax machine. "How do I turn it on?"

"No idea."

She blew on the keyboard, puffing dust into the air, then punched a random key. The monitor stayed dark. She reached around the back of it, groped blindly, and flipped a switch. The monitor made a staticky pop, and a moment later an amber cursor blinked to life.

"I'll be damned," I said. "It works."

A word appeared. A single word on a single line at the top of an otherwise black screen.

Command: ___

Noor whistled. "This thing is *old*."

"Told you."

"Where's the mouse?"

"I don't think they were invented yet. It wants you to type something."

Noor typed *Warn.*

The machine bleeped unhappily.

Command not recognized.

Noor scowled. She typed *Mail.*

Command not recognized.

"Try 'directory,' " I said.

She did. "Nothing." And then she tried *message, root, help,* and *loop.* None of those worked, either.

Noor sat back in the chair. "I don't suppose your grandpa kept the instructions."

I went to the supply locker and poked through the books. Most were spiral-bound, softcover, homemade-looking. A few were old mission logs belonging to my grandfather, and I promised myself to one day read them all. Between a worn-looking pamphlet titled *So You Want to Build a Hollowgast Shelter* and a couple of the spy novels my grandfather liked to read was a laminated volume with a little bird insignia on the cover and four letters in red: FPEO.

I had seen the same letters inside certain editions of the *Tales. For peculiar eyes only.*

I flipped it open. The inner title page read:

Syndrisoft pneumatic teleprinter OS 1.5 operating instructions

"Noor! I got it!" I shouted so loudly that I startled her, though with half a second's reflection I didn't know what I'd gotten so excited about. The thing was almost certainly disconnected from whatever network it had once been a part of.

We pushed back the heavy keyboard to make room on the desk and opened the manual. From over our heads came a roar and another crash, the sound muted only slightly by twenty feet of dirt and reinforced concrete. I wondered how much of the house would be left standing after the hollow had finished with it.

We attempted to ignore the apocalyptic noises and thumbed through the manual. In the table of contents was a chapter labeled "Communications and Connectivity." I flipped pages and read aloud while Noor typed.

"Try typing this," I said. "*Outgoing CC.*"

She did. The cursor typed a reply: *Outgoing communications unavailable.*

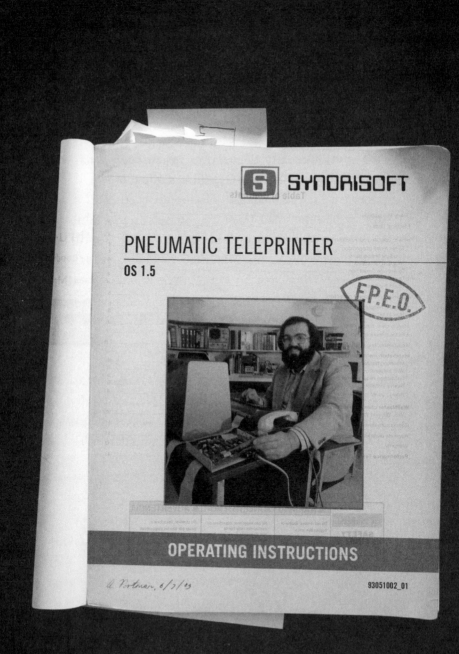

S SYNDRISOFT

PNEUMATIC TELEPRINTER

OS 1.5

F.P.E.O.

OPERATING INSTRUCTIONS

A. Portman, 6/7/03

93051002_01

SO YOU WANT TO

Build a
Hollowgast Shelter?

Revised and Updated Edition

F.P.E.O.

I read more commands to Noor. She tried *Query outgoing* CC. The cursor blinked fast for a few seconds, then came back with *CC lines cut.*

"Dammit," she said.

"It was a long shot, anyway," I said. "This thing probably hasn't been used in decades."

She slapped the desk and got up from the chair. "We can't wait down here much longer. That hollow isn't going to just leave voluntarily."

I was starting to think she was right: that the beast would never leave; that eventually whoever had sent the yellow-jacketed man would notice he hadn't returned and come to check on him; that every minute we hid down here was a minute stolen from our allies in the Acre, who could've been making plans for escape from, or defense against, whatever onslaught Caul was no doubt preparing. If I protected Noor only to let my friends be slaughtered in a surprise attack, was that any victory at all?

Maybe. Maybe it was, in the coldest possible calculus, because Caul was a threat not just to the peculiars I loved, but all peculiar-kind. And really, to the world.

Then again, my friends *were* my world.

I was about to say *screw it, let's go* when I heard Noor mutter, *"Holy shit."*

She had returned to the desk and was bent over the ancient monitor. The cursor had typed something of its own volition. Two lines of amber text.

Threat detected.

Activate home defense: Y/N ___

Noor did not wait, did not ask my opinion. Her index finger stabbed the Y button.

The screen blanked. I thought for a moment it had shut down—had just been teasing us—but then the cursor reappeared and drew a new screen.

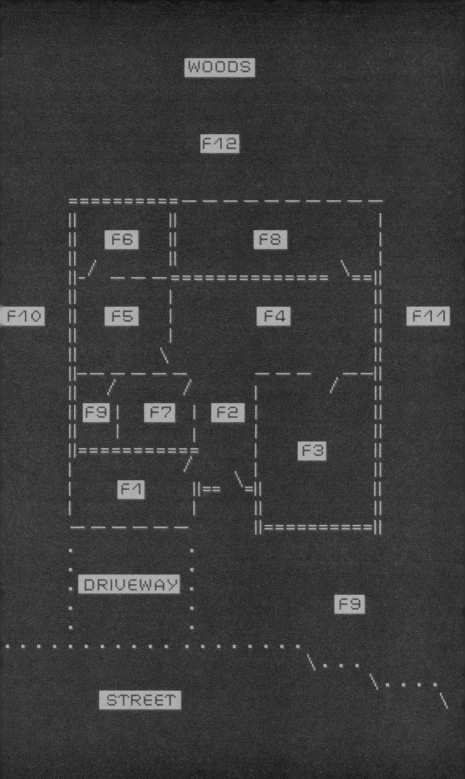

WOODS

F12

F6　　　　F8

F10

F5　　　　F4

F11

F9　　F7　　F2

F3

F1　　||==　==||

DRIVEWAY

F9

STREET

It was a map of the house crudely drawn in keyboard characters. The map was divided into twelve zones, marked F1–F12, eight zones for the house and four for the yard. There were twelve function keys on the keyboard. A cursor blinked, waiting, at the bottom of the screen.

"What do you think they do?" Noor said. "Shoot fireballs? Open trapdoors?"

"In a suburban retirement community?"

She shrugged. "Let's find out." Her finger hovered over the function keys. "Think it's still above us?"

I felt the hollow's proximity, but couldn't sense exactly where he was. I went to the periscope—what was left of it—and pulled it down again. Through the viewer's cracked glass I saw a distorted rendering of the yard. The hollow had stomped down the grass enough for me to glimpse the house and the street beyond, but there was no sign of him. I rotated in a circle. My view raked the yard, past a fallen tree and a downed power line sparking on the sidewalk, to the neighbor's roofless house. And then I felt my inner compass needle flicker and heard the beast howl, sharp and loud, as the periscope yanked violently upward, knocking me to the ground before it smashed against the ceiling again.

Noor leapt out of the chair and rushed to me. "Oh my God, are you okay?"

"It's right above us!" I shouted.

She helped me up and we stumbled to the computer together.

"What part of the yard is that?" she said, peering at the monitor. I tapped the screen. "I think . . . it's that side."

Noor rested her finger on the corresponding key. F10. "Mind if I do the honors?"

"Yes! I mean, no! Just push it!"

She pushed it.

At first nothing happened. Then the walls around us began to rattle, and there was a sound like the creak of some giant old radiator, and a moment later there was a deafening boom and the room shook. The bunk bed fell over and everything we hadn't taken out of the supply cabinet went flying onto the floor.

The compass needle inside me spun. I couldn't tell how hurt the hollowgast was, but I was sure it had been thrown some distance by whatever had just happened aboveground. Which meant—

"We got it!" I shouted.

Noor cautiously uncovered her head. "Is it dead?"

"It's hurt, I think, not dead. But let's not stick around to find out."

I ran to the wall and started prying open the door that was partially hidden beside the supply cabinet. "Another exit," I explained. "This leads to a different house, and a car we can use."

"What about V?" Noor said.

I tried to imagine dragging her body down tunnels and up ladders while an injured and furious hollowgast chased us. But then Noor seemed to read my mind without me having to explain, and she shook her head and muttered, "Never mind."

"We'll come back," I assured her.

She didn't say anything, just dug her fingers into the doorjamb and started to pull.

CHAPTER THREE

*W*e sprinted through the low-ceilinged tunnel that ran below my grandfather's suburban street, then climbed another ladder and up through a hatch into the bedroom of the dummy house. There was no time to look out the window to check the damage to my grandfather's house, no time for anything but the motion of our legs and my hand pulling Noor's, and thank God the house was a mirror of Abe's so I could find my way quickly down the hallway and into the living room with no unnecessary expenditure of thought. The living room was howling and wet, gauzy curtains flapping at the shattered bay window, a fallen oak branch reaching into the room like a monster's hand.

A glimpse, barely registered, of flames across the street.

No sign of the hollowgast. Despite myself, I felt a surge of hope that it was dead.

We burst into the garage. The boatlike Caprice was just where it had been, the spot beside it vacant. (The Aston had been abandoned weeks ago in Brooklyn and was now surely in the wights' hands or had been stolen and stripped for parts.) We threw open the Caprice's long doors and sank into its seats. The keys were in the cup holder, the garage opener clipped to the visor. I reached up to touch the button, but Noor snatched it before I could.

"One thing," she said. It was the first time my eyes had come to rest on anything since we'd started running. Even in the unflattering glare of the Caprice's dome light, even soaked to the skin, hair tangled, breathing hard, she was a vision. A vision.

She said, "You don't stop. Whatever happens, you have to get back to the Acre. Even if I'm in trouble."

It took me a second to process what she was saying. "I'm not leaving you behind."

"Listen. Listen." Her body was coiled with tension. She took my hands, twined our fingers together without unlocking her eyes from mine. "Someone has to warn the others, and there's nobody but us to do it. Nobody else knows what's happened."

My whole mind rejected the idea, cringed at the thought of abandoning Noor for any reason. But I could conjure no more articulate an argument against it than "No."

Her hand stole onto my leg. "I already cost V her life." Her fingers dug in. "Don't let me be the reason our friends die, too."

My heart was beating in my throat. "You have to promise the same thing," I said. "No stopping."

Her eyes flicked downward and she nodded, an almost indiscernible movement. "Okay."

"Okay," I said.

It was a lie. I would never have left her behind.

She offered up the clicker. I hit the button. The garage door motor kicked on, complaining as it began to roll upward. My grandfather had backed the Caprice in, so we were facing the street, and the door opening was like the curtain's rise at the start of a play.

My grandfather's house was burning. The side yard was blackened. A hole smoked in the grass; another had been punched through a wall of the house, exposing the bathroom's pink tiles.

I'm pretty sure I muttered, "Oh, *shit*," and Noor said something about starting the engine, but a sudden, sharp pain in my gut demanded all my attention. It also told my eyes where to look: at the hole in the yard, where a black tongue was reaching up into the rain from a shifting pile of pink-tiled rubble.

Noor was staring, too, had followed my eyes to the pile.

"Jacob?" she said quietly. "I think it survived."

The hollowgast rose from the rubble. It was enormously tall despite its hunched back, and it stretched and cricked its neck as if just waking from a nap rather than unburying itself from a house. Pulverized concrete had dusted it ghostly white—making it visible to Noor.

"Start the engine." Noor was reaching over, shaking me. "The *engine*, Jacob!"

I twisted the key, then racked the shifter down to *D* and punched the gas. We lurched into the driveway, bottomed out in the gutter with an attention-grabbing scrape, and swerved into the street.

"I *see* it, I can *see* it, GO," Noor shouted, body angled back toward my grandfather's house.

I floored the gas pedal. The car's engine howled with a fury that old, boatlike Chevy Caprices were never meant to have. It was too much power; the back wheels spun on the wet pavement as the rear end swung sideways.

The hollow was loping across the yard, nearly to the street now. It was even taller than the one I'd fought at the deadrisers' loop in Gravehill, and spattered with impressionistic puffs of concrete dust and black blood.

"GO, GO, GO, *GO*!" Noor shouted. "Forward, not sideways!"

I let off the gas until the back tires stopped spinning, cut the wheel the other way, and eased down the pedal again.

"*Right behind you—*RIGHT *behind you—*"

We took off just as the hollowgast's tongue tried to lasso our bumper, but it bounced off with a loud metal *thwang*. A moment later another of its tongues punched out the back window. It shattered, raining glass into the rear seat. We were tearing down the street now, and it was running after us, limping and injured but still fast.

Noor opened the glove box and rifled through it. She was

looking for a weapon, or maybe a secret panel of James Bond–style buttons. But there were only registration papers and a pair of old reading glasses. We were going as fast as I dared, given the wet streets and fallen branches and uprooted yard ornaments that had made an obstacle course of the neighborhood—that and the endless circles of Circle Village, which was nothing but curves and curlicues and cul-de-sacs that kept trying to throw our fast-but-heavy car into retention ponds and the sides of houses, and I had to keep braking and turning and braking when I was dying, *dying* just to floor it. We were beginning to lose the hollow despite all that, but only because it was hurt, forced to use one tongue as a crutch.

But then I felt the compass needle jerk away, and in the rearview I saw the hollow skitter off the road and disappear behind a house.

"It's trying to cut us off," I said, and we both leaned right as I swerved to avoid a tipped-over golf cart in the road.

"Then go a different way," Noor shouted.

"I can't! There's only one way out of this labyrinth . . ."

For the next couple of turns we didn't see it, but I knew it was close, tracking us, running as fast as its injured body could carry it. Then, up ahead, the guard gate. The exit. Beyond that a main road, a straightaway where I could finally reach an uncatchable speed.

I felt the hollow before I saw it, streaking out along our right side to block the way. We were heading straight for it, down the little alley that ran between a low curb and the unmanned guard gate.

"Hang on!" I shouted, and I stamped down the gas and swerved sharply right.

We hit the curb. My unbelted body lurched forward, slamming the wheel as we launched over. One of the hollow's tongues grazed the side of the car. The other managed to punch through my driver's side window, and as we sailed onto the putting green that fronted the neighborhood, we swept the hollow off its feet and pulled it with us.

We spun across the clipped grass, turning a wide half circle before I cut the wheel and straightened us out, and thank God, thank *Abe* this was no ordinary old car but one he'd clearly modified, because the engine had enough grunt and its back wheels enough grip to keep us skidding across the soggy putting green, enough momentum that instead of diving nose-first into the ditch we jumped it, the back tires slamming its outer edge before finding traction again, then sending us off like a shot down Piney Woods Road.

All good, all fine, but for one thing, which Noor couldn't see because the hollow had now been washed clean by the storm: Its tongue was inside my window, had wrapped itself around my door's inner handle. We were pulling it behind us, dragging it down the road at forty, fifty miles an hour, and still I did not feel it dying, could only feel its rage.

That tongue was tensed hard as steel. It was not only hanging on, but slowly reeling the hollow in, up off the road that was surely skinning it alive.

Because I could think of nothing else to do, I punched the gas all the way down.

"Have you got anything sharp?" I shouted.

Noor looked at me in horror, realizing at once why I had asked. I prayed for an oncoming car, something I could use to peel the monster off, but Englewood was a ghost town now and the roads were empty. No one but us was stupid enough to be driving in the middle of a hurricane.

"Just this," she said, and once again offered me the bronze-handled letter opener: the ever-useful, Swiss-Army-knife, totemic thing that wouldn't leave me alone.

The hollow was howling with pain and from the effort of pulling itself to my door. I didn't dare take my foot off the gas, even as chunks of debris forced me to swerve all over the road.

I grabbed the letter opener. Asked Noor to take the wheel,

which she did. I stabbed the hollow's tongue. Once, twice, three times. Hollow blood spattered me, black and hot. The creature screamed but wouldn't let go, wouldn't let go, and then, when it finally seemed about to—

"Jacob, *brake*!"

My foot had been planted on the gas but my eyes had been on the hollow. I turned to see an abandoned pickup truck and a downed tree blocking most of the road and stomped the brake. The Caprice did a dopey back-ended swerve that almost missed the pickup but not quite, our tail connecting with a jolting smash. We kept going, the branches of the downed tree raking us, cracking our windshield and tearing off the side mirrors before we finally cleared it and skidded to a stop.

We had ceased to move but the world still spun. Noor was shaking me, touching my face—she was okay, had been wearing her seat belt. The letter opener was gone, torn from my hand, and the hollow's tongue was gone, too.

"Is it dead?" Noor asked, but then she frowned as if embarrassed by her optimism.

I turned to look out the shattered rear window. I could feel the hollow still, steady but weakened, but couldn't see it. It was far behind us, knocked loose in the crash.

"It's hurt," I said. "Bad, I think."

On both sides of the road were darkened strip malls. Up ahead a snapped traffic light twisted dangerously in the air. On a different day I would've turned the car around and gone back to finish off the hollow. But today I couldn't afford the time or the risk. One hollowgast running loose was the least of our worries.

I touched the gas. The car wobbled forward, the Caprice's nose angled slightly downward and to the left.

We'd popped a tire but could still roll.

◆　　◆　　◆

I didn't dare push the damaged Caprice too hard, lest I risk popping a second tire and stranding us completely. We limped along at what my grandfather used to call "after church speed," wobbling through a town I hardly recognized. It looked like the end of the world: shuttered stores, abandoned parking lots, streets littered with wet trash. Traffic lights blinked, heeded by no one. The small boats people docked in creeks and canals had snapped their moorings, and in the heavy chop their masts tick-tocked like wagging fingers.

Under different circumstances, I would've been narrating the drive for Noor, would have enjoyed playing tour guide in the town where I'd grown up, relished the chance to measure the extraordinary turns my life had taken against the straight and stultifying path I'd once seemed destined for. But now I had no words to spare. And the hope and wonder such musings had once made me feel had been extinguished under a suffocating blanket of dread.

What was waiting for us on the other side? What if the Acre was already gone, and my friends with it? What if Caul had simply . . . wiped it all away?

Thankfully, the bridge to Needle Key was undamaged. Thankfully, too, the storm had begun to let up, so that as we climbed the wide, frowning arc of the bridge there were no sudden gusts, nothing to push us over the flimsy guardrail and into Lemon Bay, that stripe of whitecapped gray below. Key Road was still passable, if strewn with downed branches, and with some effort we were able to navigate past the shuttered bait shops and old condos to reach my house.

I had assumed it would be empty. Even if my parents were back from their Asia trip, they would probably have evacuated to Atlanta, where my grandma on my mom's side lived. Needle Key was a barrier island, practically below sea level, and only the crazies stuck around during hurricanes. But my house was not empty. There was a police cruiser in the driveway, its rollers flashing silently, and next to it a van with ANIMAL CONTROL emblazoned on it. A cop in rain gear stood beside the cars, turning as soon as he heard our tires crunch the gravel.

"Oh, great," I muttered, "what the hell is this?"

Noor sunk down into her seat. "Let's hope it's not more wights."

We could only hope, since there was no way the hobbled Caprice could outrun a police cruiser. The cop signaled for me to stop. I parked, and he walked toward us while sipping from a thermos.

"The loop entrance is in the potting shed in the backyard," I whispered. *"If you have to, make a run for it."*

If it's still there, I thought. *If the shed didn't blow away in the storm.*

"Names."

The officer had a trim black mustache, a square jaw, and pupils in his eyes. Pupils could be faked, of course, but there was something about his manner, so bored and irritable, that struck me as distinctly non-wightish. The patch on his official police rain jacket said RAFFERTY.

"Jacob Portman," I said.

Noor gave her name as "Nina . . . Parker," and luckily the cop didn't ask for ID.

"I live here," I said. "What's going on?"

Officer Rafferty's eyes darted from Noor back to me. "Can you prove this is your residence?"

"I know the code to the alarm system. And there's a photo of me and my parents in the front hall."

He sipped from his thermos, which had a Sarasota County Sheriff's Department logo on it. "Were you involved in an accident?"

"We got caught in the storm," said Noor. "Skidded off the road."

"Anyone injured?"

I glanced at the black hollowgast blood that had run down my door and my arm, and realized with some relief that he couldn't see it.

"No, sir," I said. "Did something happen here?"

"A neighbor reported seeing prowlers in the yard."

"Prowlers?" I said, exchanging a glance with Noor.

"It's not uncommon during evacuations. You get thieves, looters, individuals of that nature lurking around, looking to burglarize abandoned properties. They most likely noticed your alarm signs and moved on to greener pastures. We didn't find anyone . . . but we *were* attacked by a canine." He indicated the animal control van. "Some folks stake their animals outside during storms. It's damn cruel. They get scared, break their leashes, run off. The animal's being collared now. Until it's secure, you should remain in your vehicle."

There was a sudden burst of loud barking from behind my house. Two more officers rounded the corner, one young and one gray, each grappling the end of a long pole. At the other end of the poles was a collar, and inside that collar was a furious dog. It was giving them hell, snarling and trying to shake them loose while they dragged it toward the animal control van.

"Give us a damn hand here, Rafferty!" the older officer shouted. "Get that door open for us!"

"Stay in your vehicle," Rafferty growled. He jogged to the animal control van and started trying to open its rear door.

"Let's go," I said as soon as his back was turned.

We got out. Noor rounded the car to join me.

"Back in your car!" Rafferty shouted, but he was too busy struggling with the door to come after us.

"Quick now—before we get bit again!" the gray-haired cop yelled.

I led Noor toward the backyard. We heard a bloodcurdling snarl and then the younger cop shouted, "I'm gonna tase it!"

The dog's barks took on a new, louder urgency. I fought an urge to intervene, and then I heard someone say, in a crystal clear British accent: "It's me!"

I stopped cold and turned. So did Noor.

I knew that voice.

It belonged to a tan boxer dog with a spiked collar, his muscular legs dug into the gravel. In the chaos the officers hadn't seemed to hear him.

Rafferty finally got the van open. The older animal control officer held on to his pole while the younger one brandished a taser.

Then I heard the dog say—saw his lips form the words— "Jacob, it's Addison!"

The cops heard *that*—and then they were all gaping, open-mouthed. So was Noor.

"That's my dog!" I shouted, running toward him. "Down, boy."

"Did he just . . . ?" said the younger officer, shaking his head.

"Stay back!" Rafferty called, but I ignored him and knelt down a few yards from Addison, who was looking a bit ragged and very glad to see me, his docked tail wagging so hard it shook his whole rear end.

"It's okay, he's trained," I said. "He does all sorts of tricks."

"He's yours?" Rafferty said doubtfully. "Why the hell didn't you say that before?"

"I swear to God he *said* something," said the gray-haired cop.

Addison snarled at him.

"Put that away!" I said. "He won't bite if you don't threaten him."

"He *already* bit me!" complained the younger cop.

"The kid's lying," Rafferty said.

"I'll prove he's mine. Addison, *sit*."

Addison sat. The cops looked impressed.

"Speak."

Addison barked.

"Not like that." The young cop frowned. "He said *words*."

I looked at him like he was crazy.

"Beg," I said to Addison.

He glowered at me. That was going too far.

"We're going to have to take him in," said the older cop. "He bit a police officer."

"He was just scared," I said. "He won't hurt anyone now."

"We'll take him to doggie training school," Noor said. "He's a total sweetheart, really. I've never seen him even growl at someone before."

"Make him talk again," said the younger cop.

I gave him a concerned look. "Officer, I don't know what you thought you heard, but—"

"I heard him say something. Now make him apologize for biting me."

"It's just a *dog*, Kinsey," the older cop said. "Hell, I seen a Doberman on YouTube once that sings the national anthem . . ."

And then Addison, who'd had quite enough of being insulted, drew up on his hind legs and said, "Oh, for heaven's sake, you provincial boob, I can speak better English than *you* can."

The young cop let out a single sharp laugh—"Ha!"—but the other two were speechless. Before their brains could unfreeze, there was a loud, shattering crash behind us. We spun around to look, and there was Bronwyn standing at the edge of the driveway. She'd thrown a potted palm tree through the animal control van's windshield.

"Come get me!" she taunted them, and I had not even a second to appreciate the joyous fact of her being alive, or to wonder what she was doing here, because she took off running behind the house, and Rafferty shouted at her to stop and chased after her. The other two cops dropped their poles and did the same.

"To the pocket loop, friends!" Addison cried, and he shook the poles off his collar and started to run.

We chased him into the backyard. I looked for the potting shed by the oleander hedge, but the storm had carried it into Lemon Bay, and where it had been there was now just a rim of splintered boards.

Bronwyn barreled into view around the opposite corner of the house. "Jump in! Jump in where you see the shiny place!"

Addison led us to the spot where the shed had been. In the middle of it, in the dark heart where the pocket loop entrance was, a strange and shimmering distortion hung in midair. "It's a loop in its most elemental form," Addison said. "Don't be afraid—just go."

The cops were twenty steps behind Bronwyn, and I had no doubt that if they reached us, there would be nightsticks and tasers and Bronwyn would have to seriously injure them, so without stopping to warn her, I shoved Noor into the mirrored air. In a flash of light, she disappeared.

Addison jumped in after her, and with another flash was gone.

"Go, Mr. Jacob!" Bronwyn yelled, and because I knew she could hold her own against any normal ever born, I did.

Everything went black, and for the second time in as many hours, I was weightless.

CHAPTER FOUR

*W*e tumbled out of the broom closet in a tangle of flailing limbs and sprawled across thick red carpet. I caught an elbow on the chin and felt a wet dog nose swipe my face, then narrowly missed getting punched by Bronwyn as she thrashed free of the pile. "Unhand us, you animal-torturing bastards!" she was shouting, her eyes wild and unfocused, and she pulled back her fist and was about to knock one of us unconscious when Addison tackled her with his forepaws and pushed her backward.

"Get ahold of yourself, girl, we're back in the Panloopticon!"

He licked her face. Bronwyn's arms went limp at her sides. "We are?" she said meekly. "It all happened so quickly, I lost track of where I was." She took us in. A smile bloomed across her face. "My goodness. It's really you."

"I'm so happy to see you guys, I can't even—" Noor started to say, but the rest was muffled by the folds of Bronwyn's homemade dress.

"We thought we'd lost you for good this time!" Bronwyn cried, hugging us both. "When you disappeared *again* without telling anyone we thought for certain you'd been kidnapped!" She stood without letting go, hauling Noor and me up with her. "Horace had a dream you'd gotten your souls sucked out through your feet! And then the desolations began, and—"

"Bronwyn!" I shouted into the sandpapery fabric of her dress.

"For heaven's sake, let them *breathe*," said Addison.

"Sorry, sorry," Bronwyn said as she released us.

"It's nice to see you, too," I wheezed.

"So very sorry," she said. "I get carried away, don't I?"

"It's fine," Noor said, and she gave Bronwyn a light side-hug as proof there were no hard feelings.

Addison chided Bronwyn, "Don't apologize so much, it makes you seem timid."

Bronwyn nodded and said "Sorry" again, and Addison clicked his tongue, shook his head, and turned to Noor and me. "Now, where have you been?"

"It's kind of a long story," I said.

"Never mind then, we've got to get you to the ymbrynes," Addison said. "They need to know you've been found."

Noor asked if they were okay.

"They'll be better now that you're back," Bronwyn allowed.

"Everything's still here?" I cast a wary glance down the hall.

"Yes . . ." Bronwyn began to look worried.

"There hasn't been an attack?" Noor said.

Addison's ears pricked up. "An attack? By whom?"

A tightness that had been building in my chest began to loosen. "Thank God."

"There's been no attack," Bronwyn said, "though honestly, we've been so preoccupied with finding you that we might not have noticed if bombs started falling."

"I want to know what you mean by all these strange questions," Addison said, raising up on his hind legs to squint at me.

Noor glanced at me, uncertain.

"Maybe nothing," I said, rubbing my face. "It's been a long night. I don't mean to be mysterious, but I think you're right, we should talk to Miss Peregrine first."

I didn't want to spread panic. And there was still a small part of me that hoped I was wrong about Caul. That he was still where he belonged, condemned to spend forever trapped in the Library of Souls.

"At least tell us where you've been," Bronwyn pleaded. "We've been working day and night to find you. The ymbrynes have had us patrolling every loop where you two might conceivably have disappeared to. Emma, Enoch, Addison, and me have been on rotating shifts of your house in Florida since yesterday evening."

"Even in that tempest!" said Addison. "And then those sadistic, pole-wielding constables surprised us—"

"Since yesterday?" Noor said. "That can't be right . . ."

"How long have we been gone?" I finally thought to ask.

Addison's furry brows pinched together. "These are odd questions indeed."

"Two days," said Bronwyn. "Since the afternoon before last."

Noor fell back a step. "Two *days*."

That's how long we were falling, I thought, and for a moment I felt that weightless, bodiless sensation come over me again. *Two days*.

"We went to find V," I said, "that much I can tell you."

"And we did," Noor added, which was more than I wanted to say.

Bronwyn gasped, but didn't interrupt.

"It didn't go well," I said. "We got ejected from her loop somehow and woke up on my grandfather's porch in Florida."

"By our winged elders," Bronwyn said quietly. "That's unbelievable."

"Quite literally," Addison agreed. "It violates every known law of loopology. Now let's go before we ruin the carpet with our wet." And he nudged us down the hall, washed in the wan gray light of a Devil's Acre morning.

"You really found her?" Bronwyn asked as we walked.

Noor nodded. Bronwyn seemed to understand that something terrible had happened, but didn't pry. She cast a worried look in my direction. "I'm really sorry," she said again.

Passing a window, I looked outside and was met with a strange sight: a dusting of grayish fluff coated the streets, the rooftops, the Acre's few stunted trees. More fell gently through the air. It was snowing in Devil's Acre. But the Acre was a loop, and the weather did not change from one day to the next, and so it couldn't have been snowing.

Bronwyn caught me staring. "Ashes," she said.

"It's one of the desolations," explained Addison. "That's what Miss Avocet calls them."

So all was not as we had left it; all was not well.

"When did that start?" I asked.

But then someone was screeching, "Is it them? Is that *them*?" and two people came racing out of the stairwell.

Emma. Emma and Enoch, running toward us in black raincoats smeared with ash. My heart expanded at the sight of them.

"Jacob! Noor!" Emma was shouting. "Thank the birds, thank the heavenly peculiar *birds*!"

Again we were wrapped in arms, spun in circles, peppered with questions. "Where the devil have you been?" Emma demanded, her mood flipping between ecstatic and angry. "For a visit to your parents, without leaving so much as a note?!"

"You ruddy idiots, you had us thinking you were dead!" Enoch berated us. "Again!"

"We nearly were," Noor said.

Emma attacked me with another hug, then shoved me to arm's length and looked me up and down. "Well? You look like drowned rats."

"They've been through hell," said Bronwyn.

"We should really talk to Miss Peregrine," I said apologetically.

Enoch curled his lip. "Why? You didn't bother telling her you were leaving."

"She's in her new office, upstairs," Emma said, and we started down the hall again.

"They found the hollow-hunter," Addison blurted, apparently unable to contain himself.

Emma's eyes lit up. "Really?"

"Where is she?" Enoch said suspiciously.

"Don't ask," muttered Bronwyn.

Emma blanched. She was about to ask me something more when we came to a throng of people lined up in the hall, and we stopped talking as we passed them. They looked like new arrivals, both wide-eyed from the strangeness of their surroundings and dazed from recent loop crossovers, all dressed in clothes from different eras and parts of the world. Some could easily have passed for normals: a young couple who looked like English gentry and had the bored expressions to match; a boy tapping his foot and checking his pocket watch; a glaring baby in an old Victorian baby stroller. Others were so manifestly peculiar they'd have had a difficult time living anywhere outside of a circus sideshow or a loop: a bearded girl and her mother, a man in fancy dress who had a parasitic twin growing out of his chest, a freckled girl who had piercing eyes but lacked a mouth. They were lined up to get their transit papers stamped by one of Sharon's passport control functionaries.

"*New joiners from the outer loops,*" Enoch whispered. "The ymbrynes have been inviting all sorts to the Acre, not that we can fit many more. We're cheek by jowl as it is." I asked why and he gave an irritable roll of his shoulders. "I've no idea why anyone would want to come here. Any other loop would be better than this."

It made me wonder if the ymbrynes already knew something bad was coming and were gathering the most vulnerable peculiars in the Acre for their protection.

We were nearly past the crowd when I thought I heard my name and looked back, and caught about half of them staring at me. The moment I turned away again I swear I heard the glaring baby say, in a distinctly not-baby voice, "That *is* Jacob Portman!"

BEARDED GIRL AND MOTHER.

When the throng was behind us Emma finally asked her question. "What happened to V?"

"I promise we'll tell you everything," I said, "just as soon as we talk to Miss P."

Emma sighed. "Tell me this, at least. Did you have something to do with the hail of bones yesterday?" She touched a purpling bruise behind her ear, the sight of which made me wince.

"The *what*?" Noor said.

"The desolations," Addison stage-whispered.

"There was a hail of bones yesterday morning," Bronwyn said matter-of-factly. "Rain of blood last evening."

"More of a drizzle," said Emma, shouldering open the stairwell door and holding it for the rest of us. "And now the ashes."

"Something is rotten in the state of Denmark," Addison said. "That's *Shakespeare*."

◆　　　◆　　　◆

On the top floor of Bentham's house, above the libraries and dormitories and snaking halls of Panloopticon doors, were his attic of peculiar treasures and his office, which in his permanent absence Miss Peregrine had claimed as her own. "She comes here to think," Bronwyn explained, her voice echoing in the stairwell. "She says it's the only place in the whole bloody Acre she can get a moment's peace and quiet." At the landing she pushed the door open and bellowed down the stairs for Enoch to quit lagging.

We wended our way through rooms containing Bentham's museum of peculiar objects. When I'd first seen the attic the displays had been hidden under sheets and stowed away in crates, but now the boxes had been pried open and the sheets torn away. The effect of seeing his entire collection at once, uncovered and washed with ghostly, ash-filtered light, was dizzying. If the snaking Panloopticon hallways were the peculiar world's Grand Central Station, then the attic floors above them were its mixed-up and mothballed Museum of Natural History. Pathways had been cleared by double- and triple-stacking many of the displays, and my gaze tripped from case to case as we shuffled single file through the narrow aisles.

I tried to stay focused on our meeting with Miss Peregrine and how we would break our awful news to her, but the oddities passing inches from my face conspired to distract me. Something rattled inside the shadows of a fancy dollhouse locked inexplicably inside a barred cage. A case filled with glass eyes stared back, shifting in their display rests to follow me as I hurried by. A hum drew my attention to the ceiling, where a ring of small rocks slowly orbited a thick black book that hovered in the air.

I turned to Noor and whispered, *"You okay?"* and she returned a tiny smile and a shrug that said, *As I can be.* Then she narrowed her eyes at something over my shoulder.

It was an apparently empty glass box. Above it a sign read THE ULTIMATE AND PENULTIMATE FLATULATIONS OF SIR JOHN SOANE, BUILDER OF THIS HOUSE.

"What was this Bentham guy's deal?" Noor said. "Why'd he collect all this crap?"

"He was an obsessive, clearly," said Addison. "With far too much time on his hands."

"It ain't *crap*," a sharp voice said from across the room, and we all snapped our heads to see Nim appear from a patch of shadow. "Master Bentham's peculiarium is *treasurous* and *precious* and I'd like to you leave *at once*, if it pleases you—or even if it don't!"

He chased us onward, flicking at our heels with a broom.

As the others laughed about Nim, I wondered about Bentham. Was he just another obsessive nerd who, thanks to the Panloopticon he helped develop, happened to have access to vast swaths of the peculiar universe? Or was he squirreling away evidence of a world he feared his brother might one day obliterate? And if that was something he'd worried over, why hadn't he done more to stop it?

Shoved into a corner, I spied the person-sized cases that had once contained people—living ones—paralyzed by some obscure temporal reaction and imprisoned here in a kind of sadistic wax museum. The kernel of pity I'd begun to feel for Bentham evaporated. Granted, in some sense he'd been a prisoner himself, kidnapped and forced against his will to work for the wights. And yes, he hated his brother and worked in various subtle ways to subvert Caul's aims. But his efforts had not been enough. Noor and I weren't entirely to blame for Caul's resurrection. In the years he lived here Bentham must have had opportunities to destroy the Panloopticon or, better yet, kill his brother. But he hadn't. What might he have achieved for peculiarkind if he'd been toiling alongside his sister for all those years rather than Caul?

The last of Bentham's museum rooms had been turned into a photo studio, its walls covered in framed portraits. A cross-eyed photographer was dashing between his camera, a giant black box stamped with the words MINISTRY OF PHONO- AND PHOTOGRAPHIC RECORDS, and his subject, a small girl posing woodenly on a chair. A cluster of nervous kids waited nearby to have their turn, several clutching newly stamped temporal transit papers. The Ministry was documenting them almost as soon as they arrived, which wasn't the usual procedure. As if they worried there might not be another chance.

We left the studio and came into a high-ceilinged vestibule. The walls here were so thickly covered in gilt-framed paintings that I could hardly tell where the door to Bentham's office was, until I heard Miss Peregrine's voice shouting from the other side of it: "Well then, what the devil are you up to down there? It certainly doesn't *seem* like you know what you're doing!"

"I think that's Perplexus she's slagging off," Emma said.

"Yes, obviously the work is important!" Miss Peregrine said. "But you're going to break Devil's Acre if you continue failing this way, so either fix it, or find somewhere else to do your blasted experiments!"

"Maybe we should come back later," Bronwyn said.

Enoch shushed us all and cupped his ear against the door—which then flew open. Miss Peregrine stood in the frame, the color high in her cheeks. "You're back!" she cried, and, flinging out her arms, she engulfed us in a flutter of black fabric. "I thought . . . I thought . . . Well, never mind what I thought. You're *back*."

I caught a glimpse of Perplexus in the room behind her, but whatever drama we'd interrupted had been all but forgotten.

"I'm so glad to see you," I whispered, and her stack of inky hair brushed my cheek as she nodded vigorously in reply. I'd often felt relief at seeing Miss Peregrine but never so much as I did right then, having spent the past several hours trying and failing to imagine the world, and my life, without her. And it struck me, in a way that seemed both obvious and profound, that what I felt for this strange, small woman was love. I clung to her for another moment after Noor disengaged from a nervous hug, both to assure myself she was there and because I was realizing with some astonishment how frail she seemed through the voluminous folds of her dress. It frightened me how much weight rested on such slight shoulders.

She let me go and stepped back to take us in. "My goodness, you're soaked to the bone."

"Me and Addison found 'em at Mr. Jacob's house just ten minutes ago," said Bronwyn, "and brought 'em straight to you."

"Thank you, Bronwyn, you did the right thing."

"Oh, you dears, you poor creatures!" called Miss Avocet from inside the room, and I looked past Miss Peregrine to see the elder ymbryne sitting by the window in a wheelchair. She gestured for us to come in, then snapped at two ymbrynes-in-training hovering nearby. "Ladies, fetch some clean towels, fresh clothes, Russian tea, and something hot to eat."

They chorused, "Yes, miss," and dipped their heads. One was named Sigrid, a serious-looking girl with perfectly round glasses, and the other was Francesca, Miss Avocet's promising favorite. Enoch sighed and turned his head to watch Francesca go as she slipped past us. Then he caught me looking and immediately resumed his usual scowl.

"We need to talk to you in private," I said to Miss Peregrine.

She nodded, and I wondered if she already knew what we'd come to tell her.

"Private?" Enoch's scowl deepened. I could see he wanted to argue, but held back; perhaps the memory of her shouting at Perplexus was too fresh.

"I need you to go round up the others," Miss Peregrine said to our friends. "Tell them Jacob and Noor have been found. Bring them all back to Ditch House and wait for us there."

"Millard and Olive are searching the New York loop," Emma said, consulting a thin watch on her wrist. "But they should be back any minute."

"Go get them now, please," Miss Peregrine said. "Don't wait."

"Yes, miss." Emma gave Miss P a look that seemed to beg her not to keep them in the dark too long. "See you soon."

Emma, Enoch, Bronwyn, and Addison went out. Perplexus cleared his throat irritably, reminding me he was in the room. "*Mi scusi*, Signora Peregrine, we haven't finished—"

"I believe we have, Mr. Anomalous," Miss Peregrine said in a pleasant but clipped tone, which coming from her was practically a shove out the door. He turned red and left muttering curses in Italian.

Miss Peregrine saw Noor rake rain-plastered hair from her neck and asked us if we wanted to change.

"That's kind of you," Noor replied, "but if we don't tell you what happened soon I think I'm going to have a nervous breakdown."

Miss Peregrine's mouth tightened into a thin line. "Then by all means," she said, "let's begin."

In lieu of fresh clothes we were given blankets to wrap ourselves in, and the ymbrynes-in-training returned with tea and snacks that were laid out on a table but went untouched; we had no appetite. And then we were finally alone with the two ymbrynes, perched on a small sofa between Miss Avocet in her ornately carved wheelchair and Miss Peregrine, who stood beside us, apparently too anxious to sit.

"Tell us everything," she said. "I think we know much of it, but tell it anyway, and leave nothing out."

So we began our awful story. I told them how we'd decided that if Noor was going to stay with us permanently she should have more of her own personal things, and so we'd gone to her foster parents' apartment in Brooklyn via the New York loop.

"Without telling a single soul where you were going," Miss Avocet said, her long fingernails drumming the arms of her wheelchair.

It seemed indefensible now, but I tried to explain anyway. Things had calmed down in the Acre, I said. The dark clouds of danger that had hung over our heads the past few weeks had seemed to clear. Our friends had been coming and going, using the Panloopticon with some freedom, and Noor and I felt we'd earned enough leeway to do the same.

"We really thought it was safe," Noor added, sounding genuinely apologetic. "We thought we'd be back before anyone noticed."

I told them about the postcard we'd found in a stack of mail at her foster parents' place. That it seemed to have been written by V and invited Noor to come visit her. The address was a place that was only a few hours away by car. "We were already out of the Acre when we found it," I added, feeling like a kid trying to wheedle his way out of being grounded. "And rather than coming all the way back—"

"It was something we wanted to do ourselves," Noor cut in.

"We don't need your justifications," Miss Avocet said. "You're not on trial here." And then she muttered, *"Yet."*

I wasn't sorry, in retrospect, that we'd done it alone. I tried to imagine Noor leading not just me but several of our friends through the Waynoka loop and its dual tornados. The odds of everyone surviving were slim at best. And even if a number of us had managed to reach V, would it really have changed anything? Murnau would still have taken us by surprise, and in that hostage situation, with his gun trained on V, would it really have mattered how many of us had been there?

Maybe, maybe not.

Noor took over the telling. She described driving into Waynoka, and the strange feeling of déjà vu that had come over her. She described the storage facility, and the odd man we met among the cages who was toiling in pain. As we described him I saw Miss Peregrine and her mentor exchange a knowing look. Noor described the tornado-plagued loop. The song she remembered from childhood, taught to her by V, which had seen us through the loop's trials, one near-death experience after another, until we reached V's little cottage.

Here Noor stopped, her face tightening, and she fell silent. She could not continue, so I did.

"V wasn't expecting us," I said.

"It wasn't she who sent that postcard, was it?" Miss Avocet asked.

I shook my head slowly. "She was angry when she saw us," I said. "Terrified, too."

"'What the hell are you doing here?'" Noor said quietly. "That's what she said when she saw us." Her lip quivered. "What she said to me." She nodded at me to keep going.

"She took us into her house," I said, "which was practically an arsenal, and started locking it down like she was expecting an attack. And before she could finish, one came."

"Murnau," muttered Miss Peregrine.

"He was the man we'd helped in the storage warehouse," I

said. "He'd disguised himself." I paused. Shifted uncomfortably. "The last ingredient on Bentham's list wasn't the heart of the mother of birds. He was never after either of you. It was the heart of the—"

"Mother of storms," Miss Avocet said. "Francesca noticed Bentham's intentional mistranslation last night. I suppose he hoped it would throw Caul's people off the trail."

I shook my head. "It didn't."

"Murnau killed her," said Miss Peregrine. She didn't need to ask; she could read it on our faces.

Noor's chin dipped to her breastbone. She took a shuddering breath, and when she began to steady, I continued.

"He shot her. Then he shot the two of us with some kind of sleep dart. And when we woke up . . ."

I stopped. Couldn't make myself say it in front of Noor. Even speaking the words aloud seemed a kind of violence. Miss Peregrine sat beside Noor on the sofa and put a hand on her back.

"He took her heart," Miss Avocet said, staring at her liver-spotted hands, now balled to fists in her lap.

"*Yes,*" I whispered.

I told them how Murnau took the heart and his leather bag of unholy trophies and ran straight into a tornado that was raging across the road. How he'd been swept up, and how shortly thereafter the face of Caul had appeared in the wind and among the whipping branches of an uprooted tree, and how his voice had boomed my name in the form of a thunderclap.

Miss Peregrine straightened. "Horace dreamed it," she said. "That very image: Caul's face in the whirlwind. He dreamed it two nights ago."

My throat tightened. "Just as it was happening," I said. Not a prophetic dream, more of a channeling. A supernatural livestream. I looked at my ymbryne. "Then you already knew."

She shook her head. "We feared the worst. But we didn't know—until just this moment—that Caul had truly been resurrected."

"May the elders help us," Miss Avocet said.

Noor's head sank.

"We did know *something* was terribly wrong," Miss Peregrine said. "There have been . . . disturbances."

I nodded. "Emma said it's been raining . . . bones?"

"Bones, blood, ash. There was a squall of larynxes very early this morning."

"Perversions in the fabric of the loop," said Miss Avocet. "They can mean a loop is breaking down, beginning to fail in telltale ways."

"We thought it might be a result of the temporal experiments Perplexus has been conducting recently," Miss Peregrine said, and flashed a guilty look at the elder ymbryne. "I believe I owe him an apology."

"I have wondered," Miss Avocet said, "whether these phenomena could be the result of a hostile force attempting to sabotage our loop from outside."

Noor's head rose. "Like a hacker messing with the code."

The ymbrynes looked at her blankly.

"The elders called these irregularities *desolations*," said Miss Avocet. "Such phenomena often heralded a loop's demise."

"I'm so sorry," Noor said miserably. "I'm so, so sorry."

"Oh, nonsense," Miss Peregrine said. "Why?"

"This is my fault. I led Murnau to V. It's my fault she's dead. My fault Caul's back."

"Well, if it's your fault, it's just as much his for helping you," said Miss Avocet, poking a finger at me, and Noor's mouth fell open in surprise. "And Fiona's for allowing herself to be captured so they could slice out her tongue," she went on. "And those deadrisers who sat on their backsides while the wights turned their precious graveyard inside out looking for the alphaskull. And mine and Francesca's, come to think of it, for not catching Bentham's sneaky mistranslation of *storms* earlier, which would have tipped you off the moment you realized V's loop was infested with tornadoes."

"All right?" Miss Peregrine said to Noor. "Enough of this *my fault* business. That is self-pitying piffle, and helpful to no one."

"All right," Noor said, forced by their good-natured bullying to agree. But I knew the question of blame was more complicated for her than they'd made it out to be.

"But has Caul *attacked* anyone?" I said, the question I'd been dying to ask finally bursting out. "Has he shown himself?"

"Not yet," said Miss Avocet. "Not that we know of."

"But he will," I said.

"Oh yes. Most certainly he will." Miss Peregrine rose from the sofa and crossed to the window. She studied the view briefly, then turned to face us. "But if I know my brother, this attack will come in a way we're not expecting, at a time we're not expecting. He won't rush. He's careful, methodical—like all wights."

"Just a moment," said Miss Avocet, sitting as erect as the parenthetical curvature of her back would allow. "How did the two of you escape the loop before it collapsed? You haven't told that part of the story yet."

"I think it had something to do with this," Noor said, and she dug V's strange stopwatch out of her pocket.

Miss Avocet's rheumy eyes flashed with interest. "May I examine that?"

Noor passed it to her. The old ymbryne fished up a monocle that hung from a thin chain around her neck and held it close to the watch. After a moment she exclaimed, "Why, this is a temporal expulsatator!" She flipped the watch over in her hand. "I was told this never made it to production. Too unpredictable. It had a tendency to turn the user gut-side-out."

"I think V kept it just for emergencies," I said, trying not to picture the oozing mess we might've become had the thing malfunctioned. "We found it in V's hand after we woke up on my grandfather's porch."

"In Florida?" Miss Peregrine's gaze had wandered out the window again, but now it snapped back to me. "Yes, that makes sense. Abe trained her, after all. And they worked together for some years . . ."

"She was an ymbryne," I said. "V made that loop herself. Did you know?"

Miss Peregrine frowned at Miss Avocet. "I did not."

"I knew," Miss Avocet said, answering Miss Peregrine's unasked question. "Abe introduced me to Velya when she was just a teenager. He asked me to train her in secret. As a favor to Abe, I agreed."

"You might've told me, Esmerelda," Miss Peregrine said, sounding more hurt than angry.

"My apologies. But it would not have helped the children's search. Only made it seem impossible, and discouraged them."

"Because how do you find a loop that's never been mapped?" I said.

Miss Avocet nodded. "When I heard Velya was hiding in America, I did wonder if she'd made her own loop, so that she could hide without having to entrust her whereabouts to another person. But I never suspected she would create such a dangerous one, intentionally, as a means of defense. It's brilliant, really."

"Quite," Miss Peregrine agreed. "But what a lonely life that must have been."

"I'd like to bury her," Noor said quietly.

"We had to leave her behind," I explained. "Her body's in my grandfather's bunker."

"We don't bury ymbrynes, at least not in the usual way you're accustomed to," Miss Avocet said. "But she deserves a funeral at the minimum." She looked away and muttered what sounded like a prayer in Old Peculiar, her downturned mouth and pinched brow transforming her face into a topography of creases.

"We'll send a team to retrieve her body," Miss Peregrine said.

"I'd like to go," Noor said.

"Me too," I said. "There's a hollowgast lurking around. A pretty injured one, but still."

"Out of the question," Miss Avocet said flatly.

"A hollowgast?" Miss Peregrine stiffened. "You mean you were attacked?"

"There was a wight patrolling my grandfather's yard," I said. "The hollow was off in the woods. It seemed like they were waiting for something, but I don't think it was us. The wight was pretty surprised when we showed up."

"He was even more surprised when I stabbed him in the neck," said Noor.

Miss Peregrine looked frustrated. "Sometimes it seems as if my brother's forces are inexhaustible. I truly thought we'd killed or captured most of them."

"Most, but not all, it would appear," said Miss Avocet. "We've kept a careful count of the hollowgast over the years. I think the one you encountered today really must have been the last of them. Now please, children, finish your narrative."

I told the rest quickly: our escape into Abe's bunker. His teleprinter-activated home defense system, a detail that impressed the ymbrynes but made me think, yet again, about the sacrifice my grandfather had made for me the night he died, by leading that hollow into the woods and fighting him there with just a letter opener, rather than sheltering in his bunker. I told them about our mad dash across Englewood in my grandfather's unwieldy car, in a hurricane, with an injured and furious hollow chasing us.

Having recounted it all, I could hardly believe we were here, safe, breathing the same air as our friends. I thought we'd lost our lives, this world, everything.

"So?" I said. "What now?"

Miss Peregrine's face darkened. "Now we try to prepare for what's coming. Something we don't yet know the shape or size of."

"War," said Miss Avocet. "I wish I could say it was none of

your concern. That this is the province of ymbrynes and the senior-most among us, the battle-hardened, the veterans. The grown." She turned her body toward us. "But it is not. It concerns you intimately. Especially you, Miss Pradesh."

Noor met her gaze unflinchingly. "I'll do anything that's needed. I'm not afraid."

Miss Avocet reached out and patted her hand. "That's good. Though a modicum of fear wouldn't hurt, either. It's the absolutely unafraid who tend to die first, and we need you, dear. We need you badly." She picked up a cane that was leaning against her chair and rapped the brass tip on the ground twice. The door flew open and her two ymbrynes-in-training came inside. "Call an emergency meeting of the Ymbryne Council. And when that's done, escort me to the council chamber."

"Yes, madam," they said in unison, then quickly went out again, petticoats shushing.

"I'll escort Jacob and Noor back to the house and meet you in the council chamber shortly," Miss Peregrine said. "Their friends are all waiting, and they're about to receive some very alarming news. I'd like to help break it."

Miss Avocet looked pained. "Do they have to be told right now? I'd rather inform all our citizenry at once, after the Council has had a chance to talk things over."

"I can't ask Jacob and Noor to lie to their friends, and I haven't the heart to keep them in suspense any longer."

Miss Avocet nodded. "I suppose they deserve to know first, anyway, after all they've done. But they mustn't spread word around about . . . *him*."

"Understood," said Miss Peregrine, and conducted Noor and me out into the hall, where Enoch had been shamelessly eaves-dropping.

"*Him* who?" he said, trailing after us. "Who's *Him*?"

"I thought I asked you to return to the house, Mr. O'Connor,"

Miss Peregrine said through her teeth. "And you'll find out soon enough."

"I don't like the sound of that at *all*," said Enoch. "By the way, you two should really wash up. You're a mess, and frankly, you smell. Coming from me, that should tell you something."

Noor looked down at her shirt, partially dried and gone stiff with mud and blood, and grimaced. There were a pair of washrooms opposite Bentham's office, and Francesca had left a pile of towels and fresh clothes for us beside them.

"Change, by all means, but be quick about it," Miss Peregrine said. "I've got a meeting to attend."

*   *   *

I felt a bit guilty, taking an extra thirty seconds to soak my hands in hot water, to clean caked mud from my face and inside my ears, but I needed it badly—a few seconds alone, a moment to breathe. I stripped off my torn shirt and wet jeans and changed into the clothes Francesca and Sigrid had given me. I would've donned a pink bunny suit rather than spend another minute in a shirt stained with V's blood, but happily I didn't have to stoop to that. They'd given me an old suit to wear: a white collarless button-down shirt, black pants, black jacket, black boots. My shaky hands kept fumbling with the buttons, and I had to force myself to slow down, to breathe, to concentrate on the tiny careful motions required of my fingers. After a few tries, my breathing evened out. It all fit, even the shoes. A vest and tie were part of the outfit, too, but I didn't feel the need to compete with Horace for best dressed, so I left those folded on the wooden vanity, and my ruined clothes piled in the corner.

Time to go, I told myself, but my feet wouldn't turn toward the door. I ran a hand through my hair and looked at myself in the gold-trimmed mirror. I felt as creaky and tired as an old man, but I looked okay, I thought.

The pictures covering the vestibule outside continued throughout the bathroom, and I noticed a framed photo of Bentham above the vanity. *Strange*, I thought. In the photo, he was wearing the very suit I had just put on—plus a top hat, tie, and watch chain—and he sat between two presumably peculiar animals, a baby goat and a small dog. And he was, arrestingly, staring right into the lens, his expression humorless and severe, as usual.

What happened to you? I wondered, locking eyes with him. Bentham and Caul were trapped together in the collapsed Library of Souls. *When your brother was resurrected, did you come back, too?*

And then I swear I saw his lip twitch, and I felt a cold charge go through me and hurried out of the washroom.

Noor was waiting for me outside, looking uncomfortable in a black-and-white striped dress that brushed her ankles. Her hair was pulled into a hasty ponytail, her face washed and shining, and I thought how remarkable it was that it took so little effort for her to be beautiful.

"You look great," I said.

She shook her head and laughed like I'd told a corny joke. "I look like I'm going to a circus funeral." She gave me a genuine smile. "I like you in a suit, though." Then she sighed. "You okay?"

It was the question we asked each other most often. We lived in trying times, and there were so many ways to not be okay.

"Yeah," I said. "You?"

This small exchange of words held a hundred potential shades of meaning. In this case: *What took you so long in the bathroom?* and *Have you been able, for even a minute, to stop the horror movie playing on repeat in your head?*

"I had mud in places you wouldn't believe." She shrugged. "I'm okay." She closed the small gap between us and leaned her head against my shoulder. "Sorry, I complain when I'm nervous."

I pressed my cheek to her hair. "I thought you hummed when you were nervous."

"I'm testing this out instead."

I put my arms around her, hugged her tight. There was a meter somewhere inside me, a confidence gauge, a bravery indicator, and every time I touched her it bounced upward.

"Ready?" I said.

"To confess my sins," she said, and before I could argue with her word choice, Miss Peregrine and Enoch whooshed into the hall and escorted us out.

CHAPTER FIVE

*O*ur trip across the Acre was surreal. More surreal than usual, that is. It wasn't just the strange sky, which was a bruised purple rather than its normal shade of sickly yellow, or the deep drifts of ash that swirled around our feet as we walked, or the dark rivulets of drying blood weeping down the walls of buildings. It was the idea, easy to forget from moment to moment, that we were now living in a nightmare, walking through a world in which the worst thing I could imagine, short of everyone I loved dying, had come to pass. It was a hard and immutable fact. And we were about to break this awful news to all our friends.

Enoch kept pestering me: "Who's *Him*? Is it who I think it is? Is that why I almost got knocked unconscious by hail bones yesterday? Is he *back*?" But I wouldn't tell him anything, and finally Miss Peregrine had to separate us so that he'd leave me alone.

It had not fully struck me how unwise the architecture of their house was until, crossing the last footbridge over their narrow tributary of Fever Ditch, I saw the place again. It was twice as wide at the third floor as it was at the ground, like a pyramid stood on its head, and was prevented from tipping into the Ditch only by a forest of wooden struts and stilts that stretched to the upper stories. In an attempt to brighten things up, Fiona had covered the leaning house in flowers—reinforced it, really, with long, winding cables of purple dogrose. They trailed up the stilts and spilled from window boxes. But they only filled me with dread, a reminder of the vines that held me down on Gravehill, and of the horror of being forced to watch helplessly as Murnau committed his atrocities.

The front door flew open. Olive bounded out and stomped down the rickety steps. "You must—stop—*disappearing like this*!" she cried, attacking me with a hug. And then the others all came flooding out, Horace and Millard and Claire and Hugh, so many at once that they bottlenecked in the doorway and had to struggle free of one another, and then they were rushing down the steps, crowding us, shouting questions.

"Is it really them?" Horace cried.

"It's really them!" Olive sang, twirling to hug Noor.

"We've been looking *everywhere* for you!" said Claire, gaping at me with wide, frightened eyes. "Were you kidnapped?"

"They'd better have been!" Hugh said, pulling me into a hard embrace. "Not even a *note*!"

"They'll tell you everything," said Miss Peregrine, glancing at the curious faces peering from nearby buildings, "once we get indoors."

We were bundled inside amid a cluster of nervously chattering friends. And there was Fiona, covered in blankets and chickens, on a daybed in the middle of the hay-strewn kitchen. She liked it better down here in the cozy mess, Hugh explained, and while she was recovering, Miss Peregrine had told her she could sleep wherever she liked. She beamed at me as I crossed the room and bent down to hug her.

"I hope you're feeling better," I said, and though she didn't respond with words, she nodded and then kissed my cheek. The chicken in her arms clucked and ruffled its feathers possessively.

Miss Peregrine asked for quiet. She waved Noor and me to the center of the room, and our friends sat around us on wobbly wooden chairs and on the floor. They all looked as anxious as I was feeling. I was anxious to get this over with, to tell our story for what I dearly hoped would be the last time; anxious, too, about their reactions. Would they hate us? Would they despair?

We told it. They listened in grim, stunned silence. When it was over the air in the room felt leaden. Claire and Olive had scooted across the floor to Bronwyn and curled into balls against her legs. Claire was crying. Horace had crawled underneath the kitchen table. Hugh sat stone-faced on the daybed beside Fiona, who was holding his hand and staring at the floor. Emma—I cared most about her reaction—Emma had twisted her hair into a knot and was several shades paler than when Noor and I had started talking.

"You left out that part at the end," Emma said, "when you told it before." She blew out her breath.

"So he *is* back," said Enoch. "*Him* is . . . *him*."

"He's back," I said, nodding grimly. "Him is him."

"Oh my bird, oh my God, oh hell," Horace moaned from under the kitchen table. "It *was* his face I dreamed."

Millard rose from where he'd been sitting. "I'm broken-hearted. I'm shattered."

"V's really . . . gone?" Olive asked meekly.

Noor nodded and said quietly, "Yeah. She's gone."

Olive ran to her, attached herself to Noor's side. Noor rubbed Olive's shoulder as the little girl began to cry.

"So, what does this mean for us?" Hugh asked. "What will happen?"

"Then it's Caul who's behind the desolations?" asked Bronwyn. "Not Perplexus?"

"Yes, we think so," said Miss Peregrine.

"Oh, *absolutely* he is," said Emma.

"I'm sure it's only a taste of what he can do," said Horace. "An amuse-bouche."

"He's warming up the orchestra," Millard agreed. "He'll be coming for us soon, and when he does you can be sure he'll bring a lot more than bloody rain down on us."

"We're doomed! We're sunk! This is the end of everything!" Claire wailed.

"He's only one man," said Addison, who I'd just noticed sitting by the door. "And aren't most of his adherents dead or in prison? As for his hollowgast, can't young Jacob polish off whatever few remain?"

"You don't understand," Emma said. "He's not a *man* anymore, not really. You weren't there, in the Library of Souls, when he transformed into that . . . *thing* . . ."

"I'm not allowed in most libraries," Addison said with his muzzle raised, "so I boycott them on principle."

"This isn't a normal library," said Millard. "It's a repository for thousands of ancient peculiar souls, many of them extremely powerful. It was hidden for millennia, ever since certain evil peculiars discovered how to break into it and steal its souls, and their abilities, for themselves."

"They tried to fashion themselves into gods," said Miss Peregrine. "And they succeeded, to a degree. But they warred with one another, causing famines, floods, plagues. They would have destroyed the whole world if our ancestor ymbrynes hadn't managed to hide the Library from them. It stayed hidden so long that its existence faded to legend . . . until my brother broke into it again. We were able to collapse the loop and trap him there, we thought forever. Until, as you just heard, his top lieutenant resurrected him."

"A scenario that was prophesied long ago," said Horace. "Along with an apocalyptic war, similar to those ancient ones, that would leave the earth a cratered ruin. And us, presumably, dead."

"*Exceedingly* dead," said Enoch. "Caul despises us."

"So, let me get this straight." Addison raised an eyebrow. "You believe he's absorbed some of these terrible powers for himself. And thus no longer needs an army of toadies and shadow-creatures at his beck and call."

"That's our general working presumption, yes," said Millard.

"But none of you have actually *seen* him," said Addison, "except the American boy, in a cloud, and that boy cowering under the table there, in a dream."

"We saw him in the Library of Souls just before it collapsed," said Emma. "He was a giant tree-monster." Then, more quietly: "It was a lot scarier than it sounds."

"And that was after absorbing just *one* soul-jar," I said. "Who knows how many he's absorbed since then."

"Maybe all of them," said Emma. She looked fearfully at Miss Peregrine. "Is that even possible?"

Miss Peregrine pursed her lips. "We're treading in the realm of the hypothetical. We simply don't know."

"If he did then he'll be absolutely unstoppable," Horace cried.

"Don't lose your wig," said Enoch, rolling his eyes.

"I will, I *will* lose my wig when it's appropriate!" Horace shouted. He crawled out from under the table and stood next to it, gesticulating wildly. "Caul had been trying to get his hands on Bentham's resurrection ingredients for *years*. He *wanted* this. He planned for it! To get trapped in the Library, and then to be brought back again. He would never have put himself through that kind of hell unless he was sure it would make him better, stronger, *eviler*. He's a lot more than a tree monster now, I can assure you. Not because I dreamed it—because I have a brain!"

Everyone was staring. His lip, and then the rest of him, began to quiver. "I'll just go back under the table."

"No you won't," said Emma, popping up to grab him. "We won't be doing any more hiding, cowering, or running away. Right, Miss P?"

"I was hoping one of you would say that," the ymbryne replied.

"Yes, I thought you people had more spine," said Addison.

"Running away gets an unfairly bad rap," said Horace. "The best offense is a good defense, don't the American footballers say that?" He looked at me; I shook my head no. "No matter—it's true. Does it really make sense for all of us to stay here in Devil's Acre, where he can get us in one swat? Not only does he know just where to find us, he knows this loop inside and out. It was his headquarters for years."

"We shouldn't ever show him we're *scared*," said Bronwyn, her expression curdling. "Even if we are."

"We're stronger here, together," said Hugh, and Fiona nodded along. "Besides which, we can't abandon this place and let him have the Panloopticon again. It's our most powerful tool. And it could be his."

"You're worried about what he'll do with the *Panloopticon*?" Horace said, his voice rising again. "He could be omnipotent, omni-*present* at this point. What does he need a hallway of loop doors for?"

"If he was *omnipotent*, we'd already be dead," said Emma. "You must calm down a bit, and try not to scare the young ones."

"*I'm* not scared," Olive announced, and banged her little fist against her chest.

Miss Peregrine cleared her throat. "There's one thing you must understand about my brother. I seriously doubt he wants to kill us. Well"—she winced briefly—"he may want to kill me, and perhaps Jacob as well, but not all of you, and not the rest of our people. He wants power and control. All he's ever dreamed of, his whole bitter life, was to be the king and emperor of peculiarkind, to be worshipped by all the peculiars who mocked him as a child."

"So he'll just enslave us all," Enoch said, "make us lick his boots and sing his praises and go on retreats at the weekend to murder normals, or whatever gives him his jollies."

Emma climbed onto the kitchen table and stomped her foot, which made the silverware jump. "Can everyone *please* stop spinning out these terrified worst-case scenarios. We're not seriously about to give up hope before we even understand the full dimensions of what we're up against! Caul may be very powerful—we don't even know how much yet—but *we* are powerful, too. Powerful enough to have spoiled his plans and dealt him bad setbacks two or three times now. And we're not just a handful of peculiar children anymore. We have something like a *hundred* peculiars to fight him with—all our many allies who live here in the Acre, and who are reachable via the Panloopticon, not to mention all our abilities, all our experience, a dozen ymbrynes, and—and—"

"And Noor," said Horace. "We have Noor."

Noor's head snapped as if she'd been startled from sleep. "Sure," she said. "You have me, whatever good I am."

"What good *is* she?" asked Addison.

"If the prophecy is to be believed," Horace said, his voice deepening, "and given how much of it has already come to pass, I think it is, then Noor may be the most important asset we have in the coming struggle."

"Not without the other six," Noor said.

"I'm afraid I'm lost," said Addison.

"You get used to it," muttered Claire.

Horace went on. "The prophecy says that together, the seven foretold peculiars, of which Noor is one, may close the door."

"Notice it says *may*," said Enoch, "not *will*."

"To end the strife of war, seven may seal the door," Horace recited. "That's the best translation we have. There's also something about the 'emancipation' of peculiardom, but that part's a bit fuzzier."

"Seal the door to what?" asked Addison.

"We don't know," said Horace.

Addison stared him down. "Seal it *how*?"

"Don't know."

"And do we know where the other six are?" Addison looked around at the rest of us.

Miss Peregrine shook her head. "Not yet."

His voice rose. "What *do* you know, for pup's sake?"

"Not a great deal, as of now."

"All right, you've convinced me," said Addison, collapsing to the floor and covering his eyes with his paws. "We are all in very serious trouble."

❖   ❖   ❖

Before excusing herself to the emergency meeting of the Ymbryne Council, Miss Peregrine made everyone promise not to breathe a word of what they'd heard to anyone else in the Acre. "Not a soul," she warned. "Until we have a solid plan of action, it will only spread panic."

"And that's what you're going to do?" Hugh said with just a touch of sarcasm. "Develop a solid plan of action?"

Claire gave him a look that would curdle cheese.

"Yes, Mr. Apiston," Miss Peregrine said patiently. "We are." She scanned our faces. "It would be best if you all remained in the house until I returned. Do I make myself clear?"

I got the impression she was starting to regret telling everyone the news; that their reactions had been too scattered and frightened, and that we were all now filled with questions she was not prepared to answer, which only made us more anxious. And anxious, highly independent peculiar children who were prone to ignoring her orders were a headache she didn't need. So we were to be sequestered until further notice. Maybe a few hours, maybe longer, depending on how long the ymbrynes' meeting lasted.

After she left there was some grumbling about how Miss Peregrine still didn't trust us and treated us like children. Claire, who always took the ymbrynes' side, argued that we *were* still children, and as long as we kept doing things like disappearing into the Panloopticon without telling anyone—she gave me a long glare—maybe we did deserve to be treated as such. That sparked a debate about physical versus actual age, and whether living in an unchanging loop for eighty years was anything like living in the real world, and what effect it had on the state of one's mind and heart, at which point I started to feel overwhelmingly tired and snuck upstairs to sleep.

I collapsed in what I assumed was Horace's bed—it was the

only one that was made, the corners tucked tight, pillows fluffed. I lay on my side facing the window, watching ash fall gently while listening to a voice murmur from a small radio on the nightstand. A DJ was reading the morning news. I wanted to turn it off, but the knob was out of reach and I'd gone boneless with exhaustion. I wondered idly how a radio inside the loop could pick up a station from outside it, and then I heard the DJ say, "In rugby, the Devil's Acre Cannibals crushed the Battersea Emu-raffes for their fourth consecutive win this season."

The broadcast was coming from *inside* the loop. How long had Devil's Acre had a radio station? The DJ had a voice like an oil slick, low and hypnotic, and I listened in sleepy fascination as he went on about peculiar sports for a while.

"In a stunning upset, Miss Flycatcher's Aberdeen Eels were forced to give up the bog-swimming title they won last month against Miss Titmouse's Killarney Blighters after judges decided that the Eels' top swimmer having gills was a violation of the Poseidon rule. In local news, the lead and *the understudy in Miss Grackle's production of* The Grass Menagerie *have fallen ill with a touch of plague, so tonight's performance has been cancelled. In weather, the desolations continue, with a squall of horned snails reported on Attenuated Avenue in the late hours of last night and flurries of ash expected through the afternoon. Still no definite word on what's causing the disturbances, though plenty of rumors. Stay safe, peculiarfolk, it's weird out there. And not in a good way. This is Amos Dextaire, and you're listening to WPEC, the voice of Devil's Acre. I've got a pile of wax to spin you through the morning. Let's kick it off with a cozy old favorite of mine, the unsettling disharmonies of Krzysztof Penderecki's 'Threnody for the Victims of Hiroshima.' "*

A piece of classical music began to play—I think it was music, anyway—except the violins sounded like they were being tortured in hell, which finally motivated me to scooch all the way to the edge of the bed, stretch my arm out from under the womblike covers, and switch it off. And then I noticed a small picture leaned against the wall behind the radio—a framed photo of Amos Dextaire signed to Horace by the man himself. He seemed to be winking at the camera from behind dark glasses while managing an ice cream cone and a cigarette in the same hand.

I fell asleep dreaming about an orchestra of tuxedoed musicians burning alive while they played, and woke up sometime later to a vibrating bed.

Enoch had plopped down next to me. "I know you need your beauty rest, Portman, but there's a hollowgast at the door who seems really keen to chat."

"What?" I shot upright, covers flying off me.

"Just kidding, but it's getting boring down there without you. Goodness, you're high-strung."

I punched him on the arm. "Don't *do* that!"

He shoved me and I nearly fell off the bed. "Can't you tell when I'm joking?"

"Next time it'll be true and I won't believe you. You'll get eaten and deserve it."

I heard feet on the stairs, and a few seconds later Emma burst in. "Ulysses Critchley from Temporal Affairs just came to fetch us. They've called a meeting."

I slid my feet out of bed. "The ymbrynes?"

"Yes. But it's not just for us; the whole Acre's supposed to come."

"They're going to tell everyone *now*?"

"I suppose they want to beat Caul to the punch." Her fingers drummed the wall. "Get your shoes on!"

To a big fan,

Amos
Dextaire

CHAPTER SIX

A mandatory all-Acre assembly had never been called before. Instructions rang out from loudspeakers for everyone to drop what they were doing and attend, and peculiars were streaming into the streets from every building we passed. A great swarm converged on the lecture hall where it was to be held. The line to enter was long, and as we jostled into the queue and shuffled closer, Millard noted that it wasn't just the size of the crowd that was causing the slowdown, but that a pair of home guards were searching every single person before they were admitted inside.

"What are they looking for?" asked Noor. "Weapons?"

"We *are* weapons," Hugh replied.

"Some of us more than others," said Emma.

One of the guards started patting down Enoch's thighs. "Aww, no kiss first?" he said.

"What's this?" the guard said, peering into a cloudy glass jar he'd pulled from Enoch's jacket.

"A murderer's heart pickled in Himalayan salt brine."

The guard bobbled the jar, nearly dropping it.

"Careful, you clod, that was a gift!" He snatched it from the guard's hands. "Let us through already, don't you know who we are?"

The guard reared back. "I don't care if you're an ymbryne's grandmother, every single person is to be—"

The other guard leaned to him and whispered something in his ear, and the first guard gritted his teeth, unhappily swallowed his pride, and waved us through. "Go on." He gave me a forced smile and said, "Apologies, Mr. Portman, I didn't see you there."

Emma patted Enoch's shoulder. "Sorry, E. Guess you're just part of the entourage."

Enoch laughed and shook his head.

As a final precaution, we were made to stand in front of a strange young man with misaligned eyes and let him stare at us. ("Sorry, even you," the second guard had said to me.)

So I let the young man stare, his eyes roving up and down my body before coming to rest on my face.

"What's he doing?" I asked.

"Scanning your intentions," Millard said. "Be they good or ill."

I felt a mild heat building in my forehead, where the young man's eyes were focused. I was about to complain when he looked at the guards and nodded.

We were allowed inside, then ushered down a stone hallway flickering with gaslights and echoing with the murmurs of a crowd.

Noor walked beside me. "That was extremely thorough," she said suspiciously.

"They must be worried about crazies," I said.

"I don't blame them," replied Horace. "Imagine if someone set off a bomb in this place. That'd be ninety percent of the ymbrynes in Great Britain, not to mention several from around the world, wiped out in a blink."

"Thanks for that comforting thought," Noor replied. "I'm feeling much calmer now."

Enoch teased me the rest of the way down the hall, bowing and scraping, until I turned red from embarrassment. "Apologies, Mr. Portman, right this way, Mr. Portman! There's a spot of mud on your boots, Mr. Portman, might I lick it clean for you?"

"Don't be an ass," Noor said. "He never asked anyone to treat him like that."

Enoch bowed lower. "I'm so sorry if I ever offended you, madam."

She gave him a playful shove and he pretended to stumble into the wall, which he apologized and bowed to, and then we were all laughing. It was good to laugh, and to see Noor laugh, if only for a moment.

The passageway ended and we came into the top level of a large lecture hall, which wasn't really a lecture hall at all, Horace informed me. It was an old operating theater, designed so that an audience could observe surgeons at their grisly work. The seating was level upon level of rough wooden benches, arranged concentrically and looking down on a circular floor below, at the center of which was a body-sized platform. Gaslights shone everywhere, in giant chandeliers hung from the ceiling and from iron sconces that ringed the walls.

We descended to the second level and sat on a long, curving bench that had been reserved for us. The rest of the theater was filling up fast.

"This room was built as part of a medical school," Horace said, "but the wights used it to do horrible experiments on peculiars. Grafting animal parts onto human bodies. Trying to create hybrid hollowgast. Switching people's brains just to see what would happen. See the metal grate below the platform there? That was to catch all the—"

"I get it," I said, holding up a hand.

"Sorry. Sometimes the only way to get bad pictures out of my head is to share them with other people. Which I know is selfish."

"It's okay," I said, feeling a little guilty now. "You can tell me."

"No, no, I don't have to. I know it's disgusting."

He was quiet for a few seconds. His knee jiggled. He looked like he might burst.

I looked at him. "Go ahead."

"It was to catch all the entrails and blood," he said quickly.

"That's what the grate was for. And the smell was supposedly indescribable." He let out a sigh.

"Feel better?"

He gave me a sheepish grin. "Profoundly."

The hall was almost half full. There were over a hundred peculiars staying in the Acre now, and nearly all of them were in attendance. Everyone was freaked out by the desolations, and they weren't about to miss what they hoped would finally be an explanation.

To my surprise, I recognized a lot of people in the crowd. Ulysses Critchley had gone to sit beside his black-suited cohort from Temporal Affairs, who were noisily shushing the people around them. Sitting across from us was Miss Grackle's theater troupe, who had just come from practice and were still dressed from the neck down in outlandish animal costumes. In the row below them were Sharon and his burly cousins, all in matching black robes, though only Sharon wore his hood raised; the four cousins never did. They had fine silver hair but their faces looked young, and their strong jaws and high cheekbones were attracting long looks—though the cousins, whispering among themselves, hardly seemed to notice. Beside them squirmed a klatch of half-fish Ditch dwellers: Itch, his wife, and their two scaly kids. They sat grumbling in ill-fitting clothes and a spreading puddle of water that had made a little stream down the steps, occasionally spritzing themselves from a muddy seltzer bottle and looking like they were counting the seconds until they could strip off their clothes and return to the Ditch.

At the top level of the room stood a half dozen home guards and the young man who had scanned us with his eyes. They were watching the crowd intently.

I was surprised, too, to notice some Americans: Antoine LaMothe, too proud to sit, wearing a raccoon coat that was stirring on its own; a lanky bodyguard in Western-style chaps and a fringed leather jacket; a few more from his Northerner clan whom I recognized from Marrowbone but whose names I didn't know. I was even more surprised to spot a few of the diviner kids: Paul, Fern, and Alene, all of them in their Sunday best, Paul looking nervous and the girls surveying the scene coolly in wide-brimmed hats. I made a mental note to find them after the assembly and welcome them, and ask how they'd reached the Acre. It was no small journey getting here from their loop in Portal, Georgia; it would have meant either a plane ride or that same long road trip to New York that my friends and I had made to reach the Acre's connector loop there.

A few rows away were even more Americans I hadn't seen in a while, including several of Dogface's so-called Untouchables: the boy with the pulsating and possibly sentient neck-boil; the half woman, Hattie the Halfsie, who sat propped in the lap of the tusk-cheeked warthog girl; and two others who I'd only met briefly and in the dark. They sat whispering to one another, pointing at this peculiar or that. I got the feeling they were sizing us up, and I couldn't help but wonder what they thought.

Emma saw me looking at them. "I don't know why the ymbrynes let them into the Acre," she said. "They may have helped us a little when things got really dicey, but they're still just a bunch of mercenaries, as far as I'm concerned."

"I trust them about as far as I can throw them," said Enoch.

"Me too," agreed Bronwyn.

Enoch rolled his eyes. "*You* could throw them a long way."

"It's true," she said. "I have a trusting nature."

I was wondering whether Dogface himself was here when I heard someone bark my name, and I turned to see him coming down the row above us, mouth curled in a furry grin. "Well, if it isn't the celebrated Jacob Portman and his sycophantic friends. You've always got everyone in a tizzy, don't you? '*Where is he, where's he disappeared to now?*' Especially your many female admirers." He winked at Emma, and my jaw clenched while her color deepened.

"What do you want?" she snapped at him.

"What kind of greeting is that?" he said. "Didn't I save your life the last time I saw you?"

"The last time we saw you, you extorted us for an exorbitant sum of money just to do what any decent peculiar would've done out of kindness," said Emma.

"I never claimed to be decent. And by the by, the interest on that half-paid debt of yours is fast accruing. But I ain't here to collect. We just came to pay our respects before the show begins."

Coming up behind Dogface were Angelica, pursued as usual by a small dark cloud and an air of grumpy affliction, and by Wreck Donovan, lanky in a suave brown suit and red tie, his hair a pomaded wave. Watching them, I realized I had no idea who else was in Angelica's gang of peculiars, nor what Wreck's peculiar ability was, other than extreme overconfidence.

"I thought you all hated one another," Emma said.

Angelica looked down her nose. "We can put aside our differences when the situation demands it."

"And what's the situation?" I asked.

"That you've come to live with us in the Acre?" asked Olive, smiling. Olive was automatically nice to everyone, and clearly had no idea that these Americans had, at one point, tried to buy us.

Wreck broke out laughing. "*Live* here? With you?" His glancing Irish accent turned "with you?" into "witchou?"

Angelica shot him a black look, as if they were supposed to be on their best behavior, and Wreck stifled his laugh. "Leo Burnham couldn't be here," she said, "so he ordered us to come on his behalf. He's asked us to study how your ymbrynes run things. Observe your, er"—she cast a glance around her and couldn't hide her repulsion—"way of life."

"To see whether you've made any innovations, politically or organizationally, we might want to adopt for ourselves," Wreck said.

"*Whether they can take us down, more like,*" Enoch whispered in my ear.

"Come to see how the other half lives, eh?" said Hugh.

"Squalidly, from the looks of it," Dogface countered.

Hugh spat a bee at him. Dogface ducked as it zinged past his ear, curved around his head, and boomeranged back into Hugh's mouth. "It's a lot more civilized than the way you barbarians do things, I can tell you that," Hugh said, chuckling as Dogface growled at him.

Across the big room, one of the Ditch dwellers belched loudly enough for everyone to hear, and a fountain of dirty water sprayed from his mouth onto Sharon's cousins, who turned around and threatened to spit-roast every last one of them.

"It's the most singularly hideous loop I've ever set cloud in!" Angelica burst out, then looked relieved—as if holding that in another moment might have killed her.

"You can't judge our way of life by *this* place," Emma said irritably. "So many of our loops were destroyed when the wights raided them a few months ago, and we've all been shoved together here like survivors on a lifeboat. We've hardly begun rebuilding."

"Sure, sure," Wreck said. "And when that's done, what?"

"We go back to the way things were," said Claire. There was such hope in her voice that none of us had the heart to crush it, but it was utter fantasy in light of what the ymbrynes were about to announce.

Dogface knelt down to Claire's level. "And you liked the way things were?" he said in a childish voice. "With the ymbrynes treating you like schoolchildren?"

"They don't!" Claire protested.

"Don't they?" Angelica said.

"We'd have more say in things than we used to," Bronwyn said defensively.

Wreck's substantial brow shot up.

"The ymbrynes promised," said Claire.

Dogface stifled another laugh. I was getting impatient for the ymbrynes' presentation to begin.

Emma stood up from her seat and squared her shoulders to confront Dogface. "And do you think it's so much better in America? With a few strongmen acting like gang lords, controlling everyone with threats and intimidation? Forced to steal to earn your living? Warring and fighting with one another all the time? Afraid to cross into rival territory for fear of being taken prisoner? How could anyone live like that?"

Angelica tossed her head proudly. "Spoken like someone who would never make it a week in peculiar New York."

Wreck was more tactful. "I'm not saying there isn't room for improvement. That's why we've come. But at least we call the shots inside our own loops."

"You're trapped in a vicious cycle of vice and crime," Millard said. "Your freedom is an illusion."

Dogface chuckled. "At least we get to choose our own bedtime, you coddled, infantile—"

"We didn't come to fight with you," Wreck interrupted.

Dogface sulked. "*I* did."

"Can't you just be decent?" Claire said to him. "You'd have an easier time in life, don't you think?"

Dogface's perpetual grin vanished. "When you look like my Untouchables and I do, there is no easy time. Maybe pretty little girls like you can afford to be *decent*"—he said it with utter disdain—"but I cannot. So I'm a businessman, a survivor. They call me a stain on the world, a cockroach with fur. That's all right. I'll be the cockroach still standing when this world crumbles to dust." He turned to leave, then stopped. "Oh, and I take issue with the notion that we're *forced* to steal. For me, it's a passion." He opened his hand and dangled from it a small locket on a silver chain.

"Hey!" Olive shouted. "That's mine!"

He grinned, dropped it into her lap, and left, taking the other two Americans with him.

"*Most* unpleasant," said Horace, waving his hand in the air as if to dispel a stench.

"They've got some nerve," Emma said. "If it weren't for the ymbrynes, they'd all be at war right now, killing one another over some dusty old argument."

"Eh, forget them," Enoch said. "Looks like we're about to start."

On the operating stage below, a door had opened, and one by one, the whole Ymbryne Council filed out.

The crowd fell quiet as nine ymbrynes filed somberly onto the stage: Miss Peregrine was first, looking even more serious than usual. Then came Miss Cuckoo, whose gold pantsuit and metallic silver hair reminded me of David Bowie. Miss Babax followed her in a white dress and white gloves, a bold choice for this filthy loop. Then came Miss Blackbird with her third eye open, scanning the room for danger. Miss Loon and Miss Bobolink, who I knew little about, stuck close to her heels, and were trailed by Miss Gannett, from Ireland. Addison stood on his hind legs and raised a paw in salute as Miss Wren entered, and lastly came Miss Avocet, wheeled onto the stage by Francesca and Bettina, her two favorite ymbrynes-in-training.

Esmerelda Avocet was the most senior and powerful ymbryne of them all, the mentor who had trained most of Great Britain's living ymbrynes and all those before us now. But she was looking older and more feeble than ever, a skinny wisp of woman cocooned in a thick shawl. She looked almost as frail as she had the first time I'd met her, when she'd flown into Miss Peregrine's house with shocking news of a hollowgast raid, and worse than when I'd seen her earlier in the day, as if whatever the ymbrynes had discussed in their meeting had sapped much of her remaining strength. I just hoped she could hold it together long enough to get through the assembly.

Last through the door were four more home guards, who took up positions around the stage and stood at attention. Francesca and Bettina left, closing the little door behind them, and Miss Peregrine paced to the center of the operating stage, stood at the gruesome body platform as if it were a lectern, and began to speak.

"My fellow peculiars. Some of you may have guessed why we've called you here today, and others will be wondering. I do not intend to keep you long in suspense. Only recently, we were celebrating our victory over the wights at the Battle of Gravehill. We fought bravely and prevailed, and I can speak for all the ymbrynes present today when I say that we are intensely proud of you: those who fought, as well as those who persevered here in Devil's Acre despite the danger, who with tenacity and firmness of purpose kept working to rebuild our loops and our society even while menaced by such a dire threat."

She paused. I could feel everyone in the room lean forward in their seats, on tenterhooks.

"But—I'll tell it plainly—a terrible thing we tried mightily to prevent has come to pass." Her voice boomed, aided by the unusual acoustics of the room. "One wight escaped our grasp at Gravehill. His name is Percival Murnau, and he was Caul's top lieutenant. We thought we had stopped him from achieving the wights' goal, and while we dealt him setbacks and decimated his fighting force, I'm sorry to tell you that we failed to put an end to his plans."

Whispers rippled through the room.

"Two days ago, desolations began to plague the Acre. There's been a great deal of speculation about what might be causing them. Now we can be certain: Two days ago, Percival Murnau resurrected Caul, my brother, the leader of the wights."

Murmurs turned into shouts, shouts into cries of despair. The ymbrynes pleaded for quiet. Slowly, the crowd settled to a volume that allowed Miss Peregrine to continue.

"Our fiercest adversary has returned, in some form, and while all but a handful of the other wights have been killed or captured, Caul himself is more powerful than ever. How much more powerful, we don't yet know." The murmurs were growing louder again, and she raised her voice. "But he is still just one person, and as of now there have been no reports of attacks by Caul on any loop, any peculiar—"

"And when the attacks begin?" a familiar voice boomed. The crowd's gaze shifted to LaMothe as he rose, imposingly, to his feet. "What will you do?"

Miss Cuckoo stepped forward to stand beside Miss Peregrine. "We've organized a defense for Devil's Acre that will be impenetrable, we believe."

"You *believe*?" someone called out, and I saw Miss Cuckoo wince at her own word choice.

"How could you let this happen?" another person yelled.

"We have everything under control!" Miss Blackbird shouted, jittering hands cupped around her mouth, but she could hardly be heard.

Next to me, Emma was shaking her head. The assembly was in danger of slipping into chaos. I could hear people around me shouting, not just at the ymbrynes, but at one another, arguing about who was to blame and what should be done. One thing was clear: These people needed leaders. Though the fractious and diverse peculiars of Devil's Acre had complaints about the ymbrynes, they would be lost without them.

Then Sharon's thundering cry cut through the noise: "QUIET!" The crowd settled again. "I, too, have questions," he said, booming a bit more softly. "I, too, am angry, but now isn't the time to dissect the lapses that led to this moment. There will be time for that once this crisis has passed. We may not have long to organize a defense, and if we waste time squabbling, we will live to regret it. Or die to regret it, as the case may be. Now, please." He extended his long arm graciously toward the ymbrynes and a rat tumbled from his sleeve. "Let the good ladies speak."

Miss Peregrine gave Sharon a nod of thanks, then gripped the edges of the body platform. "We ymbrynes don't claim to be infallible. I wish we had predicted this. I wish we could have prevented it. But we did not. I readily acknowledge our error."

This seemed to cool some tempers in the crowd. I glanced at Noor. She was staring at the floor, looking ill.

"Now, I won't ask you not to worry," Miss Peregrine went on, voice rising. "But I insist you not surrender to fear. I won't insult your intelligence by telling you this will be easy, but no good thing ever was. We have lived under the shadow of the wights and their hollowgast for a century, and it should be no surprise that such evil cannot be shed in a few weeks, or in a few minor engagements. Our victory at Gravehill, savage as it was, was perhaps too tidy. The final trial is yet to come: a battle the magnitude of which we can't yet know. But this I do know . . ." Miss Peregrine let go of the platform and strode to the front of the stage, hands clasped behind her like a military commander. "He will come for us. He will come here. This loop was my odious brother's home for many years, and you can be sure he's still furious that he and his people were driven from it. But we will not allow him to take back Devil's Acre. We cannot, and will not, relinquish control of our only refuge, nor of the Panloopticon. We will make this loop impenetrable, and then we will find a way to drive him back into the underworld he came from. But we need your help. Stand with us. Stay and fight." She pounded the air with her fist. "Our resolve is strong. We will not let him in. We will not—"

For some time, a low rumbling sound had been building, but I'd been so entranced by Miss Peregrine that I'd hardly registered it. Now I could feel it shaking the floor, and all at once it doubled in strength and was joined by a sudden wind that blew out all the gaslights and plunged the hall into blackness. There were screams, but they were drowned out almost immediately by an overwhelming voice:

"GET OUT!" it bellowed. "Get out of my house! Get out while you still can!"

The voice seemed to come from everywhere and produced a sour stink that blew with each syllable from the center of the room. People began scrambling to escape, tripping over one another in the dark. I heard crashes and screams that sounded like people tumbling down stairs. "Stay put or we'll be trampled!" shouted Emma, and I felt her hands pushing my shoulders down. I turned to Noor and pulled her down, too, and she pulled Fiona next to her.

"*I am born agaaaaain!*" the voice thundered, so loud it seemed to shake my eyes in their sockets. And then from the darkness there shone a sudden, brilliant light at the center of the room—a face, giant, blue, and glowing, that hovered in the air. It was Caul's face, his face and nothing more, ten feet high and sneering, his thin lips and beaked nose, his mouth open and blunt round teeth shaking as he cackled at the pandemonium he had caused. Everyone was falling over one another, climbing, clambering for the steps and the door and outside, but the steps were jammed with splayed and reeling bodies and the door was blocked. The ymbrynes, directly below Caul on the stage, had scattered to the walls but had not fled. The home guards were stunned, frozen in place.

The laughing stopped. Caul grinned and said more softly, "How's that? Have I got your attention?"

There was a sudden bang as one of the home guards fired a weapon at Caul, but the projectile passed through his ghostly face and ricocheted off a wall.

"Silly man, I'm not actually *here*," Caul said. "But I *will* be. I am coming. I am inexorable. I am inevitable!" His voice was rising again. "I have harnessed the power of the ancient souls, and I will use it to crush all who stand against me!"

Just when I thought my eardrums would break, his voice fell to a childlike wheedle. "Oh, jeepers creepers, the bad man's coming to get us! What do we do, Poppa, what do we *do*?"

Caul's face turned slightly, and his voice deepened into a loony caricature of a 1950s-era American dad. "It's simple, Johnny. We need to choose the path of righteousness!"

The demented "kid" voice again: "What's that, Poppa?"

The dad: "Well, Caul is our god now, and it's a real good thing he's a *merciful* god. You're a sinner, Johnny-boy, and so am I. We've been worshipping these half-bird charlatans instead of him all these years! Oh, it was a *bad* thing we did. Denying our true natures, our true power, our destiny to *sit at the head of the human table* rather than hiding underneath it!"

"The human *what*, Poppa?"

Through it all, Miss Peregrine was shouting to be heard over Caul's insane spectacle: "He can't hurt us! It's only a projection! Everyone stay calm!"

"The human table! Why, we peculiars are the most evolved humans there ever were, and here we've been hiding in loops rather than running the show—for two thousand years! Isn't that a *shame*?"

"Yes, Poppa! That must make Caul SO MAD!"

"Don't be scared, Johnny. All you've got to do is ask forgiveness and pledge your undying loyalty to him, and you'll be spared."

"Gosh, really?"

"Well, there's one more little thing."

Caul's face flickered, then appeared to melt, skin sliding off bone into a glowing puddle in the air, then swirling up again to form a new face: mine.

I went cold, certain I was hallucinating. The wheedling child's voice disappeared, replaced by the low, rattling snarl of a demon summoned from hell:

"KILL THE BOY."

I heard Emma gasp. Noor clasped my arm. The face changed again, the skin bubbling to mush, then forming a different face: Noor's.

"KILL THE GIRL."

Now it was my turn to clasp Noor's hand. She was silent, grim-faced. The image of Noor changed quickly back to Caul, and he said, in his own mocking voice, "And for *extra* brownie points . . ."

His image exploded into a thousand points of blue light, then rapidly coalesced into a picture of our ymbrynes, the nine who cringed on the stage below mirrored in blue above.

"KILL THEM ALL!" Caul screamed, the voice so loud I slapped my hands over my ears, so loud I could see the glass ceiling rattling, threatening to shatter.

I heard screams from the crowd, and then the ymbrynes' blue doubles turned into birds. Caul's voice, his own again, cackled and said, "Crawl away, little bugs, fly away, little birds! Scurry and scatter, fly, fly, fly, get out of my kitchen!"

The spectral image of the birds flew upward toward the glass ceiling, and as they reached it they evaporated into nothing and the ceiling shattered. A hundred thousand shards of glass rained down on us, and everyone was cut to ribbons and shrieking, Emma screaming with a head full of broken glass, Noor screaming as blood ran down her arms and her neck, Horace screaming as he spun around, taking in the horrific scene.

And then the image before me flickered . . .

And the screams began to fade . . .

And the sky above the broken glass ceiling darkened—*strange, I don't remember a glass ceiling in this room*—and then the gaslights around the room flared to life again, and there was no glass ceiling above us now, broken or otherwise, just a normal painted one, and we had not been cut to ribbons.

It had all been an illusion.

The gaslights brightened.

Caul was gone.

Then, other sounds: cries of relief, cries of pain from those who'd fallen on the stairs and in the doorway, who'd been caught in the crush. The sobs of the overwhelmed, the terrified. Claire was crying softly as Bronwyn cradled her. Noor had my hand in a death grip. The ymbrynes begged for calm. Miss Peregrine, now wielding a megaphone, declared that Caul's manifestation had been merely visual, that he was only trying to scare us, and to divide us, and we could not allow him to do that. She again assured the crowd that the ymbrynes were working on a defense for the Acre that would shortly be ready, then handed the megaphone to Miss Wren, who began to direct an orderly exit from the hall, one level at a time. The sobs and cries began to subside. The ymbrynes climbed up from the pit and went to console people individually. Their assurances were easier to dismiss from a distance, as a passive member of a skeptical audience, but in person, up close and one on one, you believed it. It's why an ymbryne's wards never numbered more than ten or fifteen. They would never win us over as a mob. Their work would be accomplished going house to house, peculiar to peculiar, methodically undoing Caul's terror one person at a time.

As we waited for Miss Wren to call our row, I noticed someone walking against the crowd's flow, elbowing and shouldering his way toward us. It was the cockeyed scanner boy. He was one level below ours, and when he came even with us, he climbed up onto the lower bench and stood atop it, his head inclined toward me, wearing a blank look.

"Are you going to ask me something?" I said to him.

He reached behind him and pulled something from his waistband. I had only just registered that someone was shouting—"He's got a knife!"—when I saw it in his hand, long and curved, and he lunged at Noor.

She dove across my body as he buried the knife in the bench where she'd just been. The boy's hat fell off as he yanked at the knife. Someone grabbed him by the waist as he flailed. Horace slapped him in the head and Noor kicked him in the face. Soon a couple of home guards had separated him from the knife and were dragging him away by the arms. He was silent, not even struggling.

"Are you okay?" I said to Noor, and she nodded and lifted herself off me.

Then Miss Peregrine was there, asking if we were hurt; we said no. She looked relieved, but only fleetingly. As she looked past us to scan the room, I saw a new kind of fear in her eyes.

It said everything had changed.

CHAPTER SEVEN

*J*he ymbrynes got Noor and me out of there as quickly as they could. Miss Peregrine, Miss Wren, and three home guards escorted us from the hall while our friends clamored to make sure we were all right and the crowd gawked. I tried to pull our friends along, too, but Miss Peregrine, whispering behind me as she guided my shoulders, said it would look like special treatment if all her wards were evacuated first. Only Noor and I had been called out. Marked for death.

Beyond that, we were in the dark. We didn't know whether more would-be assassins would be waiting for us. Didn't know whether the scanner boy's attack was premeditated or if he'd been inspired by Caul's bizarre rant. I knew the ymbrynes well enough by now to see that they were just as rattled as the rest of us, but since a hundred terrified peculiars trapped together in one big room was the definition of a powder keg, they were doing their best to feign, and maintain, calm.

Noor and I were hurried across the Acre to a location deemed safe: the Ymbryne Council chamber inside the asylum/peculiar ministries building. Along the way we could hear the effortlessly calming voice of Amos Dextaire through the loudspeakers: "Hey now, Acrefolk, let's all do our best to remain calm. We're safe. Caul is not here. If you can walk, go on back to your dormitories. If you're injured, stay where you are and a bone-mender will come to you. Ymbrynes will be paying visits to each house and dormitory throughout the day. I repeat, we're safe. And be sure to tune into Amos's Hit Parade this afternoon, when you and one lucky friend could win a draft horse!" In a lightning-fast undertone he added: *"Winners will split horse. Aliveness of horse not guaranteed. No returns or exchanges."*

I saw Miss Peregrine mutter something to Miss Wren and shake her head.

We arrived at the ministries building and were brought upstairs to the council chamber, where we waited with Miss Peregrine and Miss Wren while the home guards stood watch outside the door. Other ymbrynes would be coming soon. In the meantime, we tried to make sense of what had happened. Noor and I sat at the long, polished conference table, Miss Wren stood beside a corkboard of loop maps on the wall, studying it like it might hold a clue to Caul's plans, and Miss Peregrine treaded the floor, backlit by a triple-height window wreathed in vines.

"It was largely a visual manifestation," she was saying, "with a few mind tricks tossed in for effect: The glass ceiling that wasn't there, the bloodied crowd. A loud magic-lantern show, all sound and fury."

"He's only trying to scare us," I said.

"Job done," said Noor. "Everyone was freaking out."

"He's trying to divide us," Miss Wren replied.

"That's nothing new," said Miss Peregrine. "He's been doing that for decades."

"But he's never been able to project himself and his propaganda into our midst before. That *is* new. If he can turn some of our own wards against us, he'll hardly need to wage much of a battle for Devil's Acre, will he?"

"Do you really think that could happen?" Noor said. "That peculiars here would turn against you?"

"Absolutely not," Miss Peregrine said dismissively. But I couldn't help remembering the loop freedom protest that had broken out just recently, and the underground meetings Sharon had invited me to. It may not have been a fiery-hot resistance movement, but even our mild divisions were cracks Caul could exploit and pry into gaping fissures.

"He got to at least one person," Noor pointed out.

"We'll see," said Miss Peregrine. "It's possible the boy was just weak-minded, and Caul was able somehow to invade his thoughts."

"Perhaps," Miss Wren said doubtfully. "But we're dealing with an increasingly disaffected population of peculiars here, and Caul's message of peculiar supremacy is perniciously attractive to certain people. That's how he attracted his earliest followers. And remember, some of our number are ex-mercenaries who lived in the Acre while it was under wight control. I doubt they would welcome Caul's return, but they might not dread it, either. Nor fight very hard to prevent it."

"That boy has been Miss Bobolink's ward for fifty years," said Miss Peregrine. "He's no mercenary. It could only have been mind control."

She said it like she needed it to be true. Mind control sounded a lot more problematic to me than one bad apple succumbing to Caul's poisonous rhetoric, but to the ymbrynes, a traitor was infinitely worse. Loyalty was everything; we were supposed to be family.

Miss Wren shook her head. "Well, we're questioning him now, so we should know soon enough. Until then, no more all-Acre assemblies. We make too easy a target when we're all together." She turned to face me and Noor. "Also, you both must be guarded at all times."

Noor's expression soured. "Is that really necessary?"

"I'm afraid it is," said Miss Peregrine. "Your lives are too valuable, and Caul has just put a bounty on them."

"And where there is one assassin, there may be more," said Miss Wren.

I sighed. Though I knew they were right, I didn't relish the thought of being trailed by home guards everywhere we went.

Just then the door opened, and the guards let in Miss Cuckoo,

Emma, Horace, and—announcing himself with a "Hello, it's me"—
Millard. They were in the middle of a heated discussion of their own.

"But he projected himself right into our midst," Emma was
saying. "If he can do that, he'll know everything we're planning!"

"No, it was as if we were watching him in a film," said Horace.
"We could see him, but he couldn't see us."

"How do you know?" I asked, and then they noticed me and
Noor, and rushed over to make a fuss over us. Once we'd assured
them we were fine, Horace answered my question.

"If Caul had spotted Miss P, don't you think he would have
taunted her?"

"That's true; he never misses an opportunity," Miss Peregrine
said, and motioned for our friends to be seated.

"And neither should we," said Millard, whose nakedness no
one seemed to mind at the moment. "We need to dissect every word,
every syllable, every visual clue that Caul's little show just gave us,
and use them to form a picture of what he is now."

"He's completely *mad* is what he is," said Emma. "Did you
hear the voices he was making?"

"He's always been mad," said Miss Cuckoo. "That hasn't
changed."

"And it's never stopped him from achieving his wretched
goals," said Horace.

Emma turned to face the door. "Where's Miss Blackbird with
Fern?"

"Can you really make the Acre impenetrable?" Horace said.
"And *soon*?"

"Yes, we think so," Miss Peregrine replied, though she sounded
less certain now than she had in front of the whole assembled Acre.
She seemed about to explain further when Emma said, "Hi, there
you are!" and in came Miss Blackbird and Fern, one of the diviners
from Portal, her big hat now in her hands. I said hello and she gave
a tiny wave, too shaken for pleasantries.

"Fern's a guest from America," Miss Cuckoo said. "Her peculiarity allowed her to make a very useful observation about Caul. Go on, dear."

Fern cleared her throat nervously, then hesitated.

"You're a diviner," Emma prompted her. "Start there."

"Awful sorry," Fern said in her soft Southern drawl. "I'm not used to . . . being so proximate to . . . er, in the company of . . ."

"Ymbrynes," Emma said. "She's rarely been around real ymbrynes before."

"I'm sure she can speak for herself," Miss Cuckoo said, and Emma looked chastened.

Fern cleared her throat again. "I'm a diviner. And the thing I divine is other peculiars. Whether they're close or far, here or there."

"Like my Addison does," said Miss Wren.

"Not quite," said Fern. "Your dog smells peculiarity, but I can *see* it. Our peculiarities emit a certain kind of energy, you see, which I'm sensitive to." She looked down shyly, as if embarrassed at having spoken so much. I'd never known her to be timid; she must really have been intimidated by the presence of so many ymbrynes.

"And what did you observe today?" Miss Cuckoo prodded.

"In the beginning, when he first appeared, the blue man was real strong. But by the end, just before he turned into birds and disappeared, his energy was weak. He was all worn out."

"Fascinating," said Miss Wren. "So it cost him something to project himself that way."

"Which means he is exhaustible," said Miss Cuckoo.

"Finite," Millard added. "Therefore, not quite the god he claims to be."

Miss Peregrine grimaced. "Don't rejoice yet. My brother's only just been resurrected. I imagine he's still gathering his strength." She glanced at our visitor, whose eyes were widening by the second. "Thank you, Fern, that was enormously helpful. Vernon, would you see she gets back to her dormitory safely?"

"Pleased to meet y'all," Fern said, curtsying as one of the guards showed her out.

The moment the door closed, Horace was out of his chair and tugging at Miss Peregrine's sleeve. "You were saying? About making the Acre impenetrable?"

Miss Peregrine accompanied him back to his chair and made him sit. "We'll need three more ymbrynes than we have here to do it. Twelve altogether."

"We'll have them," said Miss Wren. "I know for a fact Miss Waxwing and Miss Troupial are abandoning their loops to bring their wards here. Safety in numbers, you know. Raise the drawbridge."

"And I will recall Miss Merganser from Mozambique today," said Miss Cuckoo. "She's freelance, with no wards to concern herself about."

"*If* this can be done," Miss Wren cautioned. "It's an untested technique. Untested on such a wide area as an entire loop, anyway."

"What is it?" I said.

"It's a sort of shielding web that's woven around the loop," Miss Peregrine explained. "We call it the Quilt."

"How soon can you create it?" asked Horace.

"As soon as the other three ymbrynes arrive," replied Miss Cuckoo.

"What about the Panloopticon?" Millard said. "It'll have to be disconnected, won't it? It's like a hundred back doors into this place."

"He's right," Miss Peregrine said. "It's a terrible vulnerability."

"Close it now!" Horace cried, but then he looked perplexed. "But then we'll be stuck here . . . under siege with no escape route . . ."

"We can't turn it off," said Miss Wren, her eyes pinning Miss Peregrine. "Not until we find them."

"Nor before our three ymbrynes arrive," Miss Peregrine replied.

"Them?" Emma said.

"Aren't you forgetting something?" Noor said to the ymbrynes. "What about the prophecy? What about the other six?"

"I'm so glad you mentioned it," said Miss Wren, turning to Noor with just a hint of a smile. "That's just the *them* I was referring to."

There was a knock at the door.

"Who is it now?" Miss Peregrine sighed.

It was Miss Avocet and two trainees, a guard announced, and the old ymbryne came wheeling in with Francesca and Sigrid.

"Your timing is excellent," said Miss Wren. "We were just discussing the prophecy. Or were about to."

"Is there something new?" Horace asked eagerly.

"First things first," said Miss Avocet, wheeling herself toward Noor and me. "How are you both holding up?"

She was only looking at Noor, though Noor glanced quickly at me before answering, "We're all right."

"You've only just arrived, and there's been such drama, much of it aimed at you," she said pityingly. "I'm sorry to say it doesn't look as if that's going to change anytime soon."

"Thanks for worrying about me, but you don't have to," Noor said. "It's my fault all this is happening, and I'm going fix it. Just . . . tell me how."

"My dear, that is utter nonsense," said Miss Avocet.

Miss Peregrine looked exasperated. "I keep trying to tell her."

"*Please*," Noor said sharply. "Stop trying to tell me how to feel, and just tell me what I can *do*. Tell me what you know about the other six."

Miss Avocet sighed. "Yes, all right." With some effort she wheeled herself to the head of the conference table, proudly refusing Francesca's help. "The minute I heard Caul had been resurrected, I ordered all my ymbrynes-in-training to scour the *Apocryphon* in all its various translations for references to the seven. Francesca?"

Miss Avocet's star pupil stepped forward. "As you all may

remember, there were specific references to Noor's birth, but little mention of the other six—nothing that might've helped us pinpoint their nationality, location, or era. We cannot assume they are all modern children, born recently. The prophecy was written some four hundred years ago, and it's entirely possible some of the prophesied children may now be very old. We just don't know." She allowed herself a dramatic pause. "But we may soon." She turned expectantly to Sigrid, the owlish girl in round glasses. "Sigrid?"

The girl blinked rapidly and smoothed her dress, suddenly aware that everyone was looking at her. "Yes, yes. There was a breakthrough about an hour ago."

Miss Peregrine seemed surprised. "During the assembly?"

"Yes. I work part-time in the communications room, in the basement level of Bentham House?"

"The room with all the radios?" I said, remembering the people I'd seen there wrapped head to toe in wires and antennas.

"That's the one. We've been monitoring our networks for encoded communications from the wights, and while that hasn't been fruitful, two days ago we picked up a series of late-night, long-distance loop calls. Or rather, it was the same call, made a series of times to different numbers. It was a young girl's voice. We have a recording of what was said." Sigrid's hand had been hidden behind her back, and now she raised it to her face and read something written on the palm. "'He's back. Meet at the meeting place. Fast as fast can be.'"

Francesca said, "She spoke the same words, in the same order, in each of the calls."

"We don't know who the caller was, or where she was calling from," said Miss Avocet. "But we know she made six calls to six different loops around the world."

"Six?" I said. "Not seven?"

Miss Peregrine held up a finger as if to say *We'll get to that.*

"Only one was made to America," Sigrid continued. "While we can't pinpoint the location of the call with a great deal of accuracy, we know it was to a loop, previously unknown to us, in eastern Pennsylvania."

Noor, who had been standing, sat down. "My God."

A shiver went through me, the same eerie sensation I got whenever big pieces began falling into place. "They tried to call V," I said.

"This happened two days ago?" said Miss Peregrine. "Why are we just hearing about this now?"

Sigrid shuffled her feet. "We didn't understand its true importance. But when we learned Caul had returned—"

"'He's back' is fairly telling," said Emma.

Miss Avocet said, "Our communications people think the calls were made to six ymbrynes. We know now that V was one. We also believe that ymbrynes were assigned to protect each of the prophesied children."

"Assigned by who?" I said. "Wouldn't you have known about this, Miss Avocet?"

"Wasn't it you who assigned V to protect Noor?" Emma asked.

"No," answered Miss Avocet. "I asked V to accompany Noor safely to America so that she might escape the hollows pursuing her here, but that's all. I had no inkling of the other six, or any knowledge of how important Noor really was." She shrugged, an oddly casual gesture for such a serious woman. "As we've well established, we ymbrynes are not altogether perfect."

Miss Peregrine resumed her nervous pacing and lit her curved pipe, which meant her mind was hard at work. "We didn't know how important she was, but someone else did. They took the catastrophes prophesied in the *Apocryphon* seriously and made preparations to protect the seven. They were waiting for this. The question is"—her heels clicked as she stopped and blew out a cloud of purple smoke—"who placed the calls?"

It seemed no one wanted to repeat the words *I don't know*

again, so everyone was quiet until I asked: "Why did they only make six calls, if there are seven children?"

"Perhaps because whoever made the calls already had one of the seven in their safekeeping," said Millard.

"Or maybe the girl who made the calls was herself one of the seven," said Miss Avocet.

Miss Peregrine frowned skeptically, but stopped short of disagreeing out loud with her senior ymbryne.

"Either way," said Millard, "surely all that matters now is locating their meeting place, 'fast as fast can be.' Sigrid, are we absolutely sure none of those calls was traceable?"

Sigrid nodded. "But their destinations were. Aside from Pennsylvania, USA, there was a call placed to Slovenia, one to the Andaman Islands off the western coast of Thailand, one to Namibia in southern Africa, one to the Amazon basin in Brazil, and one to the Kelardasht region of northern Iran. But their origin is a mystery. The radio operator said he'd never seen anything like it. He said it was as if the calls came out of the aether."

"So the six could be out there, waiting for Noor to join them," Emma said. "And she could, if only we knew where the meeting place was."

"You can be sure it was a secret known only to the six ymbrynes themselves," Miss Peregrine said. She left a trail of smoke in the air as she crossed to Noor, then perched lightly on the edge of the table beside her. "One of whom we have access to."

"You mean . . . V?" I said, a tingle of dread crawling up my neck.

Noor looked puzzled. "But she's . . ."

"That doesn't mean we can't ask her a few questions," Miss Peregrine said delicately. "You're familiar with Mr. O'Connor's gift?"

"He can resurrect the dead." Instead of revulsion, there was a faraway look on Noor's face. "How long would she be awake for?"

I realized what she was imagining, and my heart broke a little.

"Not long," Miss Peregrine said. "A few minutes at most. But I must warn you, she won't be the woman you remember."

"The whole thing is pretty . . . horrible," I said, which was a mild word for what it was. To see a person you loved turned into one of Enoch's meat puppets would be downright scarring.

"Would you consent to it?" Miss Peregrine said. "If you don't, we'll find another way."

I saw Miss Wren's eyebrows rise—*what other way?*—but she kept silent.

Finally, Noor said, "Do what you have to do. Even if it's horrible."

Miss Peregrine thanked her and patted her on the shoulder. "We'll send a team to retrieve her body within the hour."

Noor looked up sharply. "I said I want to be part of it."

"And I told you it's a risk we can't take." Miss Peregrine looked sternly at me. "Same goes for you, Mr. Portman."

"What about the hollowgast that's hanging around?" I said. "He's pretty banged up, but sometimes an injured hollow can be even more dangerous than—"

"We were evading hollows long before you arrived," said Miss Wren.

I saw Emma wince. *Ouch.*

"Don't feel useless, *mon garçon*," said Miss Cuckoo. "We'll have dangerous things for you to do soon enough."

CHAPTER EIGHT

*J*ust hanging around the Acre was dangerous enough on an average day, what with its many natural hazards (Smoking Street's jets of flame; flesh-eating bacteria in the canals) as well as various malefactors, both normal and peculiar, who lurked in its shadows. But now that Noor and I had nearly been assassinated, the ymbrynes were taking no chances, which was why a pair of guards stuck to us like glue as we walked back to Ditch House, then posted themselves outside the front door.

Most of our friends were inside, burning off residual stress from the disastrous assembly with household tasks. Emma boiled water for laundry in a big metal tub, and when the clothes were cleaned and wrung out, they were hung beside the coal-burning radiator in the basement; hanging them outside in the Acre's ashy air would've only made them dirty again. When they were dry, Horace starched and ironed them, all the while waxing rhapsodic about the modern miracle that was fabric softener. Obtaining it, he insisted, was one of the few compelling reasons ever to venture into the present day. Olive removed her leaden boots and polished the ceiling with a rag and a feather duster. Fiona tended to the vines, nipping them back where they had begun to invade the interior of the house, which was almost everywhere. Anything Fiona grew, Hugh explained, was forever after attracted to her, and would inch steadily in her direction whenever her back was turned. The rest of us busied ourselves with making beds, mopping floors, cleaning up after the chickens, and sweeping away the ash that drifted into the house every time a door or a window was opened.

I found the work calming. It helped restore a small sense of normalcy to a world that was teetering precariously. But some of my friends were only growing more jittery. After an hour Hugh threw down the broom he'd been wielding and cried, "I can't take it anymore!"

"Me neither!" Enoch said. "This floor polish smells like kerosene."

"No, I mean, why are we being made to just wait around? We've just been told that Caul is coming, and who knows what sort of fighting force he'll arrive with. Shouldn't we be assembling one of our own? Preparing for battle?"

"I bet you could round up a battalion of killer bees," Olive said. She pushed herself down from the ceiling and grabbed onto a chair. "There's a loop door that leads to some flowering fields in Paraguay . . . second-floor hallway, third door left from the loo."

"There's a town on London's outskirts full of invisibles trained in guerrilla warfare," Millard said.

Horace turned to Fiona. "Have you had any more contact with the tree people from the Great Hibernian forest? An army of trees, think of that!"

Fiona whispered something to Hugh, who said, "No, but she says she could drop a line."

"We already have an army," Claire said. "They're called the home guard."

"What's left of it," Hugh said with a sigh. "The hollows tore them to shreds during the raids."

"I wouldn't trust them to defend my lunch, much less my loop," said Enoch.

Olive pressed a finger to her lips. "Shh, they're outside the door. You'll hurt their feelings."

"I feel the same frustration as the rest of you," Emma said, "but right now we need to set an example for all the other peculiars in Devil's Acre, like Miss P said, and not run around like the sky is falling. When the ymbrynes need us to assemble a peculiar army, you can be sure they'll let us know."

Grumbling, Hugh announced he was breaking for lunch and stomped off toward the kitchen.

❖   ❖   ❖

A little while later, Miss Peregrine arrived with Miss Cuckoo in tow. Noor and I spoke to them in the little sitting room near the kitchen. We told them everything we could about how to find V's body and the challenges their team might face along the way, including but not limited to the injured hollowgast, more wights who may have gone to check on the one in the yellow raincoat, and the dopey but potentially troublesome cops at my house who had witnessed our exit through the pocket loop. "Might need to be memory-wiped," Miss Peregrine muttered to Miss Cuckoo, who nodded.

There would also be the remnants of the hurricane to deal with, I said, which could make driving tough. "You'll need a car. My grandfather's is in my parents' driveway, but it needs a new tire."

"Let us worry about that," Miss Peregrine replied.

We were excused and went out into the kitchen, and the ymbrynes emerged a short time later. They laid out the basics of the mission and asked for two volunteers. Emma's hand shot up. So did Enoch's, but Miss Peregrine refused him. "You're the only irreplaceable part of this operation, Mr. O'Connor, and I need you here, rested and ready to work, the moment we return with V's body."

His eyes gleamed with excitement. "I'll be ready." He patted the jar-shaped protrusion in his jacket. "These murderers' hearts are tops if you need your resurrectee to do something physical, but for strength of mind, a poet's heart would be ideal . . . if I can lay my hands on one . . . Might need to sneak down to Westminster Abbey with a spade—"

"Don't you dare," said Miss Peregrine.

"All right, all right."

"I mean it."

He winked at her.

She chose Bronwyn and Emma to join them on the retrieval mission, and Miss Wren asked Addison if he felt up to making the trip again. He snapped to attention and said, "Anything for you, madam." He was the most loyal peculiar I knew, though that loyalty belonged to one ymbryne in particular. He would have died for Miss Wren, as several of his loop-mates already had when their menagerie was raided by the wights. If only every peculiar felt as he did, I'd have had no doubts about our chances against Caul.

Their team assembled, the ymbrynes said they hoped to be back within a few hours, but not to worry if it took longer.

We wished them luck and they set off. It was strange to imagine my friends going to Englewood without me. Stranger still to imagine what they'd be bringing back.

*   *   *

The two ymbrynes hadn't been gone twenty minutes when news broke of a new attack, and this time the aggressor was more than just a trash-talking hologram. We clustered around Horace's radio to hear Amos Dextaire, whose usually silky voice was raw and rattled:

"We're hearing reports of an assault on Miss Plover's loop in Squatney, East London. She's just flown in, and we have her in the studio now. Miss Plover, thank you for being with us. Can you talk about what's happening?" There was some shuffling and the sound of wings flapping. "She's only just now turned to human form . . . Bear with us a moment, listeners . . ."

Horace wrung his hands nervously. "Even Amos sounds shaken. Miss Plover must be a sight."

"Her loop was one of the few survivors of the hollow raids in London," said Millard. "Makes sense that it was Caul's first target."

The voice of a frightened woman came through the speaker. "Yes, Adrienne Plover 'ere. They came smashin' in through the walls of our house—"

"Who did, ma'am?"

"Leaves and branches and wind. Caul, I think it was. I heard his voice, and the house came rippin' apart . . . I dunno what he is now, couldn't get a good look, but he ain't human nummore. I was able to get my littlest ones out safe, except for Sheena and Ruzzie . . ."

She broke down crying. Amos quickly took his microphone back. He thanked the ymbryne for stopping by the studio, then introduced Miss Bobolink, who instructed everyone listening to keep calm and carry on. "All Acre business will continue as normal until further notice. You're expected to report to your work assignments and classes as usual. Curfew will be in effect after dark, but until then, go about your day as you would any other. Rest assured, we are taking every measure to ensure your safety and security."

"The more they say that, the less I believe it," muttered Emma.

"It's official, then," Millard said glumly. "Caul can do more than just project a hologram of himself. Now he can mount a physical attack."

"We're sure that was him?" Horace said.

Noor said, "Monstrous tree? Tornado winds? That's him."

"Caul two-point-oh," I concurred.

"It's nothing to worry about," Hugh said. "Miss Plover's loop was fairly isolated and only lightly defended. Easy pickings."

"*Claire* could have run Miss Plover out of that loop," Enoch agreed.

"And I can bite your toes off with my backmouth while you sleep tonight," Claire growled. "Would you like that?"

Enoch ignored her, as he usually did.

"He knows he can't *really* turn us against the ymbrynes," Hugh said, "so Caul's plan B is to scare us away. Get as many of us to abandon the Acre as he can, and then he'll able to waltz into a nearly undefended loop."

"*Nothing to worry about*," Horace muttered. "He's only just beginning. He'll pick off one loop after another, growing stronger as he goes, and then he'll come for us." He looked around, eyes wide. "Does that sound like nothing to worry about?"

"Sounds like nothing to be *done* about, so why worry?" said Hugh, his voice cracking on the word *worry*.

"There's plenty to be done, and I don't mean laundry," said Enoch. "I need that poet's heart if I'm going to resurrect a body who's going to be asked questions, or the answers will be half gibberish. I'm not just going to sit around and wait."

Hugh rose from the bed and moved toward the door. "Me neither. What do you say, Fee, feeling up to a little adventure?"

She was already waiting for him in the doorway, long-stemmed flowers curling excitedly around her ankles.

Claire jumped up and stomped over to them. "Where do you think you're going?"

"That loop door Olive mentioned before," Hugh said. "Twenty-one-Q, third from the loo. Just scouting; we'll be back in a jiff. And if you tattle to Miss P about it, I'll chew off *your* toes."

"Well . . . I officially object!" Going a bit red, she stamped off into a corner to sulk. But I knew she wouldn't rat out her friends, even to curry favor with Miss Peregrine.

"But the Panlooopticon's closed until further notice," said Olive. "There's no getting in without special permission."

"Sharon owes me a favor," Enoch said, joining Hugh and Fiona by the door.

I caught him by the arm before he could turn the handle. "Wait—go out the back or the home guards will see you."

"Thanks, mate." He smiled and gave me a brotherly elbow to the ribs, and then the three of them went up the stairs to slip out an upper-floor window into the alley.

An invisible hand tapped my shoulder. "I don't suppose you and Noor would be amenable to a bit of sneaking around, as well?" Millard asked. "Unless there's something here you'd rather be dusting."

Noor smirked. "What did you have in mind?"

"I was hoping you still had V's stopwatch. The expulsatator."

Noor checked the pocket of her striped dress. "Right here. It's fried, though."

"Well, that's just it. Maybe it's not. I'd like to show it to my tinkerer friend, if you don't mind. He's got a knack for these things, and . . . if we really do have to close the Panloopticon, it would be a good thing to have a working expulsatator on hand. For emergencies."

"I guess it's worth a try," Noor said. "And it's a hell of a lot better than going nuts waiting around here. What do you think, Jacob?"

My feet were itching to move. There had only been guards at the door for a short time and already I felt like a prisoner. "Yeah, it's worth a try. Let's just make sure we're back before . . ."

I trailed off, the words stalled in my throat.

Before they come back with V's body.

"It's a promise," said Millard.

❖   ❖   ❖

We snuck out the rear second-floor window like our friends had a few minutes before. After shimmying down a ladder of wobbly stilts, we dodged a stream of ashy sewage and darted down the narrow, crooked alley that ran behind the house. The guards wouldn't have let us go even if we'd been able to convince them the trip was necessary, and we agreed that the fewer people who knew about the existence of a potentially repaired expulsatator, the better. It had saved Noor's life once. If Caul closed in and the situation here in the

Acre got really dire, it might be called upon to do so again; I couldn't have some panicky peculiar trying to steal it. I especially didn't want the Americans to find out about it. Desperation could make good people do bad things . . . and morally ambivalent people do *really* bad things.

Once we'd gotten a few blocks from the house, we veered back onto Doleful Street, which was divided down the middle by Fever Ditch. On each side of the festering water, peculiars were out and they were busy—but this wasn't an average day in the Acre. In spite of the ymbrynes' instructions to carry on as usual, it looked like nearly everyone had forsaken their jobs and classes to prepare for an attack any way they could. The Ditch was a liquid parking lot of skiffs and barges, and boatmen were off-loading crates onto trucks and horse-drawn carts.

"Food, clothing, tools, medicine," Millard said. "Your basic siege survival supplies."

A few cases were stamped with the word EXPLOSIVES, which made me wonder if they were also bringing in conventional weapons. As if guns would do any good against a proto-demon like Caul, or whatever he'd become; I was pretty sure a flying slug of metal wasn't going to stop him. But the worrying truth was that most peculiars' abilities were not well-suited to combat. We weren't soldiers. We weren't superheroes. In the face of an organized assault, the best most of us could do was to hunker down and hope for the best. Maybe ten percent of us could muster any kind of aggressive defense. It's why we needed the home guard, relatively useless as they were. And why we'd depended for so long on the protection of ymbrynes and their loops.

The group most equipped for battle was the Americans. They'd spent the last half century in a Darwinian fight for survival that had privileged those with weaponizable abilities and forged the rest into fearless brawlers. So I was both surprised and grateful to see a number of them doing more than just watching bemusedly. LaMothe and

< THE DESOLATIONS OF DEVIL'S ACRE >

a cadre of his Northerners were helping the boatmen roll supplies onto trucks. Farther down the banks, Parkins was barking orders from his levitating wheelchair as a group of his Californio cowboys looked for good ambush blinds: a rooftop here, a bridge stanchion there. One of them, a sour-faced lady with a long braid trailing one shoulder and a shotgun in her hands, stood guard outside a small house while another Californio brought armful after armful of weapons inside. Peeking through the door as we passed, I could see a growing cache of guns, knives, swords, and clubs, easily accessible in case of attack.

Leo Burnham was notably absent but had sent some goons in his stead. Noor shied away as we walked by four of them at the Shrunken Head, just visible through an open window. One was polishing his pistol, while the others had taken knives from the kitchen and were making Molotov cocktails from bottles of liquor.

"I can't believe the ymbrynes let them in," Noor muttered.

"Nor can I," Millard said. "All they care about—Burnham's people especially—is expanding into other peculiars' territory. It can only mean the ymbrynes don't fear them . . . or don't fear them as much as they fear Caul."

"Then they don't know who they're dealing with," Noor said.

Rounding a corner, we came upon Wreck Donovan and Dogface, who were working with a gang of Untouchables and some peculiars from the Acre to fortify the entrance of the peculiar ministries building with sandbags and gun emplacements, while Angelica was using her cloud to try and blow a bothersome squall of bones away from the workers.

"I thought you were just here to observe!" I said, approaching Wreck.

He grinned. "Well, *someone* had to get you people ready for battle. Your ymbrynes certainly aren't lifting a finger."

Just as he said it, a scattering of finger bones rained onto the cobblestones nearby.

"They're working on something more important," Millard said testily.

"Ah, right, their secret plan to save everyone!" Wreck looked around with exaggerated eagerness. "Which will happen . . . when, exactly?"

"I didn't realize you cared what happened to us," Noor said.

Wreck picked up one of the skeletal fingers from the ground and wagged it at us. "Don't confuse our assistance for caring. The dominoes are starting to fall, and if this one goes"—he circled the finger in the air—"then the cancer your ymbrynes have failed to quash could spread to our side of the Atlantic. We can't allow that."

"How noble of you," Millard said.

"Heroes are rarely acknowledged in their own lifetimes," Wreck said, flicking the finger away. "So it goes."

"But don't expect us to stick around if things get really hairy," said the half-warthog Untouchable as she passed carrying a sandbag. "We're here to protect our investment, not die for you."

My head snapped toward Wreck. "What investment?"

A flicker of irritation crossed his face, but he recovered quickly. "Our investment in *you*," he said with saccharine sweetness, "who we hope to remain friends and allies with for years to come."

But they'd let something slip, and now we had even more reason to distrust them.

"Come on, fellows, we don't have all day to waste on this swaggering gasbag," said Millard.

Wreck flashed us a cocky two-fingered salute goodbye. Then with a lift of his arm a sandbag rose into the air and followed him as he walked off toward the ministries building.

So that's what he can do, I thought.

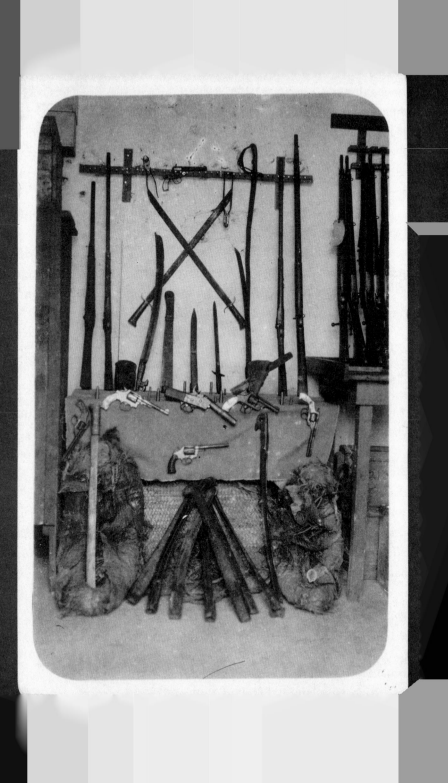

The tinkerer's workshop lay on the Acre's outer edges, a zone that ringed this loop's peculiar heart like bathtub scum. With each zigzagging block Millard reassured us it was only a little farther, that the place we were heading was just around the next corner. Meanwhile, the streets kept narrowing and the grimy tenements leaned at ever more precarious angles and the glares from the normals who lived in them grew darker and more murderous.

I was starting to wonder if we'd made a mistake ditching our two guards.

From a doorway an old crone hissed, "Begone, ye cursed strangers!" and then spat at us while furiously scratching her head.

We darted across the street as she retreated into a basement bolt-hole. "God, what's eating her?" Noor said.

"Lice, worms . . . possibly rats," said Millard. "You'll want to give all these looped normals a wide berth. It's been raining blood and bones here for days, and I suspect they think it's the end of the world."

"They might be right," Noor said.

"I didn't know any peculiars lived out here," I said, eager to change the subject.

"Only Klaus," Millard replied. "Says he doesn't like people breathing down his neck. He's a bit eccentric. Though I suppose that's the pot calling the kettle black."

We found the tinkerer's house, at long last, in the middle of a deserted-looking block. A hand-lettered sign above the weathered door read CLOCK REPAIR. The door swung open before any of us had a chance to knock, and the next thing I knew there was a gun in our faces, a giant double-barreled blunderbuss wielded by an old man with wild white hair.

"Whaddaya want? Go away! I'll kill ye!"

"Don't shoot!" I cried, and I heard Millard drop to the ground while Noor and I flung our arms in the air.

"It's me, Klaus, it's Millard Nullings!"

He looked down at the ground. "WHAT?"

"MILLARD NULLINGS!"

The old man squinted at the empty air from which Millard's voice had issued, then slowly lowered his blunderbuss.

"Hell. Why didn't you tell me you was coming?"

His every word was delivered at high volume, and his mouth hung open even when he wasn't speaking. He seemed to be very hard of hearing.

"Because you shot at the last parrot I sent," Millard half shouted in reply. "These are my friends, Klaus. The ones I was telling you about?"

Klaus nodded, then picked up the long gun again, raised it over our heads, and fired off a blast. We threw ourselves to the ground.

"Jest so's none of ye's gets any ideas!" he shouted to the empty windows across the street. When I dared to uncover my head, I saw that the only thing he was aiming at us now was a wide smile, his lips a pale, chapped crescent in the bushy nest of his great white beard. *"Don't fret, she only shoots blanks,"* he stage-whispered, then motioned for us to follow him into his workshop. I peered after him. It was pretty dark inside, and all I could make out from where I lay were teetering piles of clutter.

Noor looked around and hissed, "Millard, where are you? I owe you a slap in the head."

"Don't mind Klaus, he's mostly harmless," Millard said from inside the workshop door. "He wouldn't hurt a maggot . . . He's just an old-fashioned American."

"What does *that* mean?" I said, helping Noor up.

"He also happens to be a genius," Millard said, ignoring me. "He kept half of the un-ymbryned loops in California ticking before the wights' people tricked him into coming to work for them here."

"Well?" Klaus roared from somewhere inside the workshop. "You want to let in every dad-blamed fly in Fever Ditch, or will you come in and drink my whiskey?"

I got up and helped Noor to her feet.

"I'm going back to Ditch House," she said. "If the wights trusted him, how can we?"

Millard sighed with irritation, then came close and said in a low voice, "He was lured to the Acre and *forced* to work for the wights. Sharon told me they held Klaus's wife captive in one of the Panlooopticon's prison loops, which was the only reason he helped them. He lived out here, as far away from them as he could. So far away that he didn't realize the Acre had been liberated until a month ago, if you can believe it. But he's a genius, like I said. For some time now I've worked at befriending him. Bringing him little gifts, mostly alcoholic, spending hours listening to his interminable stories. And I think he just might be able to help us, if I can pique his interest."

We heard a clink of glasses from inside, then something smashed on the floor and Klaus swore.

"Okay, okay," Noor said under her breath, "if you really think he can fix the—"

"Excellent!" Millard sang out, and he nicked V's device from Noor's pocket and darted inside.

"Hey!"

"Klaus, I've got something here I think you'll find very interesting . . ."

Noor and I shook our heads at each other. It was hard to be mad at someone so well-meaning, as frustrating as Millard could be sometimes. We stepped inside the shadowy workshop and shut the creaking door behind us.

◆   ◆   ◆

The inside of Klaus's workshop looked like a giant clock had exploded its guts onto every available surface. Chairs, tables, whole sections of the floor, and several long workbenches were piled with disassembled gears. There were functioning clocks, too—legions of them—tall grandfather clocks and tiny round tabletop clocks, simple wall clocks and elaborately carved cuckoo clocks. The sound of their pendulums ticking away was maddening and omnipresent.

Klaus stomped out of a back room with a tray of mismatched mugs and cleared the section of the workbench nearest us with a sweep of his massive arm. "Who likes rye whiskey? Made this batch myself." He shoved a mug into Noor's hand, then one into mine, then waved a third in Millard's general direction until our invisible friend took it from him.

"Welcome, *skol*, *sláinte*, to yer health!" Klaus said, upending his own mug into his mouth. Millard's glass rose and turned, and a stream of green liquid dribbled out and then disappeared as it passed his lips. Noor shot hers back, then coughed and looked as if she'd been struck across the face. I took a tentative sip—it tasted like fire— and held on to the mug, hoping Klaus wouldn't notice that the booze he'd poured me was still mostly there.

"A lot better than the swill they serve at the Shrunken Head, eh?" said Klaus. "*And* it'll shine the tarnish off a pocket watch better than any solvent you can buy." The fiery trickle of alcohol down my throat gave me a flashback to the Priest Hole, that malodorous dive on Cairnholm where my dad and I had stayed. It was unimaginable that it had all happened less than a year ago. That such a short time ago I hadn't met Millard yet or Emma or Miss Peregrine.

The boy I'd been then was a stranger to me now. That was another life.

"This is quite the piece of history you've got here," Klaus said. Millard had handed over the expulsatator and Klaus was bending over to examine it, a magnifying loupe strapped over one eye, which made him look like a myopic cyclops. He flipped the device over in his hands, then used a tiny screwdriver with a head the width of a needle to pop it open. Despite his recent intake of high-proof liquor—or perhaps because of it—his hands were steady.

"Hmmmmm," he said, peering through the loupe. "Fascinating." He flipped away the loupe and snapped his head toward Millard. "Have you shown this to Perplexus Anomalous?"

"No. Perplexus has no interest in mechanical things. Paper and maps and differential equations, yes, but—"

"The man's got sticky fingers," Klaus said abruptly. "Show him something shiny and you're not likely to get it back. He toured my shop last week and next thing you know I'm missing a femur from my best and oldest bone clock!"

I couldn't see Millard's expression, but I was sure it was one of disbelief. "I'm quite sure Perplexus had nothing to do with your missing femur, but I'll inquire about it next time I see him—"

A sudden cacophony shook the workshop, hundreds of clocks marking the hour all at once. Noor and I held our ears. Klaus had turned his attention back to the expulsatator and hardly seemed to notice.

It was clear why he was so hard of hearing. He'd been made deaf by his own clocks.

When the ringing stopped, Klaus said, "You know this doo-hickey is shot, right? Single use only."

"Yes, we know," said Millard, "but we're hoping there's some way it can be refurbished, so that it could be used a second time."

His eyes went wide and he let out a giant laugh. "No, no—no way, no how. It's not possible. I wouldn't do it even if it were. This is some bad business."

"What is?" I said.

He leaned back on his stool and pointed an accusing finger at the stopwatch. "You know what powers this thing?"

"Springs?"

"The *dial* runs with springs. No, the expulsion reaction." Now that we were discussing his area of expertise, he sounded less like an ornery old prospector and more like a scientist. "The thing that kicked y'all down the eastern coast of the United States, and forward through time a couple days, in a flash-blink."

"I don't, Klaus," said Millard. "Why don't you tell us?"

He leaned toward us and lowered his voice. "A very hard-to-come-by, ethically dodgy dollop of extracted and concentrated soul. You know, suulie, as the addicts call it."

It was a word I hadn't heard in a long time and it made my pulse quicken. It was the stuff the wights had extracted from my grandfather. That they'd peddled to weak-willed peculiars, addicting them so they could be controlled.

"You mean ambrosia?" I said.

Klaus's grotesquely magnified eye flashed at me through the loupe. "Aye, that's the word," he said and nodded. "It's why they could never mass-produce these little miracles." He tapped the expulsatator gently. "The fuel comes too dear."

"What if we could get you a vial of it?" Millard asked.

"How?" he said, cutting his eyes at me. "He a dealer?"

Noor laughed.

"No, no, Klaus, we chased them all out of the Acre. Don't you know who this is?"

"Don't know, don't care. And I won't deal with anyone who deals in suul, either."

"He doesn't," said Millard, "but if I understand what Jacob's hinting at, we might be able to get our hands on a vial that was requisitioned from the wights after their stronghold was captured. They had a stockpile, though I believe most of it was destroyed before the battle ended."

"I wouldn't touch the stuff even if you could get it."

Millard thought for a moment, then said, "What if we can recover your bone clock femur?"

Klaus scratched his white beard. "You know the story of that bone clock? It's a very special piece of peculiar horology."

"I don't," I said, and glanced in the general direction of Millard, who shook his head.

"Then I'll tell you," Klaus said. He settled his bulk onto a stool and folded his meaty arms. "A long, long time ago, there was a pe-culiar clockmaker named Miklaus who lived in Prague. He built the clock in the main city square, and it was the most amazing thing any-one had seen. Rival cities all wanted Miklaus to build them a clock just like it, but the Councilors of Prague were jealous men, and to ensure that he would never make another, and that the pride of their city would never be bested, they had him blinded. Well, Miklaus lost his mind, and one night he threw himself into the guts of that great clock and was crushed to death in its gears."

"*Damn,*" whispered Noor.

"His son was a clockmaker, too, and to honor his father he exhumed Miklaus's bones and made another clock from them—an even greater clock than the one in Prague, it's said. Never been to Prague, so I couldn't tell you. But the clock made from Miklaus's bones is s'posed to be haunted, and vested with certain peculiar abil-ities I ain't quite sussed out yet. It's been a pet project of mine for years, something I tinker with when I have the time."

"How did you come into possession of the clock?" Millard asked.

"I inherited it. Miklaus was my great-great-uncle and my name-sake." He said it so casually it took a moment to catch his meaning. Klaus sighed, looking a bit defeated. "I tried busting down Perplex-us's office door to get it back, but the guards chased me out, and some muckety-muck told me that if I tried anything like that again, I'd be kicked out of the Acre. I didn't want to come here in the first place, but . . ." He shrugged, and his shoulders sagged, and for a moment he looked very small despite his hefty frame. "But now it's home."

I wondered what had become of his wife—the one who'd been a prisoner of the wights. But if she wasn't here now, I didn't have to ask. His reaction to the idea of using suul for any purpose was telling.

"If we can get you that bone," I said, "and bring you a vial of suul, would you reset the expulsatator?"

< THE DESOLATIONS OF DEVIL'S ACRE >

"I don't like it, not one little bit," he said. His forehead had sprouted droplets of sweat. He drew a dirty rag from his jacket and mopped his brow with it. "Tell me what you need it for."

I looked at Noor, who shifted uneasily. "Your call," I said.

"It saved our lives once," she said. "My friends seem to think we might need it to save our lives again."

"Noor's the key to everything, Klaus," Millard said in an undertone. "Without her, Caul might be unstoppable. So if the worst happens, and he manages to break through the ymbrynes' defenses—"

"You need a fail-safe," Klaus said. Even his stentorian voice had dropped to something like a whisper. "You get me the bone and the suul, and I'll do my best. *But*"—he raised a crooked finger in warning—"I make no guarantees. I've never touched an expulsatator before today, and you know they ain't built to be used twice. It could blow up in your face."

"If anyone can do it, Klaus, you can," said Millard. "You're the best there is."

Klaus grinned. "Where's your hand at, boy?" Millard's sleeve rose to shake Klaus's outstretched hand, and then Klaus bent to dig around under the workbench. He emerged holding a bottle of muddy liquid. "Nip for the road?"

"No, thank you," said Millard. "Today we need our wits about us."

A look of vague dread crossed Noor's face. "I'll take one," she said. Klaus poured more into her mug.

I leaned close to her. "You sure?"

A long and brassy *bong* sounded from the top of the work-bench, and an intricate cuckoo clock began to sound the hour, a few minutes late. A small door opened and a platform popped out with a black-robed executioner and a supplicant on his knees. With each toll of the hour the executioner brought down the axe, the victim's lopped head hinged away from his body, and a spring-loaded spout

< 155 >

of red felt shot out from the neck-hole. Noor tipped back the drink as the beheading was replayed ten times over, and then she grimaced and slapped down the mug.

◆　　◆　　◆

I was starting to worry about Noor. As we hurried through the dark streets of the Acre's outer ring, she hardly spoke. It might've been the home-brewed lighter fluid she'd just consumed, but it seemed more likely that she was lost in her own head, thinking about what we were about to do. How do you ask someone if they're ready to see a long-lost loved one resurrected? Gently but directly, I decided.

We were passing through a sunken place where the cobblestones were torn up and the street was carpeted with sodden trash when she stumbled. I caught her arm before she could fall.

"Face-plant in this stuff and you'll catch a flesh-eating rash for sure," I said.

"Another day in paradise." She laughed darkly.

"So, are you ready for this?" I asked, still holding her arm. "When Enoch does this thing, it could be really . . . rough. I've seen him do it a few times before, and it's not pretty." I thought of Bronwyn's poor, dead brother, Victor. And Martin, the man who'd run the little museum on Cairnholm, who woke up with half a face, quoting poetry. Scenes that had haunted my dreams ever since.

Noor shrugged. "I already watched her get murdered. How much worse could this be?"

"Sometimes you don't know until it happens."

We walked in silence for a little while, and then quietly she said, "Did you ever wish you could talk to your grandfather again?"

"You mean Enoch's way?"

"No, just . . . *any* way."

"For a while after I got here, I thought about it all the time. I wanted to know his opinion on everything. I wanted to tell him what I was doing, show him who I was becoming. I thought he'd be—"

"Proud."

I nodded, slightly embarrassed.

She wrapped her arm around mine. "I'm absolutely sure he would've been."

"Thanks. I hope so," I said, a sudden swell of emotion sneaking up on me. I still missed my grandfather, though it was a low, background kind of ache. But certain memories could sharpen the ache until it became, momentarily, unbearable.

I took a deep breath. She glued our sides together as we leapt over a wide puddle. The ache dulled, and in its place I felt an overwhelming gratitude for Noor. She could make me feel so much with just a word or two—because I never doubted she meant them. She was never fake with me, never for a second. She was guileless without being naive. Two more line items on a growing list of things I loved about her. "Anyway," I said, gathering myself again, "there came a point where I stopped needing that as much. When what he would have thought of me became less important than what I thought of myself. So, as much as I miss him, now I think it's better that he just . . . stay . . . gone."

"I never needed those things from V," she said. "I was too angry at her for dying. The truth would've broken me, if I'd known it back then."

"Still. I think it'd be better if you weren't in the room when it happened."

"No. I need to be there."

"Why?"

"What if she's more than just Enoch's puppet? What if there's some part of her that's actually present? Some spark?"

"There's no spark, Noor." *It's like something out of a horror movie*, I thought, though I kept this to myself. "You don't need those images rattling around your head the rest of your life."

She let go of my arm. Retreated inward for a moment. "What if she's . . . *scared*?"

"Scared?"

"Wouldn't you be?"

"She won't even know what happening to her."

I wanted Millard to jump in and back me up, but he knew we were having a private conversation and was probably a tactful ten strides ahead of us.

"I need to be there," she said forcefully, then cut a glance at me. "And you, too, please."

"Of course I will."

"Thanks." She tried to smile, I think, but winced instead. "I'll be fine." She repeated it like a mantra, armoring herself. "I'll be fine."

CHAPTER NINE

*N*oor, Millard, and I snuck into the house the same way we'd snuck out, through the back alley, up the stilts, and into an open second-floor window. We heard voices in the kitchen and went downstairs to find that Miss Peregrine and the others had already returned. Miss Peregrine was drying her hair with a dish towel while Miss Wren sat at the kitchen table, stroking a sleepy chicken in her lap. Emma was slumped in a chair by the fire, exhausted. Bronwyn stood over the sink, wiping at a stubborn smear of blood on her forearm while Olive doted on her with a first aid kit. They looked just like you might expect people who'd lugged a gory corpse across a storm-racked town to look.

Fiona and Hugh had returned, too. But where was Enoch? And where was V?

Addison was guarding the closed door to the sitting room, and barked at us as we came down the last few stairs into the kitchen. "And where've *you* been?"

"You snuck out," Miss Peregrine said, "and left behind the guards we assigned you." She sounded more tired than angry.

"I'm sorry, miss," said Millard. "It's entirely my fault. I—"

She waved a hand. "We'll talk about it another time. There are more important matters before us now." She didn't even ask where we'd been. "Olive dear, don't forget the antiseptic before you apply the sticking plaster."

"Yes, ma'am."

"Did you run into trouble?" I asked.

"You could say that," Emma grumbled, rubbing a sore spot on her neck.

"Your parents are *very* disagreeable," said Bronwyn.

"So are your uncles," said Emma.

"They're back?" I recoiled a bit, anxiety spiking. "You saw them?"

"Yes, and they don't care much for trespassers," said Bronwyn.

Emma said, "They've gotten wise to the fact that strange people have been using their backyard for . . . *something* . . . and they've taken measures."

"Hired private security persons," said Addison.

"*Aggressive* private security persons," Bronwyn added.

"We got what we went for and returned only minorly bloodied," said Miss Peregrine. "I'd classify that a success." She finished drying her hair and draped the wet towel over the back of a chair.

"Is that their blood or yours?" Noor asked Bronwyn, hovering as Olive patched her arm.

Bronwyn shrugged. "Bit of both, I reckon."

"*And* mine," Addison growled, licking a cut on his side.

"Oh no, you too?" Olive said, and hurried to Addison with her first aid kit. "I'm nearly out of plasters!"

"We're going to have to move your family," said Miss Wren. The chicken in her lap pecked crumbs of bread from her hand.

"*Move* them?" I said.

"Caul has targeted you. It stands to reason he may also attempt to kidnap your parents."

"*I* would," said Hugh. "I mean, not *me*, but, you know, if I were Caul—"

"Move them where?" I said. "And for how long?"

"Leave the details to us," Miss Peregrine said. "We'll simply persuade them to go on holiday somewhere far away."

"They just got back from one," I said.

"Then we'll persuade them to go on another," Miss Wren said sharply. "Unless you'd rather risk them being used as hostages."

"Of course he wouldn't," Emma replied, then looked at me. "Would you?"

"Of course not," I said, my temper starting to rise.

Everyone was on edge.

"Let's not quarrel," Miss Peregrine said. "Jacob, we'll be gentle as lambs with them, you have my word. And when this is all over, we'll move them back."

"And wipe their memories," I said. "It'll be as if nothing ever happened."

"Yes, precisely."

She either hadn't noticed the edge of sarcasm in my voice or had chosen to ignore it. *As if nothing ever happened* was a sweet-sounding fairy tale. My parents would never be the same. Their lives had been turned upside down, inside out, blendered on liquify. Even if they didn't remember the most upsetting chunks of the last year—assuming they hadn't already sustained some kind of brain damage from all these memory-wipes—the scars would never fade. But there was nothing to be done about it, and no reason to get mad at the ymbrynes for simply trying to protect my parents the best way they knew how. So I took a breath, centered myself, and tried to reset.

"What about you, Miss Pradesh?" said Miss Wren. "Is there anyone Caul might torment in order to manipulate you? Anyone close to you?"

Noor laughed acidly. "He already killed her."

"What about your friend?" said Millard.

Noor tensed, then turned to him. "You don't think he'd hurt Lily?"

"Caul's depravity knows no bounds," Millard replied.

A new darkness clouded Noor's features. "If anything happened to her, I couldn't live with it."

"Nor I," said Millard. "Miss Peregrine, I would like to personally dedicate myself to her protection."

"As noble as that is, we need you here," said Miss Peregrine. "I'll assign one of our best guards to watch over her."

"I wish you could just bring her here," said Noor.

"Would that we could," Miss Peregrine sympathized. "But she's normal."

"She'll know she's being watched. Maybe the guard could take her a message from me, so she'll know they're friendly, and that I'm okay."

Miss Peregrine agreed. A paper and pencil were found, and Noor began to scribble out a short letter for the guard to read to her friend. Before she could finish, the door that led to the sitting room opened a crack, and Enoch emerged wearing long black gloves and a white apron flecked with red splotches.

"She's primed and ready," he said, and looked from Miss Peregrine to Noor. "How about you?"

Noor swallowed hard, then put down her pencil. Emma stood up to join us, but Miss Peregrine raised a hand to stop her. "We don't need an audience, only those who are essential. Jacob, Noor. Miss Wren, myself, and Mr. O'Connor."

Emma sat again. "I was essential to *retrieving* her . . ."

"It's nothing personal, Em," Enoch said. "No one expects to be yanked from a sound death-sleep and questioned, and having a big audience makes it even more disconcerting. The dead can get a bit shy."

"It's okay," Bronwyn said, "I'd rather not watch, anyway. It always gives me nasty dreams."

"Bron*wyn*," Olive hissed, pointing behind her hand at Noor.

Bronwyn looked mortified. "Cripes. Sorry. Pretend you're at the cinema and it's just a scary film, that's what I do."

"I'll be fine," Noor said curtly. She seemed uncomfortable with all the pity being aimed her way. "All that matters is that we find out where the meeting place is."

"Right," said Miss Peregrine. "Enoch, if you'll lead the way."

◆　　◆　　◆

V lay upon a long wooden table that had been positioned near the window. Daylight laddered through the blinds and fell across V's body in harsh yellow stripes. She looked like a cadaver in a medical school dissection: legs straight, bare feet splayed, chest butterflied open. Blood dripped steadily into a bucket under the table. Jars of pickled organs, some opened, were lined up along the windowsill, and the smell that escaped them was sharp and sour.

"I've already emptied the hearts of two sheep, a lion, and an ox into her," Enoch was saying. "I had to requisition one fresh chicken heart, too—don't tell Fiona. A nice mix that should keep her fairly even-tempered. All that's left is the poet."

Miss Peregrine frowned. "I won't ask where you got that, Enoch."

He gave her a cheeky wink. "It's better that way."

Enoch had already begun deadrising V, and for Noor's sake, I was grateful that some of the worst parts were already done. I'd watched him work on a human only once before: It had taken several gruesome minutes and something like five sheep hearts to rouse Martin, Cairnholm's late museum curator. Noor wouldn't have to witness all that gory preamble.

I couldn't bring myself to look at V for long—it felt like an intrusion—but from the corner of my eye I noticed her foot twitch, and I thought I heard a quiet murmur, like the sound of someone half woken from sleep.

Enoch reached under the table and drew out a lump wrapped in damp butcher paper. "With such limited time, I couldn't nick one of the *major* poets' hearts, sorry to say." He unwrapped the paper and tipped out a mottled-gray lump the size of a baseball. "Just some poor penniless scribbler."

"Will she start reciting his poems?" asked Miss Wren.

Enoch laughed. "I doubt it; this is his heart, not his brain. But it should help loosen V's tongue."

Noor hadn't spoken since we'd entered the room. She appeared to be staring at the wall rather than allowing her eyes to drift toward V. I moved close to her, my arm touching hers, and she jolted slightly. She'd been quietly humming the jingle from an old TV commercial.

"Ready, everyone?" asked Miss Peregrine, though she was only looking at Noor.

"Yes," she said. "Please just do it."

Enoch needed no encouragement, but he wasn't gleeful. There were few things in life Enoch took seriously, but his work was one.

He turned to face the table. Miss Peregrine took a step back to join Miss Wren. Enoch stripped off his black gloves, took the poet's heart in his left hand, and raised it above his head. Then he leaned over V's body and plunged his right hand into her open chest.

I flinched. Noor's eyes were still locked on the wall.

Enoch squinted in concentration as his right hand rummaged around inside V's chest. Suddenly he seemed to latch onto something, and a moment later he shuddered and a violent convulsion passed through him. I fought an urge to run and help him, but there was nothing I could do; this was part of his process.

In his raised left hand, the poet's heart quivered, then started beating.

"It's happening," Miss Peregrine whispered.

V began to moan, quietly at first. She made a sound like choking. Or like a dead throat clearing.

"Rise up, dead woman," Enoch intoned. "Rise and speak."

He lowered the arm that held the heart, then quickly retracted his right hand from inside V, sucking in a quick breath like something had bit him.

V sat up. I had known it was coming but wasn't prepared for the shock. She lurched upward with a sudden, flopping jerk, like an electrified rag doll. Her head lolled to one side. Her eyes were open, but the pupils rolled back and forth. Her mouth worked soundlessly, as if chewing gum.

Enoch's hair stood in spiky electrified tufts and steam rose from both his hands. He looked briefly stunned, then slicked back his hair and looked at Miss Peregrine. "The floor is yours," he said, voice a little shaky.

Miss Peregrine stepped toward V. "This is Alma Peregrine." She paused. "V—Velya—can you hear me?"

A gurgle issued from the dead woman's throat, but that was all.

Miss Peregrine tried again. "I'm very sorry to tell you this, but you are . . ." She hesitated. Coughed lightly into her hand. "Well, there's no easy way to break the news. You are dead. Percival Murnau murdered you. I'm ever so sorry."

V's head snapped straight on her neck, but her pupils kept wandering.

"Can she hear me?" Miss Peregrine asked Enoch.

"Keep talking," Enoch said. "Sometimes it takes a while to get through to them." But his tense demeanor made me think sometimes you couldn't get through at all.

Miss Peregrine soldiered on. "We need information, V. We need to ask you something, and it's very important you find a way to answer us."

Miss Wren, running out of patience, stepped beside Miss Peregrine and cut in. "Where's the meeting place? The secret meeting place for the seven ymbrynes?"

V grimaced and jerked her head away as if in pain.

"Too loud," V said, her voice like sandpaper.

Noor jumped, then curled her fingers around my wrist.

"Miss Wren, please," Enoch said. "She's dead, not deaf."

"Too bright," said V.

"Too bright!" said Miss Peregrine. She stepped quickly to the window, twisted the rod on the blinds, and the light in the room dimmed.

V sagged forward. She moaned, took a few rapid breaths, then raised her head. Her pupils were still bouncing back and forth, settling nowhere. *"Whooooooo,"* she breathed. "Who's there?"

"Alma Peregrine," said Miss Peregrine.

"This is Miss Wren speaking."

Enoch gave a little bow. "Enoch O'Connor. Pleased to be your resurrectionist today."

V had not reacted yet. Miss Peregrine looked at me. I said my name. Her head tilted slightly. Her mouth opened, then closed again.

Noor forced herself to look at V. "And Noor."

V jolted. Her eyes stopped rolling and focused on Noor. "Baby?" the dead woman rasped. "Is that you?"

Noor looked away as if stung. *Baby*, coming from someone so vividly dead, was a shock even to me.

I clasped Noor's hand and squeezed. She squeezed back. Tapped some well of strength. Then faced V again.

"Yes. It's Noor."

"Come here. Let me get a look at you."

Noor hesitated.

Miss Wren said, "V, we need to ask you a question."

The dead woman's arm rose, grasped at Noor. "Come closer. Let me see you. Let me touch you."

Noor let go of my hand and approached the table. She reached out and grabbed V's hand in the air, and when she made contact I saw a shudder go through Noor's body.

V held Noor's hand, kneaded it.

Noor seemed frozen.

"Talk to her," Enoch whispered.

"Mama," she said. "I'm sorry."

V rocked on her hips, swaying from one side to the other. "Sorry for what?"

"For what happened to you. It was my fault."

"It's okay, baby. I'm not mad anymore. We'll get another TV."

Noor gasped and pulled her hand away.

V moaned. "Where'd you go? Come back."

"That was a long time ago, Mama."

Enoch leaned in. "You're dead now, madam," he said, as if talking to a senile old lady. "You're not alive any—"

Noor put up a hand to stop him. V said nothing for a moment, then broke out laughing like she'd heard the world's funniest joke. A fine red mist sprayed from her butterflied chest.

None of us knew what to do. Not even Enoch. When her unsettling laughter died down, she sagged like a marionette who'd had her strings cut, then let out a long, mournful cry that sent chills through me.

Enoch hissed at Noor and made a looping hurry-it-up gesture with his finger. We only had so much time.

"Mama!" Noor said loudly.

V slowly straightened, looked at Noor again. Her face was pained.

"I need to ask you a question," Noor said.

At this, I saw Miss Wren visibly relax.

"No snacks after dinnertime," V said. "You know the rules."

"Not that, Mama. Something else." Noor glanced over her shoulder at Miss Peregrine, who nodded her encouragement. "Mama, we got a phone call. It told us to go to the meeting place. I think we we were supposed to go there together. You and me. But we can't, so I have to go without you. Can you tell me where it is?"

V was quiet for a moment. We could hear the poet's heart beating in Enoch's hand. The shuffle of our friends' feet as they crowded the other side of the closed door, listening.

Then V let out a long, distressed groan. A sound of realization, and of mourning. It seemed she understood. The worst had happened. Despite all her sacrifices, the thing she'd devoted her life to preventing had come to pass.

Miss Peregrine nodded grimly. "V, listen to me. Caul has returned. We need to gather the seven . . ."

Noor stepped up to the table again. As close to V as she'd been. "Please, Mama. We're in trouble. We need your help. Please tell me where it is, Mama. The meeting place."

V stopped moaning. Suddenly, her face jerked upward to look at Noor. "It's almost tuck-in time," she said sweetly. "But we can't read stories until your teeth are brushed. Did you brush your teeth?"

Noor took a deep breath, then replied, "Only the ones I want to keep."

V's blue lips pulled upward into a smile. "PJs?"

"On," said Noor.

"And Penny?" said V. "Where's Penny-doll?"

"Got him right here," Noor lied; there was no doll.

"What shall we read tonight? *Frog and Toad*? *Eloise*? No, no—I know. Our special stories."

"We don't have time for that now, Mama."

"Get it down from the shelf. Go on. The old heavy one with the cover peeling off. I know, I know. We'll fix it, just need some paper tape and a binding edge. No, you can't put Band-Aids on books, silly goose. Good, now bring it over. That's a girl."

Noor hadn't moved; the scene playing out was entirely in V's memory.

"Turn to chapter . . . that's right, your favorite one. Now, come sit in Mama's lap."

Noor stiffened and tried to back away, but V grabbed her wrist and held on tight.

"Sit."

"My question, Mama."

V pulled her close. Noor squirmed. "Sit, sit, sit. Mama misses you."

"Please," she begged. "I need you to answer me."

"Read with me."

Noor let out a shuddering sigh. Enoch circled his finger more urgently, eyes wide.

"Okay, Mama."

"Noor," said Miss Peregrine, her voice betraying some alarm, "Are you sure you want to—"

"I'll be fine." And then she sat on the table and let V pull her into her lap. V gave a sigh of deep satisfaction, wrapped her arms around Noor's chest, and pulled her tight against what was left of her own.

Noor looked like she might pass dead away.

"Tell me," said Noor. And while the rest of us looked on with a mixture of wonder and horror, V rested her chin on Noor's shoulder and began to tell a story.

"Once upon a time, a very long time ago, there was a girl who grew spikes on her back like a porcupine. People feared and avoided her, and her parents worried for her future. One winter a sickness swept through the countryside and killed the girl's poor father. Her mother had been carried away by famine the winter before. And as the father's soul left his body, he heard the girl singing, 'Come back to me, dear Father, come back to me, as fast as fast can be!'"

The ymbrynes traded a meaningful look.

"And the man loved his daughter so much," Noor said, reciting from memory, "that rather than depart to his great reward, his soul lodged itself inside the girl's favorite doll."

"That's right, dear," V rasped. "That's exactly right." She looked spent, exhausted by the effort of speaking so much. Her head drooped onto Noor's shoulder. Enoch circled his finger. The heart in his hand was slowing.

"Now, Mama, my question . . ."

"Sorry, love, it'll have to wait till morning. Time for nighty-night beddy-bye," she said dreamily, then let go of Noor and slumped backward onto the table, motionless.

Miss Wren gasped.

"Oh, come *on*!" Enoch said, shaking the heart as if it were a stopped clock.

Noor leapt off the table, shivering. "Are you okay?" I said, pulling her into me.

Enoch threw the exhausted heart on the floor. "Is that *it*?" he shouted at V. "I go to all the trouble of bringing you back from the dead, and we get a *bedtime* story?"

"That was one of the *Tales of the Peculiar*," said Miss Wren. "The beginning of it, anyhow."

"It was my favorite story when I was little," Noor said. She was shivering. I led her to one of the floor cushions and we sat down together. She seemed okay, shaken but engaged. But Noor had a thousand layers beneath her surface and was practiced at hiding them.

"What a waste of hearts," Enoch said bitterly.

The door opened and our eavesdropping friends tumbled in, unable to stem their curiosity any longer. Miss Peregrine didn't even object; she was lost in murmured consultation with Miss Wren.

Olive rushed to where Noor and I were sitting. "Was that awful? Or wonderful? Are you all right?"

Noor looked at her blankly, as if confused by the question.

"Too soon," Olive said. "Sorry."

Miss Peregrine and Miss Wren split apart and started giving orders.

Miss Peregrine said, "Olive, I want you to go find the unabridged edition of the *Tales*. It's in section three-F on subfloor seven of the archives. Take Bronwyn to help you, as it's quite heavy. You'll need my badge to check it out of the building." As Miss Peregrine dug into her pockets and pulled out an ID shaped like an iron star, Miss Wren spoke to Millard.

"Mr. Nullings, please fetch the oldest Map of Days you can lay your hands on. Ask Perplexus for one if you come up short in the cartography stacks. Enoch, wrap V in a shroud and put her on ice, and ask the mortuary department to prepare her for funeral."

"Are we finished with her?" said Noor, confused. "Won't you need to wake her up again?"

"It'll take a few hours to arrange," Enoch said. "I'll need to collect twice as many hearts, and even better ones this time . . ."

"That won't be necessary, Mr. O'Connor," said Miss Peregrine.

"But she hasn't told us where the meeting place is yet!" Hugh protested.

"Actually," the two ymbrynes said at the same time, and then Miss Peregrine finished: "I believe she just might have."

CHAPTER TEN

V was reciting from 'The Tale of Pensevus,'" Miss Wren said. "Not one of the better-known stories."

We had gathered in the kitchen, where Olive and Bronwyn had just returned from the archives lugging a very old and very large edition of the *Tales*. "The archivist said it took the skins of three hundred sheep to make this book," Bronwyn said, panting lightly as she dropped it on the daybed beside Fiona, who grimaced as it landed with a clap and sent a cloud of chicken feathers into the air.

"The book we used to have was handwritten," said Noor, "so I always thought it was something Mama had made up, written herself. As a comfort to an orphaned kid, and to explain how I came to live with her."

"Do you think it contains a clue about the location of the meeting place?" asked Horace.

"I suspect so," said Miss Peregrine. "As you know, the *Tales* often have secrets encoded in them."

"V told only the beginning, though," said Miss Wren, seating herself between Fiona and the giant, leather-bound tome. "Let's read the rest and see what else it may reveal."

With Bronwyn's help she hefted open the cover, then flipped through dozens of waxy parchment pages until she found the story. Balancing a pair of cat-eye bifocals at the end of her long nose, she began to read.

"'Once upon a time, a very long time ago, there was a girl who grew spikes on her back like a porcupine.'" She squinted and turned the page. "Yes, yes, we remember that bit . . . ah, here we are. 'And her dying father so loved her that rather than go on to his great reward, his soul lodged itself inside Penny, the girl's favorite doll. He did it so that he could watch over her all the days of her life. She loved the doll dearly, and even though she didn't realize that the soul of her father was inside it, she felt bound to it, and took it everywhere with her, and talked to it. Sometimes, it seemed to talk back.' "

Noor closed her eyes, and her lips moved as she silently recited the story along with Miss Wren.

" 'As she got older,'" Miss Wren continued, " 'she grew careless with Penny, and one day while traveling she left it behind on a passenger ship. By the time she'd realized her mistake, the ship had departed from the port again. She saw it sailing away but was too late to catch it. She stood at the dock singing after it, *Come back to me, dear Penny, come back to me, as fast as fast can be . . .* ' "

Several of us traded glances. *That phrase again.*

" 'She looked everywhere for the doll. Listened for his voice in the wind. She didn't hear Penny, but she began to hear different voices, voices other people rarely notice or bother to listen for. The voices of animals. They felt safe speaking to the girl, now a woman, because she was not afraid of them. She took them in whenever she met them, and cared for them as if they were her own children, and built a big house to keep them safe. Her house was near the sea, and sometimes it was battered by terrible storms. One night there was a storm like they'd never seen, and in the gale a ship wrecked on the rocky beach. When the wind stopped blowing she went out to see what had happened, and there among the wreckage was a single survivor, a little boy. The boy was soaked and shivering and in his arms he clutched the doll. He ran toward the girl and embraced her, and though she'd never seen the boy before she took him into her arms.'

" 'He swore you'd be here, said the boy.'

" 'Sea monsters had chased the ship and sunk it, he said.

< THE DESOLATIONS OF DEVIL'S ACRE >

They've been after me for as long as I can remember. But Penny said you'd keep me safe. So I came, he said, fast as fast can be.'

" 'She took the boy in and kept him safe. He was an odd child who neither ate nor drank, at least not in the usual way. Under his clothes, growing out of his back and the bottoms of his feet, were roots, and when he was hungry he would go outside and lie down in the nice muddy garden for a few hours. But the woman didn't mind. She was glad of his company, and overjoyed at the doll's return— though now Penny belonged to the little boy, and she didn't have the heart to claim him again. They talked to each other all the time, the doll and the boy, the boy speaking aloud and the doll answering silently. But one morning, after the boy had been living there for several years, the woman found the boy crying by the window. When she asked him what the matter was, he replied that the doll had gone away. In that carriage, he said, and through the window she could see a horse and cart racing away down the lane. The boy sang out, Come back to me, come back to me, as fast as fast can be . . . '

" 'The woman and the boy did not see the doll again for many years. The boy grew up and the woman grew older. A terrible war broke out, a thunderous bloody war that rent the land around them and tore it to pieces. Soldiers from another country came to the house and declared it theirs. The boy was arrested and taken away. The woman was made to sleep in the stables with the animals while the officers and soldiers moved into the house. The soldiers killed some of the animals for food, and the woman wept and wept, so miserably sad she could hardly rise from the pile of hay where she slept.'

" 'The fighting went on and on. It seemed the foreign soldiers would never leave. Then one night there was a knock at the stable door. The woman, who never slept anymore, rose and answered it. It was a wounded and frightened young soldier from her own country, who would surely have been killed if discovered. She hid him, gave him food, and tended to his wounds. When he was well enough to speak, he thanked the old woman, and told her that he'd walked for

< 179 >

many weeks and crossed enemy lines to find her. She asked him why, and in answer he reached into his rucksack and pulled out her old doll, who was looking quite the worse for wear. And the soldier smiled and whispered, *Penny said you needed help . . .*'

"'*Fast as fast can be*, she finished for him.'

"'The soldier had the ability to transmute things from solid matter to gas with a certain touch of his hands, and that night he snuck into the old woman's house and proceeded from bed to bed, transforming the enemy soldiers into harmless puffs of smoke. By the time the sun rose, they were but an angry red cloud hovering above the roof, and could do nothing to the woman anymore but hiss and swirl.'

"'The doll came and went several times more, and it's said that he still roams the earth to this day, helping outcast children who need a home.'" Miss Wren took off her bifocals and looked up from the book. "And that's the end."

"So?" Enoch said impatiently. "It's a cute story, but—"

"'As fast as fast can be,'" said Emma. "That's just what the person said in those calls that were intercepted."

"That has to mean something," said Hugh. He looked to Miss Peregrine. She sat in deep concentration, eyes on the ceiling and fingers steepled beneath her chin.

"What else?" Miss Peregrine said.

"I had a doll named Penny," Noor said. "He was old and broken and missing an eye, and I couldn't stand to be apart from him."

Everyone looked at her.

"Was it *the* Penny?" Bronwyn asked. "Or was your doll named after the one from the story?"

Noor shook her head. "V said Penny was the doll from the story. But I don't know. I always imagined he could talk, but of course he didn't really."

"Or perhaps he did," said Horace in a low voice, "in your mind."

"Mama"—she caught herself—"V said he'd watch over me when she wasn't there. And if we ever got separated, he'd help lead me back to her again. But after we were attacked by wights, just before she decided she had to give me up, Penny disappeared. I was inconsolable."

"Maybe she hid him away," Emma said. "So he couldn't lead you back to her again. For your own safety." Her voice wavered, near to breaking.

Noor's face darkened, but she said nothing.

"What else?" Miss Peregrine asked again, searching our faces expectantly. "Think back to your loop history classes." No one had an answer. She frowned. "I think I let you spend too many days ca-vorting in the sun instead of studying. Miss Wren, if you please . . ."

"I was not the only ymbryne to oversee a menagerie of peculiar animals," Miss Wren said. Addison's ears perked up. "There was one other before me: Miss Griselda Tern. But her loop collapsed tragically in 1918, in the closing days of the Great War. Destroyed by artillery shells."

"Sounds a bit like the fate of our own poor loop," Emma said.

"Prior to that," Miss Wren continued, "there are stories about Miss Tern's menagerie being overrun by enemy soldiers—strikingly reminiscent of the events of 'The Tale of Pensevus.'"

"So you think . . . ," Olive said, grasping, "you think maybe it's the loop from the tale?"

"I think V told us that particular bedtime story for a reason," said Miss Peregrine, "much the same way she taught you that nurs-ery rhyme, Noor. It's a key."

Miss Wren nodded. "I believe Miss Tern's loop is the meeting place."

"Well, V was definitely an ymbryne," Enoch said. "Always talking in riddles."

"But that loop is gone," Noor said doubtfully. "You said it was destroyed a long time ago."

"It was," said Miss Peregrine. "Which, admittedly, will make it harder to reach."

"But makes it all the better a hiding place," Miss Wren said with a gleam in her eye. "Very smart, squirreling it away in a place like that."

"But how do you find a loop that isn't there?" Noor asked.

"Leave that to us," said Millard, and we all turned to see his robe floating in the open doorway. "Clear the way, please!"

He led two black-suited Temporal Affairs minions inside the room, and together they heaved a Map of Days that was even larger than the *Tales* through the door and dropped it on the kitchen table.

"Careful with that, it's older than any of us!" Millard shooed them out the door and slammed it behind them. "Do you remember," he said, turning to Noor, "when you asked whether it would be possible to visit very old, long-collapsed loops in places like ancient Rome or Greece, and I described a technique we call leapfrogging?"

Noor stood a little straighter. "Yes."

"Well, that's what we're going to have to do now, in order to reach Miss Tern's loop."

"Is it hard?" I asked. "How long will it take?"

"That depends on what and where we have to leapfrog *through*," Millard said, cracking open the atlas. "Miss Tern's original loop was in northern France, which isn't far from here as the crow flies. It was opened in 1916 and destroyed in 1918. Which is a fairly narrow window of time." He started to carefully turn the pages, each one the size of a pillowcase. "It will mean finding another loop that was initiated during those few years, then traveling across the open past to reach Miss Tern's loop before its collapse."

"Does that mean crossing through a *war zone*?" asked Claire.

"We're *living* in a war zone, Claire," said Hugh, "what's the difference?"

"It could get a bit hairy," Millard conceded, "and complicated . . ."

"Nothing good is ever easy," said Emma. "But if all six of the other prophesied ones are there, it'll be worth the danger and trouble."

< THE DESOLATIONS OF DEVIL'S ACRE >

"But what do I do when I find them?" Noor asked. "Are there any clues in the story about that?"

Miss Peregrine tried, I think, to seem reassuring. "Don't worry about that yet, dear. I'm certain it will become clear eventually."

Noor frowned and crossed her arms.

Millard was still turning pages in the temporal atlas, looking for a connecting loop, trying to figure out how much of the past we would have to cross to reach Miss Tern's loop entrance, when someone started banging on the front door.

Hugh was closest, and ran to open it.

A breathless young man was standing on the front steps. "Come quick! There's a hollowgast loose in the Acre!"

"What?" Miss Peregrine spun to face him.

I ran to the door, my heart starting to race. "Is it ours?" I hoped he was talking about the one I'd tamed, that had fought by my side on Gravehill, was formerly the Panloopticon's battery, and was now retired, recuperating—and, last I checked, imprisoned—in the former blood-sport arena.

"I don't think so," the boy said quickly. "This one's different from any we've seen before. But in any case it's wreaking havoc and hurting people, so if you aren't too busy, Mr. Portman, could you please spare a moment to go and kill it?"

Miss Peregrine told everyone to shelter inside the house, then ran outside with me, Bronwyn, and Emma to see what was going on. I noted, amid the rush, that I hadn't felt the hollow yet, which was strange, and probably bad. By now, my ability had developed such that I should've immediately felt any hollow that came within a mile's radius of us, a distance that easily covered the length of the Acre.

"This one's different *how*?" I called after the boy as we chased him down the steps.

He stopped at the footbridge and turned to face me. He looked frightened. "Mr. Portman, sir, even *I* can see this one."

< 183 >

There weren't supposed to be any untamed hollows left—and there *definitely* weren't supposed to be any loose in Devil's Acre. No one had been ready for it. The battlements we'd been prepping around the loop entrance weren't finished. It had slipped through unscathed, and now it was raising hell a few hundred yards away, near the confluence where Fever Ditch met the smaller tributary that bisected our street. It leapt from barge to barge, terrorizing the boatmen who'd been unloading supplies, sending heavy crates crashing into the water, lashing its tongues at anyone in striking distance. It had already caught someone's horse, and now it jumped atop a footbridge with the half-chewed creature hanging limp from its jaws and roared like King Kong.

"Oh, it's *awful*!" wailed Bronwyn, covering her eyes.

She could see it, too. So could Emma and Miss Peregrine, who gaped at the distant creature in fascination and horror.

We could *all* see it. And I had only just started to feel its presence, which was worryingly late considering how close it was.

"It's *horrible*," said Emma, twisting her lip. "If I'd known they were that ugly, I would've been even more terrified of them."

I gathered my courage and tried to prepare myself for a fight. "I'll take care of it," I said.

I was about to tear away from the group when Miss Peregrine latched on to my arm. "It's *you* he's come for," she said. "You and Miss Pradesh. You'd be walking right into Caul's trap."

"It's going to *kill* someone!" I protested.

"He is only interested in killing the two of you." She relinquished my arm. "Right now it's the home guard's job to deal with this, not yours. And since they can see this one, their task will be that much easier."

Bronwyn uncovered her eyes. "But *why* can we see it?"

"Perhaps it's an inferior species of hollowgast that my brother was keeping in reserve somewhere," Miss Peregrine guessed. "In any case, we can trade theories after it's dead."

She pointed out three home guards who had appeared at the edge of a rooftop near the hollowgast. They were pushing a heavy piece of machinery toward the edge. "A harpoon gun," Miss Peregrine noted. "It's modern, steam-powered, and fires a razor-sharp mesh of wire designed specially to kill hollows."

The gun was so tall it nearly overshadowed the three seven-foot men pushing it. Working quickly, they rolled it into place at the edge of the roof, swiveled the barrel around on a tripod, and took aim.

"They're only going to make it angry," I warned.

"It's not angry now?" said Noor, and we turned to see her standing behind us on the footbridge.

"It's barely even cross," said Emma.

"I asked you to stay inside," Miss Peregrine growled.

Noor did a double take. "Should I be able to *see* it?"

"Yes, we can all see it, now please go inside," Miss Peregrine snapped.

Noor stared at the hollow, ignoring her, and gagged a little. "God, he's ugly."

"Please, just let me handle it," I said. "I know they can see it, but I can *control* it. They're going to get hurt."

"Absolutely out of the question!" Miss Peregrine was close to fully losing her temper.

The guards were still aiming. The hollow leapt from the bridge onto a barge, lashed a large crate, and sent it arcing through the air like a discus. The guards saw it coming toward them and ducked; it crashed down on the rooftop not far from them.

"They'd better hurry up," Bronwyn muttered, "or they're going to be cat's meat."

The guards stood up again, then—finally—fired their weapon. There was a puff of white smoke as the harpoon gun made an explosive report. A cloud of metal wire zipped across the Ditch, expanding as it went, but flew clear of the hollow to splash down in the filthy water. A moment later, a man who'd been standing in its path collapsed to the ground, diced into a dozen pieces.

Noor and Emma gasped, and Miss Peregrine winced and muttered some quick, prayerful-sounding phrase in Old Peculiar under her breath.

"They blew it," I said. "Now it's my turn."

She grabbed my arm again. "Absolutely not," she repeated, but more weakly than before.

The hollow was on the move, jumping to the flat deck of another barge before tearing down a flimsy bridge made of planks.

"If it wants me, it'll follow me," I said, "and that means I can lead it to a less-crowded area. How easily can they move that harpoon gun?"

"Easily enough, if I help them," Bronwyn said.

Miss Peregrine frowned. She was losing this battle. "What do you mean to do?" she said to me.

"There's a tunnel near here, right?"

"There's the bridge tunnel that leads out of the loop," Emma said.

That was a half mile away down the Ditch, if not more. "I need something closer."

"There's the tunnel underneath Shank Hill," said Miss Peregrine, and she reluctantly let go of my arm to point it out in the distance.

"I have to go," I said, backing away. "Before anyone else is killed."

For a moment Miss Peregrine squeezed her eyes shut. When she opened them again, she had given up fighting me. "Go, then," she said. "I'll let the guards know you're coming, and that you need their harpoon. Take Miss Bloom with you, and Miss Bruntley."

"And me," said Noor.

"Not you!" Miss Peregrine said, latching on to Noor's arm in place of mine.

"She's right," I said, "you're too important to risk."

"So important I'm useless," Noor grumbled. Then, low and serious and close to my ear: "Come back in one piece."

❖   ❖   ❖

With a running start Miss Peregrine leapt into the air. She transformed in a blurred burst of feathers and was winging off toward the rooftop before her empty clothes had even touched the ground.

The guards had not fired their gun again. Maybe they were too horrified by what they had done. Or maybe, I thought with a sinking feeling, they'd only had one shot, and they'd wasted it.

Bronwyn and Emma followed me as I broke into a run. The rudiments of a plan were only beginning to take shape in my mind. The main thing was to get close to the hollow and try to tap into his brain. If this really was some lesser form of hollowgast, I thought, it shouldn't be difficult. Then again, assumptions like that had only ever deepened whatever trouble I was in.

We crossed the rickety footbridge to the other side of the water and ran along the bank toward the hollow. Peculiars were fleeing in the opposite direction. Leo's four goons, pale and panting. Dogface and the boy with the pulsating boil, who both looked more amused than scared.

"Go get 'em, Jake!" Dogface cheered without slowing.

"Cowards!" Emma shouted after them.

The hollow let out a scream that echoed down the street, scaring one girl so badly that she gave up running and leapt into the water. Dogface, to his credit, saw what happened and turned back to fish her out.

We reached the confluence where our filthy tributary flowed into the main Ditch. Here the streets were totally deserted. The hollowgast had clambered up to the third story of a building, and was hanging from a ledge, its tentacles sampling the air like a gourmand. Miss Peregrine had been right. It was looking for me. *Smelling* for me. And no doubt for Noor.

We entered the hollow's halo of destruction and dodged a shattered crate, from which a lifetime's supply of pungent bleu cheese had spilled across the cobblestones. Only peculiars would use bleu cheese as survival rations.

"I'll draw it toward that tunnel entrance," I shouted over my shoulder. "Bronwyn, how fast can you get that gun from the roof down to the street?"

She glanced up at the building, a block away. "Two minutes," she said, reassuringly certain.

The tunnel entrance was several blocks beyond that and down a side street. "One minute would be better," I said, "but Emma and I will buy you as much time as we can. I need you to get that gun through the tunnel before me. Post yourself at the far end and aim it back the way you came. Then wait for us."

"I hope you know what you're doing, Mr. Jacob," she said, and split off down an alley.

Emma and I kept running until we had drawn even with the hollow, which was now directly across the Ditch from us. I had assumed it would see me right away and run in our direction, and indeed it was already climbing down from the building—but not because of me. There was a woman on its side of the street: the cowgirl with the long braid over one shoulder and a rifle in her hands.

Her voice echoed off the bricks and the water. "Hold it right there! I got you in my sights!"

"Get out of there!" Emma called. "You'll be slaughtered!"

The woman ignored us. She pressed the rifle stock to her shoulder and sighted down the barrel. The hollow paused halfway down the building and gave her a vaguely curious look, as if it had never been threatened by a human before and wanted to see what she would do next.

The woman fired. The shot was loud and echoing, and the recoil threw her shoulder back. She slid the bolt on her rifle with a smooth and assured motion, lowering the barrel as the hollow began to climb down again, then fired a second time. The hollow reached the street and began walking toward her almost casually, like someone out for an after-dinner stroll.

The cowgirl held her ground and began reloading. Maybe she'd never seen a hollow in action before. Maybe she didn't know what she was up against. Maybe she was suicidal. Regardless, I didn't want her blood on my hands.

"Hey!" I shouted. "Asshole!"

The hollow froze. And then the cowgirl started firing. She got off six shots with remarkable speed, cocking and aiming between each trigger pull.

And then she stopped, out of ammo. There was a breathless moment where everyone waited to see what would happen—whether the hollow would fall down dead. Instead it calmly reached up its withered hand and, in a motion like removing lint from a sweater, plucked eight bullets from its chest and flicked them away.

"Jesus Jehoshaphat," the cowgirl said, lowering the rifle. "That was a thirty-aught-six."

The bullets hadn't even punctured its skin. It roared and lurched toward her again, faster this time, as if determined to kill a pestering fly. The cowgirl had fallen back a few steps, the first hint of fear she'd betrayed, and was fumbling to pry fresh bullets from a pocket with one hand.

"It's useless, you idiot!" Emma shouted, and began rubbing her hands together. "RUN!"

Emma worked up a fat ball of fire between her palms and launched it across the Ditch. The hollow had all three tongues out and was reaching for the woman when the fireball landed a few feet shy of it, and the hollow stopped dead in its tracks.

"*Great* shot," I yelled, and Emma clapped her flaming hands with glee.

"Over here!" I waved my arms at the hollow. "Come and get me!"

The hollow turned to look at us. The cowgirl swallowed her pride and ran. I shouted a command in Hollow across the water—*Swallow your tongues*—in the hope Miss Peregrine was right, that this hollow was so inferior that I might be able to establish control over it from a distance, without having to get close and knead its mind into submission while it tried to disassemble me.

No such luck.

I felt a quickening in the hollowgast as it recognized me, let out a scream that split the air, and spat the dead horse's head in our direction. It sailed most of the way over the Ditch, then landed short and splashed us with foul water.

"It's not working?" Emma asked, trying not to sound panicked.

"Not yet. I probably just need to get closer."

"Probably?"

I shouted, *Sleep, lie down!* in Hollow, but the hollow didn't react. It was turning left and right, looking for the quickest way across the Ditch to us.

"I *do* need to get closer."

"No *way*, Jacob. Promise me you'll exhaust every other option before you let that thing near you."

It was waiting for us to make a move. And now I'd stalled too long, and doubt was creeping in. Doubt that I could do this. Doubt that this was a hollow that could be controlled at all. And suddenly I didn't want to get within a hundred feet of it.

"Okay," I promised her. "It's a last resort."

We took off running down our side of the Ditch. The hollow bolted in the same direction, easily keeping pace with us.

"It's going to cross," I said. "We need to get inside somewhere . . . out of the open . . ."

Emma pointed to a rickety tenement. "In there!" The building was just beyond the bridge of barges. If we didn't get there before the hollow crossed it, we'd be cut off.

"We'll lead it through the building, try to slow it down once we're inside to buy Bronwyn some time, then lead it to the tunnel entrance," I said. "Get your hands as hot as you can, and stay near."

"Way ahead of you," she said, match-flames leaping from her fingers.

"Fast as fast can be," I said, panting, and we broke into a sprint.

The hollow matched us, propelling itself with all three tongues toward a traffic jam of boats that stretched across the water; an easy bridge.

We reached the tenement door just as the hollow leapt onto the first boat. I let Emma run inside first, making sure the hollow saw where we were going. There was no question: It was heading for us like a moth to a lamp.

The building's interior was an uninhabitable wreck of slumping walls and half-caved ceilings, and we navigated the rubble as nimbly as we could, running around some piles, scrambling over others. When the door behind us smashed open and flew off its hinges, I knew we were in the hollow's company.

I didn't look back, didn't need to. I could feel it now, my inner compass finally shuddering to life. It had taken a long time to generate any kind of connection to this hollow, way longer than was normal, and the feeling itself was different, I noticed, the compass needle shivering at a higher frequency. But there would be time to parse this later . . . if we made it to later. Suffice to say, I was starting to think this was no inferior hollow. This was something new, and more terrible, than before. I prayed it was killable, and that I was not leading my friends into a death trap.

We were helped by a bit of dumb luck: The crumbling tenement had plenty of trash for us to throw in the hollow's way. As we fled, we toppled an enormous wardrobe and a jumbled pile of broken chairs behind us, which slowed it some. Near the exit we led it down a short, debris-choked hallway, and while the hollow itself was slender enough to fit through any gap that Emma or I could, its slashing tongues got tangled in something, which hung him up just long enough for us to escape outside into an alley and get a healthy head start toward the tunnel.

The tunnel wasn't much taller or wider than me, and it bored through a wall where the street dead-ended ahead of us. It was not lit inside, and as we approached I couldn't tell whether Bronwyn and the guards had already entered, but I hoped to God they had.

"Emma—" I started to say, but she was one step ahead of me, as usual, flames already leaping from her hands to light up the dark.

A howl echoed off the walls of the alley behind us. The hollow was outside of the building now, and there was only open ground separating us.

We ducked into the tunnel and forged into blackness. Tree roots hanging down from the tunnel's raw ceiling slapped our faces.

A voice echoed from deeper inside the tunnel: "Mr. Jacob, is that you?"

Bronwyn. Bronwyn was ahead of us.

"It's us!" Emma shouted. "Emma and Jacob!"

We rounded a slight curve and a glow appeared in the distance—the tunnel exit. Silhouetted in the glow were four stooped figures dragging a harpoon gun. They'd been forced to turn it on its side to fit it into the tunnel.

Behind us, the hollow reached the tunnel entrance. The feeling grew more present, as if the shape of the tunnel had compressed and focused it.

We stumbled and ran and stumbled and ran, which was the best we could do hunched over like that. Then we came to a place where, mercifully, the tunnel was higher, and we could stand, and really move our legs.

The noise the hollow made was all-encompassing. We dared not look back. We just ran.

I shouted at Bronwyn to hurry. She and the guards were struggling with the gun. When we reached them, they were still twenty feet shy of the exit. The hollow was at the halfway point and closing the distance between us fast. Bronwyn was pulling the gun by its barrel while the guards were pushing, and though they were making progress, it wasn't quick enough. The heavy base kept digging into the dirt. Bronwyn was getting tired.

If this plan had any hope of working, I was going to have to find a way to slow the hollow down. I told Emma to stay with Bronwyn, to defend her, if it came to that.

"You won't be able to see it in the dark if I don't come with you!"

"I can *feel* it," I said, "and maybe that's enough." If the hollowgast didn't need eyes to hunt me, maybe I didn't need eyes to hunt it, either.

"And how do you mean to fight it?" she was saying, but I wasn't really listening now—I was turning away, steeling myself to make a run toward the hollow, when I felt someone run past *me*, down the tunnel.

"Hey!" I shouted, and Emma held up her flame too late, so that all we saw of the mystery sprinter was her back and a bobbing head of messy hair.

Hugh came running up from behind, arms wheeling as he skidded to a stop. "Did you see Fiona?" he said, panting for air. "We snuck out to help you, and a moment ago she just took off running."

"Oh God," I said, "she's going to get herself killed . . ."

I turned and shot into the dark toward the hollow, Emma and Hugh on my heels. I shouted Fiona's name, my eyes searching farther than Emma's flame-light extended. I couldn't see the hollow but I could feel it, feel the gap between us closing fast. I ran with my palms thrust out to part thickets of hanging roots, a forest of long swaying fingers that dragged across my head and my shoulders, exploring me—

We all heard the scream. Sharp and high, a girl's voice. It was joined an instant later by the hollowgast. And then Emma's light caught them, dimly at first, brightening as we closed in.

I thought we would find Fiona between the hollow's jaws, but

< THE DESOLATIONS OF DEVIL'S ACRE >

that was not, thank God, what we discovered. Fiona and the hollow were forty or fifty feet apart and facing each other like duelists. Fiona stood with her feet spread and her hands poised in the air like an orchestra conductor before the first notes of a symphony. We came to a stop and surrounded her, and while Hugh made sure she was unharmed, Emma held her flaming hands out toward the hollow and took a few warning steps toward it. I didn't understand why the hollow had stopped, couldn't see it well enough through the latticework of swaying shadows cast by the roots, didn't have an answer yet from Fiona, who was immovable despite Hugh's efforts to pull her back, away from danger.

The hollow screamed again, and this time it sounded like a cry of frustration. Emma brightened her flames.

"Hugh, wait," she said, squinting into the shadows, "leave Fiona alone!"

And he did, and Fiona raised her hands and made a motion in the air like she was yanking an invisible chain. All the roots around us curled, then pulled taut with an audible snap—and I could see what she had done.

The hollow was bound and trussed by hundreds of dangling tree roots. Roots collared it, held fast its arms and legs, wrapped its three tongues, which were all pulled as far as they would go. Fiona made two fists and pulled them apart, and the roots pulled the hollow's tongues until it squeaked.

"Fiona, you genius, you miracle!" Emma cried.

"You might've been killed, darling," Hugh said in an undertone, and though it was clear he wanted to hug her, he appeared to restrain himself for fear of breaking her concentration.

Fiona inclined her head toward him and whispered something. Hugh translated: "She says the roots are very strong. She says she can pull it to pieces right now if Jacob likes."

I said, "Can you keep him like that for a minute, Fee?"

"She can hold him like that all day if you want."

< 195 >

"Good. Before we kill him, there's something I need to find out."

I started carefully toward the hollow, parting vines as I went.

"Are you going to control its mind?" Emma said, following me from a slight distance. "Make it fight for our side?"

I was concentrating hard and didn't reply. If we were going to be facing some new kind of hollow, I couldn't pass up a chance to safely probe its mind. I approached it slowly, muttering a few words of Hollowspeak to test its reaction. If I could soften it up, pry its thoughts open a bit, then maybe I could better understand what we were dealing with.

The old familiar stench of rotten garbage came over me in a heavy wave. That hadn't changed, at least.

The hollow strained against the roots that held it, dying to wrap one of its tongues around my neck, but the roots held fast.

Relax, I said in Hollowspeak. *Don't struggle.*

It had no effect. I repeated myself, then tried a few variations on *calm down*—but it didn't react at all. Normally, I could feel a hollowgast shy away as I tried to control it. Like it could tell I was scratching around the keyhole of its brain with my lockpick. I knew the hollows' language as innately as I knew English, but for all this one reacted, I might as well have been speaking Yiddish. What was more, and worse: My failed attempts at contact and control almost seemed to strengthen it.

What the hell was going on?

Sleep, I said, still trying. *Sleep*—but instead it flexed all its muscles at once, straining against the roots that bound it. Behind me I heard Fiona groan. I turned and saw her hunched as if bearing a heavy weight, but then she straightened and tumbled her hands in the air like she was tying a knot. The roots creaked with new tension.

She had bought me a little more time. Time for a new approach. No more words.

"I'm going in close," I said loudly. "Hold it tight!"

"There's no need for this," I heard Emma say, but she must

have meant it when she said she trusted me, because she didn't try to stop me. "*Please* be careful."

Even after many encounters with hollows, I still didn't like getting close to them, even ones I had tamed. Ones I hadn't were like rabid dogs, and when they were chained and restrained, their desperate need to murder you made the air crackle. Not to mention what it did to my stomach; at this proximity, the compass needle turned into a swinging scythe.

I stopped an arm's length away and stared into its leaking eyes. Its breath came in ragged snorts, jaws ratcheted wide by the tension of its three tongues pulled to their limit in opposing directions.

This hollow was different. Not only was it visible to all, it spoke differently. The feeling it evoked in me was different, a different key, some higher register. It *stank* differently, inorganically, not like a hot summer landfill but like chemicals, bleach, rat poison, and something worse.

I spoke to it again—*Sleep, sleep you bastard*—hoping I might be able to break through at close range, and as I talked I could see muscles pulsing within the dark workings of its throat, like it was trying to reply.

And then it did. Whether I heard it with my ears or just in my mind, I wasn't certain, but a voice came to me, low and slithering, unintelligible at first, just a long, sibilant *sssssssssss* that slowly grew to a vowel (*leeeeeeeeee*) and finally, and it must have been in my head because it had no lips to make the sound with, *eeeeeep*.

Sleep, it said to me.

It could *speak*.

Sleeeeeeee, it droned—just mirroring me, that's all—but then why did I feel so heavy in the head . . . why were my knees beginning to buckle . . .

eeeeeeeeeee

What are you? I tried to say, but the words wouldn't come. *What are you doing to me?*

eeeeeeeeeeeeeeeeep.

And just as I felt myself on the verge of collapse, felt my legs going out from under me, the oily musculature of its throat tensed, pulsed, and then opened to admit one more tongue, *a fourth*, which whipped out and caught me by the neck before I could fall—and now I was hanging with my toes just brushing the ground, unable to breathe.

I heard Emma say, "Jacob? What's going on?" but my throat was too constricted to allow a reply, my arms too limp with sleep to wave. I was choking, suffocating, and my friends couldn't see the tongue tightening, tightening, until I thought my head would pop. My only hope was Fiona, that her connection to the roots might function as an extension of her own body, that she could feel and see through them. How else had she pinioned it so precisely, with three roots around three tongues? So I opened my mouth, though I couldn't speak, and turned my head as much as I could make it turn, and bit down on a stringy root that had been brushing my face.

Fiona. Help me. I formed the words with my mouth, my tongue, spoke them to the root.

"Something's wrong," I heard Hugh say. His voice sounded like it was on the other end of a bad phone connection.

The light from Emma's flame grew brighter. She was coming.

"Jacob? Are you okay? Answer me!"

I tried desperately to speak, to shout *stay back,* but the words wouldn't pass my throat. I prayed my silence would be answer enough.

And then the tongue released me; unslithered from around my neck and darted away. As I collapsed to the ground, it lashed out at Emma, whipping around her wrist and forcing her flaming hand toward her face, but she dodged and clapped it over the tongue. The hollow squealed. I tried to move, to help her, but I was still gasping for air and my body was half numb from whatever the hollow had done to me.

While Emma fought, I heard Fiona scream—not in pain, I thought, but in effort—and as her shrill cry filled the tunnel every dangling root stiffened and stretched, then contracted suddenly as if they'd reeled back up into the earth above our heads.

The roots that bound the hollow contracted, too, all at once and with great force.

It howled. I was spattered with stinging liquid, which I quickly recognized as blood.

I sat up, dazed. Three severed tongues twisted in the dirt before me like eels. The fourth was burned and useless. The hollow had been torn limb from limb.

Then my friends were around me. Hugh, Bronwyn, Emma. The guards just behind. Fiona was sitting on the ground, drained of energy. Emma was okay.

She knelt beside me. "What were you *doing*? Why take such a risk when we could have just killed it?"

"I needed to study it," I replied between gulps of air, "to find out all I could."

"And? What did you find out?"

I shook my head weakly. "I couldn't get in."

I wasn't ready to talk about what had just happened. I struggled to my feet with Bronwyn's help and went to Fiona, who was panting like she'd just run a race.

"You saved my life," I said. It was inadequate thanks but all I could muster.

She smiled weakly and murmured something.

"She says you're even," Hugh said.

Bronwyn couldn't stop apologizing. "If only I'd gotten the harpoon gun in place faster—" But I cut her off and told her that not only was she not at fault, but I was glad for what happened. If she and the guards had managed to eviscerate the hollow right away, I wouldn't have had the chance to find out about its fourth tongue. Or its most frightening new evolution . . .

It was in my head.

It wasn't anymore; whatever it had done to me had worn off the moment the creature died. Regardless, it was a worrying development, one I decided to keep to myself until I better understood what had happened.

Miss Peregrine was calling to us from the end of the tunnel. The guards, afraid there might be more enemies lurking in the dark, wouldn't let her come in after us. Before we left, I reached down and snagged one of the severed tongues, coiled it up like a garden hose, and looped it over my shoulder.

"*Must* you?" said Hugh.

"So I can study it."

"Why?" Emma asked. "Do you think there are more like it?"

"Blimey, *could* there be?" Bronwyn said.

"I hope not," I said.

But I worried that this one was just the beginning.

* * *

Miss Peregrine quickly appraised us, her chin jerking up and down as she looked us over. "Do any of you need to see the bone-mender?"

We told her we didn't.

"I'll have one examine you anyhow," she said brusquely.

She was angry at Fiona and Hugh for having left the house against her orders, a trespass that killing a hollow wasn't enough to make up for. Besides, a peculiar had been killed, a giant mess had been made, and the peculiar denizens of Devil's Acre were newly terrified. The ymbrynes had had a great deal of work to do even before our unwelcome guest arrived; now they had even more.

As we walked back to the house, I told Miss Peregrine some of what I'd learned about this hollowgast. I told her how it had been harder for me to detect, and how it had taken longer for me to pinpoint its location. I told her how the American woman's bullets had simply flattened against the creature's chest, and it had been able to pluck them off, unharmed.

"Caul found a way to armor their skin," Miss Peregrine said, her face clouding with worry. "It seems these aren't inferior models after all, but improved ones."

"Then why make them visible?" asked Bronwyn.

"To terrify people," Miss Peregrine replied.

"Where do you think Caul was hiding them?" Emma asked.

"I'm not sure he was," Miss Peregrine said. "If he'd had hollows like this a week ago, he would've used them against us then, or during the Battle of Gravehill. No, this hollow is new. I think Caul's new powers have enabled him to create an evolved breed of hollow."

"Then we can expect more," Emma said darkly.

"Yes. I'm afraid so."

I told her about the fourth tongue, too, but I didn't mention the worst part, about the hollow's influence over me. I wasn't sure I wanted anyone to know.

Miss Wren's errand boy, Ulysses Critchley, was waiting by the front steps of the house for Miss Peregrine. "The three ymbrynes have arrived, madam. You officially have a quorum. They're in the council chamber now, awaiting your arrival."

"Thank you, I'll be along presently," she said, and turned to us. "I won't waste any more of my breath imploring you not to leave the house, but I insist you don't leave the Acre. Jacob, you and Miss Pradesh should prepare for an expedition into the past. We need you to be ready to depart as soon as a suitable route to Miss Tern's loop is plotted, which could be any hour now."

Without waiting for a reply she hooked a finger toward Ulysses and they set off together for the council chamber. The rest of us went inside to get cleaned up, and to tell the others what had happened. In telling the story, I emphasized Fiona's heroism while downplaying the danger to myself so I wouldn't be fussed over too much. It took a lot of energy to be fussed over, and to have to reassure other people that I was okay when really my neck hurt and my head ached and I was feeling a little shaky. Knowing how I really felt would make them nervous, and concealing it took energy I didn't have.

Noor could tell I wasn't okay, but she seemed to know instinctively when to push through my reticence and when to let me be, and so when I told her I needed to lie down for a bit, she let me go with just a quick embrace and a kiss on the lips.

I hurried upstairs to bed—borrowing Horace's again, as I still didn't have one of my own—but couldn't make myself sleep. Every time I closed my eyes, the hollow's voice would come back to me. What would have happened if it had had longer to do its work? Might it have done more than turn my own commands back on me? How much control might it have gained? I thought of the cockeyed assassin who had lunged at me with a knife and shuddered.

A new breed. Better, deadlier, impossible to control. And which had somehow turned the power I held over them against me.

It occurred to me that this one had been sent here not necessarily to kill me. Caul knew by now that I could handle a single hollowgast—even an evolved one. It had been a warning.

Give up now. Before I send an army of them.

It was just speculation, and even if it was true, there was nothing I could do about it. The only thing to do was reach the meeting place, find the other six, and send Caul, somehow, back to hell.

Seven may seal the door.

My head was only getting foggier, but I couldn't lie there anymore. I forced myself up.

CHAPTER ELEVEN

*N*oor and I spent the rest of the day in an anxious orbit between the ministries building, where the ymbrynes were holding their emergency meeting and might emerge any minute to weave their temporal shield around the Acre, and Ditch House, where Millard and Perplexus were puzzling over loop maps at the kitchen table, working out the location of Miss Tern's loop and every possible route to reach it.

We'd been told to pack, but how could we when we didn't know what kind of territory we'd be traveling through? When we were at the house, we tried not to hover over Millard's shoulder, but failed often enough that Perplexus finally drew a line on the floor with a grease pencil and told us to keep behind it. The only one allowed to cross it was Perplexus's assistant, Matthieu, a humorless boy who carried a bamboo stick for pointing at maps and who kept his mentor supplied with steaming pots of smoky Russian tea, the only liquid Perplexus would let pass his lips besides espresso.

The goal, Millard explained while Perplexus took one of his frequent tea breaks, was to plot a quick but safe route to Miss Tern's loop. Quick meant a day or two, but so far the only one they had discovered involved traveling overland from Mongolia to France via 1917, a perilous, two week journey on horses, camels, and trains. Though Noor and I and whoever journeyed with us would have a reasonable chance of surviving the trip, there was skepticism as to whether Devil's Acre could survive a siege by Caul and his forces for that long. So the cartographers continued puzzling, and sent us away because our hovering was making them anxious.

Elsewhere in the Acre, Sharon was overseeing the strengthening of our meager defenses. The hollowgast's intrusion had convinced everyone that the home guard was far from adequate, and there was no telling how long the ymbrynes would need to create their shield. A second harpoon gun was found and both were positioned near the loop entrance. New barbed-wire fences and guard stations had been built around the prison, and Parkins's Californios volunteered to supplement the guards already monitoring our population of wight prisoners, who had been suspiciously quiet the last few days.

Dozens of peculiars lined up outside the Shrunken Head to volunteer for a new Devil's Acre Defense Corps, with a surprising number of Americans joining them. Those with combat-relevant abilities were assigned to patrols that would keep watch over the loop entrance as well as Bentham's house (though the Panloopticon was now officially powered down, doors locked). All privately owned telescopes and binoculars were requisitioned for use by the Defense Corps, to be distributed to sentries who were installed on rooftops and balconies around the Acre. Leonora Hammaker, who could see in the dark and had vision stronger than any telescope, agreed to sit in her window and simply stare down the length of Doleful Street for as many hours a day as she could tolerate.

Everyone who had a personal firearm was to keep it with them at all times. Many of the Americans already did this, but since the hollowgast's attack they'd taken their attachment a step further, refusing to unstrap their holsters for meals or trips to the restroom. Earlier in the day, one of Parkins's Californios had even been discovered napping—snoring loudly, in fact—with two cocked and loaded guns on his lap and an enormous knife gripped in his hand.

Sharon warned the volunteers that their lives would be at risk, but after this morning's brush with tragedy, no one was under any illusions to the contrary. Their lives were at risk whether they

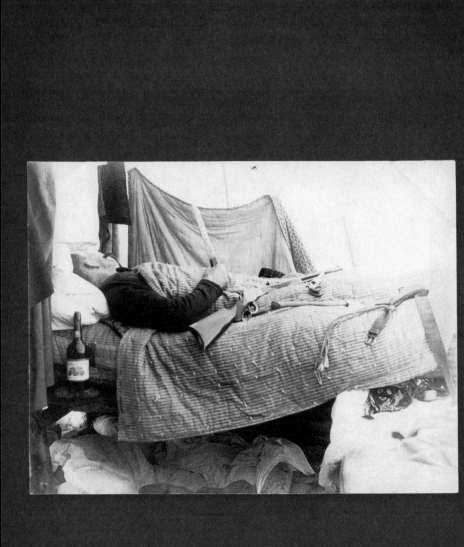

volunteered or not. A few tried to discourage the youngest peculiars from taking part in the Acre's defense, but a young boy from Miss Grackle's theater troupe jumped up on a pillar by the pub and gave an impassioned speech about how all our lives were forfeit if Caul broke through our defenses, and it was a nobler thing to risk death in defense of our loop than to give it up in defeat, which earned him a massive round of applause.

LaMothe's Northern clan would be positioned strategically around the loop entrance. Leo's goons had proved themselves cowards and were nowhere to be found, but the leaders of his three under-gangs—Wreck Donovan, Angelica, and even Dogface and his Untouchables—lined up to join the Defense Corps. When I looked surprised to see them there, they shrugged it off as nothing more than self-interest, but I was starting to think they weren't as mercenary as they let on.

Finally, just before nightfall, Francesca's voice came over the loudspeakers. The shield was ready to be created, she announced, and anyone who wanted to be present for its weaving should proceed immediately to the loop entrance.

The entire loop flooded into the streets.

* ◆ ◆

They called it the Quilt, and the ymbrynes thought it would instill some small measure of peace in us to watch it being sewn together, to see for ourselves that it was real.

We gathered near the loop entrance, along the banks of the Ditch where it disappeared into the tunnel. Torches and gas lamps cast a flickering glow over the crowd, spectators a hundred strong on one side of the water, a tight circle of twelve ymbrynes on the other, hands linked. My friends and I all stood together. Guards watched over everything from the top of the bridge tunnel, and the two who'd been assigned to watch Noor and me stood nearby, scanning the

crowd for threats. As many times as we'd evaded them, they still took their jobs seriously.

Across the Ditch, the ymbrynes began to sing in Old Peculiar and walk slowly in a circle.

"Hope they don't collapse the place by accident," Enoch whispered to a pretty, curly-haired girl standing beside him in the crowd, and she looked so alarmed Enoch had to reassure her that he was kidding.

Horace shushed him. "This is no time to joke around. If this doesn't work, we're all in trouble."

"What's deadly is how boring you are. If I wasn't here to lighten the mood now and then, everyone would've hung themselves ages ago."

Horace scowled. "If you could see the future, you wouldn't be laughing."

"Hush, both of you," hissed Millard, who I hadn't realized was standing nearby.

"Shouldn't you be off squinting at maps?" Enoch said.

"We're close to a breakthrough, I think. And I wasn't about to miss this."

The ymbrynes began singing louder and spinning faster, their long dresses fluttering in the air. A green light began to glow from the center of their circle. Some in the crowd gasped.

The ymbrynes sang louder, spun faster. The light grew brighter.

"Here it comes," I heard Millard say, and Noor, standing next to me, pressed herself to my side.

The light brightened again and expanded upward. The ymbrynes' song crescendoed in a high, wavering note that held—and then, all at once and with a sound like a thunderclap, they leapt into the air and assumed their avian forms. A collective gasp went up from the crowd. The ymbrynes maintained their formation, flying now instead of running, but its diameter grew wider and wider, and with it the pulsing green light. They were working it, pulling it like taffy.

Then they flew up into the sky, Miss Avocet first, Miss Peregrine last, the others in formation between them, the green light stretching and following. They turned a loop in the air above us, then swooped down and disappeared into the darkness of the bridge tunnel. The green glow that followed them lit the tunnel briefly and brilliantly, then was gone with the ymbrynes.

There was a brief period of silence, five seconds that stretched to ten. Murmurs of worry rippled through the crowd. Where had they gone? Were they coming back? Was it over?

Then a green light winked into view at the edge of the dark horizon. It began to draw itself across the sky like a shimmering blanket, a too-bright aurora borealis, and as it spread from one corner of the heavens to the other, veins of electric white light crackled through it. Once it had filled the sky, casting a subtle green glow over everything, a noise like a train approaching sounded from the tunnel.

After a few seconds the ymbrynes flew out of it again in a tight cluster, pulling behind them a net of green almost too bright to look at. It permeated the tunnel but went no farther, creating a semi-translucent wall. The ymbrynes did one last circle over our heads, an encouraging victory flourish, then flew off in the direction of their council chamber, pulling the crackling green net with them until it covered the whole sky.

The crowd buzzed with excitement.

"Never seen anything like it," the girl beside Enoch said.

"Three cheers for our birds!" Claire cried, punching the air with her fists. "I'd like to see nasty old Caul try and get through *that*!"

"Certainly was impressive!" Horace enthused.

"It's just some green light," Enoch said.

"I just hope it works," I said.

"It *will*," said Claire.

A guard with a bullhorn reminded us it was past curfew and began herding us back to our beds.

"What do you think?" Noor said to me as the crowd started to move. "Are we safe for a while?"

I glanced at the moonlit clouds above us, glowing pale green behind the ymbrynes' Quilt, and wondered how much of it was for show. "For a while, I think. Not forever."

We hadn't gone fifty feet when something crackled like static above our heads, and the crowd, which had been shuffling along calmly, stopped and looked up. Looming overhead was a face, giant and rendered in blue.

"Very impressive, quite the display, *very* impressive!" he boomed.

Caul, or the holographic version of him, had returned to mock us. The timing was precise: He had come to undermine our sense of security just as the ymbrynes were building it up.

"He can't hurt you! Don't panic!" someone shouted, but it was too late, and this time we weren't trapped in a packed auditorium. Everybody scrambled for cover. The stampede knocked me into Noor and we both fell to the ground, but before we could be crushed, Bronwyn heaved us over her shoulder with Claire and Olive.

Caul wailed, "Oh, what shall I do, whatever shall I do? Let me in, let me in! I am stymied, flummoxed, perplexed!"

A volley of gunshots rang out, but it was just the Americans shooting at Caul's image. Their bullets peppered the field of green overhead and got stuck, frozen in the air like a swarm of bees. The crowd was fleeing in a dozen directions, diving into nearby buildings and running for distant parts of the Acre. Bronwyn appeared to be following our friends back toward the house, but Caul's sneering face and shrill voice followed us wherever we went, omnipresent.

"I'm only joking, of course! I relish a challenge, though it won't be much of one." His voice sounded like it was right in my ear. "I would expect nothing less from my dear sister and her whelps. We haven't come to see you yet, incidentally, because we're just getting warmed up. Stretching our just-born limbs." An image of a monstrous blue-veined tree branch shot across the sky, then dissipated in sparks.

"We, we, we. Who is we, you ask? I do have friends, you know. Here they are now, in a loop you might recognize!"

Caul's face disappeared, and in its place a terrifying scene was projected against the green sky. I watched it, transfixed, while Bronwyn ran. Two monstrous creatures menaced a house as children fled screaming. Towering above the roof, one creature had a head shaped like an eel and black leathery wings sprouting from its back. It tore at the house with clawlike hands, peeling back pieces of the roof and tossing them into the air. The other looked like an amalgamation of steaming tar in a roughly human form. It shambled into a cow tied to a post, passed through it, and the cow melted into a flaming puddle. The eel-headed thing bent down on one knee and scooped up a fleeing child in its wing, then went on destroying the house.

"That's Miss Egret's loop!" I heard Emma say, running behind us.

Caul's voice narrated over the scene: "I am a god now, and these are my angels! You cannot keep us out. You cannot keep us from what is rightfully ours! And we have such *gifts* to bestow upon you, if only you'd let us! Renounce your false mothers! Give up your ymbrynes! Reclaim your dignity, your *freedom*!"

The image in the sky changed back to Caul's face as he broke into a strident, speechifying tone. "Freedom from loops, from the constraints of time that the bird-women have used to imprison you all these years. Yes, prison, prison, prison, that's all most of you have known. Join me and I will free you, my children!"

Threats and promises, manipulation and misinformation; Caul's signature style.

He disappeared, finally, in a spray of blue light, and then something was snowing down on us. Some new desolation.

We were nearly back to the house.

I realized that what was falling were papers, and something was printed on them.

We made it to the front stoop of Ditch House, where our other friends were waiting. Panting, Bronwyn eased us off her back and set us down. The papers had begun to cover the ground.

"Is he gone?" Claire cried. "Are we safe yet?"

"He was never here," said Emma. "That was another of his transmissions."

"If he wasn't here, how'd he make it rain newspapers?"

"Same way he made it rain ash and ankle bones," said Enoch.

A shaky voice rang out over the Acre's many loudspeakers. "This is Miss Esmerelda Avocet. Everyone remain calm and return to your rooms. The Quilt is fully operational now, and Caul cannot reach us. Neither can any of his hollowgast. He's only trying to scare you." There was a scratchy sound and a brief whine of feedback, and then Miss Avocet came back to the microphone sounding flustered. "And don't touch those papers, they're nothing but propa—"

There was a staticky *pop* and the loudspeakers went quiet. A breeze picked up and blew the papers in drifts around our feet.

"Propa-what?" Hugh said, and bent to pick one up.

Bronwyn snatched at it—"Hugh, don't"—but he dodged her.

"Propaganda," I said, picking up one for myself. "God, look at this."

It was a page of newspaper. Olive and Noor looked on as I turned it right side up. Across the top a headline screamed:

TWO-FACED YMBRYNES PROMISE LOOP FREEDOM TO CLAN LEADERS IN SECRET DEAL!

I looked up to see other peculiars on the streets around us also reading it.

"There's more," Emma said, tilting her face closer to the paper. Below the headline was an article, if you could call it that.

"What's it say?" Bronwyn asked, then looked sheepish. "I'm a slow reader."

Emma scanned the text and summarized. "It claims . . . let's see here . . . that the ymbrynes told LaMothe, Parkins, and Leo Burnham that they would give them all loop freedom in exchange for a signed peace deal. But only them and no one else. And then . . ." Emma grimaced and shook her head. "The rest is just ranting on about how the ymbrynes are traitors and want to keep us all subservient and loop-trapped, et cetera—"

"Would they really do that?" Olive said. She looked hurt by the very suggestion. "They wouldn't, would they?"

"Of course not!" Claire said, agitated. "Just the other day Miss Peregrine told us they still hadn't figured out how to make the reset reaction safe."

Emma balled the paper angrily and pitched it away. "It's all lies. Consider the source."

"I don't know," Hugh said. "It was a bit strange how all three clans suddenly agreed to peace, and even helped us at Gravehill—"

"It wasn't exactly *sudden*," Horace said. "They'd been negotiating for weeks."

Noor added, "And how they got Leo to forgive me, or whatever, even after feeling so insulted—"

"That's not strange, it's self-interest," Emma said. "They realized the wights were a threat to their people, too, and that we needed to work together to beat them."

"That sounds reasonable," I said, "and I'd agree with you—if anything the clans ever did was reasonable."

"Who cares if the ymbrynes *did* make an offer?" said Enoch, and we turned to see him walking toward us with one of the papers in his hand. "It got us what we needed. Peace and a partnership."

"We care because it would've meant they *lied*," Olive said. "That all the times they told the people who want loop freedom that it wasn't possible, wasn't safe yet—that that wasn't true."

Enoch shrugged. "So? We've got it, and that's all I really care about."

"Ymbrynes! Don't! LIE!" shouted a red-faced Claire.

"All right, we heard you, loudness isn't an effective argumentation tactic," said Emma.

"YES! IT! *IS!*"

The door to the house creaked open and Fiona came out in a robe. She gave us a sleepy smile and a wave, then cast a concerned look around at all the papers on the ground and the strange new green cast to the sky. She was still recovering from the strain of our hollowgast encounter, and had slept through everything.

"It's easy to forget what freedom means when you already have it," Hugh said, and he shot a glare at Enoch, bounded up the front steps to join Fiona, and disappeared into the house with her.

"What climbed up his craw and died?" Enoch said.

"Not all of us are free, remember?" Emma said. "Fiona's still loop-trapped."

Enoch frowned. "Right."

"But how do you know the ymbrynes weren't lying to the *clan leaders* about giving them loop freedom?" Noor asked.

"Because they're—" I started to reply, but cut myself short as a patrol of Americans led by LaMothe marched by. LaMothe looked furious, and had one of the papers balled in his fist. A few of his coat-raccoons glared at us in passing. When they were out of range, I whispered, *"Because they're still here."*

The two home guards assigned to Noor and I came striding toward us. "There you are," the taller one huffed. "You mustn't leave us behind anymore!"

"The ymbrynes want to see you in their chambers at once," said the other.

Just then, a paper fluttered past my face and smacked flat against the wall of the house, pinned there as if by a gust, though I hadn't felt even a puff of breeze. It was a poster with the faces of all the Ymbryne Council members in a row like a police lineup, the word GUILTY stamped across each one.

Olive said, "More propa—"

"Oh, shut up!" barked Emma. She went to rip down the poster, but it slid up the wall away from her before she could nab it, then off to one side when she tried again. She leapt at it and finally managed to tear it down, then ignited it in her hands—but as soon as she'd crumpled and tossed away the burning paper, five more just like it blew in and slapped against the wall all around her.

She let out a cry of frustration and turned to face the guards. "We're *all* going to see the ymbrynes. I need to know what's going on."

CHAPTER TWELVE

As we hurried to keep up with the long strides of the guards, the ymbrynes' faces followed us. Every few seconds another GUILTY poster flew in as if on some magical breeze to paper a nearby wall or lamppost. *Guilty, guilty, guilty,* like a drumbeat. I could see it happening all over: Posters were chasing people down the street, smacking people in the head.

Not all of us had come. Claire had refused to be a part of what seemed like a confrontation of the ymbrynes. Hugh had joined Fiona, still resting in the house. Horace was clearly exhausted by the events of the day but also said our cause would be better served by him taking a sleeping dram and going to bed, in the hopes that he might have some useful prophetic dreams.

At the ministries building a small but rowdy crowd swarmed the cobblestoned forecourt. They were waving the papers and demanding to be let in, while a phalanx of guards prevented them from reaching the massive iron doors. But they let my friends and me right through.

"I want to know what this means!" a woman shouted as she brandished the paper. "If it's true, I'm going to—"

"What?" said Emma, aiming a flaming finger at the woman's nose. "Overthrow the ymbrynes? Go out there and surrender to Caul?"

Before the woman could respond, a red-faced man shoved her out of the way. "You!" he shouted, a jet of literal steam coming out of his ears. "Tell your birds to get out here and talk to us. We deserve to know what's going on."

Enoch rounded on him. "They're working themselves to death trying to save us from Caul, that's what going on!"

Emma gaped at him in surprise.

"Let's not stop and argue with every hothead in the Acre," I said, and pushed both of them up the steps toward the iron doors, which heaved open with a great squeaking complaint.

"Haven't you got bigger things to worry about?" Enoch shouted over his shoulder as we slipped inside. "Ungrateful slobs!"

The doors thundered closed. Enoch slapped the wall in anger.

"Why, Enoch, I didn't know you cared what people thought of the birds," said Emma.

"I don't," he said, embarrassed and rubbing his hand.

"So it's fine if *you* talk rubbish about the birds," Olive said with a grin, "but if anyone else dares to—"

"I don't want to talk about it," he grumbled, and followed the waiting guards.

We were escorted through the cavernous entrance hall, empty but for a few office workers, its service windows shuttered. Then down a long, gloomy passage to the Ymbryne Council chamber room, where another pair of guards was posted outside. A sign tacked above the big wooden door read QUIET, PLEASE!

"Yes to them," one of the guards said, nodding at Noor and me. "No to the others."

"I'm not going in if they don't," I said.

"None of you, then."

"Bollocks to that," Enoch said, and then he bellowed, "MISS PEREGRINE! IT'S ENOCH! LET US IN!"

The guards began dragging Enoch down the hall while he thrashed and swore. Then the chamber door flew open and Miss Peregrine appeared. "Good heavens, Mr. Collins, just let them in!"

The guard looked flustered. "But you said—"

"Never mind that! Let them in! Mr. O'Connor, too, as long as he promises to behave."

Enoch was released and strode quickly back, brushing off his vest and casting obscene gestures at the guards, who, from the looks of it, were imagining cracking him in the head with their batons. Miss Peregrine warned us all to be quiet, and we followed her inside the high-ceilinged chamber room.

I had never seen the long conference table full before. Twelve ymbrynes were huddled around it in postures of worry and concentration: Miss Cuckoo, Miss Wren, Miss Babax, Miss Blackbird, and others who, being in the presence of senior ymbrynes, were unusually quiet. Miss Avocet sat at the head of the table, presiding from her wheelchair. She raised a hand toward us. "Mr. Portman, Miss Pradesh, please come join us. This concerns you, too—or it will soon enough."

Miss Peregrine put her hand on our backs and guided us to the table. We stood; there were no more chairs. I felt something nudge my foot and looked down to see Addison beneath the table. I whispered *hi* and he mouthed *hello*. Like us, he was not quite of a rank to be *at* the table, but as Miss Wren's trusted aide-de-camp, he was at least allowed under it.

At the edge of the room, Emma and Enoch had come with only one thing in mind—the story about the American clan leaders—but seeing so many ymbrynes in the midst of serious discussion seemed to have dampened their appetite for confrontation. At least temporarily.

"If your wards are perfectly comfortable, Alma, I will resume," Miss Cuckoo huffed. She wore a military-style greatcoat with gold stripes along the cuffs and held in her hand a thin, long-handled stick with a bit of red chalk at the end. Miss Avocet might have been nominally in charge, but Miss Cuckoo seemed to have been elected battle strategist. She and Miss Peregrine gazed intently at the table, where spread upon the polished wood was an oversized loop map of greater London.

"Caul means to surround us," Miss Peregrine intoned gravely, "and I have no doubt he will."

Miss Cuckoo rapped her chalk-stick on Devil's Acre. Its boundary was marked by a meandering green line, roughly square, near the center of the map. The Acre had become so central to my life that in my imagination it filled most of London, and it was a shock to see it rendered as a small and insignificant speck. "First he took Miss Plover's loop in Squatney." She slid her stick to the edge of the map and tapped a loop there, which was denoted by a white spiral. It had already been struck through with a foreboding chalk-marked X. "Then, as we all witnessed a short time ago, he took Miss Egret's." Her stick slid to another loop, some distance across the city, which she crossed out with two swipes of her chalk. "There are only three loops besides our own still functioning in London . . . here, here, and here." Her stick went *tap-tap-tap* in a wide circle around the Acre.

"He'll take them within a day, I reckon," said Miss Peregrine. "At most, two." She looked at Miss Cuckoo, who nodded grimly in reply.

"He'll wait for a chink in our armor," Miss Blackbird said nervously, her third eye roving. "And when one appears—"

"There will be none!" Miss Cuckoo whacked the map so hard the tip of the chalk flew off, making Miss Blackbird jump. "Our shield will hold. The Panloopticon in its powered-down state is impenetrable. Caul and his friends can surround us if they like, but they will be stalled at our gates. We will not be intimidated."

"I don't know," I heard Enoch say. "Some people seem rather intimidated."

Miss Peregrine stared daggers at him. "I asked you to be quiet. Or shall I tell the guards to drag you off to the dungeon?"

Enoch glared at the floor.

"Speaking of Caul's 'friends,'" Emma said from the back of the room, "what were those monstrous creatures he sent into Miss Egret's loop?"

Miss Peregrine turned to scowl next at her.

"It's all right, Alma," said Miss Avocet. "You children may as well come up to the table with the rest of us."

"Really?" said Olive, her eyes going wide.

"This is *most* irregular," said one of the ymbrynes who'd recently flown in from elsewhere, who I later learned was Miss Waxwing.

"We owe a great deal not just to Mr. Portman, but to all of Alma's wards," said Miss Avocet. "They've earned the right to speak."

Our friends came forward, beaming with pride, and stood beside us.

"In answer to your question," Miss Avocet said, "we believe those creatures were high-ranking wights. Or some monstrous corruption of their former selves, at any rate."

"One of them, I swear it, was certainly Percival Murnau," said Miss Blackbird with a shiver. "The slime creature. I saw his face appear briefly in the muck."

Miss Wren said, "Caul's giving the wights, the small number that remain, powers like his own. Not quite at the same level, but close. Channeling the Library of Souls' energy into them somehow."

"Creating for himself an army of lesser gods," said Miss Cuckoo.

"My brother's no god," Miss Peregrine said acidly.

"There will be more of them," said Miss Avocet. "They'll be his advance guard, his shock troops, along with this new breed of hollowgast, if he's got any more hidden away. Even with all his power, he's too much of a coward to charge first across the line in battle."

"Has anyone seen Caul in person yet?" I asked. "Because I don't think he's showing us his real form." He had looked too normal in his projections, nothing like the way he'd appeared in my dreams or in the whirlwind in V's loop.

Miss Merganser, the freelance ymbryne from Mozambique who had been sitting quietly at the far end of the table, pushed back her chair and stood up. She had rusty red hair pulled tight against her head, shining dark skin, and looked younger than the rest of the ymbrynes, hardly older than me or my friends. "One person has seen him," she said in a light, flat accent. "His name is Emmerick Daltwick. He's an escapee from the invasion of Miss Plover's loop early this morning."

"Can we speak to him?" I asked.

"He's here," the ymbryne replied. "I asked him to come and tell us what he saw. Shall I bring him in?"

"By all means," said Miss Avocet.

Miss Merganser signaled to the guards at the door. They went out and came back a short time later with a cowering boy. His face was covered with scratches, and his clothes were torn and dirty.

Miss Peregrine got up from the conference table and went to examine him. "Why hasn't this young man been to see the bone-mender?"

"Rafael's full up with stampede injuries," said one of the guards.

"This boy's been through hell. Make sure Rafael tends to him right away."

"Yes, madam."

"Thank you, miss," the boy said meekly.

"Go on, Emmerick, please tell us what you saw this morning."

He began stammeringly, perhaps intimidated by the presence of so many powerful ymbrynes.

"We only need to hear about Caul," Miss Cuckoo interrupted. "What did he look like, what did he do?"

"Well, ma'am . . . he was very . . . *big*."

"Yes? And what else?"

"The, uh . . . the top half of him looked like a person. A man. But his bottom half was like a tree. Like the trunk of a tree, with roots going down into the ground for legs? But they wasn't made of wood. They was made of . . . meat."

"Of *meat*," Miss Avocet repeated.

"Rotted meat." He squinched his nose. "And everything

he touched"—he paused, went a bit pale—"died." He shivered. Dropped his head. "After he touched Landers Jaquith, Landers turned green and black and rotted-looking. And then died."

"By the elders," I heard Miss Blackbird whisper.

"Did he kill any others?" Miss Peregrine asked.

"Yeah. Him and his . . . *people* . . . took some of my friends. Stuffed 'em into a net and dragged 'em off."

The boy was shaking badly. Miss Avocet stood up from her chair with some difficulty, limped over to him, and draped her shawl around the boy's shoulders. "Get him to a bone-mender," she told the guards. "Thank you for coming to see us."

The boy nodded and started to leave with the guards, but at the door he turned back, eyes lit with fear. "Caul can't get in here, can he?"

"No, he can't," said Miss Cuckoo. "We won't let him in."

After he'd gone and the door had closed, Bronwyn cried, "We've got to stage a rescue! Get those children back from him before he kills them all!"

"No, we can't, we mustn't," said Miss Blackbird. "It's just what Caul wants. He'll be lying in wait—"

"I'm sure you're right, but it's our duty to try," said Miss Peregrine.

"We'll assemble a rescue team," said Miss Cuckoo, nodding at Miss Avocet, who had been helped into her chair again by Francesca, and was looking spent.

Bronwyn's hand shot up. "I volunteer!"

Miss Peregrine pushed her arm down gently. "That's very noble of you, dear, but we may need you for even more pressing things."

"We've already sent orders to evacuate those three loops." Miss Cuckoo tapped the map again with her stick, *tap-tap-tap.* "But they can't come here—if we let down our shield to allow them inside, Caul could follow. So we've arranged for them to be secreted away in the night down the Thames. They'll overnight on

Foulness Island, then proceed overland to our hideaway in Ballard's Gore."

"Why weren't they evacuated days ago?" asked Miss Merganser.

"We suggested it yesterday, but all refused to leave," said Miss Peregrine. "They were worried their loops would collapse in their absence. And of course, Caul's sudden resurrection was a surprise to everyone."

I saw Noor's shoulders slump.

"These are the go-down-with-the-ship types who would rather die than flee their loops," said Miss Peregrine.

"And will they?" Olive asked timidly. "Die?"

"No," said Miss Cuckoo. "If he kills them, he will only have dead children. Now he has hostages, which are much more useful."

"I agree," said Miss Peregrine. "So long as Caul believes he can foment an insurrection in our ranks and undermine us from within, they'll be safe. So long as he's trying to win hearts and minds here in the Acre, he won't kill those children. It would injure his case."

"And if he succeeds?" asked Horace.

"Someone already tried to kill Jacob and Noor," Emma pointed out.

"That was mind control," said Miss Wren, reaching down to scratch Addison's head. "We've since developed a backstop against that—two peculiars who can detect controlled minds, and are constantly on watch."

Addison's face popped up from under the table. "Mistresses, if I may. Caul's poisonous rhetoric alone could never persuade anyone to betray you. Even the most disagreeable loop-freedom agitator understands how much we owe you. Only a mad dog would prefer Caul's rule to yours."

Miss Wren dug a morsel from her pocket and fed it to him. "Thank you, Addison."

"Many have seen firsthand what wight rule would mean," Miss Blackbird added, "in the degradation and depravity Devil's Acre endured. Slavery, drug addiction, violence. Not to mention the wanton cruelty inflicted upon our loops during the raids a few months ago."

"Still, we shouldn't take people's loyalty for granted," said Miss Cuckoo. "Especially with Caul littering propaganda all across the Acre."

Then Emma finally said what we'd all been wondering. "There's no truth to it, is there?"

"What? That we offered a secret deal to the American leaders?"

"It's ridiculous," Olive said. "Emma, how could you even—"

"It's partly true, yes," said Miss Peregrine, and Olive stopped midsentence, her jaw hanging open. "It was the only way we could get the Americans to sign the accord and avoid war. Loop freedom was the only incentive all three of them wanted."

"But, miss," said Olive, grasping for words, "you . . . you told everyone it wasn't possible . . . that the loop reset reaction isn't safe yet—"

Miss Peregrine held up a hand to stop her. "It isn't. Though we may be close to a solution."

"That's why the Americans have been such a constant presence in the Acre lately," said Miss Wren. "They're waiting for their reset."

"They're in my office every other day, breathing down my bonnet about when it's going to be ready," Miss Avocet grumbled.

"But—but—" Olive stammered, bottom lip trembling, "how *could* you! When you wouldn't give it to anyone else—even Fiona?" She was so upset she started floating despite her lead boots, and Bronwyn had to reach for Olive's ankle and pull her down again before she drifted out of reach.

Miss Peregrine looked wounded. "Really, Olive, do you think so little of us? As soon as it's viable, which could be quite soon, we'll reset the leaders' clocks. But they want it only for themselves; their expectation was that we would keep it a secret, even from their own American rank and file."

"*Especially* from them," said Miss Cuckoo.

"But that was never our intention," said Miss Peregrine. "And now that Caul has let the secret slip . . ." She spread her hands and smiled slyly.

"Everyone will get reset?" Emma asked.

"Everyone," Miss Peregrine said. "Including Fiona, naturally."

"As soon as it's ready," added Miss Avocet.

Olive nearly collapsed with relief. "Oh, thank goodness."

"I still worry," Miss Blackbird said timidly, "that universal loop freedom would cause chaos. So many of our wards know nothing of the present—"

"A few days ago I was inclined to share your concerns," said Miss Peregrine, "but the situation has changed rather dramatically since then, wouldn't you agree? Should we have to suddenly evacuate Devil's Acre—"

Miss Cuckoo whacked her stick on the table. "Which we won't."

"Yes, but if we *do*," Miss Peregrine said patiently, "our wards must be able to scatter into the great vast world and hide there for perhaps a long time. If they can only escape into loops for fear of aging, Caul will find them. And I would much rather see them lost in the present—even a present they are unprepared for—than killed or enslaved by my pitiless brother."

No one, it seemed, could argue with that.

"Well, I think one of you'd better tell the crowd outside," said Horace. "They're quite miffed."

There were shouts from the hall, the sounds of a scuffle, and before anyone in the room could react, the doors burst open. LaMothe came charging through with Parkins and several of their followers in tow. Leo's four goons pinned the home guards to the floor. I spun around, ready for a fight, and so did my friends, but the Americans stopped well short of us.

"You spilled the beans, you lyin' harpies!" Parkins shouted

from his wheelchair, then threw one of the crumpled papers on the floor.

Miss Peregrine stepped toward them and crossed her arms. "It wasn't us. We've no idea how Caul found out about our agreement. For all we know it was one of your people who 'spilled the beans'—"

"They didn't know a thing about it!" LaMothe shouted.

"If you think this changes anything, you're dead wrong," said Parkins. "You're gonna stick to the terms of our deal."

"Gentlemen," Miss Avocet said with tone of warning, "you are free to have your clocks reset along with everybody else, or not at all."

"Then the deal's off," LaMothe shouted. "It was never gonna be ready. You've been stringin' us along this whole time."

"Actually, we're quite close to a breakthrough," said Miss Wren, echoing what Miss Peregrine had said earlier.

"More lies," Parkins growled.

"Good luck fighting Caul without us," said LaMothe. "We're taking our people and going home."

"I'm not sure how you're going to get there," said Miss Peregrine. "The Panloopticon is closed until further notice."

The raccoons rose hissing from LaMothe's coat as his face deepened to purple. "You're gonna open it for us. *Right. Now.*"

"I suppose they could fly commercial," Miss Cuckoo said to Miss Peregrine, her tone conversational. "How far is Heathrow Airport from here? Ninety minutes by cab?"

LaMothe and Parkins were apoplectic, but they had nothing left to threaten the ymbrynes with. "You've made a powerful enemy!" Parkins said, spit flying from his lips.

But their underlings looked confused and increasingly alarmed. A skinny cowboy in head-to-toe denim held up the crumpled paper and said, "Boss, is it true you was gonna reset without us?"

"Who told you to pick that up?" Parkins snapped.

"Can I see that?" a man in bearskins asked the man in denim.

"Quit reading things and break something!" shouted LaMothe. The bearskin man dutifully kicked the legs off a small table.

"That's quite enough of your temper tantrums!" Miss Cuckoo shouted, and then six more home guards burst into the room and surrounded the Americans. "See them out, please. And if they break anything or threaten anyone along the way, lock them in the jail."

"Git'cher damn hands offa me!" Parkins yelled, wrenching away from one of the Guards. "I'm a-goin'. Come on, fellas."

"You ain't heard the last of us!" LaMothe shouted as they were escorted out.

Miss Peregrine shook her head. "Such disappointing little men."

As the Americans' shouts echoed down the hall, I wondered how much worse off we'd be without them fighting by our side. I didn't get far with this train of thought, though, because no sooner had their voices disappeared than Perplexus's assistant, Matthieu, ran into the room, breathless.

"Madams," he cried. "We have news!" He doubled over, panting.

Before he could say what it was, Millard came charging in as well, his blue robe billowing behind him, rolled-up maps under his arms.

"Perplexus has found a route," he announced. "Fast, but very unpleasant. He will explain."

And then history's most famous temporal cartographer rushed in behind him—Perplexus himself, muttering in Italian, arms piled high with still more maps. *"Saluti signore,"* he said, bowing to the ymbrynes.

He was trailed closely by Francesca, who was trying to catch papers as they slipped out of his hands. The whole tower began to tip, and he reached the conference table just in time for them to topple across it.

"Mi scusi," Perplexus apologized, chasing the maps into a pile and giving me a perfunctory nod hello, though I couldn't see his eyes behind the little round sunglasses he always wore.

Together he and Millard unrolled a map of Europe that covered the ymbrynes' map of London.

"Miss Tern's loop is the meeting place, we are quite sure," Perplexus said, switching to heavily accented English. He patted his pockets as he spoke, looking for something. "It existed for three years only, during the Great War, which is a *molto, molto piccolo* window of time, in terms of leapfrogging . . . very difficult to find."

"Miss Tern's loop collapsed over a hundred years ago," Millard said, "so in order to enter it we must find a loop that existed contemporaneously with hers and which also survives to this day. But there are precious few left of that vintage."

"It was a terrible time for peculiars," Miss Peregrine explained, mostly for the benefit of Noor and me. "The war was tearing apart Europe, and the hollows had only begun hunting us in earnest a few years earlier; it took some time to understand what we were dealing with and how best to defend against it."

"Long tale short," said Millard, "there are only three loops that might work."

"Do you need something?" said Miss Wren asked Perplexus, who was still searching his pockets.

"I had a vial," he said, "of espresso." A drop of sweat slid down his pale brow.

Miss Avocet snapped her fingers. "Someone get the man a strong coffee." A guard saluted her and dashed from the room.

"We were quite hoping to find a route that didn't involve crossing through any war zones," Millard continued. "Or very much of one."

"One candidate is in Mongolia," Perplexus said, dabbing his face with his heavy black coat sleeve before using Miss Cuckoo's chalkstick to point at the map. "Safe, as we discussed, but quite far away. It would require two weeks' travel to reach Miss Tern's loop in France."

"Time we can't afford to take," said Miss Avocet.

Perplexus slid the pointer southwest. "The second is in the Adriatic Sea, 1918. Much closer." It had stopped on an island somewhere between Italy and Greece. "But it's on a *lazzaretto* . . . a quarantine island."

"Not only is it heavily guarded, but it's also infested with Spanish flu," said Millard. "We can't risk you dying of sickness, and even if we could guarantee your safety in that regard, the journey would take five days, so on balance it isn't worth the risk."

The guard returned cradling a tiny cup in his hands. "Espresso," he said, handing it to Perplexus, who drained it in two grateful gulps.

"Ahhh," he said, steam escaping his lips. "When you're as old as I am, coffee's practically the only thing keeping you alive."

"And the third loop?" I said, an anxious clench building in my chest.

"Much closer," said Millard. "Practically on top of Miss Tern's loop. Only ten miles away."

"But there's a catch," Noor guessed.

"Isn't there always," I muttered.

"Miss Tern's loop is on one side of the fighting, and this circa 1918 loop, belonging to a Miss Hawksbill, is on the other." He pointed to a loop in northern France. "A sea route is out of the question; it's blocked by warships, patrolled by submarines, and would take too long, anyway. The best route is overland straight across the front lines—one of the worst hells the twentieth century ever made."

There was a pause, and after a few seconds Noor realized the room was looking at her. She stiffened. "What? I haven't changed my mind."

Enoch leaned toward her. "It's trench warfare. Bullets, bombs, gas, disease. You'd need a miracle to survive that."

She looked at him like he was a little slow. "Then we'll have to arrange for one." She turned to the ymbrynes. "It's not like there's a choice. Right?"

The ymbrynes shook their heads.

I was sure, then, that I wanted to know Noor Pradesh for the rest of my life. However short or long that turned out to be. And then a new thought entered my mind and a cold wave of dread brushed my heart.

"I want to talk to you in private," I said.

"There's nothing to talk about," she said, but I persuaded her to step away from the table with me anyway.

"You don't have to do this," I whispered.

"No, *you* don't. But I do. I let that monster out."

"You didn't—"

"We're not going to argue this again. I'm the only one here who can send Caul back where he came from. There's no choice. Not for me, anyway. If it kills me, it kills me. But you don't have to come. In fact, I'd rather you lived. *I* did this. It's my fight."

The idea of letting her do this alone, the mere thought, filled me with physical revulsion. "There's no way you're going without me."

"Or me," said Bronwyn, stepping toward us.

Emma joined her side. "Or me."

"It's too dangerous," Noor said. "You guys don't have to—"

"You won't get five hundred feet without my maps knowledge," said Millard, his blue robe swishing around the table toward us. "It's my route, and I should be there to help you navigate it."

Addison left his place by Miss Wren's side and marched solemnly over to us. "I lived in a menagerie loop most of my life. If anyone can help you negotiate Miss Tern's loop, it's me."

Enoch sighed testily and said, "I'm not about to be left here twisting in the wind. I'll be *so* bored."

"Well, if you're *all* going—" Olive began, but so many of us shouted "No!" in unison that she didn't even finish her sentence.

She looked hurt.

"Sorry, Olive," said Emma. "Big kids only."

The ymbrynes were looking at us with odd expressions, a mix of pride and fear. Miss Peregrine looked proudest of all, but she'd gone white as a bedsheet.

"Alma, do you approve of this?" asked Miss Avocet.

In reply, she only nodded.

CHAPTER THIRTEEN

*I*t was decided that we were to leave that night, in just a few hours. There was no time to waste; with every hour that passed, Caul only got stronger, and our chances of surviving the attack he was surely preparing slimmed. Miss Cuckoo, Miss Wren, and Miss Peregrine accompanied us out of the council chamber and downstairs to the costuming department. From a vast room filled with hanging racks, Gaston, the costuming department director, chose period-appropriate outfits for each of us, all shades of brown and green that would blend into the turned earth of a battle-field, and hopefully attract minimal attention from either the British and French soldiers near Miss Hawksbill's loop, or the Germans after we crossed the front lines.

While we tried on clothes, we gathered in a cluster around the dressing room and the ymbrynes talked to us about what would happen when we crossed over. They tried to hide their nervousness, but it showed in the way Miss Peregrine kept fiddling with the pins in her upswept hair, in Miss Cuckoo's tapping foot, and in Miss Wren's uncharacteristic quiet. The fact was, there wasn't a lot they could tell us. They didn't know Miss Hawksbill well, but Miss Cuckoo repeated several times that under no circumstances should we attempt to cross the front lines to find the entrance to Miss Tern's loop without her help.

"She will surely know a safe passage," Miss Peregrine said, "having maintained a loop there for the better part of a century."

But she sounded more hopeful than certain, and the fact that

I'd never heard of Miss Hawksbill before a few minutes ago made me think she might be an odd duck, and not very helpful at all.

"All wrong, Gaston, all wrong," Miss Cuckoo said impatiently, wrinkling her nose at my outfit. "The jacket makes him looks too much like a soldier."

I shrugged out of the jacket and Gaston disappeared into the racks again.

"I wish I could go with you," Miss Cuckoo said. "I'm from the north of France, and I know the area where you're heading fairly well. Not in wartime, but still—"

"I would give both my wings to accompany you," Miss Peregrine said heavily. "But all twelve ymbrynes must stay here in the Acre, or the Quilt and its protections will falter."

"Don't worry about us, miss, we'll be back before you know it," Bronwyn said, and smiled.

Miss Peregrine forced a smile in return.

We returned to Ditch House without the ymbrynes to pack and rest a little before the journey, and leaving the ministries building we were forced to pass through the restless crowd outside its doors. Behind us, Francesca made an announcement through a bullhorn that the ymbrynes would address them soon. In a few minutes, this tempest in a teakettle would fade away—but so too would the reinforcements and extra muscle that the Americans had provided, who I assumed would be leaving along with their leaders. All the more reason we had to stop Caul before he found a way to break through the ymbrynes' shield.

Back at the house, Claire started to cry when we told her about our new mission. Fiona and Hugh solemnly wished us luck. "I knew they wouldn't let you go without taking some of us along," Hugh said, translating for Fiona. She felt her place was here, standing with the ymbrynes in defense of the Acre, and naturally Hugh wasn't about to leave her side. I was sure he would've tried to stop her even if she'd wanted to go with us, having already lost and regained the

< THE DESOLATIONS OF DEVIL'S ACRE >

love of his life once this year. After all that, the idea of Fiona risking her safety in the trenches of one of the century's deadliest wars would've been too much to bear. Not that staying in the Acre was any guarantee of safety; far from it.

Horace was the last to find out. He'd been sitting in bed in a half-sleep trance, moaning and whispering to himself, and when we woke him out of it he leapt up and started chattering about how he might've discovered a way to block Caul's transmissions.

"They're on the same psychic wavelength that my prestidigitations travel on, which means they're akin to a mass hallucination, something we see with our minds rather than our eyes—" He stopped suddenly, blinking at all of us. "Hullo, what are you all doing in my bedroom?"

Emma started to tell him, but he quickly cut her off. "Never mind, you don't have to tell me—I dreamed it," he said, snapping his fingers and letting his eyes fall shut. "France. Miss . . . Cranesbill. No, Hawksbill. Death everywhere, heavy in the air." He opened his eyes. "Right. I'm coming with you."

"Um," Emma said, "that's very kind of you, Horace, but—"

"Why don't you just knit us some bulletproof sweaters?" Enoch said.

"That isn't nice," said Bronwyn, who'd been trying to fit all the books Millard said he needed into one large steamer trunk. "Horace has been through lots of battles with us. Ain't that right?"

"I detest war and fighting," he said, "but I'm coming nevertheless. You're going to need me. I'm not sure why yet, but it's not for my knitting skills." And he started to look around for a backpack to fill.

We had underestimated him yet again.

Noor had been avoiding my eyes ever since we'd left the council chamber, I think because she didn't want me to tell her, for the hundredth time, that she didn't need to do this. But I was past that now. She was the only indispensable part of all this. The ymbrynes' shield could fail and the Acre could fall, but as long as she found the other

< 245 >

six, there was a chance everything could be put right again. But she didn't need me reminding her of that. Her way of bearing the pressure seemed to be to not think too much about it. Just go, just do. So I let her go, helped her do, and let her avoid my eyes for a while.

Perplexus and Millard had lugged the maps back to Ditch House and spread them across the kitchen table again, where they were going over them one last time. Perplexus looked half avian, with map pages poking out of his jacket and the waistband of his pants, and the table was littered with drained espresso cups. We let them work in peace.

After an anxious hour, Miss Peregrine returned, pushing Miss Avocet in her wheelchair. They called Noor, Horace, and me into the sitting room to talk. A fire was kindled in the hearth and Miss Avocet was parked beside it, her head propped on pillows, her eyes tired but alert. V's body was still on the gurney by the darkened window, encased now in an ice-filled coffin. It felt wrong, keeping her like this, but there'd been too much chaos and no time to give her a funeral. And I suspected the ymbrynes wanted to keep her close at hand in the unlikely event that we needed to ask her more questions.

Miss Peregrine invited us to sit on the floor cushions. She stood backlit before the crackling hearth while she spoke. "A few final notes. We'll be restarting the Panloopticon very briefly, just long enough for you to cross over. We cannot send advance word of your arrival to Miss Hawksbill, lest we risk the message being intercepted. So you'll have to locate her when you enter her loop."

"I hope she's home," I said.

"She is," Horace replied. We didn't need to ask him how he knew.

"Isn't it dangerous to restart the Panloopticon?" Emma asked.

Miss Peregrine nodded. "Yes, but it's only for thirty seconds or so, a calculated risk we have to take."

"Does anyone know yet what I'm supposed to do when I find the other six?" asked Noor.

Miss Avocet struggled to sit up straight. "I had hoped

Francesca and our translators would uncover something new in the *Apocryphon* that might be useful in that regard, but alas. We aren't certain how the seven go about sealing shut the door, but the one who summoned you there—whoever made those six phone calls—will likely know."

"Goodness, I should hope so," said Horace.

"We'll take you all to the Panloopticon shortly," said Miss Peregrine. "No one else in the Acre must know what you're up to. We cannot risk word of your mission making its way back to Caul or the wights. We've no way of knowing whether the wights we're still holding in our jail have psychic connections with Caul. If he were to find out, he'd surely come after you. So to that end, we'll be sneaking you into the Panloopticon one by one in shipping crates."

"Excuse me?" said Horace.

Miss Peregrine ignored him. "Once you cross through into 1918, you'll have no way of contacting me or this loop, nor should you try; again, the risk of alerting our enemies is too great. You'll be cut off and entirely on your own." She'd been facing the fire for much of her short speech, but now she turned to look at us. She was nearly in tears. "If I should never see you again . . ."

Horace jumped up and put his arms around her. "You will, miss. You will."

"Are you just saying that, Mr. Somnusson?"

"I'm not. I know it," he said. And whether or not it was true, it was what we all needed to hear.

*   *   *

I was about to follow the ymbrynes and Horace out into the kitchen when Noor tugged at my hand. "Wait." She looked back toward the window, and the ice-filled coffin that lay in shadow beneath it.

I was hit by a sudden wave of shame. "We'll bury her soon as we can."

< RANSOM RIGGS >

"It's not that," she said. "I'd like to talk to her again before we go."

"She won't be able to hear you."

She hugged herself. "I know. But I still want to."

I took a breath, aware suddenly of the faint scent of formaldehyde in the air. Aware, too, that despite the loss of my grandfather, I could never fully understand what Noor was feeling. To lose a loved one you'd only just been reunited with.

She took my hand. "Will you stay?"

"Okay. If you want." We crossed the room to where V lay.

Noor knelt beside the ice-filled coffin. I stayed close enough to lend support without invading Noor's space.

"Mama, I'm going away now. I'm going to find Penny. I don't know when I'll be back again . . ." She dug into the ice with her fingers and fished out V's hand, blue from death and cold, kneading it as she talked. I think she said *I love you* and *I'm sorry*, but I was trying not to listen, because it felt too private and because it was hurting my heart.

And then the ice shifted and Noor gasped. V's fingers had curled around Noor's hand. Somewhere in her chest, a bit of blood from the poet's heart was still coursing.

V's lips parted. A noise like sandpaper on wood escaped them.

Noor leaned closer. "Mama?"

V's mouth moved and her throat rattled. I hoped she might say, *I love you, too*. Or better still, *It wasn't your fault*.

Instead, she said, "Horatio . . ."

Noor tensed, then leaned in closer. "What did you say?"

The ice shifted in the box. V was trying to sit up, but she could not, and sank back again. Her eyes stayed shut. Her words were drawn out and distorted, rough breaths barely recognizable. She said: "Horatio. He was . . . the last of us. And once was . . . Caul's . . . right hand. Find him . . ."

V's mouth went slack. Her hand opened and let go of Noor's.

And she was gone again.

< 248 >

We rushed out into the kitchen to tell the others what had happened, but they'd all gone upstairs except for Horace and Enoch, who were talking together by the sink. Enoch wore a stained apron, meat cleaver in hand, and was in the midst of chopping up a counter full of chickens, presumably for their hearts.

"Yeah, that happens sometimes" was his shrugging reaction to our news. "When there's a dollop of residual resurrecto-juice left in some ventricle or other, they'll wake up for short blips . . . though if she did anything more than grunt at you, that's very impressive. She must have really wanted to talk to you. It takes a massive effort on the part of the deceased to rise oneself."

Noor pursed her lips. "She said something about 'Horatio.'"

"Shakespeare again?" said Horace.

"No," I said. "I think she must have meant H's hollowgast. *That* Horatio. She said he used to be close to Caul, and that we should find him."

"Find him and what?" Horace asked.

"She didn't get a chance to tell us," Noor said. "I could try to ask her, if you can wake her up again."

"Can't help you there. I can't rise her more than once every few days, and each time I do it the quality of the resurrection goes down."

"Oh." Noor rubbed a hand across her tired eyes.

"Sorry, Noor." Enoch thwacked the cleaver into a chopping block and wiped his hands on his apron. "I wouldn't make too much of it, anyway. Most post-resurrection chatter is ninety-nine percent nonsense. Like dreams. No offense, Horace."

Horace turned his back on Enoch. "Offense taken!"

"I think it means something," I said. "I've been wondering about Horatio. He gave us that map scrap and clue, then flung himself out H's window. Where'd he go?"

"I don't really care," Noor said, and her bitter tone surprised me. "You know, if it weren't for that stupid map we would have never found V, and she'd still be alive."

"That's not necessarily true. Murnau knew where she was, and probably would've led us there himself, eventually. And H and Horatio meant well. They were trying to protect you. They clearly didn't know that V's heart was on Murnau's shopping list."

"I guess so," Noor said reluctantly. "So you think he's still alive? That H's old hollowgast is still out there somewhere?"

"Could be," I said. "But he's a wight now, and I kind of figured that after a lifetime of servitude as a tamed hollow he'd go on vacation or something. But you never know."

"You know who I'd like to talk to?" Enoch said. He slammed the cleaver down and a chicken head went skidding into the sink. "Myron Bentham."

At the mention of his name, a strange chill shot through me.

"As long as we're dreaming, I'd like to talk to Jesus Christ and Mahatma Gandhi," said Horace.

"I met him once," Enoch said.

"Who? Jesus?"

"Gandhi, you twit. He visited the East End once in the thirties. Nice chap. But I'm quite serious about Bentham. If you could find his body, maybe I could wake him up for a chat. He must have some useful dirt on Caul."

"He was collapsed in the Library of Souls along *with* Caul, remember?" Horace said. "There's no body to retrieve. Or not one we'd recognize, anyway. The last time I saw him, he'd turned into a giant mosquito creature."

Enoch brought down his cleaver again. Blood squirted onto the ceiling. "Sounds like he'd fit right in."

I was on my way upstairs when I heard shouting coming through a window. I stuck my head out to see Millard and Bronwyn arguing with Klaus in the alley. I shimmied through the window as fast as I could, then down the scaffolding to the ground like Millard had showed me.

"What's going on?" I said, running up to them.

Klaus was red-faced from shouting, and had a large burlap sack slung over one shoulder. I couldn't see Millard's face but he was breathing hard, and Bronwyn looked like she had no idea what was happening, but was ready to defend Millard regardless, if necessary.

"What's going *on*," Millard hissed in a half-yelled undertone, "is that I got this blackguard the bone and the vial and everything he asked for—"

"You did?" I said. "When?"

"Through some back channels I've cultivated, and let's keep it at that. And now he's refusing to give us the you-know-what!"

I started to say, "You mean the—"

"Shh!" Millard cut me off. "Don't say it out loud."

"I can't give it to ya because the damn thing *exploded*!" Klaus said, making no effort to lower his voice. "Nearly took my pinky off!" He held up a bandaged right hand as evidence. "I told you it might not work, and it didn't!"

"Then prove it, and give us back the blown-apart pieces," Millard said.

"I can't, they burned to little piles of blue ash."

Millard made a sound of disgust. "Codswallop! I don't believe you. You got it working and are keeping it for yourself."

"I should whip you for saying that!" Klaus's eyes cut to Bronwyn, who raised her fists. "But instead, I brought you a peace offering. It ain't as a good as the you-know-what, but it could save your skin in the right circumstance."

"I won't accept some booby prize."

"Just look at it, for God's sake." He lowered the sack to the ground and untied the rope that held it closed. The sack fell away to reveal a boxy wooden clock about two feet high.

"Is that . . . ?"

"That's right. The bone clock."

I looked closer. The face looked like stretched and tanned skin, and the hands were made of long, delicate-looking bones.

"Why would you give this away? I thought it was made from pieces of your ancestor."

"Well, that's just how bad I feel about this whole deal," he said. "You'll bring it back to me, of course, this is just for loansies, while you're away on your trip."

"And how'd you hear about that?" said Bronwyn.

Klaus grinned. "Secrets have short half-lives in the Acre."

"What's it do?" I asked, bringing our discussion back to the clock.

"It helps you hear the whispers."

"What whispers?" said Bronwyn.

"Don't fall for his tricks," said Millard, but Bronwyn shushed him.

"Of someone who's just passing on," Klaus said. "After the heart and brain have given up the ghost but the ghost itself is still clinging to the body. They whisper, see, but faster than the mind can grasp and quieter than the ear can hear, so you can't understand it unless you slow down the world and listen *real close*—"

"And what good will that do us?" Millard said impatiently.

"The bone clock is what does the slowing, and that slowing is what allows you to hear the whispers. Everything comes to a snail's crawl. That can serve a lot of uses, even beyond listening to ghosts. You unlock the case with the ring finger key, wind the clock with the thumb key, then crank the mainspring with the index finger." He dug a key ring from his pocket and held it out. The ring was iron and the jingling keys were bone.

Millard snatched it. "This doesn't make up for the you-know-what," he said reluctantly. "If I catch wind of you using it, you'll be caught and thrown in jail before you can say *I'm a traitor to my people*." Millard knelt beside the bone clock, ran his hand over its carved top, and sighed. "And, um, thank you," he said quietly.

Klaus nodded. "Hope you never need to use it." He took a flask from his pocket. "Good luck to you all," he said, and drank.

* * *

We were halfway up the scaffolding when a shout came from below: "The hell do you think you're doing? Get away from there!"

We looked down to see Wreck Donovan and Dogface goggling at us from the alley. When Wreck saw me, he squinted and said, "Is that you, Portman?"

"What are you doing there?" said Dogface.

"Keep your voices down!" Millard hissed.

"We live here," I said.

"Then why you breakin' in?" Dogface said with a sneer.

"We're *sneaking* in," said Bronwyn. "And never mind why."

"What are *you* doing here?" I asked them. "I thought you'd all have left with Parkins and LaMothe."

Dogface spit on the ground. "To hell with those gutless traitors."

"We decided to stay and cast our lot with the only peculiars that got any honor at all, and that's you," said Wreck. "You're welcome and God help us."

They continued on their way, and we resumed our clambering.

"I guess we misjudged them," I said.

"We shall see about that," Millard replied.

We went back in through the window we'd snuck out of. No one inside had heard the shouts, and we decided not to tell them. Bronwyn wedged the bone clock into the same trunk that contained Millard's books and maps, which she had outfitted with ropes that would allow her to carry it like a big, bulky backpack. She'd only just fastened it shut when we heard a commotion downstairs, and rushed down to the kitchen to find all twelve ymbrynes talking with our friends amid the hay and chicken feathers.

It was nearly time to leave, and they'd come to see us off. Some gave us their feathers as talismans, which we tucked into our pockets or poked through the metal grommets of our period-accurate backpacks. Horace distributed the bulletproof sweaters he'd made from peculiar sheep's wool. These had become indispensable; at this point I would've felt naked going on a dangerous outing without one, itchy as they were.

And then the moment came, and we followed Miss Peregrine out of the house and around to the alley again. Klaus was gone; instead there were six large crates waiting for us. Mine was big enough to fit two people, and since Noor had already been closed into a smaller crate by herself, Emma squeezed in beside me. We sat shoulder to shoulder, knees hugged to chests, our backs against the crate walls. Horace was describing to the ymbrynes his new theory about how to stop Caul's transmissions—something about playing a specific frequency through the loudspeakers, a note that tended to disrupt hypnosis—but then the crate lid closed over our heads and his voice muffled.

Emma and I jostled against each other as our crate was loaded onto a wagon.

"Did you ever think it would get this bad?" I said, my teeth clacking as the wagon began to roll along the Acre's pitted streets.

"You mean with Caul getting resurrected and coming after us? And all the power of the Library of Souls at his disposal?"

"Yeah. That."

I felt her shoulders rise, then fall. "Truthfully? I never thought it would get this *good*."

I thought I'd misheard her.

"It doesn't feel much different than having the hollows hunting us at every turn," she went on, "which was our reality for years and years. Before you came along, we had no way to defend against them. We were trapped and helpless. So, in a way, that piece of things doesn't feel like it's changed much. At least now we're all together, instead of split apart in dozens of different loops. At least now we can fight as one. And we're not helpless anymore. We have you, and we have Noor. We have a chance."

I felt a surge of pride expanding in me, immediately followed by a deflating prick of fear.

"But it might not work," I said. "We could fail."

"As with any great endeavor," she said. "Better to die trying. Better to burn out than fade away."

" 'Hey hey, my my,' " I said.

"Your what?"

"Neil Young," I said. " 'Better to burn out' . . . I played his record for you once, in my room."

"I remember. We danced."

She leaned into me, and I felt her hair fall onto my shoulder. I leaned into her, just a little, just briefly. Just friends. Though I loved her still, in a dimmed and dusty way.

Out on the streets, people were laughing. Distantly, someone sawed away at a violin. People were trying to forget the sword hanging over them, the wolf at their gates, if only for an evening.

Emma said quietly, "Do you regret it?"

"What?" My breath stalled.

"Your decision. Choosing this, our world, over your family. If you could be a regular kid again, fretting about grades and schoolgirls—"

"I wouldn't. I don't regret any of it. Not for a second."

Then I really thought about it. Tried to imagine what I'd be doing now if none of this had happened. If I'd never gone to the island, never met Emma or the other children. But I couldn't. I'd come too far and changed too much. I had evolved into a different kind of person.

But there was one thing I regretted.

"Maybe it would've been better for everyone if we'd never met," I said.

"What's that supposed to mean?" she said, hurt. "Why?"

"Then none of this would've happened. I wouldn't have been at the Battle of Devil's Acre, which means Caul would never have dragged me into the Library of Souls, and I wouldn't have been able to give him one of the soul jars."

"Stop being ridiculous."

"It's true. He wanted the Library's power, and he never would've gotten it if it wasn't for me."

"You can't think that way. You'll drive yourself mad."

"Way too late for that," I said.

"And anyway, Caul never would have needed all these terrible powers to get what he wanted if not for you. He had just developed hollows who could break into loops, remember? He would've invaded them one by one until all of us were dead or captured. I'm sure he would have preferred *not* to have died and come back as half a hell-beast, all things being equal. But you forced him to with all your derring-do and badassery. To borrow a slang term from you modern people."

We hit a pothole so deep I felt my brain slap the inside of my skull, and the incisive argument I was going to make turned into "Yeah, I guess so . . ."

"And if not for you, we'd all still be loop-trapped and in constant danger of aging forward. I can't tell you what a relief it is not to worry about going gray overnight or turning into a bag of dust while doing some out-of-loop grocery shopping."

"I didn't do that. It was the ymbrynes. And Bentham—"

"But it was *because* of you. If not for that, we wouldn't have known it was even possible to do. So thanks to you, someday soon everyone in the Acre will be free of loops, too. Hopefully."

The wagon jolted to a stop.

"You ready?" I said, grateful for a change of subject.

"I'm serious, Jacob. Please take this to heart. You only ever helped us. You were the best thing to happen to us in a long time."

I was feeling a hundred different things but didn't know how to say any of them. Three weeks ago I would have kissed her. Instead, I found her hand in the dark and squeezed it. "Thank you," I said. "Regret retracted. Compliment accepted."

"*Good,*" she whispered, and squeezed back.

And then the lid creaked open. I pulled my hand free just as Miss Peregrine's face appeared, peering down at us.

"Why, Jacob. You're bright red."

I jumped up and got out of the crate as fast as I could.

· · ·

We were snuck into Bentham's house through a back alley carriage entrance. The arrivals were staggered so as not to spark too much curiosity along the way. Bronwyn used a crowbar to pry open each crate as it came into the little stone-walled basement room. It reminded me of the way vampires transported themselves from place to place in stories, packed away from the sun inside their cushy, crated coffins.

Only Miss Peregrine, Miss Wren, and Miss Cuckoo had come to see us off. There were eight of us altogether including Addison. He had flatly refused to be sealed into a crate and was strutting around like a general. Once we'd all emerged and stretched our cramped limbs, we were given tan coats made from heavy wool, which, combined with Horace's sweaters, I worried would quickly became suffocating. It was the middle of November in Miss Hawksbill's loop, Millard said, and we would need the extra warmth.

We were handed our backpacks. I shrugged into the straps of mine and felt the weight, which was considerable. The ymbrynes had repeatedly assured us we'd find Miss Tern's loop with no problem, but the things they'd stuffed our packs with told a different story: thermal blankets, canned food, ice picks, binoculars, first aid.

"Just in case you run into a delay," Miss Wren said.

"Or have trouble finding Miss Hawksbill," Miss Cuckoo added.

Noor rifled through her pack. "No weapons," she noted.

"Guns would only arouse suspicion, if you should run into trouble with any soldiers," Miss Cuckoo said. "If they think you're combatants, you could end up in a military prison camp, or worse."

With that cheerful thought to comfort us, we proceeded up a staircase to the lower Panloopticon hall. I'd rarely seen it so empty. Usually there were a dozen people coming and going, transit officials stamping passports and checking documents, Sharon stalking around to make sure everything was shipshape. It reminded me of the first time I'd seen it, when Emma and I had stumbled into this hallway by accident, before we ever met Bentham. Now it was even quieter: There were no drifts of snow spilling across the carpet, no piles of sand collecting around the jambs of desert loop doors. No echo of whistling wind or crashing surf. The doors were dead, blank. Deactivated. At least for now.

The ymbrynes escorted us nearly all the way down the hall, around a corner into an even narrower hall, to a door built into a dead-end wall. Its paint was flaking and the plaque read FRANCE, NOVEMBER 1918. Sometimes you could tell how often and how recently a particular loop door had been used by checking the frame around it, because Sharon had gotten into the habit of putting subtle notches in the wood.

There were no notches in this door. It hadn't been used in a long time. Certainly not since the ymbrynes had occupied the Acre.

"Coats on, everyone!" Miss Peregrine said.

We shrugged on our long wool coats and antique boots that went halfway up our calves. There was even a coat for Addison, a little green number with short sleeves and faux-fur trim, which Miss Wren helped him into. Millard, who would freeze if naked but attract way too much attention if he was anything other than

< THE DESOLATIONS OF DEVIL'S ACRE >

mummified in clothes, pulled on a muffler, earflap cap, and gloves, and hung a pair of smoked goggles around his neck that he could pull over his eyes at a moment's notice.

"It had better be *arctically* frigid over there—I'm sweltering," said Millard.

"You look dashing," Horace said to him. "Like one of the polar expeditioneers."

"Which? The one who got lost and had to eat his crew?" Millard loosened the muffler and fanned himself. "You're *sure* Miss Hawksbill will be waiting for us?"

"I saw it in a dream. She's in her house right now, not far from the loop entrance. We shouldn't have much trouble finding her."

Miss Wren announced that we'd have only thirty seconds from the time the Panloopticon restarted to get inside the loop before the door would shut behind us. Sharon was down in the machine-clogged guts of the building, standing ready for the signal.

"Are you ready?" asked Miss Peregrine.

"I'm ready," said Noor, and down the line we all answered the same. *Ready, ready, ready.*

"All right, then."

We waited. I glanced out a window, and beyond the yellow sky I could see the Quilt glowing green. I thought of old Miss Avocet, and how exhausted all the ymbrynes were. Until we succeeded none of them could sleep, or that green shield keeping our enemies at bay would shatter.

The floor began to rumble. The candle-shaped electric sconces along the wall flickered. I wondered for a moment if it was an earthquake, but then a puff of something like steam escaped from the crack under the door in front of us and from every door down the hall, and there was a faint *ding!* that sounded like an egg timer hitting zero.

The Panloopticon was back online.

Miss Peregrine and Miss Wren exchanged an anxious glance,

< 259 >

and then Miss Peregrine reached out her arm and turned the knob of *France, November 1918*. It blew inward, the knob sucked from her hand, and slammed hard against the inner wall. She fell back, startled.

I ventured a look inside. It was the usual Panloopticon sameness: an uninviting bed that never tempted you to linger, a wardrobe and a nightstand, and the red poppy carpeting that ended at a missing fourth wall. Beyond that, a shimmering image of a snowy forest was materializing. Emma started toward the door, but Miss Peregrine held out her arm to stop her.

"Wait for it," she said. "It's not quite born yet."

We watched the forest. It brightened, and the shimmer stopped, and then it looked every bit as real as the view out the window.

"Godspeed, children," Miss Peregrine said. "May the elders watch over you."

CHAPTER FOURTEEN

*S*even teenagers and a dog said goodbye to the three ymbrynes and marched through the open door. Our boots clomped to the edge of the carpet, then across a blanket of fallen leaves.

"Go quickly now, my pets, we must shut the door," Miss Wren called, shooing a clingy Horace after us. When he was fully clear of the room, the ymbrynes waved at us from the hallway and pulled the door shut. There was no time for long, tearful goodbyes. They had to shut down the Panloopticon before Caul or any of his monsters could slip through.

The three-walled room wavered in the air like a heat distortion, then dimmed away and disappeared. And we were alone in a forest in France with no obvious way back home—or to the place I had started to think of as home, anyway. A gust of wind flurried the leaves around us and made a lonely sound through the trees. Emma clapped her hands, cutting through the heavy silence that had begun to accrue. "Right!" she barked. "Job one: Find Miss Hawksbill."

We looked around. There was no path, no trail, no signage. The forest thickened into dense brush ahead of us and climbed over a blind hill in the other, so we couldn't see far in any direction.

Noor turned to Millard. "I saw you packing maps."

"Reams and sheaves of them," he replied. "But since we don't know where we are right now, they won't do us much good."

"We're in a forest," said Bronwyn.

"Thank you, I can see that. We've got to find a landmark."

From the direction of the brush came a distant rattle of gunfire.

"War's over that way," Horace said, pointing.

"That settles it, you're all geniuses," said Enoch.

Addison popped up on his hind legs. "If Miss Tern's loop is on the other side of the front lines, why don't we simply follow the shooting and cross over?"

"Because," Horace said slowly, "we could get *shot*." The low boom of an explosion rumbled from the direction of the front.

"Or blown up," Enoch added.

"Well, try not to." Addison harrumphed. "For supposedly heroic people, you worry an awful lot about things like that."

"Heroic isn't the same thing as stupid," Horace said.

Addison growled at him.

"Can he be muzzled?" Enoch said to no one in particular.

Emma separated them before the situation could escalate. "You're *all* being stupid. Look, we'll find our own way across if we have to, but before we resort to that we must try and find Miss Hawksbill."

"If only Olive were here to float above the trees and spot for her house," said Millard.

"Or we could try this," I said. I cupped my hands around my mouth and shouted, "MISS HAWKSBILL!"

Horace leapt at me and tried to clap his hand over my mouth—"Be quiet!"—but I shoved him off. "When has *that* ever been an acceptable way to find an ymbryne?"

"When no one has a better idea?" I said.

"But *soldiers* might come!"

"If you're going to do it that way, you've got to be much louder," said Bronwyn, and then she threw her head back and bellowed at the top of her lungs. "MISS HAWKSBILL!!!"

Horace clapped his hands over his face and muttered, "You're dreaming again. Wake up, Horace."

Emma shrugged. "Perhaps we should all shout?"

And so we did, Horace included. We screamed until we ran out of breath and the woods echoed Miss Hawksbill's name, and in the quiet that followed, we listened.

Even the distant guns had fallen silent, and I began to wonder whether we'd made a mistake, and a squad of soldiers was about to burst through the trees to mow us down.

Instead, from over the hill behind us we heard a small voice call, "Hello?"

We turned to see a figure in a dress and a large hat at the top of the hill. I couldn't see her face. Whoever it was must not have liked the looks of us, because she immediately turned and darted back into the trees.

"Don't let her get away!" Millard shouted.

We took off running, loaded down with heavy packs, feet thundering in heavy boots. I crested the hill to see more forest stretching out ahead of us. Addison barked, his body forming an arrow. The figure disappeared behind a stand of brush. We ran after her until we came to a clearing and a small thatch-roofed cottage. It was ringed by burned trees and singed shrubs, and in the front yard what had once been a flower bed was now a pair of bomb craters with a narrow gravel path threading between them to a front door—which slammed shut just as I laid eyes on it.

We could hear someone rattling around inside the cottage.

A large sign staked into the yard read KEEP OFF GRASS in three languages, though there wasn't much grass left to keep off of.

"Miss Hawksbill!" Bronwyn shouted. "We need to talk with you!"

A small shuttered window slapped open and an old woman's face peeped out. "*Va te faire cuire un oeuf!*" she shouted. "Go away, I have nothing to say to anyone!" She slammed the shutter closed, then opened it again to bark "And stay off my grass!" before pulling it shut.

"We need your help," Emma shouted. "Please!"

"The ymbrynes sent us!" I yelled.

The shutter opened again. "What did you say?"

"The ymbrynes sent us."

She gaped at us. "You are *peculiar*?"

"We're in your loop, aren't we?" Enoch said.

She frowned doubtfully, stared at us for a moment longer, then disappeared from the window without a word.

We looked at one another dumbfounded. What kind of ymbryne *was* this?

We heard a heavy lock turn and the front door swung open.

Miss Hawksbill said, "Well, you'd better come in, then. And step lively!"

We hurried in single file between the craters. One was still smoking and smelled like fresh earth; the bomb had fallen only recently. Which, since this was a loop, meant that it exploded thirty feet from Miss Hawksbill's front door every day.

She stood propping the door open with her foot, glaring as we went inside. She might've been in her seventies, physically, but if I knew anything about ymbrynes she was probably twice as old, if not older. She kept her hair in a gray bun so tight it looked painful, and wore a long, blanketlike dress that was the color of dried blood. But what caught everyone's attention was her right hand, which was wrapped in a cast and hung from a sling around her neck.

"Hurry up now and get inside, and don't sit on my furniture, damn you," she growled in a French accent.

Her little cottage was just a single wide room: against one wall hulked a midnight-black cooking range and a rough dining table; in the center was a lumpy sofa; and some bookshelves and a massive wood-framed bed occupied another wall. When the last of us was inside, she slammed the door shut and shouted, *"Protégez vos oreilles!"* and clapped her hands over her ears, and a moment later a blast rattled the house. The lanterns swung from the ceiling and dirt came flying into the room through the small window she'd left open.

"*Sac à merde,*" she swore, running toward the pile of steaming dirt that had landed on her floor.

Horace uncovered his head. "Was that another bomb?"

"I *told* you to keep off the grass! I opened my shutters because of you, and look what's happened! Who's going to clean up this mess?"

"We will, of course," Bronwyn said, rushing to help.

"And your wards?" Emma said, scanning the room curiously.

"My wards"—Miss Hawksbill flung two more shutters open, and daylight poured in—"are useless."

"*Mange tes morts!*" said a low, booming voice. "How dare you." It had come from a giant, mounted moose head propped on a table by the bed.

"Oh, don't be so sensitive, Teo," Miss Hawksbill said.

The moose head's lips curled. "I wasn't the one who left the window open," it replied tartly.

"Oh, *shut up*, Teo," said a shrill voice, and then another voice concurred in French. In the bright new light I could see that the walls and much of the ceiling were covered in stuffed and mounted animal heads. They were talking to one another.

"What wicked sorcery keeps them bodiless but alive?" Horace cried.

"My God," Addison shouted, backing away from the ymbryne, "she's a serial murderer!"

"Don't insult her," Emma hissed at him.

"These are your wards?" Millard asked her.

"A menagerie of the dead!" Addison wailed.

"We aren't dead!" roared the mounted head of a bear, which set off a chorus of arguing voices—"We *are*, technically!" "No we aren't!"—and a volley of French insults (*"Bête comme ses pieds!"* *"Con comme une valise sans poignée!"*) until Miss Hawksbill raised her arms and shouted, "BE SILENT!" and the bickering ceased.

She turned to us with a sigh. "I suppose I must explain."

"At the risk of being rude, we don't really have time," Emma said. "Do you know a Miss Tern?"

The ymbryne struggled to suppress a look of shock. The heads began to mutter among themselves, until Miss Hawksbill gave them a vicious shush.

"Miss Tern's loop has been gone a very long time," she said.

Emma nodded. "Her loop was destroyed a few years after yours was created, and—"

"Yes. Miss Tern was my sister."

Emma's eyes widened. "Really?"

"Do you mean in the way that all ymbrynes are sisters?" Bronwyn asked. "Or by blood?"

Miss Hawksbill drew up her chin proudly. "In the way of having shared a mother and a womb. And when we fledged into full ymbrynes we made adjacent loops so we could be close to each other."

We were all stunned. It was one thing for Miss Peregrine to have a pair of somewhat peculiar brothers. It was a much rarer thing for an ymbryne to be sisters with another ymbryne.

"My sister was a true prodigy and graduated from Miss Avocet's academy two years before I did. When I eventually completed my training I came here to establish a loop near hers, as we had planned. I meant to collect a group of wards like yourselves, human peculiar children from all walks of life." Miss Hawksbill looked away. Her face fell into shadow. "Before I had the chance, a mere week after this house was completed, a hollowgast killed my sister. When her life ended, so did her loop. The bombs she'd been holding at bay fell on the house. I took it upon myself to rescue all her animals who survived—and many that did not. A talented taxidermist was able to save many I had feared beyond saving, and preserve their lives and voices, if not the entirety of their bodies." She gestured to the walls with a sweep of her hand. "I brought them here; they became my wards."

So this loop was a kind of memorial to that lost one, filled with the animated remains of peculiar animals. What a strange, sad place.

"If you don't mind me asking," Bronwyn said, "why didn't you leave here after Miss Tern's loop was destroyed? Take the heads elsewhere?"

"So I could visit her now and then," she replied. "Though it's a bit like calling on a forgetful ghost, as it's always the same day for her and she never remembers my last visit."

"We need to reach her," Noor said. "And soon."

Miss Hawksbill turned to study her. "And what's your peculiarity, young lady?" The way she said it made it seem like she already knew.

Rather than explain herself, Noor scooped a handful of light from the air, tucked it into her cheek, and swallowed. Miss Hawksbill gazed at the churning black spot between them for a moment, then broke into a smile. "You came," she said. "Finally."

Noor's eyes narrowed. "What do you mean, finally?"

"Are you familiar with a book written by a madman named Robert LeBourge?"

Bob the Revelator. Author of the *Apocryphon.*

Noor sucked in her breath, then tried to cover her surprise. "You know about . . ." She lowered her voice. *"The prophecy?"*

"All I know is, you're expected."

"I told you they would come," intoned the moose head gravely, "in due time."

Millard tossed his arms up and cried, "We were right! We've done it!"

"Am I the first?" Noor asked excitedly. "Or have other people already come?"

The heads were all murmuring among themselves about Noor.

"Maybe," replied Miss Hawksbill mysteriously. "But they didn't come this way. There are other avenues to reach my sister's loop, if you're not in such a hurry."

"But is there a way from here to there?" said Emma. "A safe one?"

"Well, naturally." She squinted at us. "Can any of you fly?"

Emma frowned. "No."

"Oh. Then, no. But there is a dangerous way."

Emma's face fell. Horace shrank back against a wall.

"That'll have to do," Millard said. "Will you show us?"

"But of course," said Miss Hawksbill, plucking a furry hat from her bed and clapping it onto her head. "You'd never make it without me."

"*Au revoir, mes enfants!*" she called to the heads. "*Vous avez l'intelligence d'une huitre!*"

"*Casse-toi!*" they chorused in reply.

And then she hiked up her dress and opened the front door.

◆　　◆　·　◆

Miss Hawksbill led us past the smoking craters in her yard, which now numbered three, and into the woods. We headed for the sound of distant guns, which had gone from occasional to regular, trudging toward a war while Noor hummed "We're Off to See the Wizard." A clammy blanket of dread settled over me.

Twice in five minutes Miss Hawksbill stopped at a fork in the path and seemed briefly confused before choosing one. "I normally travel this route by wing," she said apologetically.

We began to trade worried glances. Millard unfolded a map from his coat pocket and attempted to read it while walking. "I think we're about *here*," he mumbled, "and the front lines are somewhere over that way . . ."

The path broke through the trees and followed the edge of a hill. In the distance below us we could see the fighting for the first time. Confused lines of trenches and barbed wire ran like sutures through fields so blown to hell they resembled the surface of the moon. In the middle was no-man's-land, a rutted cavity of smashed tanks and splintered trees. A shroud of smoke hung thickly over it all.

"My God," I heard Bronwyn murmur behind me.

"This side here, closest to us, is the British and French," Miss Hawksbill explained as she walked. "The Germans occupy the opposite side. My sister's loop entrance is over there." She gestured toward the German side. "In that town."

"What town?" Noor asked, squinting into smoky distance.

A mortar shell landed in no-man's-land, sending up a fountain of brown mud.

"See that patch of rubble behind the German lines?"

"If that was ever a town, it's not one anymore," Emma said. "It's just a big hole in the ground."

"This entire countryside's a hole in the ground," said Millard.

Addison began to recite: " 'They sent forth men to battle, but no such men return. And home, to claim their welcome, come ashes in an urn.' "

"Aeschylus," Millard said appreciatively, and Addison nodded.

"Isn't there some way *around* the fighting?" asked Horace. "Must we really go straight through?"

"Not unless you grow wings," said Miss Hawksbill. "The front lines stretch to the sea, and a hundred miles in the other direction."

"You aren't suggesting we simply *walk across* no-man's-land," Horace said. "We'll be shot to bits the instant we pop our heads over the berm!"

Miss Hawksbill stopped. Poked a finger to his chest. "You will not, if you heed me." She pointed to the trenches below. "At this moment, on this day in history, that pitch of ground there is the deadliest place in the world. From here on you must watch me very closely. Mirror my actions. Tread in my footsteps. Do exactly what I do, and we'll have a safe crossing. Otherwise"—her eyes traversed each of our faces, searing with intensity—"we won't."

We assured her we would, and we meant it.

The path sloped downward and soon our view of the front was obscured again behind trees. We descended into a forested valley of ghostly fog, where we joined a dirt road. It was tough to see more than a hundred feet ahead, but Miss Hawksbill walked with such confidence that we never doubted she knew where she was going.

It occurred to me that, at some point, we must have passed through a membrane and exited Miss Hawksbill's loop into the outer past—unless Miss Hawksbill's loop was miles wide, which it almost certainly wasn't—but the transition from inner loop to outer past had been subtle enough, or had happened while we were distracted enough, that we hadn't noticed. The change wouldn't have affected the ymbryne's timing or her foreknowledge of events; it only meant that after twenty-four hours had passed, Miss Hawksbill's loop would repeat itself while the bygone world beyond its membrane would tick on into the future—or the later past, or whatever you wanted to call it—if you were still there to experience it.

Thinking about it was starting to make my head ache, and I was grateful to be spared further contemplation of it when Miss Hawksbill suddenly veered us off the road and behind a tree.

"Wait," she said, raising her good arm to hold us back.

We waited. After a few seconds she furrowed her brow, puzzled, and pulled a watch out of her dress pocket. She tapped it and held it up to her ear.

"Is something the matter?" Horace asked.

"Damn thing's late," she muttered.

"What is?"

That's when we heard the sound of an approaching engine, and leaning around the tree, I could see the shape of a massive truck gathering in the fog.

"That troop transport," she said. "It's nine seconds late." She shook her head in frustration.

"Is that bad?" Noor said, mostly to me.

"I'm afraid I've let my loop shift a tiny bit." Miss Hawksbill popped open the watch's case and twiddled its dial as the truck rumbled by. "I haven't been as diligent with my resets as I used to be . . . Sometimes my wards let me sleep late . . . but I only have to make this slight mathematical compensation . . . Now see here! *Pothole!*" she sang out, and the truck banged loudly through a hole in the road. She nodded at her watch. "Nine and *one-quarter* seconds."

Millard corralled us in a private huddle. "Not to worry. Everything will happen in exactly the same order she's used to. Just a bit later than before."

The truck disappeared into the fog. Miss Hawksbill snapped shut her watch. "Come on, then."

We had, as usual, little choice but to entrust our lives to a person who in the normal world would be considered deeply unwell.

We continued along the road for a while, then jogged down a footpath. The sound of the guns grew less frequent but louder as we approached the front. The fog began to clear.

"The battle has mostly moved on from here," Miss Hawksbill said, "but it's still quite possible to get your head shot off. *Watch. Me. Closely.*"

We passed remnants of fighting. Empty crates that had contained rations and equipment. A splintered wagon. An exhausted medic sitting with his head on his knees near some bodies covered by a tarp. Through a break in some trees, we saw a line of soldiers laboring to dig a new trench in half-frozen ground. A grim thought occurred to me: that would become their home. And, perhaps, their grave.

Now and then a soldier would pass us trudging in the opposite direction. "Walk as if you belong here, and they won't bother you," Miss Hawksbill told us.

Some gave us curious looks. But she was right: They all had more important things to deal with than an old lady and some kids. All but one soldier paid us no mind. He marched up to Miss Hawksbill with his eyes full of fire. "No women and children!" he shouted, but as he began to turn away, she put a hand on his cheek and swiped a feather under his nose in what was the quickest memory-wipe I had ever seen, and then he stood blinking and befuddled as we continued on our way.

The path flattened and the woods thinned out. We hugged the edge of a clearing where two soldiers were operating a massive artillery gun. As we were passing, one of them shouted, "Fire in the hole!" and we just had time to clap our hands over our ears before the gun went off. It shook the ground and sent such a shock wave through the air that my vision briefly distorted, but hardly a moment later the gunners were joking and helping one another light cigarettes.

Miss Hawksbill glanced at us over her shoulder. Addison looked a bit unsteady, but my other friends, who'd lived with bombs dropping near them for most of their lives, seemed as unfazed as the two gunners.

We walked on.

◆   ◆   ◆

The road began to sink and then to narrow, its sides rising gradually around us. A scarred sign read CATACOMBES. Two more, in English: CROUCH PERPETUALLY and HELMET AT ALL TIMES.

Miss Hawksbill stopped us. "Have you got gas masks in those packs of yours?"

We did not. "Do we really need them?" Emma asked.

"Only if you don't want to go blind," she said. "But I know where we can get some. Come on."

The sides of the road kept rising until they became walls made of sandbags and sawed logs. And then suddenly we were entering the trenches. Their walls continued to narrow until you had to squeeze against the sandbag wall to let someone pass going the other way. The composition of the ground degraded from dirt into mud, a gluey morass that sucked at our feet. Soon we were covered in it from the shins down, and Miss Hawksbill's dress was one-quarter filth.

It amazed me how deftly she navigated here, despite her wildly inappropriate clothes.

The trench was mostly, but not completely, abandoned. We passed soldiers tucked into nooks and stretched out on benches cut into the wall, sleeping, smoking, and reading. A few looked no older than me or my friends. At least one looked younger, his cheeks smooth but his eyes ancient with pain. No wonder most of them didn't look twice at me or Enoch or Horace. We could've *been* them. They stared at Emma, though, and Noor most of all, who was not only young and female but brown-skinned.

Only a skeleton crew of soldiers remained in this section of trench. The big action, Miss Hawksbill told us, was miles away. But that didn't mean the machine gun nests on either side of no-man's-land had been abandoned, or that the mortars had stopped falling, or that it would be much easier to cross here than it was a mile down the line. And I still had no idea how Miss Hawksbill was going to get us across that patch of hell in broad daylight.

I bumped into Noor, who had just collided with Miss Hawksbill's back. "Wait," the ymbryne said, her good hand signaling us to stop. "Nine and one-quarter . . . now duck!"

She waved us down and we all squatted in the mud. A percussive blast shook the ground, and then a fine rain of dirt fell over us. Then she waved us up and we were moving again. We clambered over a mound of smashed wood and a half-collapsed trench wall. I nearly tripped over a man's leg poking out from the debris.

"Do not stop!" Miss Hawksbill said loudly, and Bronwyn, who had hung back to dig the man out, gritted her teeth and forced herself to keep walking. "I know it's all ancient history," she said, "but I can't help it, I have feelings."

"Do not look at anything but me," Miss Hawksbill said. "Unless you want all these bygone horrors to live in your memory forever."

I did not. I did my best to lock my eyes on Noor's backpack

and the back of Miss Hawksbill's head and nothing else. We ducked under a series of wooden bridges built across the top of the trench. Miss Hawksbill stopped our line and disappeared through the door of a small, dark bunker. She rummaged noisily, then came out with a stack of gas masks and handed them out.

"Let's hope these fit," she said dubiously.

It wasn't the first time an ymbryne had handed me a gas mask; I was reminded of the night I first witnessed a loop reset, cowering in Miss Peregrine's garden as rain and bombs fell from the sky and she timed her watch to a children's song.

"Put them on now?" asked Bronwyn.

"I'll tell you," Miss Hawksbill replied.

I slid my arm through the straps and let it dangle from my elbow as I walked. A short time later we came to a row of ladders leaned against the sandbags. There were dozens of them, spaced twenty feet apart down the length of the trench. Miss Hawksbill slowed, bending to inspect each one. "We cross . . . here," she said, stopping decisively by a ladder with a broken rung and a speckling of cigarette butts around it.

Horace peered down the row of ladders. "You're sure?"

She gave him a withering stare. "As sure as any ymbryne can be who's walked the environs of her loop for a hundred years." She nodded behind her. "That crossing gets you shot to ribbons." She nodded the other way. "That one gets you blown to cassoulet. I have seen every potential route attempted, often at the cost of life and limb, so yes, I am sure. Unless you'd rather wait seven hours and twelve minutes for the scout at German watch post seven-B to drink himself into a stupor, though I've had complaints about that route, as it involves swimming through a soup of choleric corpsewater and taking refuge for twelve minutes inside the remains of a horse."

Horace looked at his boots. "This route will be fine."

Addison lifted his paws onto the ladder's first rung. "Could someone boost me, please?"

"Not quite yet," said Miss Hawksbill, reaching down to pat him. "Be ready in four minutes and . . ." She consulted her watch. "Seven seconds. Until then, make yourselves comfortable."

A rattle of gunfire somewhere down the trench made me startle.

"Let's get cozy," Enoch said with a snicker. He unshouldered his pack and dropped it in the mud. "Anyone want to give me a shoulder rub?"

Bronwyn proceeded to, but Enoch flinched away, yelping, "Oww, not so hard!"

Miss Hawksbill was flicking mud blobs from her dress and re-adjusting her sling when she looked up as if she'd just remembered something. "Does anyone need a pep talk before we go up and over? I'm not very good at them, but I'll have a try if it would help . . ."

Distantly, a man was screaming.

"I'd like to hear your pep talk," Bronwyn said.

Miss Hawksbill cleared her throat. " 'Death comes for us all,' " she began in a loud voice.

Bronwyn grimaced. "Never mind, I think I'd prefer some quiet."

"Suit yourselves," Miss Hawksbill said with a shrug.

Enoch straightened one of the stubbed-out cigarettes and held it toward Emma. "Light?"

Emma made a gagging face. "That's disgusting, Enoch."

Miss Hawksbill walked away to memory-wipe a soldier who'd been staring at us a little too long. As she was coming back, Noor hooked me around the arm. "Come talk to her with me," she said.

We intercepted Miss Hawksbill while she was still beyond hearing range of the others. "Could I ask you something?" Noor said in an undertone.

"You have two minutes, three seconds," Miss Hawksbill replied.

Noor leaned in close. "Is there anything else you can tell us about the prophecy? We found out I was one of the seven. And we found out about this meeting place. But . . ."

Miss Hawksbill looked at Noor expectantly.

"When we're all finally together, the seven of us, what do we *do*?"

The ymbryne's eyes narrowed. "You're one of the seven . . . and *you* don't know?"

Noor shook her head. She'd missed out on so much, not having V in her life. "The ymbryne who was supposed to bring me here died before she could tell me anything." She didn't mention the part about resurrecting V's dead body to prime her for clues.

"I'm sorry, dear, I don't have any more information to give you. *Bullet!*" She pointed to a sandbag just above and to the side of Noor's head, and with a soft *piff!* it was struck by a German round. She glanced at her watch, which she'd pinned to her sleeve. "Well. It's about that time, isn't it?"

◆   ◆   ◆

Miss Hawksbill insisted we put on our masks. Before strapping on her own, she stood on the ladder's first rung and said, "The two hundred fifty meters that lie between here and the German line are, in the words of a poet, 'the abode of madness.' So please corral your eyes, pin them to the back of the person in front of you, and do not let them roam." She counted down on her watch. "Nine and one-quarter . . . *right!*"

She began to climb. At the top of the ladder she didn't hesitate, didn't pause to peer over the breach, but hauled herself over the top. "Up and over!" she cried, out of sight now. "Watch that broken rung!"

I cut in front of Noor and climbed the ladder after Miss Hawksbill, though Noor objected with a mask-muffled "Hey!" I figured if Miss Hawksbill's nine-and-a-quarter-second calculations were off a little, it would be better if I took the bullet rather than Noor. Of course, if a bomb landed on us, it wouldn't matter what order our line was in; we'd all be dead.

I could hear my friends yelling to psych themselves up as

I launched myself over the top of the sandbag wall. The sky reappeared, such as it was, a whorl of shifting smoke framed by walls of barbed wire. I picked myself up and ran in a crouch after Miss Hawksbill, who was yelling, *Go, go, go!* All I could see was her back and an inky moonscape of mud, haze, and the blackened stumps of trees. *This used to be a forest,* I thought.

We clustered together in a tight line and followed Miss Hawksbill at a jogging pace, which was as fast as any of us could go. There was no flat ground anywhere. Every step was a calculation, a potential broken ankle. Shredded wood and shrapnel stippled the ground. Noor banged into my pack as I crouched down to follow Miss Hawksbill through a hole in some barbed wire. Gunfire sliced through the air, but if someone was aiming at us, their aim was way off.

We'd made it maybe halfway across when Miss Hawksbill held up her good arm. "Now . . . stop!" she shouted, and waved us down. We all dropped to the ground except Enoch, who had turned to stare at something as a patch of smoke cleared. "My God, I could raise such a fearsome army of dead here—"

I tackled him around the waist and we slammed into the mud.

"Hey! What are you—"

A shell landed not far from us. The blast felt like a kick to the head, and the world turned black for a moment. My ears rang as the sky cleared of falling dirt, and before he could thank me, Bronwyn pulled us to our feet again and we were running after Miss Hawksbill. She took sharp, seemingly random turns, cutting left or right for no obvious reason, until a short time after we'd left a certain path, a volley of bullets cut the air or a mortar shell dropped in a place we'd recently been.

Miss Hawksbill knew every hazard by heart, every minuscule event down to the moment, had committed to memory the timings of a hundred thousand interlocking occurrences. The farther we went, the more I was in awe of her.

My lungs burned, both from running nonstop and from bad air

that had seeped through my mask's imperfect seal, smoke and death and traces of residual gas. Ahead of us I could see a wall of barbed wire, and beyond that more trenches. The German line.

Miss Hawksbill guided us to a collapsed trench wall and we slid down into the trench. She was moving almost casually at this point and seemed no more stressed than if she'd been on a moderately strenuous hike. Meanwhile, my heart was clattering in my chest; now that we were in the enemy's domain, I expected at any moment to get shot at close range by a surprised German soldier. But this section of trenches was even more sparsely populated than the British ones we'd recently left.

We did have to hide once, Miss Hawksbill shoving us into a bunker while two soldiers passed. Then, another fifty paces or so down the line, she stopped at a junction. "This bit is unpleasant but necessary," she hissed over her shoulder, and then she picked up a wooden board from the ground, raised it, and five seconds later brought it down on the head of an unhelmeted soldier as he rounded the corner. He slumped to the ground.

"Good show," Horace said admiringly.

Soon we were out of the trenches and past the front line. Miss Hawksbill took off her gas mask and tossed it aside, and the rest of us followed suit. We came into the crumbling town Miss Hawksbill had pointed out from the hilltop. If it had once been a bustling place, it was now little more than a ruin, bombed and sacked and almost entirely deserted. Except for a few skinny dogs rummaging through the wreckage of buildings, we saw no living creatures at all.

The entrance to Miss Tern's loop was inside the town zoo. We entered through a still-standing iron gate. We made our way to the bear pit, climbed down into it, and went through a wooden door in the side wall. Inside, we felt a rush of time and gravity. We had crossed over.

CHAPTER FIFTEEN

*N*o sooner had the door opened than a bear's face appeared in the crack. There was a sudden rush backward against the wall to escape it—except by Addison and Miss Hawksbill, who the let bear sniff them.

"*Bonjour, Jacques,*" Miss Hawksbill said pleasantly. "*J'ai amené des invités pour rendre visite à ma sœur.*"

The bear stepped back from the door to let us pass.

"Jacques is one of my sister's grimbears," Miss Hawksbill explained. "He guards this loop entrance."

"Pleased to meet you," Addison said. Jacques growled, and Addison looked offended. "No, I'm not making fun. Some of my best friends are bears."

Jacques moved back to let us pass.

"Not everyone thinks as highly of grims as we ymbrynes do," said Miss Hawksbill. "Now come on, step lively. No more bombs to watch out for here. You're all safe in this loop."

We climbed out of the bear pit, to the great surprise of some workers peering down from the viewing platform above. The grimbear roared behind us, and Miss Hawksbill shouted goodbye and waved to him, and then we made our way out of the zoo.

Here, the sun was out, the sky cloudless and smokeless. I couldn't hear any guns or explosions, a welcome reprieve for my overtaxed nerves. It was 1916 in Miss Tern's loop, and while the war was close, this town had not yet been overrun. The front lines weren't far away, though, and the townspeople must have known that the tide could turn against them at any time.

As we walked out of the zoo and into the town, Addison muttered unhappily about the cages, though most were empty. "Most brutal thing in the world, zoos," he said. "How would humans like it if we displayed them in cages?"

"Bentham had a plan for a human zoo," said Millard. "Normals collected from round the world, penned up in habitats that mimicked the places they'd lived. I read about it in his book."

"He wrote a book?" I said.

"Part of one. I found an unfinished copy in his office. *Myron Bentham's Menagerie of Unextraordinary Children*. Part museum catalogue, part encyclopedia, part peculiar history."

We walked through the town's peaceful streets, talking about Bentham's museum and the morality of zoos both human and animal. I was grateful for any conversation that distracted my mind from the horrors we'd just hiked through. My nerves were still jumping from the ceaseless crash of bombs and guns, my chest still clenched from it, and with every break in our chatter my mind filled with scenes from no-man's-land. So we kept our mouths moving along with our feet.

We passed a crowd in the town square that had gathered to watch a strangely somber parade of elephants. There was no calliope music to accompany them, no clowns or acrobats, just a glum pair of trainers to prod them along.

"They're being evacuated to England," Miss Hawksbill told us. "In a few weeks a lot of these townsfolk will wish they'd joined them."

We walked on toward the outskirts of town, where Miss Hawksbill pointed out the roof of her sister's house, peeking up from the trees at the top of a hill. To reach it we climbed a winding forested lane. Animal sculptures made of iron and wood were half hidden in the bushes, and in deeper shadows I thought I could see creatures scurrying to follow us. Peculiar ones, no doubt.

"I can't believe we made it," said Bronwyn. "For a while there I wondered if we would."

"Bronwyn, you'll jinx us!" Emma scolded her.

"Seriously," Noor said. "Save it until we actually meet them."

"If this gets written up in the *Muckraker*, we're going to look like heroes," Enoch said. "Do you think they'll print pictures of us? Maybe that vixen Francesca will finally go on a date with me."

"I'll be sure and tell Farish Obwelo how Jacob saved your life on the battlefield," said Emma. "Francesca will love that."

"Oh, shut up. He did not."

"I can't believe you're talking about publicity," said Horace. "There won't be even *be* a *Muckraker*, much less any vixens to impress, if Noor can't manage to—" He caught himself and awkwardly changed tack. "Look at that fascinating sculpture, is it a crane?"

Noor kicked a stone with her boot. "Thanks, Horace, a little extra pressure is just what I needed."

"For what it's worth, we all believe in you."

"That makes one of us."

"Come now, don't be defeatist," said Miss Hawksbill.

Noor sighed. "It might be easier to believe in myself if I had any idea what was expected of me."

"I daresay you'll find out soon enough. Now, when you meet Miss Tern, please play along; to her it's still 1916, and she knows nothing of Caul's death or resurrection, or that her loop will collapse in a week. I'd ask you to please not inform her. She tends to get very upset." She saw something ahead of us, then brightened and quickened her pace. *"Ah, ah, ma chérie!"*

A young woman ran down the driveway toward us, her pretty face lit by a wide smile.

"Maud! Tu m'as manqué!"

She seemed to be in her late twenties and wore a fashionable army-green coat with a floppy beret. Miss Tern's smile faltered as she took in the sight of her sister, who must have looked much older than she remembered, but Miss Hawksbill pulled her into a double-cheek kiss and a hug before she could say anything.

Enoch gaped. "That's the old crone's *sister*? But she's so—"

"Young?" Noor said.

"This is a collapsed loop, remember," said Millard. "Miss Hawksbill probably looked equally young when this loop was new."

"Dead a week hence," Enoch said with a sigh. "What a waste of beauty."

"She never would have gone for you anyway," Bronwyn said. "Not to mention she's an ymbryne, for bird's sake."

"Ymbrynes need love, too. Just because they're not allowed to marry doesn't mean—"

Emma stopped him with a dig of her elbow. "Don't be revolting."

"There's nothing revolting about love, you Victorian prudes."

Miss Tern's smile had vanished, and she was looking her sister up and down while speaking animatedly in French.

"She wants to know what happened to Miss Hawksbill's arm," Millard whispered. *"And why she looks so old."*

"I'm testing a new disguise from the skin tailor," said Miss Hawksbill, replying in English for our benefit while giving us a subtle wink. "And my grim rolled over on me in his sleep." She patted her sister's arm, then drew her in for another hug. "I'll tell you about it later."

The ymbrynes walked toward us arm in arm.

"My, such a lot of visitors today," Miss Tern remarked, which got my attention. "To what do I owe the pleasure?"

"They are on a grand tour of the Continental loops," Miss Hawksbill answered for us, "and heard about your wonderful menagerie."

"It's a must-see," Miss Tern said proudly. "Did you know we were partially fictionalized in one of the more recent *Tales of the Peculiar*?"

"That's why we're here," said Millard, and then he bowed and introduced himself. "We had to see this famous place for ourselves."

" 'The Tale of Pensevus,' " Noor said, to which Miss Tern nodded. "Is Penny here now?"

Her brow arched. "You know him?"

"He was mine, for a while, when I was young."

She looked impressed. "Well, you must be someone very special. I'm sure he'd love to see you again. He's in the house with a girl named Sophie, who rarely lets him out of her grip."

There was a rustle from the bushes, and a flock of chickens darted across our path. "No, thank you!" Millard yelped, scurrying behind Bronwyn. "Are those the exploding type?"

"I see you're familiar with peculiar zoology," said Miss Tern.

Addison trotted to the front. "Armageddon chickens only lay eggs early in the morning," he said, "and only in their coops." Addison rose up on hind legs and extended a paw. "Addison MacHenry, seventh pup of the seventh pup in an illustrious line of hunting dogs."

Miss Tern was clearly delighted. "You're one of Miss Wren's." She shook his paw. "Your mistress is a close friend of mine. I owe her a visit. I hope you'll feel at home here, though I'm sure my menagerie pales in comparison to that of the great Miss Wren."

Addison tried to smile, but looked pained. "Oh, I don't know about that." His home, like ours, was lost, along with many of his friends. "Thank you, I'll pass along your regards."

"You said something about visitors?" Noor said, flashing Miss Hawksbill an urgent look.

"Er, yes," said Miss Hawksbill, taking her cue, "we'd be curious to meet them, and perhaps freshen up from our journey across the line—"

"Yes, it's a most unpleasant trip on foot," said Miss Tern. "Like passing through the gears of a great meat grinder . . ." She shuddered in a way that seemed distinctly birdlike, then looked perplexed. "My visitors tell me they arrived a few days ago, but strangely I don't remember it. They were here when I awoke this morning." She shrugged. *Peculiar things happen all the time in loops.*

"Her memory resets every day along with the loop," Millard whispered to Noor and me.

"They've sequestered themselves in the upstairs parlor," Miss Tern continued. "They are having some sort of meeting, at which I am evidently not welcome." She briefly frowned, bothered but trying not to show it. "But you can *try* to meet them."

Miss Hawksbill put a hand on her sister's back. "Sister, if you'd show us the way."

"*D'accord,*" she said flatly, and I could see in her pinched expression the weight of the strangenesses that were piling up: her unfriendly visitors; her sister's inexplicable aging; us. But she walked on and asked no more questions, at least not of my friends and me, speaking quietly with Miss Hawksbill in French as we continued up the drive.

There was so much waiting for us, it was hard not to break into a run. Noor hummed to herself, tension rounding her shoulders and practically crackling the air. And then we came around a bend and the house revealed itself. It was a grand old chateau that, architecturally speaking, had been given the works: triple-peaked roof, beautiful domed entryway, fancy woodwork, a colonnade framing the ground floor. But much of it was hidden beneath a drape of leaves and vines, which made the house look like it was being eaten by the forest.

"Pardon our appearance," Miss Tern said. "It's meant to camouflage the house from bomb-dropping airplanes. I didn't get a chance to remove it before making the loop, so now we're stuck with it."

"If Miss P had gotten some camouflage, maybe we wouldn't have had to get soaked standing outdoors every night at our loop reset," Enoch said sourly.

"Wouldn't have been worth the aesthetic trade-off," Horace remarked, wrinkling his nose at the scene before us. "Our house was much too beautiful."

A pair of horses grazing on the front lawn watched with muted interest as we walked past them to the porch. When they were behind us I thought I heard one of them whisper, and the other gave a nickering laugh in reply.

We followed a trail of grimy hoofprints inside the house. "The animals live downstairs; I live upstairs," Miss Tern explained. We scooted around a donkey in the foyer and came into a palatial living room that had been turned into a stable. Goats with long horns munched garbage beneath grime-dimmed windows. An intricate parquet floor was mostly hidden under a tide of dirt and straw. Velvet curtains had been torn down and spun into nests for a flock of honking, long-necked birds. A winged monkey leapt onto a grand chandelier, sending it swinging as he howled at us, but after Miss Tern chastised him he dropped to the floor again, tucked his wings away, and rejoined two monkey companions who were having tea around a little table. I understood now why Miss Wren's loop had mostly been outdoors, just simple structures on a wide hilltop.

"Everyone's a bit on edge today," Miss Tern apologized. "They're not accustomed to having so many strangers about."

"Where are they?" Noor said sharply, her eyes scanning the room.

"In the drawing room, through that door there . . ." She pointed to a tall door across the room. "I don't suppose you'd like a tour of the house first, or something to drink—"

Only Millard had patience and manners enough to politely decline; the rest of us were already walking toward the door, desperate to finally meet the other prophesied kids.

Miss Tern tried to follow, but Miss Hawksbill held her back. "Let's sit and talk awhile," she pleaded, and led her outside.

The tall door opened onto a smaller room, considerably cleaner and free of animals. Free of people altogether, at first glance, with a great curving staircase leading up to a balcony landing, where daylight streamed down through a glass ceiling.

"Hello?" I called out. "We're looking for—"

Suddenly everything went black, the light stolen from the room so fast that the words stalled in my mouth.

"What's happened?" Horace shouted.

"Someone turned out the damned—" Enoch started to say, then in a clatter I heard him trip and fall.

"We come in peace!" Bronwyn called.

Emma sparked her hand-flames, which lit her face, etched with fear. Then a brighter light drew my eyes up to the balcony. The source was a woman who appeared not just to be illuminated by fire, but *made* of it, and the sight of her made several of us gasp. She was toweringly tall, wore the plate armor of a medieval knight, and in her hands she wielded a huge broadsword, also flaming. We took a collective step backward, but none of us turned and ran.

"Who are you?" the woman said in a resounding voice. "Why have you come?"

"We're the wards of Alma Peregrine," shouted Emma, attempting to match the woman's volume.

"We're accompanying one of the seven," said Horace, his voice loud but wavering. "You know, from the prophecy of the—"

The woman's flames burned brighter as her voice rang out. "Which of you is the light-eater?"

The light-eater. They already knew.

Instinctively my hand shot out to stop Noor, but she shook off my grasp. "I am!" she said, taking a step forward. "Are you one of the seven?"

"You were meant to come with only an ymbryne. Where is Velya?"

At the mention of V's name, Noor stiffened, but quickly recovered. "She died."

"Then how did you find this place?"

"V—Velya gave me a clue, and we followed it here."

"Without the ymbryne to vouch for your name, you must prove yourself. Come forward and meet me, if you truly are one of the seven."

The fire-woman moved to the staircase and started down it. I grabbed one of Noor's elbows and Bronwyn hooked the other.

"It could be a trap," I said through my teeth.

"Let her go," said Horace. "I think this is what needs to happen."

We did, reluctantly. Noor met the fire-woman at the bottom of the stairs. For a moment they only stood, tensed and facing each other, and then the woman heaved the sword above her head—it flamed brighter as she raised it, throwing light to the corners of the room.

"STOP!" I screamed, but it was too late; the sword was already coming down. Noor brought up her hands and caught the blade between them, and in one smooth motion she stole the sword from the woman's hands, then collapsed it into a ball of light between her palms and shoved it into her mouth.

The woman stumbled, righted herself, and let her arms fall to her sides. "Very good," she said, smiling. "Very good indeed."

Noor swallowed. Her throat glowed as the sword's flame traveled toward her stomach. "How did you know I was a light-eater?"

"Because," said a young man's voice from the dark, "we all are."

He appeared in a pool of light below the staircase—light that appeared to be emanating from inside his head—then drew a breath and blew out a roomful of daylight. In a few seconds his head returned to a normal shade and the space around us was transformed from night-black to midday, rays of sunshine streaking down through high windows.

The young man looked about eighteen. He had smooth dark skin and was dressed immaculately in a pinstriped suit, bowler hat, and thin leather gloves, which he was pulling onto his hands as he strode toward us. "My name is Julius," he said, "and that's Sebbie."

I assumed he meant the fire-woman, but she was shrinking before our eyes, dimming out and collapsing into a ball of scintillating orange light. It flew up the stairs and into the hands of a small, pale girl on the balcony, her arm extended like an outfielder catching a fly ball. It smacked into her palm, and then she smashed it flat with her other hand, stretched it into a rope, slurped it quick into her mouth like spaghetti, and let out a little belch.

"Hello," she boomed, and I was shocked to hear the fire-woman's giant voice coming from a tiny girl of no more than ten. "It's about time you showed up."

＊　　＊　　＊

"Sorry about the unfriendly welcome," said the girl, Sebbie, as she descended the stairs. "Had to make sure you were really one of us." She wore a white flapper dress and a dour expression, spoke with an Eastern European accent, and seemed to hate bright light. Stepping into a pool of sun by a window, she swiped the light away, leaving her face in a dim shadow she would take with her everywhere.

Julius joined us at the base of the stairs, where we had all gathered. "We were expecting one girl and one ymbryne. Not a party."

"It's a long story," said Noor.

"We've got time." Julius crossed his arms. "Are you people hungry?"

"We really *don't* have time," said Millard. "Where are the others?"

Sebbie shrugged. "This is all of us, so far. Our ymbrynes dropped us off here a couple of days ago."

Emma looked confused. "Dropped you off—and went away?"

"They worried their presence here might attract too much attention," Julius explained. "We don't require babysitting."

"There was another boy," Sebbie said. "But he got bored of waiting around and left."

Noor's eyes bugged. "What do you mean, left?"

"We need *seven* to shut the door," Horace fretted.

Julius waved a hand. "He'll be back, I imagine."

Noor looked like she was ready to pull out her hair.

"What about the other three?" I said. "Where are they?"

"Sophie says they're on their way," Sebbie said.

"You people seem very on edge," Julius said. "I really think you should come upstairs with us and eat something."

I began to wonder whether they had any idea why they'd been called here.

"How much do you know about the prophecy?" Noor asked them.

"That there is one, and that's why we're here," Julius replied.

"Our ymbrynes didn't tell us much." Sebbie batted away a ray of light that had strayed across her face. "Do you know what all this is about?"

They'd been spared the details, their ymbrynes apparently afraid of scaring them. Of course, until recently, the prophecy had been unknown to most, and taken seriously by very few.

"Have you never heard of Caul?" Emma asked.

They had, of course. "Why? Does this concern him?" Julius asked.

"I thought he was dead," Sebbie said.

They were starting to look worried.

We gave them the short version of the bad news. Caul had been trapped in the collapsed Library of Souls, fulfilling a major part of the prophecy. Had been recently resurrected, and was now more powerful than ever.

"And he has new hollowgast," I said.

"And he's coming for our loop of last refuge, Devil's Acre," Horace added. "If he gets control of it, and the Panloopticon, no loop anywhere is safe, not even the most remote ones."

Julius nodded pensively. "So it's down to us, you're saying." He still didn't sound *very* concerned.

"It very well might be," said Millard. "Other than holding him off and hoping he goes away, you seven are the best hope we've got."

"Except it's just three of us," Noor said.

"The others are coming," Sebbie insisted. "As for the boy who went walkabout, Sophie and Pensevus said he couldn't have gone far. They went out to retrieve him a few hours ago."

"He had the personality of a warthog anyway," Julius said.

Noor was getting jumpy, picking at her hands. "Okay, we can't control that right now, so whatever," she said. "But do any of you even know what we're supposed to *do*?"

Julius cocked his head at her. "Do?"

For a moment she looked like she might scream. "*How* do we fight Caul? *How* do we shut the door? None of you have any idea?"

"Well, the answer seems a little more clear than it did an hour ago," Millard said.

"It does?" she said, spinning to face him.

"Mm-hmm." He turned to Julius and Sebbie. "The one who came before you—what did he do?"

Julius said, "He was a light-eater, like us."

"Ah!" Millard clapped his hands. "Then I'd wager all seven of you are. So, it's no stretch to assume that 'shutting the door' has something to do with eating light."

Noor's eyes went wide and she nodded slowly.

"Maybe Caul's made of light now," Emma hypothesized. "And you just need to, you know . . ."

"Eat him?" said Enoch.

Bronwyn winced. "Gross."

"But what about 'the door?' " I asked.

"Could be a metaphor," said Horace. "Prophecy is fifty-one percent poetry, forty-nine percent facts."

"I'm fifty-one percent starving," said Julius. "Pensevus will know what we need to do. When he comes back, we'll ask him. Now, if you don't mind, Miss Tern had just set out a lunch for us before you arrived."

CHAPTER SIXTEEN

*A*s we followed the light-eaters upstairs, my mood darkened. I was certain now that bringing down Caul would require more from the seven than simply being together in the same room and holding hands. I'd been part of the peculiar world long enough to understand that things were rarely that easy. It was likely we would have to take all seven with us back to the Acre, and at some point we were going to have to confront our enemy in person, and it would be ugly. And hard. And bloody.

I was anxious to get on with doing the hard things, not least of which would be getting out of Miss Tern's loop again. But since it looked like we had no choice but to wait for the other four to arrive, I didn't mind having some downtime. My nerves were frayed from the journey, my head was heavy with exhaustion, and I realized, as the tantalizing smell of food hit my nose, that I was ravenously hungry.

Sebbie and Julius showed us to a clean, animal-free sitting room upstairs where a banquet table had been laid with a buffet. We let our heavy packs and coats and Bronwyn's steamer trunk fall to the floor, then attacked the buffet like wolves.

We ate and talked. Mostly it was Noor and the two other light-eaters who did the talking. Between mouthfuls of ratatouille mopped up with fresh bread, Noor leaned across the table and peppered Julius and Sebbie with questions. What had their lives been like? When had they manifested their abilities? When had their ymbrynes told them about the prophecy? Were they hunted and chased, like she had been?

They had been delivered to Miss Tern's loop the previous day by their ymbrynes, they said, via slower but less dangerous routes than the one we'd taken. I was left to assume that they'd been able to reach Miss Tern's loop so quickly because they had traveled here accompanied by their ymbrynes, rather than alone, as we'd been forced to do. Millard confirmed this with a whisper in my ear: there are some temporal shortcuts available to ymbrynes and those who journey with them.

Their names were Julius Purcell and Sebbie Mayfield. Both were light-eaters, although the precise nature of their abilities varied slightly. "I can project my voice when I want to," Sebbie said, then, a bit more quietly, "and my light."

Julius's light-eating power was fearsome: He could darken huge spaces in a flash, but couldn't hold the light he'd gathered inside himself as long as Sebbie or Noor were able to. He thought his parents were from Ghana, but he'd been adopted by an ymbryne at a young age and had moved around a lot, shuffled from loop to loop for most of his life. Most recently he'd lived in China. "The loops there are wonderful, and some are quite ancient," he enthused. "You know they never had a dark age? While all of Europe was illiterate for five hundred years—even kings!—they were creating the most amazing works of art and literature." As to his age, he wasn't sure, exactly. He guessed he was about fifty-six, though he'd probably lost track of some birthdays along the way. What was clear, though, was that for a peculiar, and especially for one of the seven, he'd led a relatively sheltered existence.

"That's a lovely suit," Horace said. "Where did you get it?"

Julius smiled appreciatively. "I had it made by a tailor in Bamako. Better than can be had on Savile Row, if you ask me."

"Absolutely no doubt." Horace nodded eagerly, then looked down, embarrassed. "You can't tell from what I'm wearing now, but I'm also a devotee of sartorial, er—"

"Horace is the best-dressed peculiar I know," I said.

"Excepting yourself, I'm sure," Horace said to Julius, but

Julius had turned to talk with Millard, who was asking him some overly technical question about loop geography.

The conversation turned to Sebbie. She told us she'd spent many years hiding in caves—hiding from the daylight she hated and from villagers who, because she only ventured out at night, had decided she was a vampire. More than one had tried to hammer a wooden stake through her heart. Their persecution only drove her deeper into the caves, where she had subsisted on a diet of bats, moss, and gifts of food left near the cave entrance by the rare benevolent villager.

She stopped eating those, however, "when one of 'em tried to poison me. That's when I started developing my light-casting talent. I found I could scare people away with a fiery phantasm and by projecting my voice." Eventually, word of the light-bending cave girl got around to an ymbryne, Miss Ptarmigan, who found her and took her in. "She was a good woman, gave me a home in her loop on the isle of St. Helena."

"It's a lucky thing Miss Ptarmigan found you before a wight did," said Emma. "They hunted Noor for years."

"Oh no." Julius gave her a pitying look. "Did they?"

Noor talked about it but didn't go into much detail, because the details pained her: She mentioned the street attack that put V in the hospital and made her realize she couldn't protect Noor anymore; the wights who, years later, began following her after she manifested her power at school, then pursued her with helicopters and SWAT-style troops. She stopped short of describing the battle at Gravehill or Murnau's treachery or V's murder. She was eager to turn the questions back on our new friends.

"What about you?" she asked Julius. "Did the wights ever find you?"

He shook his head. "There were some close calls, but my ymbryne always kept us two steps ahead of them."

I asked them if they'd ever encountered a hollowgast. Both said no.

"I hear they're fearsome," Julius said blithely, his cheek full of bread.

Miss Evelyn
Ptarmigan

"Are they ever," Bronwyn replied.

"You've seen one?" Sebbie asked, eyes widening. "Or been near one, anyway?"

"Seen them, fought them, killed them . . . you name it," Enoch said. "We could tell you stories upon stories."

"My goodness," said Julius, dabbing his mouth with a napkin. "What lives you've led."

Sebbie shrugged. "I guess some ymbrynes are better at keeping their wards safe than others."

"That's not fair," Bronwyn said. "We had the best ymbryne in peculiardom!"

"I think some peculiars are just lucky," Horace said tartly.

Sebbie spread her hands. "If you say so."

"Maybe that's why they're so calm," Emma said in my ear. *"They've never even been close to a hollow!"*

"They're totally unprepared," I agreed, forming a huddle with her and Enoch.

Enoch chuckled. "Think of that. Their ymbrynes kept them *too* safe."

"I'm not hungry anymore," Bronwyn said, pushing back from the table, though it was clear she was just offended.

The meal broke up; we'd had our fill, and the conversation was starting to become contentious. I cornered Julius and asked him again when Sophie and Pensevus were coming back with the others. I felt a stab of worry every time I remembered that four of the seven were still unaccounted for. He assured me once more that they would all be here soon, but his patience with me was fraying. That and his casualness made me think they didn't fully realize what was at stake, which only made me worry more.

Julius suggested the light-eaters hold a friendly demonstration of their abilities, and that they do it outside, where there were no walls to limit them. I wasn't sure if he was more interested in showing off or in sizing up Noor; either way, she was game. With nothing better to do but wait and worry, the rest of us tagged along, too, watching from the front yard as the three light-eaters crested the hill beside Miss Tern's house.

I already knew what Noor could do, and it was a pleasure to watch her at work. She got a running start and dashed across the hilltop with her arms spread wide, gathering all the light around them, shaping it into a pulsing ball between her hands, then swallowing it in three giant gulps. There was a smattering of polite applause.

As impressive as Noor was, she was a beginner compared to Julius. He proceeded to tear vast strips of light out of the air from the ground all the way up to the clouds, carving blackest midnight from a sunny midday. I was reluctant to applaud a show-off, but he was one of the most powerful peculiars I'd ever met, and I couldn't help myself. I shouted and cheered with my friends and Miss Tern's animals, who had gathered to watch nearby, whinnying and honking and stamping their hooves.

Then it was Sebbie's turn. She began by demonstrating how she could steal light from a distance, which even Julius could not do. We watched her take all the light from inside Miss Tern's house and lift it into the air, the windows going dark while the space above the roof glowed brightly—I imagined all the ways that could be useful in a battle—and then she turned it into a glowing, winged dragon. It flapped into the black-at-noon sky, then did a loop-the-loop and dissipated into scintillating dust, lighting the rooms in Miss Tern's house again as it settled across the roof. There was more applause, and the light-eaters took a bow.

Then we heard someone shouting from behind us, and turned to see two people running up the driveway. One was a woman I didn't recognize. She was pulling a dazed-looking young girl along by the hand. The girl wore tall boots and a stained party dress, and she was holding a large, battered doll under one arm. I could tell the woman was an ymbryne just from the sight of her: her modest dress; her eyes intense as burning coals; and most of all, her hair, which fell down her shoulders all the way to her knees, like a pair of wings at rest.

Everyone converged on the lawn to intercept them: me and my friends, Miss Tern and Miss Hawksbill, Noor and the light-eaters. The animals honked and whinnied, watching the commotion from a distance.

"Miss! You're back!" Julius cried, running to the long-haired woman. She hugged him quickly. His face fell. "But where are the others?"

"My name is Miss Petrel," said the woman, addressing the group. "I'm Julius's ymbryne." She was flighty and perturbed. "We went to retrieve Hadi Akhtar, the light-eater who left here last night. He thought he could navigate on his own, but he didn't know that the road leading out of town had been mined. He tripped one, and . . ." She pulled a burned sock from her pocket and held it up.

"Oh my God," Emma gasped. "He's *dead*?"

Miss Petrel nodded.

"What about the others?" I said. Not that it mattered—if one was gone there could never be seven.

The little girl had been holding her doll up to her ear, as if it was whispering to her. Now she lowered it and said, "Penny says we can tell you. My name is Sophie, by the way. I'm the one who made the secret calls to your ymbrynes. Six ymbrynes. All but Miss Greenshank." She looked at Noor and added, "Velya Greenshank."

We hadn't heard V's ymbryne name before now. Noor stiffened, then got a faraway look.

"But only four still had living wards," Sophie continued.

"They told us their wards had been dead for years," said Miss Petrel. "One aged forward. A second was killed by wights. The third was hit by a bus in Buenos Aires in 1978. All very sad."

I was reeling. Noor was frozen stiff, like she couldn't understand what was being said, or couldn't grapple with it.

"But you said the others would come," Sebbie insisted. "You *said*."

"We only learned of their loss upon arriving here," said Miss Petrel. "And we wanted all of you present before we broke the news," she said, acknowledging Noor with a nod. "All of you who were left, that is."

And then Noor, who had been quietly simmering, blew up. "This is insane! We risked our lives to get here, and there's only three of us? Jesus Christ, that's not even half! So what's the point? What's the point of any of this? We've already lost!"

"You misunderstood," Sophie said calmly. "You know the prophecy?"

"Yeah, yeah. Seven will shut the door," Noor said angrily.

"Seven *may* shut the door." The doll was whispering to Sophie again. "That is, any of you are enough to fulfill the prophecy all on your own. You don't need seven. Only one."

"The other six," said Miss Petrel, "are fail-safes."

Julius and Sebbie looked at each other, revelation dawning. "Like, backups?" said Sebbie.

Miss Petrel snapped her fingers. "Precisely."

Sebbie rubbed the back of her head like she was kneading some intractable idea out of it. "So, you mean . . . we don't actually have to have . . ."

"Why didn't someone just *tell* us this?" Noor exploded again. "Why'd we have to come all the way across hell on earth just to find this out?!"

"Three reasons." Miss Petrel held up a hand with three fingers raised. "The information was too sensitive. It had to be told in person."

"That's true; we intercepted all your calls," Millard said. "It's a good thing you didn't say more over the phone."

"Two." Miss Petrel ticked down one finger. "We couldn't risk anyone not coming because they were 'only a fail-safe.' Each of you is needed."

"Why?" Julius said. "You've seen what I can do; I don't need help from anyone."

"Because." Miss Petrel gave Julius a sharp look and ticked down another finger. "Your powers are stronger together."

Miss Gwendoline Petrel

"Six is a lot of fail-safes," Millard said doubtfully. "You'd only need so many if the objective was unlikely to be accomplished on the first, second, or third try."

"Thank you, invisible boy, for that confidence-inspiring observation," said Julius. "But I know my own capacity, and it's second to none."

"And the unlikely objective is?" said Noor.

"To 'shut the door' and save peculiardom. No less than that."

"Yes, but HOW?" Noor said, swiping the air in frustration. Without meaning to she'd torn away a strip of light from in front of her face and had to step through it so we could see her again. "Does *anyone* know what that *actually means*?"

Miss Petrel paused, blinking. "There's another bit of prophecy that explains in more detail, but I'm trying to recall the exact wording. Pensevus, can you remember?"

Sophie held the doll up to her ear. I heard the clack of Pensevus's wooden jaws opening and closing while Sophie nodded. The light leaked slowly from Noor's hands back into the black scar she'd made. Horace held his breath in anticipation, hands clutched against his breastbone.

Sophie looked up. "Penny says you've got to eat Caul's soul."

Julius tightened his gloves and looked down, maybe hiding that he was finally starting to sweat a little. "And how are we supposed do *that*?"

Sebbie tossed up her hands, swiped a wide patch of light from the air above our heads, and slapped it into her mouth. "*Wike bis!*" she said through a full mouth, then swallowed and repeated, "Like this!"

"Yeah . . . if Caul's made of light," Noor said skeptically. "I thought he was a giant tree made of rotting meat, or something. That's what that kid who saw him said."

"Well," said Julius, like he was explaining something to a child, "then his *soul* must be made of light."

Sebbie glared at Noor. "Why would you doubt the word of an ymbryne?"

"You mean the whisperings of a doll?" said Enoch.

"He's more than just a doll," Sophie said, scowling. "Which Noor Pradesh knows very well for herself."

"Okay, we're getting way off track here," I said. "Let's just figure out how we're getting back and then get the hell going. We can argue about how to eat Caul's soul on the way."

Everyone nodded. Finally, something we could all agree on.

"Yes, there isn't time to waste," said Miss Petrel. "Caul's forces have already begun massing outside the gates of your loop in London."

Bronwyn clapped her hands over her mouth. "They have?" she said through her fingers.

"Have you talked to the ymbrynes there?" Millard asked. "Are they all right?"

We'd been gone a half day already. Anything might've happened in that time.

"Attempts have been made to breach their defenses," Miss Petrel said, "but so far they've not been successful. Their shield is strong—but only as strong as the ymbrynes who made it. If any of them are hurt, or lose consciousness, it may falter."

"You mean they can't even *sleep*?" said Julius.

"No," Miss Petrel replied. "But fortunately, we don't often need to."

Miss Hawksbill and Miss Tern came walking up. They'd been standing nearby and had heard the whole exchange.

"We stand ready to help in any way we can," said Miss Hawksbill.

"Thank you," said Miss Petrel. "Right now we need to prepare these children for their journey back to London."

*   *   *

We went back inside the house to fetch our backpacks and coats, the ymbrynes forming a plan as we walked. Miss Hawksbill suggested it was better not to risk returning to London the same way we'd come, through the front lines and no-man's-land to her loop, and the others agreed. I think if it had just been my friends and me, she might not have had the same doubts, but I worried Julius and Sebbie wouldn't survive that battlefield crossing.

Miss Tern, though tense and looking increasingly confused, suggested a safer option. It involved exiting her loop through a small tear in the membrane only she knew about. Leaving via this particular tear would lead us not into the wider world of November 1916, but back into the present—"Your present," she said, frowning. "Whenever that is."

It seemed to be dawning on her that her loop had collapsed; that she was trapped here, a looped remnant of the past, though her sister was not.

"Outside the loop you'll find a modern train station," Miss Hawksbill said, "and from there the Eurostar will whisk you back to London in two comfortable hours."

"The membrane isn't terribly far," said Miss Tern, "but you don't want to stray off track. I'll ready my fastest horses, and my sister and I will guide you from the sky."

Miss Hawksbill gave her a look of both pity and gratitude, and then they hugged, kissed each other on both cheeks, and Miss Tern leapt into the air. In a burst of wings she assumed her avian form: a great white seabird with a black stripe that resembled the beret she wore, which had tumbled to the floor with the rest of her clothes. She let out a laughing cry and flew through an open window.

"I do miss her spark," Miss Hawksbill said wistfully.

"At least you get to see her sometimes," I said.

"Aye. That's been nice. But I'm thinking of closing my loop here, packing up my heads and coming to join your ymbrynes in London. Now that the seven have come together, or what's left of you, this loop has more than served its purpose."

"But if you let your loop collapse, won't it be a lot harder to see your sister again?"

"I've hung onto this broken shard of her for too many years. It's time I let her go."

She seemed to realize that she was not just talking to me but to all of us, and she stiffened and changed the subject. "Let's not let this food go to waste." She stepped to the long table and began tossing uneaten baguettes to each of us. "Tuck these into your packs. You might get hungry on the train, and the food on board is terribly overpriced."

Miss Hawksbill made me achingly sad. Partly because her pain was so visible: It was evident in the slouch of her shoulders, the grooved lines around her eyes. But mostly because I understood. How many people would spend their lives among shades and ghosts, were they able? Every parent who'd lost a child, every lover who'd lost a mate: If they had the choice, wouldn't most do the same? We're all riddled with holes, and there were days when I would've done anything to patch mine, if just for a while. I was glad I didn't have a choice. Gladder still that I didn't have the powers of an ymbryne. The temptation to misuse them would've been overwhelming.

We gathered up our things, loading, at Miss Petrel's behest, still more of the leftover food from the table into our bags. Bronwyn hefted the steamer trunk and hitched it to her back with rope. Then we all went downstairs again to wait for Miss Tern. The big straw-floored room was almost empty now, the animals outside marveling at the stripes of dark Julius had left in the sky, which were slowly filling in again. While the others talked I tried to prepare myself for what was coming. It had been months since I'd ridden a horse, and I wasn't the best at it. *As long as we aren't riding at a full gallop*, I thought, *I'll be okay.*

I'll be okay was the last thing that crossed my mind when the screams began, sharp and panicked and coming from outside. We all ran to the soot-grimed window. A plume of fire was consuming a small outbuilding, and the animals were scattering in all directions. Miss Hawksbill and Miss Petrel turned and sprinted toward the door, but before they got there it burst inward, flying off its hinges and knocking Miss Hawksbill to the floor. Miss Petrel froze, then took a step backward.

I felt a terrible clench in my gut. I knew what was coming through the door before I saw it with my eyes: a hollowgast, down on all fours and growling like a mad dog, its eyes dripping black and teeth dripping blood. There was a collar around its neck with a leash attached. A man in a German soldier's uniform was holding the lead, and he trailed the hollow into the room.

His eyes were blank.

The hollow saw me and yanked the wight's arm straight.

"Down, boy!" the wight shouted, jerking the leash, and the hollow crouched into a coil of trembling muscle.

His accent was British, not German.

"*Wight*," Emma hissed.

"Can you see his hollow?" I asked.

She gave a quick, terrified nod. My heart dropped, though I'd known the answer already: This was one of the new hollows. The kind I couldn't control, and couldn't feel except in close proximity.

"Is there a back way out of the house?" Bronwyn hissed.

As if on cue, a gunshot rang out behind us. We spun to see another man in German army grays filling the rear doorway, the one that led to the staircase. In one hand he carried a modern-looking pistol with a gunsight, and in the other he balanced a sort of rifle, except there was a flame curling up from the end of the barrel, and it was attached via tubes to a backpack the man wore.

Not a rifle. A *flamethrower*.

"Hey!" he shouted, then shot a spray of fire over our heads. We ducked, heat crisping the backs of our necks. Sebbie knocked off Julius's hat, which had caught fire, and he dropped to his knees and beat it out against the floor.

"Turn out the lights and he'll fry you like a chicken," warned the man holding the leash.

"I—I won't," Julius stammered.

Miss Hawksbill groaned on the floor.

"What do you want from us?" Miss Petrel said, defiant.

"Merely to die," the man said. "We're not here to negotiate, and there's no use in making speeches." He drew a pistol from his belt. "Let's get this over with, Bastian. Caul's going to make us immortal for this . . ."

My mind was racing, but I could see no way out. Every exit was blocked.

"Don't do this," Emma said, trying to sound calm and controlled, trying to buy time. "We can work something out—"

Uncoiling itself, the hollow stood up to its full height.

The man wasn't listening. "Bastian, you do the honors."

"Happy to," said the man behind us, and he raised his pistol and aimed.

There was a loud pop. But instead of one of us dying, it was the wight with the leashed hollow who stumbled back against the door frame, looking shocked while his throat gushed blood from a ragged hole. He dropped the hollow's leash, gagging, and sagged to the ground.

The hollow let out a shrill, startled screech, then unhinged its massive jaws. I didn't know what the hell was going on, but my instincts told me to intercept the hollow and hope someone else would deal with the flamethrower man. I shoved Horace and Enoch aside and ran toward it. Two of its tongues shot across the gap between us and wrapped around my legs, tripping me to the floor. It sent a third tongue at Noor and collared her neck, then a fourth at Julius, handcuffing him before he could steal any light from the room.

I was being dragged toward the hollow's open mouth.

Someone was shouting in Hollowspeak.

I was about to disappear into the hollow's jaws, but just before I reached them the tongues dragging me went limp and let go of me. Then the man with the flamethrower strode past me toward the hollowgast, still yelling in a strange dialect of Hollowspeak I couldn't fully understand. The hollow had gone slack and was staring open-jawed at the man. It sucked its tongues back into its mouth and lay down on the floor next to its dead master.

The man turned to face us, his flamethrower lowered. "I've come to help you," he said. "My name is Horatio. Mr. Portman, Miss Pradesh, we've met before."

"What's he talking about?" said Julius, rubbing his wrists where the hollow had bound them. "You know this man?"

"Yes," I said, my head spinning. I could feel the hollowgast's desire to kill me, but Horatio had ordered it down, and down it stayed. "He's a wight."

Horatio didn't dispute it. "I am the former hollowgast of Harold Fraker King, known to you as H." His voice was clear and his words were crisp. His face wasn't a half-formed mass of just-born flesh any longer, but that of a normal-looking man, albeit one without pupils in his eyes. "I rejoined my former comrades and made them believe I was still one of them. They found you and tracked you," he said to Miss Petrel.

"What?" she said. "But how?"

"I can explain later. Right now you'll just have to believe me. There are more coming, and worse."

"What could be *worse*?" Sebbie asked.

And then we heard a roar from outside, a sound I associated with Godzilla or the dinosaurs from *Jurassic Park*.

"Murnau," said Horatio. "And he's bringing several more hollowgast with him."

"*Murnau?*" Noor said, not quite believing her ears.

And then I heard his voice, deep and bellowing, from the front lawn. "*Oh, children!* Come out, come out, wherever you are!"

We ran back to the window. A giant, lumbering horror was thundering up the front drive. A nightmare twenty feet tall, his bottom half a formless mass of shifting black slime, the top resembling a melted and supersized Murnau.

He was still bellowing. "My lord has blessed me with a new body and a boundless appetite . . ."

Racing up behind him, I could see, then feel, three more hollowgast. The new kind, bigger than the old ones and visible to all.

"Run!" cried Miss Hawksbill, picking herself up from the floor with help from Bronwyn. "You've got to run—take the horses—"

"Take Sophie with you!" Miss Petrel said, shoving the girl at me. "She isn't part of this loop . . . she can leave, too . . ."

And then we were running, tripping, dragging one another out of the house through a back exit, where five horses were saddled and waiting for us in a vegetable garden. They were shy and shifting, but after a little coaxing from Miss Petrel they let my friends mount.

I turned to Horatio, who was stripping off his German army jacket to reveal a neutral collared shirt. My eyes flicked to the hollow hunched behind him, slavering black drool on some tomato vines. "Will you be able to control the others, too?" I asked.

Horatio tossed away the jacket. "Not likely. This is the only one I've had proximity to for any length of time. Their language has changed, and their minds have toughened."

Horatio hoisted the flamethrower, aimed it at the house, and with one long pull of the trigger he filled the room we'd just run out of with fire.

"To slow them down a little," he explained. He was about to drop the flamethrower when I caught his arm. He snapped his head at me, a reflex presaging violence, but caught himself.

"Easy there," I said, then nodded at the hollow. "Shouldn't you do him, too?"

Nearly all of us were mounted now. Emma called after me. "Jacob! Come on!"

"It isn't necessary," he said.

I narrowed my eyes at him.

"We are damned but not unredeemable," he said, and then he turned and growled something to the hollow; the hollow skittered away toward the woods, harmless as a cat. "He won't bother us again." He mounted a horse, then reached his arm down to help Sophie on, too.

The house was filled with the crashes and howls of angry hollows. We could hear Murnau screaming at them to kill as many of us as they could—but to leave Jacob Portman for him.

I lurched onto a horse with Emma, who'd been paired with me because she knew how to ride so well. Noor rode with Enoch; Horace with Julius; and Bronwyn with Sebbie, who clung awkwardly to the trunk strapped to Bronwyn's back.

"Miss Hawksbill and I will guide you to the tear in the membrane," Miss Petrel shouted after us. "Watch the skies!"

She and Miss Hawksbill leapt into the air and transformed in a flurry of feathers, then flapped off toward some trees at the back of the property, where I caught a glimpse of Miss Tern already circling.

Our horses broke into a trot and followed them.

"Wait! What about Addison?" Bronwyn cried.

He was hurrying alongside us, still on the ground.

"I can run!" he said proudly.

"Not as fast as we can," my horse replied in plain, clear English.

Bronwyn leaned down from her saddle, scooped Addison off the ground with one hand, and pinned him under one arm while the other held the reins.

"Giddyap!" she cried, Addison howling in fear as their horse shot forward.

*　　*　　*

Hoofbeats filled the air as monstrous howls echoed behind us. I risked a look back and saw the giant slime creature—Murnau, half as tall as the house—tear the chimney off the roof and throw it at us. It arced through the air and landed in an explosion of bricks, briefly obscuring the scene with a cloud of dust.

My arms were knotted around Emma's waist as our horse

bucked and rolled beneath us. I squeezed my legs hard against its sides to keep from flying off. Emma held the reins. Not that the horse needed much guiding; it knew the terrain and wanted to escape just as much as we did.

Our five horses galloped downhill. We rode in a stampeding knot until we reached the woods' edge and the path narrowed, and our horses were forced into single file. We were at the front of the line, and Julius and Horace were at the rear. Glancing back, I saw Julius take a hand off the reins and hold it up to rake light out of the air. *Smart*, I thought, leaving a trail of dark to blind our pursuers—but the ride was too rough and he nearly flew off the horse. Horace screamed and pulled him back into the saddle before he could fall.

I searched the sky for the ymbrynes and caught a glimpse of Miss Petrel's unmistakable black-tipped wings through the trees. We were on the right track, but I could hear the hollows howling behind us. They were catching up too quickly.

We raced into a clearing. Ahead the path forked left and right. Because Emma and I were on the lead horse it was our call to make. Above us I heard a screech and looked up to see the two ymbrynes veer left, but just then, to our left at ground level, I heard a hollow's scream. Left was out of the question.

"Right!" I yelled, and Emma pulled the reins.

"Not that way!" shouted the horse.

Another howl from the left was enough to convince him. We veered down the rightward path, the others following.

"Have the hollows gotten *faster*?" Emma said, and my chin dug into her back as I nodded and hung on, and half closed my eyes. If any of the horses stumbled or any of us fell, we'd be hollow food.

For a minute we seemed to lose them. The woods thinned. We raced out of the trees and into a fallow field, the view opening expansively. To the left was a wide stretch of fields. To the right, distant and clouded by rolling black smoke, was a fleet of trucks and tanks. I knew immediately what lay beyond, because now I could hear the guns.

"Oh God," Emma said, "that isn't—is it?"

Damn it. The trenches.

It was 1916 in Miss Tern's loop, two years earlier than Miss Hawksbill's. The war had been rewound, and the front had regressed such that we found ourselves behind the British front lines. *Again.*

"Left!" I shouted, but was immediately refuted by another cry from overhead: the ymbrynes, urging us straight on. It was a path that would skirt the fighting, but only just. "Never mind! Straight!"

Then a chorus of blood-curdling howls contradicted me a second time. The hollows were out of the woods now, too, and had drawn even with us, off to our left. *Way* off to our left, but tacking toward us fast in a tight-packed blur of pinwheeling tongues.

My horse didn't need directions. It swerved right and the others followed. The hollows were herding us toward the front. And yes, they had gotten faster. If the hollow I fought in the Acre was version 2.0, these were 2.1. They just kept getting deadlier.

I heard someone shouting, *"Allez, allez!"* It was one of the horses, spurring the others on. Somehow, straining and glistening with sweat, they were able to pour on still more speed. The ymbrynes began to screech, alarmed that we were heading for the front, but there was nothing we could do about it, short of hurtling ourselves into an unwinnable fight with the hollows. All things being equal, I would take my chances on the battlefield.

Over the din of hooves and howls, I heard Julius shout to Horace, "Hold me tight," and I turned to see him let go of the reins again and raise both arms. He was steadier this time, his knees bent and flexing with the rhythm of the horse. He began to pull the light out of the air, leaving a broad streak of black behind us. I hoped it would give us some cover, enough that we might veer away from the front without the hollows seeing where we'd gone.

We rode on like that, pulling darkness after us like a cowl. The sound of bombs and machine gun fire grew louder. We passed more trucks and small tanks and clusters of shocked soldiers, who might've taken potshots at us if our wake hadn't left them in darkness.

"Now—left!" I shouted to Emma, because I hoped there was enough dark behind us to mask a direction change, and because going straight any longer would plow us into no-man's-land, where anything so strange as a moving carpet of night would surely attract a storm of gunfire.

Emma and I swerved left, but a moment later our horse screamed and skidded to a rearing stop before a wall of parked tanks, nearly throwing us off its back. The other horses piled up behind us.

"Back the other way," Emma cried, but when Julius cleared a little of the black away we saw that two tanks and a troop transport had just collided in the dark to our rear, blocking our escape.

"More," Sebbie boomed in her fire-woman voice. "Take all the light!" And together the light-eaters gathered nearly every photon around us, and we were plunged into semidarkness.

Terrified soldiers shouted out for one another. I could hear the hollows bashing around in the dark, too, not close to us but not nearly far enough away for comfort. For the moment they were confused and blinded, and I guessed that the intense smells of the battlefield—gunpowder and diesel and death—had muddied the peculiar scent trails we'd been leaving for them.

Then a light bloomed in Noor's hands, a glow that lit her aquiline features and a small area around us as well.

"Put it out!" Enoch said. "The hollows will see."

"You can't see far through this," Julius reassured him. "My dark is thick as pea soup."

A young man in uniform stumbled into the cone of Noor's glow. His eyes were saucers, his mouth trembling as he gazed up at her on horseback. "Am I dead?" he asked. "Is this heaven or hell?"

"Those hollows won't be confused for long," I said, ignoring him. In my gut, the compass points of pain that represented the hollows had stopped wandering and were drifting closer. "They're starting to catch our scent again."

"Then there's no way out," Horace cried.

"There might be," Noor said. Her eyes went to the nearest tank, a primitive hulk of metal and tread, looming at the edge of her wavering light. She locked eyes with the young soldier. "Can you drive that thing?"

He tried to speak, couldn't. Nodded instead.

"Good." Noor swung her leg over the saddle and jumped down from the horse. "We need a ride."

Enoch gaped. "In *that*?"

"That's a fabulous idea, Noor," said Emma, and she dismounted, too, then glanced at Enoch. "Unless you'd rather run through no-man's-land with just Horace's sweater to stop the bullets."

We all got down from our horses.

"What about us?" said the horse I'd been riding.

"Wait till we draw the hollows away, then run!" said Noor.

The young soldier was already climbing into the tank. We ran after him. From the rim of darkness around us, soldiers in gas masks gathered to watch. They must've thought they were dreaming.

"Smallest ones first!" Noor said, boosting Sebbie onto the tank. "Get that door open!"

The young soldier slid a bolt and threw open the tank's hatch.

"You sure we're all going to fit in there?" Bronwyn asked.

"Shrink if you have to," said Horace. "There's no other way."

The young soldier helped us in one by one. Noor and I were last, and as Noor was climbing in, the soldier asked her, "Are you angels?"

"Sure," she replied, and then we heard the inhuman howl of a hollow. They were close and coming fast. Any color that was left in the soldier's cheeks drained away. "And those," she said, "are devils."

And the hatch slammed shut over our heads.

✦   ✦   ✦

Paradoxically, the inside of a WWI-era tank looked like it was designed to kill its occupants just as much as the outside was designed to kill the enemy. Though we were packed in like sardines there was enough room for all of us, but it was hard to breathe through the engine fumes and hard to hear because of the engine roar and hard to see because there were only slits in the armor for visibility.

The young soldier wedged himself into the driver's seat. The rest of us compressed ourselves into the tight compartments around him, meant for gunners and shell-loaders, and began shouting contradictory orders.

"Go back the way we came!"

"Go wherever the hollows ain't!"

"No, follow the ymbrynes!"

"How? We can't see them from in here!"

Finally Bronwyn shouted for quiet and said, "Jacob! Machine gun bullets kill hollows, don't they?"

"I think so, if you shoot them in the head. Their chests are armored."

"But they won't destroy a tank?" This was directed to the young man in the driver's seat.

Enoch flicked his arm. "Do more than stare. She asked you a question."

"Eh, no." He rapped the hatch above him with his knuckle and it rung dully. "Armor's too thick."

Bronwyn snapped a nod. "So we lead them into a bullet storm. Let the British and Germans kill the hollows for us, *then* follow the ymbrynes."

"That's absolutely mad," Julius muttered, and then he shrugged. "You heard the lady," he barked at the soldier. "Let's go get shot at."

The soldier peered through a slit in the hull. "It's too dark—can't see where I'm driving."

"*Ach*, righto," grumbled Julius. "I'll spit it back."

With help from the soldier, Julius located the loading port of the largest gun barrel and opened it. He pressed his mouth to it, squeezed his eyes closed, and made a noise that sounded like vomiting. Peering through another of the tank's gaps I could see light shooting out of the tank's gun to fill the horizon. It must have been an amazing thing to witness, this tank firing sunlight into the sky, and I wished I could've seen it from the vantage of the gaping soldiers who surrounded us.

Now that he could see, the driver was able to quickly get his bearings. He stomped the clutch with his foot and threw the tank into forward gear. We lurched forward with a great squeal of metal.

Then there was a loud clang—one of the hollows had jumped onto the tank. It drummed uselessly against the hull with its tongues, then let out a piercing howl of frustration.

The soldier shrank down into his seat. "Cor, what was that?"

"Just drive, lad!" said Millard, half shouting over the din of the engine.

The soldier yanked the two parallel levers before him in opposite directions, which was apparently how you steered the thing, and we lurched to avoid something. A second hollowgast leapt atop the tank, while a third tried unsuccessfully to lasso and then pull us to a stop from behind. But their teeth and tongues were little use against our behemoth of iron and steel.

The soldier's state of dreamy compliance was beginning to fade, replaced by panic as we approached the front lines, but a steady stream of encouragement from Millard and threats from Enoch kept him pointed toward the battlefield.

"Put on yer splatter masks and find something to hold on to!" he shouted. He grabbed a scary-looking mask from under his seat and strapped it over his face. It had slitted metal grates covering both eyes and a chain-mail beard that hung down over the lower face and neck. There were identical masks under every seat, and we each put one on. It was heavy and reduced my visibility to almost zero, but I wasn't about to question its utility.

The tank pitched forward dramatically, then slammed into something and righted itself. We had crossed the trenches and were plowing into no-man's-land. There was a brief pause in which all we could hear was the roaring engine and the squeal of the tank's treads; even the hollows had gone quiet.

Then the guns woke up. They sounded like rolling thunder as they raked the cratered land toward us, and then a hailstorm of ear-splitting clangs filled my head. None of the bullets entered the tank, but tiny shards of metal were knocked loose and went flying, and I realized what the medieval-looking masks were for.

I felt one of the hollows die. It didn't even have time to scream. The others did, though. They were hit, and I felt them scramble from the exposed side of the tank to the sheltered one that faced the British line.

I shouted at the soldier to turn and drive the other way. I saw a flicker of hesitation on his face, but he was so thoroughly out of his depth that he did as I asked anyway. He pulled the lever on the right toward him while pushing the left one away, and we began to turn a lurching 180 degrees. The storm of gunfire passed from one side of the tank to the other. One of the remaining two hollows didn't react fast enough and was torn to pieces. The other spider-crawled around to the back of the tank, and then I felt it go underneath us, into the empty space between the treads. It scratched and pounded at the floor of the tank, rattling the metal beneath our feet, desperate for a way in. I wondered if the saliva of these new hollows was acidic enough to eat through steel. Chasing the thought from my mind, I shouted at the soldier to turn back the other way, and he shoved the levers again.

I stood up, steadying myself against the tank's violent shudder, and peered through the closest vent. Across the ruined and smoking land I saw a crater filled with tangled barbed wire.

I told him to drive straight through it.

"We could get hung up in there!" he said. "Never get out again!"

The hollow's scratching turned to a worrying *thwang* beneath us, and I pictured it peeling away loose panels in the tank's bodywork.

"We didn't come all this way just to die inside a tin can," Emma shouted. "Do as he says and drive!"

The soldier jammed down a pedal with his foot. The tank sped up, but it still felt like we were moving in slow-motion. It was hot as the fires of hell in there, the overworked engine making the air shimmer while an accumulation of fumes threatened to choke us.

Finally, we dipped down into the crater. The hollowgast began to screech as the barbed wire tore it apart. The driver poured on as much speed as he could in hopes of getting us out the other side of the crater, but our left tread bound up, tangled in wire, while the right one kept turning, which spun us in a slow circle. The bullets strafed us again, and then something snapped and we were sprung loose. A moment later the tank tipped upward and we climbed out of the hole.

There was cheering and fist pumps. And then a mortar shell landed and we were knocked sideways by a giant explosion.

Everything went black. I don't know for how long. Maybe a minute or two, maybe just a few seconds, but when I came to, one of those terrifying masks was staring down at me, and I had to suppress a scream.

It was Emma. "We got hit with a mortar!" she was shouting.

The tank had flipped onto its side; everything inside was turned ninety degrees.

The soldier was dead. His mask had slipped off just before the mortar hit, and his face was running with blood. All three hollows were dead now—I could feel it—but if we tried to escape the tank, we would be, too. Even though we'd been hobbled, the gunfire drilling us had hardly slackened at all.

I looked around, dazed from the blast and the combined voices of all my friends. Horace was tending to Enoch, who had blood flowing out of his coat sleeve. Millard and Bronwyn were frantically digging through her steamer trunk for something. Sebbie was traumatized and sobbing. "I don't want to die in here!" she wailed.

Neither did the rest of us. We had to get out of the tank before any more mortar shells landed on it . . . but the moment we popped our heads out of the hatch, we'd be as dead as those hollows.

"I could eat the light from the sky again," Julius said.

"It wouldn't make any difference," said Horatio. "They'll just blanket the air with bullets."

There were more suggestions, none of them good. Everyone was starting to panic. Then Millard cried, "Look here, friends!" and we all turned. He and Bronwyn had gotten the steamer trunk open and were carefully lifting out Klaus's bone clock. I had forgotten all about it. "I have something here that might help us, but then again it might not—"

"We'll try anything!" Horace said.

"It got a bit dinged up, but if it still works—and works the way Klaus said it does . . ." He held up a key ring of fingerbones. "Now, was it the pointer that opens the case, or the index?"

He was interrupted by an explosion that rocked the tank— another shell had landed close by and left my ears ringing.

"Just *do* it, Millard!" Noor shouted.

He fumbled the keys onto the floor, scrabbled to pick them up again, and inserted one of them into the case. Thankfully, it popped open on the first try. "I don't know precisely how this is going to work!" he shouted over the din while using another finger to wind the clock, "but whatever the effect, it probably won't last long . . ."

He gave it one last hard crank, and the clock's bony hands began to spin around the face so fast they blurred. Then there was a sudden loud *BONG* and they both stopped at twelve. As the clock's chime faded, so too did the incessant hammering of bullets against the tank's hull. I felt a nauseating drop as if the tank had just fallen off a cliff—a sensation I had come to recognize as a time shift—and then, as if by magic, the world outside went quiet.

For one panicked moment, I thought: *Are we dead?*

Millard climbed over the fallen soldier and unscrewed the hatch. Horrified, I grabbed for his leg and missed, but by then he'd gotten it open and popped his head out.

The world outside was just as quiet as the inside of the tank.

A moment later he poked his head in. "It's quite safe now!" he said excitedly.

We left the tank in the same order we'd come in, small ones first, Noor and me last. I slid out feet first. All around us was a churn of mud and wire and bits of blown-apart hollowgast.

The world was not as we'd left it. The tank's engine had died and the shooting had stopped. But even that was not enough to explain this new silence, so profound that, if not for the awestruck murmurs of my friends, I'd have thought I'd gone deaf. Had the soldiers all been magicked into some alternate dimension?

I saw Noor examining an object suspended in the air—a bullet that had been frozen mid-flight. It was stretched slightly from end to end, blurred like an object moving too fast for a camera's shutter. Swarms of them hung around us. In the distance, a mortar shell had been stopped mid-explosion, the geyser of earth it had sent up arrested in the shape of an umbrella.

Noor reached up her hand to touch the bullet.

I started to say, "Wait, Noor, I wouldn't—" but then she brushed it and it dropped harmlessly into the mud.

"By the winged elders," Sophie murmured, clutching Penny to her chest.

Enoch whistled through his teeth.

Addison hopped onto a blasted stump for a better view. "'Because I could not stop for death, he kindly stopped for me,'" he recited.

"This is no time for poetry," Emma said, and started to ford a path through the crumpled barbed wire. "Let's get out of here before that old clock stops doing whatever it is it's doing . . ."

"I strenuously agree," said Horace.

Bronwyn had strapped the bone clock to her back. It was making a loud tick-tocking that sounded ominously like a countdown, and I wondered, if I lingered near any of the dead that composed half the mud surrounding us, whether I would be able to hear them whispering.

We followed Emma out of the crater and chose what seemed the most direct path out of no-man's-land, toward the British side. Or was that the German side off in the distance before us? I was all turned around now, my brain addled from fumes and bomb-blasts, and every direction was an indistinguishable smudge of ruin and wire. I couldn't be sure anymore.

I swatted away a cloud of bullets and thought, *Where are the ymbrynes?*

"Form a chain so no one gets left behind," Bronwyn said, and she jogged up and down our line making sure our hands were linked. She picked up Sophie under one arm and tucked Addison beneath the other.

"Don't jostle the clock!" Millard chastised her.

"Remember what Miss Hawksbill told us!" Emma shouted, her voice loud and clear with no other sounds to compete with. "Eyes forward and mind your business, or it's nightmares for life!"

And then from behind us there was a tremendous bellowing roar, and we froze and turned to see what it was.

"Jesus, what is it *now*?" Noor said.

"That," said Horatio, nodding as if he'd just remembered something, "could only be Percival Murnau."

Then he came into view: Murnau, or some monstrous perversion of him, tall as two houses and made of two halves, the top nominally human, the bottom a high, churning pedestal made of the foul muck beneath us, black mud and debris and bodies, shredded bits of which flew from his too-wide mouth as he shouted my name.

The bone clock had had no effect on him. He was not of this loop.

Someone screamed. *Run.*

We did, scrambling as fast as we could manage over the ruined land, swatting away clouds of bullets as we went. Murnau traveled without legs and could move faster than us, the roiling mass beneath him sweeping over the ground like the funnel of a shrunken tornado.

After a moment the roaring behind us was joined by a screeching from above.

"Miss Petrel!" Julius cried.

"And Miss Hawksbill!" Bronwyn shouted.

Two of the ymbrynes had found us again and were circling overhead. Miss Tern *was* of this loop, and so, presumably, was frozen somewhere in mid-flight.

Miss Petrel and Miss Hawksbill began to harass Murnau, dive-bombing him, slowing him down long enough for us to get within sprinting distance of the trenches and the end of no-man's-land.

Murnau stopped to swat at the birds and missed. We ducked through a broken section of barbed wire and arrived at the trench line. Miss Hawksbill dove low in front of us, guiding us to a foot-bridge that passed over the tops of the trenches. Here the bullet clouds were thick as rain, and the sound of them falling away from our bodies as we ran was like a slot machine paying out a million-dollar prize.

I looked down into the trench as we crossed the footbridge. Dozens of soldiers frozen like grim statues, faces smeared with earth and blood, guns spitting fire.

They were German, not British. This was the German line.

There was a great thudding behind us. Murnau was close, maybe fifty yards back, and gaining. The uneven ground wasn't slowing him much, and the trenches wouldn't, either.

There was a scream from the sky. Miss Petrel dove at Murnau

and hit him beak-first in the face. He grunted and dodged away, then twisted and brought up his arm. He caught Miss Petrel in his hand, then crushed her and threw her away into the muck.

Julius screamed. Sebbie and Enoch scooped him off his knees and carried him.

She was dead. I had never seen an ymbryne killed, and the sight nearly froze me in my tracks—but I forced myself on, after my friends, over the outer trenches. We couldn't afford to waste the gift she'd given us. Miss Petrel's sacrifice had slowed Murnau down, and in a moment we were past the trenches while he was still struggling through the last wall of barbed wire in no-man's-land.

Julius was shouting as if possessed, then wrenched free of Sebbie and Enoch and ran at Bronwyn. He was hollering something like *break it, break it*, but before any of us understood what he was after, he had ripped the bone clock from Bronwyn's back, raised it above his head, and brought it down on a rock.

There was a sudden lurch in my stomach, a pressure change I felt between my ears, and the sounds of Millard screaming at Julius were drowned beneath a deafening roar as time began moving again.

A thousand guns resumed firing. The men in the trenches behind us snapped back into scurrying motion. And Murnau was caught in a hurricane of flying metal. I saw his body, or what had become of it, torn to shreds. He disintegrated before my eyes.

An ymbryne screamed—Miss Hawksbill, though I could barely hear her now—urging us forward. Sebbie and Noor gathered light as we ran to hide us. Julius had collapsed and had to be carried, this time by Bronwyn.

We sprinted through rear lines of equipment and medic tents until we came to a gauzy blur in the air—the loop membrane—and dove through it into a world of disorienting normalcy.

CHAPTER SEVENTEEN

*W*e were no longer in a battlefield, or any kind of field, but in a small, grassy park in a small French town. Miss Hawksbill did not follow us through the membrane. Maybe she couldn't, or perhaps she needed to return to the trenches to retrieve what was left of Miss Petrel. But her voice echoed after us through a slit in the air: "I can't come with you, children. Go now, go quickly, and let us mourn when this is over."

Small shops and houses ringed the park. A church bell tolled pleasantly. We had not moved through the world at all—only through time—yet we had arrived in a different country. Horatio put on a pair of sunglasses to hide his blank pupils and, in what sounded like flawless French, asked a passerby where to catch the train.

"Come with me," Horatio said to us. "Don't think, don't talk. Just walk."

We followed unquestioningly. He may have been a wight, but he had proven himself as loyal as any peculiar I knew. We hurried down a street lined with shops. It was hot, and we stripped off our heavy coats as we went, dropping them on the ground. People stared, but not for long. Maybe WWI reenactors were a common sight here. Normals didn't concern me much anymore.

"Do you think he's really dead?" asked Horace, glancing nervously behind us.

"He got shot ten billion times," said Enoch. "The Germans turned him into pie filling."

"If bullets can kill a hollowgast, it stands to reason they could kill him, too," Emma said.

I'd seen Murnau eviscerated, but something nagged at the back of my mind. He wasn't a hollowgast. I wasn't even sure he was mortal anymore. But there was no reason to burden the others with my doubts; we had enough to worry about.

We came to a train station, bought tickets to London (Horatio had money), and waited in a mostly deserted hall for our train to arrive. Julius sat moaning to himself about his lost ymbryne, and Horace sat beside him with an arm on his knee, murmuring comforting words. Emma fetched napkins from a café and tended to a cut on Enoch's arm while he winced and complained. Addison sniffed the air for trouble and tried to stay alert, but his little eyes kept falling closed.

"What happens if we fail at this?" Sebbie asked quietly.

Enoch sucked in his breath and said, "Nothing much. Caul takes over peculiardom, enslaves us all, then turns the world into a slaughterhouse."

"If he's in a good mood," added Emma.

Horace patted her shoulder. "We won't fail."

"Why? Because you dreamed it?"

"Because we can't, that's all."

We were unspeakably exhausted. The reality of what had happened was beginning to filter through. Though it had mostly been horror and trauma, I comforted myself with this: We were returning to London stronger than we'd left it. We had three of the seven, and that was all we needed. And we had Horatio. He sat ramrod straight on a wooden bench, jerking his head between the entry door and the train platform every few seconds. He was like a benevolent Terminator.

The train hummed into the station. We got on board and squeezed into a private compartment, collecting more odd looks from the passengers. Odd looks had become so common I almost didn't notice them anymore. As we took our seats, Emma worried aloud about the ymbrynes and the Acre. Miss Avocet had looked weaker than ever the last time we saw her, and the shield depended

< THE DESOLATIONS OF DEVIL'S ACRE >

on all twelve ymbrynes being okay and staying that way. Miss Petrel had said Caul's forces were massing already.

"I wonder what they're waiting for," Bronwyn said.

"For Caul's army of hollows to be born," Horatio replied. "He's making them in Abaton. Each hollowgast contains a soul stolen from the soul jars."

"I thought he couldn't manipulate those," I said.

"Apparently he can, in his resurrected form. And to such a degree that he's been able to tweak their natures."

"Which is why we can see them?" asked Horace.

"Correct," Horatio replied. "And why they're armored and larger and"—his eyes flicked to me—"harder to control."

I felt inadequate. Judged, even—though I knew he didn't mean it that way.

"*You* were able to control one," I said. "To talk to it."

"After a long time, yes. I spent days in close proximity to that hollow, and gradually was able to learn its new language. But even so, they are more intractable than we used to be."

We, meaning Horatio in his previous form.

Emma leaned forward and said in a low voice, "What's it like, being a hollowgast?"

Horatio thought for a moment. "Torture," he said after a while. "Everything feels half-formed. Your body, your mind, your thoughts. You're so hungry your *bones* feel hollow. The only relief you ever feel is while you're eating—preferably a human, and a peculiar one. And even then it's a brief respite."

"Then didn't you hate H?" Noor asked. "For keeping you that way for so long?"

He answered immediately. "Yes." He tipped his head. "And no. All hollows hate their masters. But he helped me develop my mind. Taught me to read and to understand English and to think about more than just my hunger. I understood why he kept me, why he needed me. And in time I came to love him as well as hate him."

The train juddered and began slowly to move. The benches and ticket windows of the station began to slide away past our window.

"Can you teach me their new language?" I asked Horatio.

"I can attempt to. But it's less an intellectual learning process than an intuitive one. A *tapping in*."

"I'll try anything," I said.

"One more question before you start vocab lessons," Noor said. "When you say *army* of hollows, how many are you talking?"

"Dozens, surely," Horatio replied. "Perhaps more." He lapsed into a brief, pensive silence. Out our window, the station gave way to an expanse of flowering fields. "They'll be nearly all born now. The hour is close at hand."

Enoch snorted. "*The hour is close at hand*," he repeated in a gravelly voice. "Do all wights talk like villains in a horror film?"

Horatio raised an eyebrow at him. "If I still had my tongues," he said, "I'd slap you with all of them."

Enoch paled slightly and shrank back in his seat.

A moment later, Horace jumped to his feet. "Fellows?" he said in a high voice, his nose pressed to the glass. "What is that?"

We clustered beside him at the window. Out in the fields was a fast-moving man, naked from the waist up, who appeared to be riding on a pillar of spinning wheat and yellow flowers.

"*It's him,*" Emma whispered.

"Oh, hell," Bronwyn said.

Murnau was gliding across the fields toward us, and our train was only just starting to pick up speed.

"I thought this was a *fast* train!" Enoch cried. He banged on the glass. "Go on, hurry up!"

Murnau was drawing closer, and we were speeding up only incrementally. The train bumped over a road crossing and past a parking lot, and Murnau crossed it, too. His tornadic bottom half turned gray as he left behind a trail of torn-up asphalt, and then he barreled over a car and blendered that, too.

"I'm not staying here," Enoch said, "I'm going to slap some sense into the train engineer . . ."

He ran out of the compartment. We pushed into the narrow aisle after him and ran down the length of the train in a vain attempt to get farther away from Murnau. We dashed between train cars, past baffled passengers, most of whom didn't seem to notice the nightmarish thing growing larger and larger out their windows.

The train jolted and finally began to speed up.

"Thank *God*," Horace cried.

We stopped running and pressed ourselves against a window of the snack car. Murnau was falling behind. In a last-ditch effort to reach us, he poured on a final burst of speed and lunged toward us. He disassembled in midair, pelting the train with flowers and dirt and small car parts. And then we were going fifty or sixty miles an hour, and whatever remained of Murnau was scattered behind.

✦   ✦   ✦

We collapsed back into our seats, slammed shut the door to our private compartment, and tried to calm down. Caul had nothing left to throw at us, I assured everyone, at least not until we got near the Acre. Enoch opened his shirt and out spilled a dozen sandwiches he'd stolen from the snack car. No one objected. We had jettisoned Miss Tern's bread on the battlefield along with our heavy packs, and many of us were ravenous. Sustained terror had that effect on people.

Speaking of terror, I had stopped even attempting to process the things that had happened to us. They just washed over me in a tidal wave of horrifying events. If we survived these ordeals I'd probably develop a twitch or resume the crippling nightmares that used to plague me. Maybe one day a therapist would help me unpack it all. And not some quack my parents had hired, or a wight in disguise. A peculiar one. I asked my friends if there was such a thing as a brain-mender, but they looked at me strangely, and I didn't feel like explaining why I'd asked.

It would be a two-hour trip to London. Addison and Bronwyn slept. Others were too keyed up and had to talk, and there was a constant low buzz of chatter as people recounted all the insane things that had occurred in the past day. Sophie huddled with Pensevus against the window, soaking in the pastoral landscapes that whizzed past. Julius and Horace sat side by side with their knees hugged to their chests and their shoes off, heads touching now and then as they spoke in low voices.

Noor and I took the opportunity to talk more with Horatio. The last time either of us had seen him he was a deformed half hollow who could barely speak, and he'd leapt from the window of H's sixth-floor apartment in New York—we had assumed to his death. How had he reached a collapsed loop in France and how had he managed to embed himself—now a fully formed wight, and not a bad-looking one—among Caul's faithful servants?

"Yeah," Noor said, head bobbing as she stared at him. "What the hell happened to you?"

Horatio conjured a weird smile, a facial expression he was clearly still mastering. "Yes, it's been . . . eventful. After dropping from the window, I hid myself in the sewer. I stayed there for several days while completing my metamorphosis from hollowgast to wight. I had cultivated certain disciplines of mind during my long years with Harold Fraker King, and by employing them I was able to retain my memories, which many hollows lose." His language was clinical, he enunciation precise. He had a subtle New York accent, which, combined with his grammatically perfect English, made him sound like an AI bot trying to imitate a cab driver. "I never forgot Harold Fraker King or the generosity he showed me. I was determined to continue his mission—to protect Noor Pradesh and assist in the fulfillment of the prophecy of the seven."

"Well, thanks," Noor said.

"Your timing could have been better," said Enoch, edging in.

"And it could've been worse," Emma added.

"At least his aim was true," Sebbie said, massaging her throat in the approximate spot where Horatio had shot the wight.

Now everyone had joined our conversation.

"One question," Millard said. "If you knew so much about the prophecy, why didn't you tell us V's heart was on the list of elements needed to resurrect Caul?"

"Master King did not know, because Mistress Velya never told him," he answered plainly.

"If she had, H never would have sent us to find her," I said.

"It would've meant admitting she was an ymbryne," Emma said. "Which she probably didn't want to do."

"That's a very boring mystery," said Enoch, flapping his hand impatiently. "I want to know how you infiltrated the wights. Didn't they know who you were?"

"They did not," Horatio said, "because I disguised myself. This was not the face I emerged with, but a sewn-on one."

Emma's lips twisted in disgust and Noor mouthed, *Whaaat?*

"When my transition was complete, I found a wight and killed him, then removed his face and took it to Ellsworth Ellsworth, the Untouchables' celebrated skin tailor. And this was the result." He turned his cheek and raked the back of his hand across it like a model in a skincare ad. You could just make out a fine line of stitches that disappeared beneath his blond hairline.

"I stole his identity," Horatio continued. "Mimicked his mode of speech and joined a band of wights operating in New York, among the last in America. At that point it was too late to stop the wights' plot to break Percival Murnau and his comrades out of your Devil's Acre prison, and too late again to prevent them from resurrecting Caul. But I learned that they intercepted one of your phone calls"—he gestured to Sophie, who hid her face in shame—"and I learned that they were planning to track

Ellsworth
Ellsworth

Miss Pradesh in an attempt to discover the location of the meeting place."

"So Caul knew about the seven," Bronwyn said, newly awake and blinking groggily. "And the prophecy."

"Of course," Emma said. "That's why he sent wights after Noor in the first place, when she was a little kid."

"It was right there in the *Apocryphon*," Horace said.

"Caul's no fool," Millard said. He turned to the light-eaters. "I don't believe he's losing sleep over you three—no offense intended—but he wasn't about to go through all the pain and bother of getting himself resurrected without killing you as an insurance policy."

"So we walked into a trap," Noor said to Horatio. "And you came all that way to save us."

"Yes," Horatio replied, with no trace of either modesty or pride.

Noor clasped her hands together. "Thank you."

"He's going to keep trying to kill us," said Julius. He had recovered his composure, and I noticed that his fingers and Horace's were interlaced on the seat between them. "We slipped his trap, killed his hollows, humiliated his chief lieutenant monster. *I'd* be intent on murdering us if I were him. Wouldn't you be?"

CHAPTER EIGHTEEN

brittle paranoia crept over me as our train slowed into St. Pancras Station. We were in the center of present-day London now, and there were too many people, too many eyes, and too many bodies, though not so many that we could disappear into the crush. We were a noticeable bunch, to put it mildly, despite each of us having spent an eternity in the train's cramped bathroom trying to wipe battlefield mud from our faces and our clothes.

Caul and his agents could be anywhere, and we had to assume they would be looking for us. We had to assume Murnau had told Caul where we were heading. Or maybe Caul, invested now with powers beyond imagining, just knew.

We filed off the train in a protective clump. It was disorienting to be thrust into such a buzzing hive of twenty-first-century-ness. There were bright screens and signs everywhere, and nearly all the people flowing around us were staring at phones while they walked. At least they weren't looking at us. Emma held a humiliated Addison at the end of a leash improvised from twine because there were rules about animals in public spaces, and rule-breaking could cause a scene, and we needed to disappear as well as a bunch of strange-looking kids dressed in mud-stained clothes from another era could.

"We need a phone," I heard Millard say. He had pulled a scarf over his head and put on big dark glasses. He looked like old photos I'd seen of Jackie Kennedy.

Enoch went to snatch one from a passerby, but Millard caught his arm. "Not that sort of phone. A *real* one, inside a booth. I need to call the Acre."

We left the platform area for the vast ticket hall, which looked like a sci-fi cathedral where people came to worship fast food. We were a cluster of swiveling heads, on the watch for attackers and analog phones from the previous century. As it turned out, most of the red phone booths, which are so iconically famous in London, no longer had actual phones inside them, but had been converted into charging stations and private spaces to make cell phone calls. After several minutes of fruitless searching we finally found an old phone booth with an old phone inside it, in a dingy corner near some bathrooms.

We crammed as many of us inside as would fit, which was less than half our number. My face was uncomfortably adjacent to Bronwyn's armpit. Millard paged through a chunky phone book that dangled from a cord. "Most of the pages are torn out," he grumbled.

My attention drifted through the glass. Outside, a crowd was gathering around a big flat-screen TV, but I couldn't see what they were watching.

"What's he doing?" Noor whispered in my ear.

"The ymbrynes have their numbers listed under fake names," I explained. "He can connect to some of their loops if he whistles the right birdsong."

She slipped her arms around my waist from behind and my hands rose instinctively to grip hers. How something so simple could feel so reassuring was both a mystery and a miracle.

"Miss you," she whispered, and I nodded. *Me too.* I'd hardly left her side for days, but we'd had so little time to be alone and ourselves, she'd begun to feel distant. This thing between us was still new, still forming, and I worried that if we starved it now it would wither, never to be revived. But there was no time for dinner and a movie. Hardly even a minute to talk to each other, let alone hang out—something more important, be it planning or fleeing or

fighting or catching a rare hour of sleep, was always taking precedence. Maybe one day, if this fighting ever came to an end, I could love Noor Pradesh the way she deserved to be loved.

Millard tapped the book excitedly. "Gee jolly jingo, here we are." He squinted at the page, then plucked the phone from its cradle, pulled away his scarf, and held it to his invisible ear. After a couple of false starts he whistled a high and uncannily realistic birdcall. "It's going through," he said.

I heard a tinny voice on the other end say, "Ahoy."

"Ahoy there, this is Millard Nullings. I need to speak with Alma Peregrine *at once.*"

She must have been waiting near the one room in Bentham's house that contained a phone, because she came on the line almost immediately. Several of us pressed our heads together and strained to hear her.

"Millard, is that you?" The connection was tinny and crackling, but even so I could hear the breathless worry in her voice.

"Yes, it's me, miss."

After that, I couldn't hear Miss Peregrine for a while, only Millard's end of the conversation: "We're all right. Yes, we've got the seven. Well, not all. Two more than we had before, so three altogether. Right. But that's just fine . . . as it happens we didn't need all of them. The other two are spares." Julius scowled at this. "Yes, that's right. We were chased out by Murnau and some hollowgast . . . Uh-huh . . . Say, we were wondering if we should—well, there was talk of *eating his soul* . . . Oh? All right, let me relay that." He pulled his head away from the receiver and covered it with his hand. "Miss P says we mustn't under any circumstances attempt to engage Caul on our own. We should come back to the Acre right away."

Bronwyn snatched the phone from Millard. "Miss, it's your Bronwyn. Please, you've got to evacuate all the little ones from the Acre. Caul's got a whole army of hollows on the way and they're extremely nasty and Jacob won't be able to control them. There must be some Panloopticon loop where the kids would be safe for a while—what's that?" Her brow furrowed. "Oh." Her voice deepened in shock. "Oh no."

"Let us *hear*," Enoch said, and managed to yank the receiver far enough away from Bronwyn's ear that a few of us, crowding around, could make out Miss Peregrine's voice.

" . . . just after you went through to Miss Hawksbill's loop," she was saying, "and only moments before we shut down the Panloopticon again, one of Caul's monstrous enhanced wights snuck into the house through one of the upper-floor loop doors. It wreaked havoc. Killed two home guards and seriously wounded Miss Plover and Miss Babax, though, thank the elders, they weren't killed or our temporal shield would've disintegrated instantly. We mobilized a lot of people to fight him, and in the end he was felled—though much was damaged in the doing. I'm afraid the Panloopticon is inoperable, and far too risky to use even if it weren't."

"So you're stuck there," Emma said. "With nowhere to run."

"We have no interest in running."

"And there's no way to reach you other than going through the loop entrance," Enoch said, "which is probably surrounded by now—"

"Perhaps you should surrender?" said Addison. "Preserve lives in the face of what is clearly a superior and overwhelming force?"

We looked at him like he'd gone batty.

"Never!" Emma said. "I'd never surrender to Caul!"

"Even if it meant dying? And everyone you love dying?"

A flicker of hesitation crossed her face. But she maintained that death was preferable to becoming Caul's prisoner or slave, and the rest of us agreed.

"Good," Addison said. "I was just testing you."

We discussed strategy with Miss Peregrine. There was talk of us "softening up" Caul's forces from the outside while the Acre prepared a surprise attack from within. Millard suggested waiting until

Caul and his forces tried to break through the shield, then assaulting from the rear while they were distracted—at which point the ymbrynes would drop the shield and attack.

"A classic pincer formation," said Millard.

"Or we three light-eaters could find Caul and attack him," said Julius. "I think you're overcomplicating things."

Miss Peregrine reiterated that we were not to fight Caul on our own. "You're not to attempt *anything*. I want all of you to return only when it's safe to do so. Until then, I want you to hide in our safe house near the Acre's loop entrance and wait for *us* to come to *you*."

"But, miss, the new light-eaters and Sophie are loop-trapped," Bronwyn said. "They can't stay in that safe house more than a day or they'll age forward—"

"We won't let that happen," I heard Miss Peregrine say. "When the time is right, we'll come. In the meantime, there are things we can do to harass Caul's forces. We can make some desolations of our own."

I'd been so focused on the call that I hadn't noticed until then what was going on outside the booth. The crowd around the big TV had grown to several dozen, and they seemed frozen in place. I craned to see the screen through the tinted booth glass and caught a glimpse of a man with light shooting out of his eye sockets.

"Oh my God," I said, pushing out of the booth for a closer look. I shouldered my way to the middle of the crowd, my blood going cold. The screen was showing footage of people running terrified down city streets. Then it cut to an aerial shot from a helicopter or a drone of a man and a woman who had clearly just ingested huge doses of ambrosia. They were in the middle of a bridge, beams of light from their eyes blackening the concrete as they swung their heads from side to side. The woman ripped the door off an abandoned car and flung it at a couple of people crouched behind a delivery truck. Then a man jumped out from behind the truck and raised both his hands, and the car the woman had been ripping apart slid suddenly toward the edge of the bridge, pushing her with it. She dove out of its way just before it tumbled into the river below.

We were watching a battle between peculiars unfold live on television. "They're fighting!" Bronwyn cried, running up beside me. "And everyone can *see*!" My friends had left the phone hanging from its cord in the booth. They gathered around me, mouths open in disbelief.

A chyron rolled across the screen: FREAK ASSAULT ON CENTRAL LONDON.

"I recognize one of them," Emma said. "The one throwing car parts. It's that horrible woman . . ." I realized I did, too. She was the chain-smoking proprietor of a peculiar flesh market who we'd interrogated for information about the wights. Lorraine. She must have escaped the Acre before the ymbrynes started making arrests. She'd once been a mercenary with no loyalties. Now she'd sunk even further: She was an ambro addict fighting for Caul.

"I know the ones hiding behind the truck," Millard said. "They're part of the rescue team we sent to free Caul's hostages."

The man beside Lorraine turned toward a police cruiser that had just arrived and projectile-vomited a stream of something at it— it glinted silver in the sun, like hot liquid metal—which melted a hole in the hood of the cruiser and sent the two police officers inside running for their lives.

"This is awful, this is terrible, someone turn this off before we're exposed!" Horace cried.

"It's too late for that, mate," said Enoch, and he pointed to three more screens nearby that were showing the same footage.

And yet the people around us seemed more skeptical than frightened. "This has got to be a joke," said a man near us as he turned away.

"Promotion for a film, innit," someone else agreed.

They just couldn't believe it was real.

And then I heard a voice say, "*Freak* assault? Why, this is tame! Wait till they see what's coming next!"

I turned and saw a man standing next to me in the crowd, a normal-sized man in a normal-enough shirt and tie connected to the ground by what appeared to be legs, and I was so shocked I froze for a moment.

It was Caul. His beaklike nose and jutting chin. His white eyes, full of laughing malice even in their blankness. He grinned, revealing sharpened canines. "Hello again, Jacob."

And then Emma, fast to move and quick on the draw, slapped him in the face with a hand full of fire, and Caul spun around and collapsed to the floor.

There were screams of panic around us, and the crowd flooded away in a wave. Caul was writhing on the floor and howling, "The freaks—they're here! They're here!" He appeared to be melting into a black puddle on the floor. "I'm melting!" he screeched. "*Meltiiinggg!!!*"

In a moment only his empty clothes were left. The pool spread quickly, approaching our feet as we scrabbled backward away from it.

"Do something!" Sebbie shouted at Noor and Julius. "Now's our chance."

"To do *what*?" Noor said.

As if in reply, the black puddle began to pulse blue light in the rhythm of a heartbeat. Julius took the cue. "This," he said, and spreading his arms he stepped forward. He moved to swipe the light from the puddle when an impossibly long arm shot up from it, and a clawlike hand wrapped its fingers around Julius's throat.

A loud cackling laugh issued from the black pool. Julius fell to his knees, choking, his skin turning a deathly gray.

"Julius!" Sebbie screamed.

Noor broke away from me, though I tried to hold her back. She ran for the puddle, arms extended, but before she could steal the light from it the blue glow disappeared. A second arm rocketed out of the puddle at her. I tackled her to the floor and it missed her by inches.

Emma flared her hand-flames at the arm and it retreated like an angry snake. Millard screamed that no one else should touch the arm, and Bronwyn, who had been about to wrestle the one still choking Julius, stopped short. Then Sophie ran forward with Pensevus held high. The doll's face was suddenly alive, its eyes aflame with anger and its mouth chomping hungrily. She flung Pensevus at the arm. The doll sunk a rack of razor-sharp teeth into Caul's skin and bit straight through the bone in one bite. There was a piercing howl as the severed hand fell away from Julius's throat. Julius slumped into Horace's arms and Bronwyn dragged them both away.

And then something began to rise from the puddle, coalescing as it did. It was Caul, bigger now, dripping black liquid like a hollowgast, naked to the waist. He rose slowly as we gaped in horror. He was vaguely human but all wrong: his head was stretched vertically, his neck barely there, his chest concave and his back arched like someone being electrocuted. His arms were too long, thick and grasping like hollowgast tongues, and the right hand that had been severed was quickly growing back. His top half was nominally human but below that he was all trunk, a tree made not from wood but from what looked like mottled-gray flesh, the roots somewhere deep inside the puddle. He towered over us, growing taller until his head nearly bumped a rafter fifteen feet overhead. This was the horror Caul had become, his true form.

"We don't have to fight," he cooed softly. His voice was doubled, both high and low, like a child and a man mated to one soul. "Just kneel before me, children, and pray to your new master."

We kept backing away, unwilling to run but with no idea yet how to fight him.

"A pity," he said. "Have it your way, then."

He swept out one of his long arms, narrowly missing us and crashing into a flower shop's window display. The glass shattered and huge sprays of flowers turned instantly black at his touch. I glanced at Julius, who was leaning on Horace, struggling to breathe.

Emma shaped a fat new fireball between her hands and threw it at Caul. His neck and spine contorted grotesquely and it sailed past him. He roared, emitting a blast of rotten air that nearly knocked us down, and then he came at us, the black pool beneath him churning as it carried him across the floor.

It was a decision made collectively and without discussion: We turned and ran. Until we knew how to fight him, or could identify some weakness in him, it was our only option.

His arms shot out, grasping for us and missing. We sprinted past a coffee kiosk and an instant later heard it tip and crash. We bolted down a narrow alley of shops, and heard glass shattering behind us in an endless cascade. A quick turn and we were heading for the exit and the street outside. Shocked bystanders fled for their lives.

We burst through the exit, dodging tourists pulling suitcases and crowds waiting for taxis. There was an immense crash behind us—I risked a look back to see Caul flying through a plate-glass window—and the crowds scattered. Bronwyn stopped to pick up someone's suitcase and fling it at Caul; it bounced harmlessly off his chest. We ran downstairs to street level. His lower half raced after us with no trouble. The street was blocked off for a farmer's market, and he dragged his hands along the stalls, his necrotizing touch turning all the fruits and vegetables rotten in an instant.

Caul began shouting after us in his strange doubled voice: "Look how they run! Look how they fear us! But how quickly fear turns to hatred, and hatred to killing and purges. Oh, they'll come for us, no mistake, come for *you*, young ones, they'll burn you and hang you and drive stakes through your hands just as they always have!"

There was a wide, shallow fountain in front of us and a surging crowd of terrified market-goers blocking either side. We jumped the fountain's short lip and splashed straight through, then raced past a barricade and out of the market, where a terrified cop was standing with his gun drawn and aimed at Caul. "Don't!" Emma shouted. "Just run!" The cop squeezed off three rounds as we ran past him. A few seconds later, I heard him scream. I looked back to see him convulsing on the ground. Caul's black pool flashed bright blue, then quickly faded.

We skidded around a corner onto a side street. Caul was still sermonizing. "Our war with one another is over! You've lost the battles; all that's left to lose are your lives. But our war with *them* is just beginning!" He paused to sweep his arms over the heads of some bystanders huddled in a bus shelter, and with a collective groan they all turned the color of lead and slumped to the ground.

I am become death, the destroyer of worlds.

"Someone *stop* him!" Sebbie screamed.

"We can't just throw ourselves at him," Noor said, panting, her eyes flicking to Julius. "We're not ready."

"And we've got to get Julius to a bone-mender," Horace said.

Caul rounded on us, his arms raised like bat wings, and our group faced him from the opposite end of the short street. We were ready to run if we had to, but we'd never beat him if we couldn't study him.

"Pledge me an oath and I will make you my soldiers!" Caul bellowed. His back arched and his black pool pulsed bright blue again. Was that the light—the soul—the light-eaters needed to steal? "Defy me and I'll make you suffer the most painful death imaginable. I am a benevolent god, but this is your last chance at salvation!"

"I don't think he can cross water," said Millard, who had shed his clothes as he ran and was now invisible. "That fountain we cut through—he took the long way and went round it."

"Regent's Canal isn't far," said Addison. "Perhaps we can lose him there!"

Caul was growing again before our eyes. He had raised his

arms and thrown back his head as if to channel power from the sky, and now his trunk was fattening as it rose higher out of the inky pool. "Children!" he roared. "Come to me!"

"I don't think he's talking to us anymore," Emma said, her face full of dread.

A wind began to coalesce into a miniature tornado around his trunk, and in the pit of my stomach I felt a queasy hitch.

"He's calling his minions," I said.

"More hollows?" Noor said.

"And God knows what else."

We turned and ran. Caul roared behind us. I was finished looking back. I only cared about getting away with our lives intact.

❖   ❖   ❖

The canal was a murky swath of dark water bounded by crumbling brick walls. It looked to be thirty or forty feet across. But for the hell-beast behind us, I would never have considered jumping into it.

The water was cold and filthy. We began to swim, but halfway to the other side I heard someone shout from the opposite bank and looked up to see one of the ambro addicts who had recently been on TV. He didn't make any demands or give us a chance to beg for our lives. He just opened his mouth and began to vomit a stream of silvery liquid metal at us.

"DIVE!" Enoch shouted, flailing in the water.

The addict's first shot missed: The hot metal sprayed the water near us and sent up a giant plume of steam. We used it as cover and swam down the middle of the canal away from him, Bronwyn pulling the little ones while kicking her powerful legs. Ahead of us the canal disappeared beneath an overpass. Another stream of liquid metal flew over our heads, the blowback spraying us with painfully hot water. Emma flung a fireball through the steam in the addict's direction—she was getting good at that—while Sebbie dragged light from the air, further obscuring us from view. I could hear Caul raging somewhere nearby, but couldn't see him through the steam and Sebbie's dark. Millard had been right: He'd avoided the water.

Meanwhile, I could feel a hollowgast somewhere close by, though I still couldn't pinpoint it.

We paddled frantically into the overpass tunnel. There was no way for the addict to follow unless he jumped into the water, too, which he must have known would put him at a disadvantage. Once inside the tunnel Bronwyn kicked us toward a wall, and Sebbie coughed up some of the daylight she'd swallowed to give us some light. Bolted to the wall was a small platform, above it a rusted door. We couldn't swim out through the other side of the underpass; our enemies would be waiting for us there. It was better never to emerge.

We hauled ourselves up onto the platform. Bronwyn gave the door a couple of kicks. It dented, then flew inward to expose a cramped passageway. "I hope none of you's phobic of small spaces," she said, but even if any of us had been, our fear of Caul would have won out.

Sebbie ventured in first, blowing new light through her lips in a thin stream. Julius hobbled after her on Horace's arm. Bronwyn stooped and led Sophie into the passageway by the hand, then Millard, Enoch, Addison, Emma, and Noor followed. Horatio and I took up the rear.

"Can you feel the hollow?" I asked him.

"No," he said. "But I can smell him."

"Which means he can smell us, too."

The passage was long, low-ceilinged, and smelled like urine.

"If this is a dead end, I'm going to be very upset," I heard Horace say.

It was not. The passage terminated at a ladder, and the ladder climbed a long way up a concrete tube to a hatch. Which, Bronwyn discovered while wedged up there with her back against the tube and her feet on the ladder rungs, was locked from the outside. She swore—something she almost never did—and began hammering it with her fists as we waited at the bottom.

That's when I felt it. It was always at the most inopportune times, and in the worst places: A hollowgast had entered the passage with us.

"Hurry up and open it!" I yelled. *"Hollow!"*

Her banging grew more urgent. I shoved my friends toward the ladder and told them to climb. I could hear the creature running down the passage toward us, the unmistakable triple-step echo of its two feet plus a tongue.

There was a loud metal bang. A shaft of daylight fell down the ladder. Bronwyn had gotten it open, and my friends began climbing toward freedom—or whatever was up there. But there were a lot of them and the rungs were slippery and the hollow was close now. A few of us would have to fend it off while the rest escaped.

Emma shoved Noor up the ladder before she could protest, then lit flames in each hand and assumed a fighting stance beside me. Horatio pulled something the size of a large flashlight from his waistband. With a flick of his wrist, a long, glinting blade extended from it. "One of Master King's tools," he said, and then he began shouting commands in the new Hollow dialect that I couldn't understand. As for me, my words didn't work on hollows anymore. I was unarmed. But killing hollows was my job, so I stood my ground while my heart hammered against my rib cage.

There was a flash of white teeth in the dark. From our vantage the hollow was just a mouth full of razors racing toward us. Horatio raised his sword. Emma stepped in front of him and cast a wall of fire that filled the passage. That slowed the hollow for a moment. Then Horatio lunged and jabbed his sword through the dissipating wall of flame like a fencer. I heard the hollow screech.

One of our friends shouted from halfway up the ladder—it was our turn to climb. Emma lobbed another fireball down the hall, then nudged me toward the ladder with her back. "GO," she said, and because at this point arguing would have only slowed us down, I turned, scooped up Addison, who was cowering at the base of the ladder, and climbed with the dog under one arm.

Below me, I could hear Horatio shouting, the hollow growling, and what sounded like a metal blade deflecting off brick. Emma started up the ladder after me. Bronwyn's hand reached down from the open door overhead and yanked Addison and me up into daylight. We tumbled into her and the three of us rolled. A moment later a commuter train bombed past, so close the wind from it knocked us back. We were in the middle of a busy train yard, and the hatch was smack in the middle of some tracks.

Once the train had passed, we raced back toward the hatch. I peered down the ladder to shout Emma's name, and a hollowgast tongue shot out of the dark and narrowly missed my face. We stumbled away. A moment later, the hollowgast climbed out, two of its tongues whipping ahead of it to keep Bronwyn and me at bay. Its third tongue was holding Emma by the waist. She hung limp in the air, blood running from a cut on her forehead.

I screamed and ran at it. One of its tongues punched my throat and knocked me down, and I was briefly unable to breathe. Bronwyn grabbed the tongue with both hands and tried to yank it, but it was too slick to hold and slipped right out of her grasp. Then Horatio climbed up from the ladder. He was bleeding from the chest, his shirt torn wide-open. The hollowgast sensed him and spun, and in one balletic motion Horatio swung his sword and sliced off the tongue that had been coming for his throat. It flew clear of him, spraying black blood. While the hollowgast was stunned, he raised the sword with two hands, ran at the hollowgast, and brought the blade down on the tongue holding Emma. It severed the tongue like a hot knife through butter, and Emma fell to the tracks in a heap. Before Horatio could strike again, the hollow's two remaining tongues knocked the sword from his hands, lassoed him around the neck, and dragged him into its waiting jaws.

The jaws bit down. Horatio's face contorted into a mask of pain. I tried to stand but could still hardly pull air into my throat. Bronwyn skittered forward and scooped Emma off the train tracks—another train was fast approaching. The hollow crouched down and began to chew his meal, his own inky blood and Horatio's mixing around his feet.

We would have been forgiven for abandoning Horatio to his death, accepting the sacrifice he'd made for our lives. But I could not, and my friends could not. Noor, knowing all this wight had done for us, could not. She took off sprinting toward the hollow. I shouted after her to stop, but it was no use. Her cheeks were puffed with concentrated light, and it looked like she meant to get close enough to spit it right into the hollow's face—but she never got the chance: Its two remaining tongues swept her legs out from under her and she hit the gravel. But the attack had left the hollow off balance and momentarily distracted, and Horatio—still in the grip of its jaws but not as dead as he'd been pretending to be—raised his arm and jabbed something into one of the hollow's eyes. The hollow squealed and fell onto its back. With the next train nearly upon them, and in a move that must have caused him incredible pain, Horatio wrenched his body upward, which forced the hollow's head down—and onto the track.

The train trumpeted its horn. A cloud of black blood filled the air as the train rocketed past. When it was gone, the hollow was missing the top half of its head, and Horatio, his chest scissored open and his left arm severed at the elbow, lay slack atop what remained of the hollow's dying body.

We scooped him into our arms, Noor and I, and as we ran out of the train yard, Horatio moaned into my ear. *"He showed me things."* His words were slurring. *"He showed me . . . everything."*

◆   ◆   ◆

We ran, hobbling, shoving one another on, until our lungs were bursting, then ran across an open yard of parked train cars, through a peeled-up section of chain-link fence, and down a concrete embankment. Finally, our muscles failing, we collapsed in a pile at the boundary of what looked like an old neglected park, our backs against some stones stacked around the trunk a graceful, wide-boughed tree.

Horatio had slipped into unconsciousness. Blood had darkened his clothes. Emma was awake but groggy, and there was a big fuss over where she was hurt and how badly, but she seemed to have suffered no more than a knock to the head.

"In my pocket," she said, wincing as she reached her hand into it. She brought out a small package wrapped in cotton and string, which her shaking fingers couldn't quite untie. Horace's, deft from decades of sewing, quickly got it open. Out fell a pinky finger and a little toe.

"Is this from Mother Dust?" Millard said.

Emma nodded. "She found me in Bentham's house, just before we left, and practically forced me to take them."

Bronwyn rolled the toe carefully between her palms, crushing the toe and finger to powder. She sprinkled some of it onto the cut on Emma's forehead. Then Enoch, who had no squeamishness about open wounds, spread dust onto the stump of Horatio's severed arm and the deep cuts in his chest, and right away the bleeding stopped. Next, Horace made a paste by combining the dust with water from a puddle, and that was applied to Julius's throat and then a bandage improvised from a torn shirt tied over it. His skin was a shade or two closer to normal than before but still ashen, and finger-shaped bruises collared his neck where Caul had gripped him. As the paste sunk in, his eyes fluttered and he began to relax.

Horace eased him back against the stones. "You look better," he said kindly.

Julius let his eyes fall closed and slowly shook his head. "I can feel his poison spreading," he said calmly.

Horace bit his lip and turned away.

< 376 >

We sat for a minute, letting our hearts gradually slow. Listening to the breeze move through the trees. A pleasant tingling numbness passed through my head, maybe a symptom of extreme exhaustion. Then I remembered something that jolted me from my half sleep.

"What's the matter?" Noor asked me.

"Horatio said something in my ear before he passed out. He said, '*He showed me everything.*'"

Emma frowned. "Who showed him? Caul?"

"No—the hollow. I think."

"Well, wake him up," Enoch said with a shrug.

"He nearly died just now!" said Bronwyn.

Horatio's lips were blue and his chest was rising slowly and shallowly. "He may still," I said. "Let's give the dust a minute to work."

"Did you see those lights in Caul's muck-puddle?" Sebbie asked. "Julius, can you hear me?"

"I can," he said through his teeth. "And I did."

"They flashed every time he killed someone. Like, when he swallowed their soul, that glow was the soul going down." Sebbie was talking fast. She had torn some of the light away around her head to shield her sensitive eyes, so I couldn't quite see her expression.

"Perhaps that light is the force which animates him," suggested Millard. "I remember a similar light suffusing the Library of Souls, glowing from every soul jar."

"We have to find a way to take it from him," Noor said. "To steal it—and eat it."

Sebbie leaned toward Sophie, mute and staring into the distance, and spoke loudly to Pensevus. "Is that right, Penny? We have to eat his little soul-light?"

Sophie's eyes shifted. She had a deserted look about her. "Penny's asleep," she mumbled. "Maybe forever."

Noor's head snapped toward her. "What? Why?"

Sophie had been clutching Pensevus to her chest, but reluctantly turned him over to show us that he'd been sliced wide-open and lost half his sawdust stuffing.

Noor scooted closer, her brow pinched. "Is he fixable?" she said quietly. It was the first concern she'd shown for her old doll.

Sophie shook her head. "I don't know."

"Here." Enoch picked a handful of grass and offered it to Sophie. "Stuff this into him. Fixed."

"He doesn't work that way. He had something old and special inside him, and now it's gone."

"I'm sure one of the ymbrynes can help," said Emma, starting to come out of her grogginess.

"Oh, for dog's sake, it's just a bloody toy," said Addison.

"*Thank* you," Enoch agreed, and the girls all glared at them. "Now, can we worry about how you light-eaters are supposed to get anywhere *near* Caul? If he so much as touches you . . ."

His eyes cut to Julius.

"No one promised this would be easy," said Sebbie.

"Exactly," said Millard. "That's why there are seven of you."

"We're expendable," Julius murmured.

Horace shot an evil look at Enoch. "You're *not.*"

I heard a strange noise coming from Emma. One I couldn't remember her making before. She had started to cry.

"Oh, Miss Emma." Bronwyn slid close and put an arm around her.

Emma sniffed and wiped angrily at her tears. "I'm so tired of fighting," she said. "So very tired of it."

"Me too," said Millard, slumping against one of the stones stacked behind us. "It seems our trials will never end."

"They will," said Horace. "For good or ill, in victory or death . . . soon enough, they will."

"It's looking more like death with every passing hour," said

Enoch. "Your life took a bad turn when you found us, American boy. You should never have stayed on. Look what it's got you: a no-return ticket to the graveyard." He nodded his head at the stones behind us, which weren't just slabs of rock, I realized, but dozens of weathered grave markers. They were tilted in long rows against the tree's trunk, greening with moss and so old the names had been worn away. "If Caul has his way, we'll soon be as forgotten as them. And all of the hard, horrible things we've had to do will have been for nothing."

Seeing Enoch so hopeless scared me. He was insufferable most of the time but unsinkable, too, and until then I hadn't realized how much I'd come to count on his indomitable spirit.

Noor ran her hand along the time-smoothed stones. "Just because no one remembers your name doesn't mean your life wasn't worth something."

"But if Caul wins and becomes the ruler of the peculiar world," said Enoch, "then it was all a damned waste."

"What are you suggesting?" Emma said sharply. "That we should give up? Go and surrender to save our own lives?"

"No! I'm just saying we'll be *dead*."

"It won't have been a waste, even then," Millard said, "because we'll be the ones who fought. Years from now, when whatever peculiars Caul decides to keep alive have to pledge allegiance to his evil empire, they'll gather in private to tell the story of the ones who fought to stop him. And perhaps it will inspire them to try again."

Enoch sighed. "That is some icy-cold comfort, Nullings."

" ' 'Tis better to have fought and lost, than never to have fought at all,' " Addison said, reciting again.

" 'Better to burn out than to fade away,' " said Emma.

"Hey hey," I said.

"My my," she replied.

◆   ◆   ◆

"We can't stay here much longer," I said. "If Caul was able to find us in that busy train station, he'll find us here, too."

"But Julius and Horatio—" Horace protested.

"I can walk," Julius said. But he still looked weak. And Horatio was out cold.

"I can carry the wight on my back," Bronwyn said.

"We don't even know where we're going yet," said Addison.

"To the safe house," said Horace. "Just as Miss Peregrine instructed."

"You sound like Claire," said Enoch, "and no, I don't think I'll be doing that. Miss Peregrine is brilliant at protecting us, but rubbish at planning battles. You can't win a war if you refuse to put your soldiers in harm's way."

With a sudden cry, Horatio woke up. His eyes flew open and he gasped like someone who had been holding his breath for minutes. Emma and I scrambled to him. He sat straight up, his body rigid as a board. He was mumbling fast but seemed to be speaking Hollow.

"We can't understand you," Emma said.

He went quiet for a second. He seemed haunted, possessed. And then he began to speak, disjointedly, in English. "When that hollow had me in its mouth . . . I nearly died." His eyes narrowed. "*Did* die."

"Welcome back," said Enoch, arching one eyebrow.

Bronwyn hissed at him to shush.

"My mind . . . and the hollow's . . . merged." His eyes searched the air. He seemed briefly confused. "They are all one. All their minds. A great, writhing hive."

He paused. Gently, I prompted him. "You said he showed you something."

His eyes narrowed again, then closed. He nodded. "I know where they are. Caul's army of hollows. *They're close.*"

"How close?" I said. "Where?"

He grimaced and pushed a knuckle into each of his temples. "They were born in the Library of Souls," he said. "They were supposed to go through a door . . . but the door was blocked. So they left on foot. Walked through a desert to a sea, where they were loaded onto a ship. That's where they are now."

"On their way here," Noor said. "On a ship?"

Horatio nodded. "They won't be long, either. They're plying down the Thames as we speak."

"My God," Millard said. "They must have tried to come through the Panloopticon. But they couldn't because the ymbrynes shut it down."

Emma shuddered. "And thank the birds they did. If they hadn't, the battle would already be lost. They would have overrun everything."

"Instead they had to go the long way," Millard said, "and leave the Library by its actual loop entrance—wherever that is—and travel here via ship. Which bought us time enough to collect you light-eaters."

"We've got to intercept that ship before it reaches central London," I said. "And sink it."

"Cracking plan," said Enoch. "The Thames is crawling with boats—shall we sink them all?"

"If we have to."

All of a sudden Horace jumped up, moaning and stumbling as if drunk. Bronwyn leapt to her feet and caught him before he could fall. "What's the matter, Mr. Horace?"

He squeezed his head between his hands and shook it. "I'm having *intense* déjà vu," he said. "I dreamed this conversation—dreamed it exactly—the boat, the hollows, Horatio on the ground, just like that . . ." He looked up, eyes sharp. "What we need are—"

"A fast boat and a lot of explosives?"

We whipped around to see Sharon striding toward us, his vast black cloak ripping in the breeze. I thought for a moment I was dreaming.

"Sharon!" Emma cried. "What are you doing here?"

He marched up to Horace and put a bony hand on his shoulder. "This boy came to me in a most agitated state yesterday."

Horace was shocked. "I did?"

"You told me to meet you by the Hardy Tree in St. Pancras's churchyard, have my fastest boat at the ready, and bring a load of powerful explosives."

"But I don't remember that at all!"

"Horace, you must have been sleepwalking," Emma cried.

"And did you?" Horace said, blinking into the black hole of Sharon's hood. "Did you do what I asked?"

"I did. You were quite adamant. You said all our lives depended on it, and that I must keep it a secret." A rat poked its head out of his sleeve and squeaked, and Sharon replied, "No, of course not, Daddy keeps nothing secret from *you*, Percy."

Horace broke down in grateful tears, and Bronwyn enveloped him in a massive hug.

"But how did you get out of the Acre without being seen?" Emma asked Sharon.

"My boat has a stealth mode, you'll remember. I've been sneaking in and out of Devil's Acre for my whole long career." Sharon pretended to check a nonexistent watch on his wrist. "You should know there are a lot of nasty peculiars roving not far from here, and I'm fairly positive they're looking for you. They've been making rather a mess of the city, too. We should get on with whatever it is you need me for."

"We need to intercept a boat on the Thames and sink it," I said.

"And I have rough idea of where that boat will be," said Horatio.

"Stellar, but what does it look like?" asked Sharon.

Horatio said, "It's pink and green and has an, uh . . ." He traced an S in the air with his finger, but struggled for the exact words.

"An . . ." Enoch copied his gesture as sarcastically as possible. "Are you sure you aren't describing an ice cream van?"

Horatio glowered at him. "No. It's a ship. I saw it through the hollow's own eyes."

"If you say so." Enoch gave an I-give-up sigh. "In any case, I won't be coming with you."

"What?" Emma said. "Why not?"

"I'd be of more service to the cause by staying in this churchyard to raise an army of the dead. Or at any rate, a small squadron of them. And when I have, I'll meet you at the Acre. Also, I get sick on boats."

"Don't be daft, we can't split up now," Horace said.

"My boat is quite small," Sharon said, surveying our group doubtfully.

"A big group will only make this task harder," Millard said. "You'll need to move quickly and silently, not as a traveling circus."

"What do you mean, *you'll* need?" said Horace. "You're not thinking of splitting off, too?" He grabbed at what he thought was Millard's arm, but missed.

"I'm afraid so. I've been in regular contact with a detachment of invisibles in Croydon. They've been waiting for my call to action, and I think it's time I went to round them up."

"And I know of some local grimbears who would just love to sink their teeth into Caul's minions," said Addison.

"Some of you should go directly to the safe house," said Emma. "Sophie, Sebbie, Julius. We'll meet you there when the ship's sunk. Horatio, you'll come with us?" She glanced at the wight; he nodded. Then she turned to Noor. "And, Noor, I think—"

"No way," Noor snapped. "No way I'm sitting this out."

Emma knew better than to argue.

"It's probably better not to have all of us light-eaters in one place," said Sebbie. "Just in case—"

"I don't like this splitting-up business one bit," said Bronwyn with a sigh. "But I'll go wherever I'm most needed."

And as much as I would've loved to have Bronwyn with us, it was more important for her to protect the other light-eaters, and I told her so. "I think you should take Sophie and Julius and Sebbie to the safe house and guard them until the rest of us get there."

"And me?" Horace said miserably.

"Why don't you come along with me," Millard offered. "I could use a good lookout."

Horace cast a regretful look at Julius.

"This isn't goodbye," I said. "This is 'see you after we kill a dozen hollows.'"

I saw Horatio wince at my guess. The real number was probably a lot higher.

"Don't worry about us," Emma said.

"That's like telling us not to breathe," said Bronwyn.

Sharon tilted his head sharply and crouched to a normal person's height. "We mustn't linger," he said, low and urgent. "Enemies are near."

"In that case," Enoch said, looking around, "I'll catch a cab to Highgate. Draft as many of its residents to our cause as I can."

We said a hurried goodbye and split: Millard and Horace to a suburb to find invisibles; Bronwyn to the safe house with the two light-eaters and Sophie; Enoch to Highgate Cemetery across town; and Addison in search of grimbears. After so long traveling in a big group we were suddenly half our number, and it felt like we were missing limbs. We remnants took off running after Sharon—Emma, Noor, Horatio, and me. We hugged a series of shadowed walls, leaving the churchyard a different way than we'd entered.

CHAPTER NINETEEN

I moored the boat by the Temple of Satan," Sharon said as we approached a clutch of squat buildings. Emma gasped.

"Yes, people are often surprised when they learn I'm a vegan."

"A *what*?"

We were jogging past a restaurant with tie-dyed curtains. The sign on its awning read THE TEMPLE OF SEITAN. "The Acre's meager selection of dining establishments are all practically swimming in animal blood," Sharon explained as he ran, "so I used to sneak out here in my fast boat, when I wasn't ferrying passengers thus and fro, to prevent myself from starving to death. Hullo, Steven!" He waved to a guy with a ponytail who was leaning in the doorway, and to my amazement the guy waved back as we passed.

We proceeded down an alley between the Temple of Seitan and the building next to it. At the end appeared a hidden bend of the canal. We stopped at the edge of the bank.

"Your chariot awaits," Sharon said.

We stared at the murky water. There was no boat.

"Are you having us on?" Emma said.

"My mistake. One moment." He extended his arm and said, "Where's my dongle?" A rat popped out of his sleeve with a key ring in its mouth, dropped it into Sharon's open hand, and disappeared again. On the key ring was a small black object about the size of a modern car door remote. Sharon pushed a button and an electronic chirp sounded from the canal. Sharon's boat materialized into view, moored to the closest bank.

It was a strange, steampunk marriage of an old wooden boat, slightly larger than the one he'd used to ferry us through the Acre, mated to an engine that looked like it belonged on a speedboat in *Miami Vice*. In the back a wooden crate was tied down under a tarp. My guess was that it contained the explosives Horace had requested.

We hurried down steps built into the bank, hopped on board with Sharon's help, then slid into two rows of bench seats. "This craft has seat belts," Sharon said as he settled into the captain's chair. "I suggest you use them." He clicked his remote again, and after another chirp the air around us rippled. Though we could still see the boat, Sharon explained it had become invisible to everyone else. He turned a key and the engine roared to life, and then he pushed the throttle forward so hard our heads snapped back. We shot away from our mooring, a five-foot wake slapping the canal walls behind us.

We whipped around bends in the canal so quickly the world blurred. On my left, Emma clenched her jaw and went pale. Addison hid himself under his seat. After a few nauseating minutes we exited the canal into a body of water so wide it was almost a sea by comparison: the River Thames. Horatio squatted next to Sharon and shouted directions in his ear. He was doing remarkably well considering his injuries, and it made me wonder again if wights weren't part robot. Mother Dust's dust was powerful stuff, but it didn't work *that* well.

We flew down the river, shredding past barges and cargo ships, tourist cruises and yachts, while Horatio scanned the water ahead. Our path straightened and my nausea faded. I thought of the friends we'd left behind in the Acre. Claire and Olive, both probably paralyzed with worry. Hugh and Fiona, who had vowed to sneak out of the Acre and rouse a fighting force in the way only they could; I imagined them riding into battle on a wave of attacking bees and marauding trees. Their lives all depended on us, and whether we could stop a ship filled with hollowgast from reaching the Acre. It was a task so monumental and so unlikely that I couldn't imagine what it might entail, even though my brain was always racing ahead to grapple with future impossibilities and demoralizing worst-case scenarios.

This time, I didn't have long to wait. After just a few minutes, Horatio stiffened and raised his arm to point at something. I had to blink a few times to make sure I was seeing clearly. He had said it would be pink and green, but somehow I'd forgotten that detail and had been picturing a cross between a ragged pirate's galleon and some kind of rusted-out ghost barge. Anything but what Sharon was steering us toward now: a cruise ship the color of a piña colada with a huge spiraling waterslide rising from its main deck. (There it was: the S Horatio had traced in the air.) Emblazoned across one side was the name *Ruby Princess*.

"The hollows got here on a *cruise ship*?" Noor said. She leaned forward to ask Horatio: "Are you *sure*?"

He nodded. "I saw it very clearly in that hollow's mind."

"Of course they did!" Emma said, laughing coldly. "It's the last place you'd expect to find them."

"It's a classic wight move," I agreed.

The closer we got to the *Ruby Princess*, the taller it seemed. It had to be five stories high and several hundred feet long. Which meant . . . *damn*.

"Guys, we have a problem," I announced. "Explosives won't blow up a ship that big. Just sink it."

"And?" Emma said.

"Hollows can *swim*."

Her face fell. "Right."

"We're going to have to board the ship, find where the hollows are being kept, and blow *that* up," I said.

Horatio turned to face us. "They're in a dark place. All together. I caught a brief glimpse of it, before that hollow's head got smashed."

"Sounds like a cargo hold," said Sharon.

"Yes," said Horatio. "I believe so."

We talked through the plan, which was alarmingly light on detail and depended altogether too much on chance and luck. We would climb the ship's emergency ladder, find the cargo hold, toss in the explosives, and run like hell back to Sharon's boat. Oh, and avoid heavily armed wights along the way.

Sharon cut the engines to a putter as we got close to the ship, a green-and-pink monolith that towered vertiginously above us. We could see no activity on board, no faces in its rounded stateroom windows, no life at all. Our boat rolled sickeningly as we rounded the stern and crossed the big ship's boiling wake, and then we sped up briefly until we pulled even with the emergency ladder. It was bolted to the hull and nearly reached the water. It climbed several stories to a rickety platform, and from there metal steps led up to the lower deck. Just following it with my eyes gave me a touch of vertigo, my old fear of heights rearing its head at the worst possible time, as usual.

Sharon instructed me to remove the tarp from the crate of explosives. I guess I was expecting some cartoonish pile of dynamite sticks, but the crate was filled mostly with straw packing material, on top of which lay a small bundle of yellow bricks bound together with duct tape. I'd seen enough crappy action movies to know these were plastic explosives. Next to them sat a little remote with a safety latch and a grip trigger—the detonator. The whole thing weighed maybe five pounds, which wasn't much, but the only one of us still wearing anything with pockets large enough to carry it was Horatio, who hadn't yet shed his WWI coat, even though it was soaked in blood and missing an arm. I felt only the slightest hesitation as I passed a handful of deadly high explosives to him.

He noticed. "Do you trust me?" he asked, both our hands holding the five yellow bricks.

"I do," I said, and retracted my hand. And I did.

Horatio tucked the explosives into his inside coat pocket. He paused for a moment, then gave me the detonator. "You keep it."

I weighed it in my hand, then slid it into my pants pocket.

Without the detonator, Sharon explained, the explosives were no more dangerous than a box of matches. "With it, you'd better be at least a hundred feet away before you hit that trigger. In fact, it would be best if you were back on this boat and we were speeding off in the opposite direction."

With that, it was time to go. Sharon steered the boat as close to the emergency ladder as he could manage, and then there was nothing to do but climb. Emma went first, grabbing the bottom rung and pulling herself up with ease. Noor followed. I nearly asked her to stay behind on the boat, but I knew what she'd say and decided to save my breath. Horatio used his remaining arm to pull himself up *one-handed*, and then it was my turn. I gathered what little courage I had left, stood up, and almost fell out of the pitching boat. Sharon caught my arm, tsked, then boosted me by the waist so I could grab a rung and pull myself up, legs pedaling the air. When I'd gotten my feet hooked in and climbed a few rungs, I looked down at Sharon, bobbing in the rough current.

"I'll be waiting right here," he called, white-toothed grin gleaming from his hood. He waved a paperback book. "Take your time. I brought a novel!"

❖   ❖   ❖

I swung my legs over the railing and dropped onto the deck of the cruise ship, my knees still rubbery from the climb. The first thing I noticed was a festive poster on the wall inviting passengers to a luau. It was splattered rather spectacularly with blood. A single red high-heeled shoe lay abandoned on the deck nearby.

No matter. We had made it on board without being seen, with-out falling from the slippery steps, without setting off any alarms. I

still had my doubts whether this was really a ship filled with hollowgast; our plan had depended on the hallucinatory near-death visions of a wight who'd only recently been a hollowgast himself, and I half expected to find nothing more than boomer-aged tourists pounding margaritas. But there seemed to be no one on board at all. No one on the narrow promenade the ladder had led us to, no one in the triple hot tub we passed as we snuck along the deck to another set of stairs. It climbed to a catwalk that had a view across the whole main deck, where the garish corkscrew waterslide fed into a giant swimming pool—

There. Someone was in the pool, floating in the shallow end. In a black cocktail dress. Facedown.

And someone else, splayed in a lounge chair, limbs twisted as if they'd fallen there from a height. And another, slumped over the open-air tiki bar, blood in a wide smear around them. And then I felt it, a creeping discomfort that spiked as soon as I recognized it, multiplying until it felt like a million needles in my gut. The others saw me wince and knew what it meant.

"Down!" Emma hissed, pushing our group behind a planter of fake palms. Through their branches we could see a man in black tactical clothes patrolling the deck below. He wore a machine gun strapped across his chest.

"He's a wight?" I asked.

"Mind-controlled normal," Horatio said. "But there are a few wights on board somewhere, you can be sure, and a turncoat peculiar who's doing the mind controlling."

Emma's face clouded. "I despise wights as much as the next peculiar—no offense, Horatio—but I hate these traitors with a passion. They should all be strung up by their heels and flayed."

"There can be no justice before victory," said Horatio.

"Could we please find the hollows and blow them up and get out of here?" said Noor.

The sensation in my gut sharpened to a directional point. I

whispered for the others to follow me. Once the guard had passed, I guided my friends back down the steps. We snuck from hiding spot to hiding spot, and luckily there were many. My inner compass led us through a dining room: a chaos of flipped tables, broken glasses, and vivid dark splashes across the carpet that could have been either food or gore. What had happened on board was becoming clearer: The ship had been commandeered by wights, and the passengers and crew had been fed to the hollows.

"I'm ready if you need me," Noor said, pulling a bit of light from the air as we walked.

"So am I," Emma said, rubbing her hands together.

We hurried down a hallway lined with staterooms, through a heavy door marked CREW ONLY, and down a staircase into another hall, this one unadorned and utilitarian. There was a long blank stretch with no doors to duck into, then a quick turn down a short hall that ended at a cage door, toward which my compass pointed unmistakably.

That was it. The cargo hold.

"In there," I said, probably too loud, but before we could reach it the door slid open and a man walked out. He was dressed like a tourist in blood-splotched yellow pants and a Hawaiian shirt. He was drying his hands with a shop towel when he looked up, saw us, and froze.

His eyes were blank.

"Hey, what the—"

Horatio grabbed my arm and pulled me roughly toward him. *"Malaaya, eaxl gestealla,"* Horatio said, a greeting I didn't understand but recognized as Old Peculiar. "I found him hiding in one of the kitchens."

It was just me and Horatio; Emma and Noor were behind us and had stayed hidden around the corner.

I tried to act hurt and terrified. The wight relaxed. "I just fed them," he said, "but they're insatiable."

Horatio said something else in Old Peculiar and both men laughed. Then Horatio dropped my arm and punched the wight in the throat. He gagged and dropped to his knees.

"STOP!" I heard a voice shout, and we spun to see Noor and Emma being pushed down the hall by two men with guns. My heart kicked into high gear.

"Get in there!" one of the men yelled, gesturing to the cargo hold door. "Now!"

Horatio tried to play it off. He said something angry in Old Peculiar, then added in English, "Unless you want to explain to Caul why you fed the Prelate of the Loops to the hollows!"

It didn't work. One of the men fired a bullet into the floor. There was nowhere to run, no peculiar trick their guns couldn't best. Nothing to do but go through the door and let them lock us into the cargo hold with the hollows.

The man shot the floor near us a second time, and this bullet came close to Noor's feet and made her scream. We all backed up through the cage door, Horatio included. Now the other man fired a shot, his bullet biting the air just above our heads.

We retreated into the dark. The men threw the door shut and locked it. Then they pulled a second door down over the cage, this one solid and heavy, and it blocked out the light as it slammed closed.

It felt like bolts of lightning were shooting through my stomach. We could hear the hollows moving around farther inside the hold. I cursed myself for letting Noor and Emma come with us. Now they would die needlessly, when the only sacrifice required was Horatio and me. And at that moment I would have happily given my life to rid the world of every last hollow. But no victory was worth Noor's life, or Emma's.

First we smelled them, an enveloping wave of rotten meat stench choking us. Then we heard their teeth crunching through bone, slurping and grunting as they finished whatever meal the

Hawaiian-shirted wight had just delivered to them. Then Emma lit a flame and we saw them, all massed together at the other end of an enormous cargo room. They were crouched on a rusted floor with their backs to us, feasting. I looked for any possible exit or escape, but there were none. The floor was a seamless expanse of iron and the walls were ribbed metal curving up to meet a high ceiling. There were no doors but the one we'd come through, nothing at all in there but us, the hollows, and a few metal crates stacked in a corner.

"*Jacob,*" Noor whispered. "Please tell me you figured out how to control these—"

"I didn't," I said, feeling terrified and pathetic. "And even if I had, it would only be one at a time. And there are—"

"*Dozens,*" Emma hissed. Because she could see them, too. We all could.

"*What do we do now?*" Noor whispered. "*Use the explosives?*"

"*They're too powerful,*" I said. "*We'll all die.*"

"*I don't know that we have a choice,*" said Horatio.

And then one of them spun, locked its black eyes on us, and spat a half-chewed limb from its mouth. It had smelled us. *Felt* us. And then another hollow turned, and another, and soon they were all staring, their half-finished meal forgotten.

We weren't just another morsel. We were peculiar. Our souls were the sustenance hollowgast craved more than anything.

They started toward us. Unhurried, because it was clear we had nowhere to run.

"*You* talk to them . . . ," said Noor, gripping Horatio by the elbow.

"I'll try," he said. He barked something at them. The hollows shuffled to a confused stop, pausing like a crowd waiting at a DON'T WALK sign. "At best I can keep them at bay only a short time. My power over them is nothing compared with Jacob's."

"I told you—I don't *have* any power over them!" I shouted,

frustrated with Horatio but furious at myself. "I don't know their language!"

The hollows moaned strangely, then started toward us again, slow and wary.

"Your connection is deeper than language," Horatio said. "If you can manage to access it." He shouted at the hollows again, but this time only some of them stopped.

"Jacob." Emma turned to look at me, her expression wooden with fear. "Remember in the wights' fortress, when you fell into that nest of hollows and came out able to control all of them at once?"

I shook my head. "That was different. We'd all gotten knocked out by sleep dust . . ."

She'd extinguished one hand and was using it to dig frantically in her pocket. "This is the last of her—I saved it for an emergency," she said, fishing out a thumb half wrapped in cotton and thrusting it at me. "Do it again. Just like last time."

I hesitated. "But that was different. There are too many of them, and no way to spread the dust—"

"Yes, there is." Horatio pushed the explosives into my hand. "Tie that thumb around this brick. Then repeat after me."

I knew what he was thinking, and it was madness. The explosives were too strong. This would kill everything in the room, not put us to sleep. But since there was no alternative except waiting to die, my hands obeyed. I took the thumb from Emma, the brick of explosives from Horatio, and bound them together with string. As I worked, Horatio was shouting at the hollows, trying to slow them down. Then he shouted at me, slotting English phrases between the ones in Hollow: "Repeat after me!"

I tried. He was talking so fast, using words my mind didn't recognize.

"You're thinking too much!" Horatio barked.

I finished tying the thumb to the explosives, which freed up all my attention. My words started to flow, began to match his. I didn't know what we were saying, but the doubling of my commands with his seemed to have more effect on the hollows than Horatio's voice alone.

While he shouted, he used his shoulder to push Emma, Noor, and me into a tight huddle. Then he snatched the explosives from me, wound his arm back, and threw them as far as he could. I heard the bundle bounce off the back wall and land somewhere in the opposite corner.

The hollows were close now. A wall of them was shuffling toward us, hungry and slavering, my and Horatio's shouts the only thing keeping them from tearing us apart that very moment. But I could feel their will gaining strength and Horatio's beginning to fade.

Noor pressed into me and Emma. "I love you guys," Noor said, crying. "You're like my family. Okay?"

I was shouting guttural commands at the top of my lungs. But I nodded and hugged her tight, and Emma, who couldn't put her arms around us without setting us on fire, held her hands away while pressing her back into the little knot we'd formed.

"We love you, too," Emma said. "This is going to work, right?"

"Of course it's going work," I said, because I didn't want despair to be the last thing they felt before dying.

"HAND ON THE DETONATOR!" Horatio shouted between commands in Hollow.

I began to understand, slowly, what he was saying. Not *stop*, or *sleep*, or *get back*, but *gentle, easy now, slowly*. And then, as he turned to face me and pressed himself into our huddle: *arms, gentle, give me your arms*.

Horatio reached up his own arm and touched Emma's, and told her with a look and a nod that it was time to extinguish her flame. She did, plunging the room into dark again, and I felt one of her still-warm hands on my back.

And then, still echoing Horatio's every shout, I felt a hollowgast wrap its arms around us, and its tongues. I prayed for a quick death as its noxious breath rolled over us.

But the hollow didn't close its jaws, didn't bite down, didn't squeeze the breath and life out of us with its encircling tongues.

Gentle. Come forth. Gentle. Give me your arms.

And another did, and another, all wrapping their bodies around us. I could feel their hunger like the desperation of a starving man, could feel them dreaming of killing us, cracking open our skulls, draining our souls. But one after another, they merely added themselves to our knot, and after a minute we were ringed around with their open, ragged-breathing mouths, gagging in their hot stink.

I realized then what Horatio was doing. He was fashioning their armored bodies into a shield. But he was tiring, his voice growing hoarse. I felt a row of teeth dig into my shoulder and start to bite down, and a ripple of sharp pain made me scream, *Stop, stop, stop,* in this broken Hollow dialect I hardly knew, which was enough to stay his teeth but not to make them retract.

"NOW?" I shouted to Horatio.

"Not yet!" he said. Then between commands in Hollow, he said, "Think of yourself as a bridge . . . a conduit . . . a vessel to contain their minds . . ."

The tongues tightened around us, suddenly and viciously, and I heard Noor gasp and Horatio shriek, along with the sound of breaking bone—and his voice dropped away. I didn't need light to see that he was badly injured and didn't need him to tell me what to do.

I clenched the trigger in my palm. And all went black.

◆   ◆   ◆

For a long time there was only darkness, and the sound of rushing water, and the hazy sensation of floating. I had lost myself, though I couldn't remember how.

My ears rang, sharp and constant, like feedback from a

microphone. That and the dark and the rushing water were all there was, for a long time, until another sound joined them: a girl's voice.

Arms tugged at my body. And then someone slapped me, and a constellation of stars flashed in the dark, and with them new sensations:

I am cold.

I am almost completely submerged in cold water.

My vision began to return. I was in a room filling with rolling water and reeling shadows. I saw a frightened face cowled in strands of wet hair. Her dark eyes flashed in a glimmer of firelight. They widened when she saw me look at her, and she shouted my name. I opened my mouth to reply and swallowed salt water instead.

My vision came and went. I vomited. I heard my name again, shouted by another. Caught glimpses of a room filled with waves and dim, thrashing forms, and a girl cupping a living flame in her palm.

Someone was holding me from behind, preventing me from drowning.

I am here but elsewhere, too:

I was spidered into a corner, deaf and terrified, my lower half flowing a river of black blood

I was underwater in pieces, fading

I was floating on my back in the churning water, two hundred pounds of angry, taut muscle, waiting

I was all of them at once

Jacob, can you hear me?

Yes, I tried to say, but my mind was splintered fifty ways; I couldn't find the body that my voice lived in

Jacob, God, please.

We were in a boat. Trapped in the lightless belly of a ship. In a room filling fast with water.

Ah. There I am.

Jacob, we're going to drown.

I found my tongue
I said: *No, we're not.*
I could move my arms. My legs.
My body.
And then,
      splintering,
       I can move
          all
              of
                  them.

CHAPTER TWENTY

hey were still alive. Noor, Emma, and Horatio. By some miracle we had all survived the blast, wrapped in an armor of hollows—who were themselves armored, chests and backs thickened by a steely exoskeletal plate. Many had been killed, and many more had been injured beyond usefulness, but judging by the dizzying number of paths into which my mind diverged, there were at least a dozen undamaged hollows now under my command.

The feeling was not altogether alien. It had happened once before: a collective brain reboot that had fused my mind with a nest of hollows, allowing me to move beyond my shaky grasp on their language to tap into the unconscious heart of my power—and into them. It did not seem to matter that these hollows were new. Despite their differences with hollows of the past, their deepest minds were the same. This was not merely control, but inhabitation. I acted as them, experienced a dulled version of their pains, saw through their eyes as well as my own. At first it was terrifying, this feeling that I was at once nowhere and everywhere, my *me*-ness rippling through all of them like a deck of cards being shuffled.

One of me, underwater, was staring at a star-shaped hole in the wall where the sea was rushing in, pale, filtered light gleaming on the other side.

Our escape.

Grab on to me, I tried to say as Jacob. *Take a deep breath.* But the words came out wrong, through the wrong mouth, and I had to stop thinking for a moment, and focus, and find myself. There I was: staring vacantly while my friends panicked.

Dropping back into myself felt like slipping into old, comfortable clothes.

"Everyone grab on to me and take a deep breath!"

This time they heard me and did as I asked.

I gathered my hollows. They clustered around us in a pod, lassoed our waists, and pulled us underwater. I hardly even had to think about what I wanted them to do, and it was done.

I hadn't lost my touch.

The hollows were surprisingly agile swimmers. Their tongues rippled like fins and grabbed hold of things to pull us along. In a moment we were gliding through the jagged hole that had been blasted in the wall, then down a hallway that was flooded to its ceiling. If we'd tried to swim it on our own we surely would have drowned, but the hollows powered us through the water so quickly my cheeks fluttered against the current.

We shot up a flooded staircase, breaking through to the surface halfway up. After that we were carried in a nest of withered arms and muscled tongues, our feet never touching the ground.

We burst through a door and onto the deck. The ship was listing badly to one side, the deck tilting like a ramp. The hollows swarmed around us, thrilled to breathe open air again, angry because anger was their nature, hating me but ready to do anything I commanded. There were so many of them—more than I'd thought, more than I'd been able to count—thirty-five, maybe forty hollows. They leapt in the air, drummed the deck with their tongues. A wight ran into their midst and started shouting orders. Before he could finish his sentence, they'd wrenched his head off and thrown it into the Thames.

I had the hollows set us down. There was a burst of gunfire from the tilting waterslide and a ricochet answered behind us. I pushed my friends back into the sheltering stairwell and blocked the entry with two hollows, then sent the rest to go clear the ship of enemies.

Within a minute it was done: three men with guns disarmed and torn to pieces, the turncoat peculiar who'd been controlling them flung onto the shuffleboard deck with his back shattered. Another wight had surrendered at the ship's controls with his hands up and his knees trembling.

The ship, or what was left of it, was ours. Now we just had to find a way off it.

"Climb aboard," I said, kneeling two hollows for Noor and Emma to mount.

"I'd rather walk," said Noor.

"It's perfectly safe when Jacob's in control," Emma said. "And much faster." She hopped onto the hollow's back, and it secured her with a quick wrap of its tongue around her waist.

"It really is," Horatio agreed, climbing on behind Emma.

"You can ride with me," I offered, and when I mounted the second hollow she gave in and climbed on behind me.

"This is a dream, right?" she whispered in my ear.

And then we took off.

*   *   *

A police helicopter was circling the ship at low altitude. Sirens were approaching. At some point while my friends and I were trapped in the cargo hold, the ship had docked at an industrial port along the Thames, where enormous oil tanks loomed beyond a maze of ships.

My squadron of hollows carried us to the edge of the railing. I hoped they could swing us down to the dock, but it was a long way. I sent two hollows to find some rope—*shouldn't be hard to come by on a boat*—while I exercised the rest, making them jump and tumble around the deck to shake off the last of their dust-induced sleep and strengthen my connection to them. It was a surreal scene, no question, though its strangeness was dulled somewhat by my fractured state of mind. My connection to so many hollows at once occasionally threatened to overwhelm me, and mental noise faded in and out like a staticky radio signal.

"Jacob! Where have you gone?" I'm not sure how long Emma had been trying to talk to me, but the alarm in her voice made me think it had been a while.

"Sorry," I said, shaking my head and popping my jaw, which had been clenched tight in concentration.

Horatio sat astride his hollow's rounded back like a master horseman, and he was smiling. At me.

"What is it?" I said.

"You're quite a specimen, Jacob Portman." He watched a hollowgast do an acrobatic flip off the top of the waterslide, then turned again to face me. "I think Abraham Portman was right about you."

"My grandfather?" I said, leaning forward. "Why, what did he say?"

"That you could be the most powerful peculiar of our times, were you given the opportunity to prove yourself." His smile faded. "But it would come hand in hand with terrible danger."

Danger he never wanted me to face.

The hollowgast did another flip off the waterslide. The two I'd sent to find rope hadn't returned yet. I made the hollow that was guarding the surrendered wight in the control room drag him out, and thirty seconds later they appeared, the hollow pulling the wight along by his hair, the wight screeching and pathetic.

He was begging for his life.

I ignored him, because a tug at my attention told me that the two hollows who'd gone to find rope had encountered someone unexpected.

I heard his voice through their ears.

"Hullo, my lovelies, what are you doing out and about? Oh, you've been *very* bad . . ."

And then he rose into view off the side of the ship, suspended in midair upon a tornadic pedestal of racing black wind.

Caul.

Noor stiffened at the sight. Emma swore.

He was giant now, a stretched and distended corruption of a man from the torso up, a violent storm from the waist down. His arms were normal, but his fingers were ten thick and wriggling tree roots, turning whatever they touched to rot.

He was screaming something about revenge, something about living forever, and as he did, he turned his hands upward and his long fingers shot toward the sky. And then a gang of deranged, ambro-enhanced peculiars began scrambling over the railings of the ship to attack us.

The first to make it on board spat a stream of liquid metal at the nearest hollow, and as the creature's brain melted under the spray, I felt its consciousness wink out. But then three more leapt on the ambro addict and in an instant he was dead. Then more of Caul's minions came, and with each a new scourge: One called down a cloud of acid that burned one of my hollows, another had incredible strength, two of them working together made a bolt of red lightning that left a hole in the chest of another hollow and streaked close over our heads, sizzling the air and leaving a scent like burned hair. My hollows swarmed them like rabid animals, overwhelming eight, nine, ten of these powerful, ambrosia-enhanced traitors in the space of a minute while the two hollows that my friends and I rode fell back to a safer distance.

When that wave of the attack had ended, I had lost three hollows, and no less than ten of Caul's addicts lay sprawled on the deck, dead or nearly so.

Caul was furious. With a roar of wind he flew across the gap and onto the boat, where he hovered just above the deck while his miniature tornado ripped apart the wood below him and sucked chairs and debris into its funnel.

So much for not being able to cross water. It seemed Caul too had evolved, and quickly.

Before he could get his bearings I sent three hollows sprinting toward him. Caul reached out his arms and entangled them in his long fingers, then lifted them off their feet and clutched them to his upper body—now twice their size—like they were babies. I forced their mouths open, but couldn't get their tongues to attack him; Caul was whispering to them, and their will to obey me was quickly fading.

"What's going on?" Noor said, panicking as they all went limp in Caul's arms. "Why aren't they killing him?"

I wanted to explain, but my mind was too occupied. Something bad was happening. I felt the tendrils of Caul's influence flowing backward through those three hollows and into my own brain.

Hello, Jacob.

I closed my eyes and put everything I had into pushing Caul out of my mind. But my attention was too divided.

Kill the girl.

At this, I felt the hollow Noor and I were riding flinch, then tense, and I had to devote all my focus to reasserting total control over it, lest it unwrap its tongues from our waists and circle them around Noor's throat.

After a moment, it relaxed again. But Caul's influence was insidious and his possible entry points into my brain were scattered across the deck.

I had thirty-four hollows left, but I let go, temporarily, of thirty-one of them to put everything I had in the two we were riding and the hollow closest to Caul's face. All the rest went limp and slack as I relaxed my grip on their minds, and there was a great collective *thud* as they collapsed to the deck.

"Oh my God!" Emma cried. "What's happening to them?"

I didn't have the bandwidth to reply. I had narrowed all my focus to Caul and the two hollows. It was enough: I shoved Caul out

< THE DESOLATIONS OF DEVIL'S ACRE >

of my mind, stopped the hollow we were riding from trying to kill Noor, then regained control of the one most immediately in Caul's grip. As I wrenched open that hollow's mouth I could hear Caul yelling, "Stop there, what are you doing—"

I sent all four of its tongues at him. One each through his blue-glowing eye sockets, the other two into his open mouth, with such power that they punched through the back of his throat.

Caul lolled backward drunkenly, gagging. His wind slowed and he began to crumple, the life going out of him. He sank into the puddle and was swallowed up by it, taking with him the three hollows in his arms; I could feel them dying as they all disappeared together.

For a moment, it was quiet but for the helicopter and the whine of approaching sirens.

"The blue light!" Noor cried, and I could feel her body starting toward it. "If I can just—"

"Don't fall for it!" Emma said. "He's pretended to be dead before. That's how he got Julius!"

As if on cue, Caul burst from the hole like some nightmarish Jack-in-the-box, the blast of wind that propelled him blowing back our hair and tumbling chairs across the deck. He seemed even larger than before, and absolutely unscathed. He'd retreated to his hole and regenerated himself in mere seconds.

"A thousand hollows couldn't stop me!" he bellowed. "Death only makes me stronger!"

He was really starting to piss me off.

"Yeah?" I said quietly. "Let's test that theory."

I bowed my head, closed my eyes. I felt a strange power course through me as my mind split, fled itself, and flew into the limp bodies of twenty-nine hollowgast. They shuddered awake like old cars starting in the cold, then rose to their feet, one after another.

Despite his claims, twenty-nine was apparently more hollowgast than Caul wanted to tangle with at once, and he began rearing backward toward the railing. "It's been such fun seeing you again,"

< 413 >

he called out. "I'd love to stay and play, but I've got a date with old friends—"

"You'll never get through their shield!" Emma shouted at him.

A smile flickered across Caul's face. "That reminds me. Carlo, if you wouldn't mind?"

The wight I'd forgotten about shoved back his sleeve and barked into a smartwatch: "Vigsby, this is Eagle! Strike now! I repeat—"

I caught his wrist with a hollow's tongue and wrenched it so far behind his back I heard the arm break. But it was too late: Whatever message he'd meant to send had been sent.

Briefly distracted, I hadn't noticed Caul entangling the hollow closest to him with his long fingers, and immediately I felt its life fading. Through its ears I heard Caul whisper, *"Come home, sweetheart, you were always my favorite."*

The other twenty-eight were running at him flat-out, but before they could reach him, Caul's wind propelled him high into the air. Nearly a hundred tongues whipped at him but all missed. He let the dead hollow drop, then waggled his long fingers at us in a teasing *toodle-oo.* "To be continued, eh?"

With that, he arched his back and flung himself farther skyward—because of *course* he could fly now—then flipped his tornado's funnel at the rotors of the police helicopter that had been buzzing overhead.

It lost control and began to spin toward us.

I made the hollows we were riding dive for cover as the helicopter tumbled, decapitating the waterslide before it fell out of sight and crashed into the river.

The moment plastic debris stopped raining down, Noor wriggled out of the tongue-belt's embrace, slid off our hollow's back, and ran to the broken-armed wight. He was on his knees. Whatever call he'd made on his watch was still connected. On the other end I could hear screams and chaos.

"Who's Vigsby?" Noor shouted in his face. "What did you do?"

His blank expression spread into a grin.

Emma ran up beside us, panicking. "I just placed the name. She's one of Miss Babax's wards!"

"I suppose there's no harm in telling you now," said the wight. "She was one of ours. And a skilled assassin."

Through his watch we heard a name shouted crisply in anguish: "Ravenna!"

"That's Miss Babax's name," Emma cried. "Oh my God—"

Noor gasped. "That means our shield—"

"Is no more!" the wight said. "And soon Master Caul will reclaim our rightful home—and make a stack of your bodies for the fire!"

Emma smacked him in the mouth with a ball of flame. He stumbled away howling, head like a lit match, then tripped backward into a hot tub.

"We have to get to the Acre *now*," Emma said. "Before it's too late!"

But we all knew the awful truth: It was probably too late already.

CHAPTER TWENTY-ONE

*T*he hollows surrounded us, keyed up and mouth-breathing heavily, their dripping black eye sockets slicking the deck beneath our feet. Noor edged against me, rigid. I assured her I had them under control, and she claimed to believe me, but I knew from experience that it was next to impossible to switch off the instinct to run from a hollowgast—especially one you could see.

There was no rope to be found. I would have to improvise a way to reach the docks below. I told my friends to hang on tight. We mounted the hollows. Sharon had almost certainly fled in his boat after Caul appeared.

At my command, twenty-eight hollows ran down the slanting deck to the rail and leapt overboard. They chained themselves together while falling, unfolding themselves into a bridge leading down to the docks. I had the two remaining hollows strap us onto their backs tighter than ever, and then we leapt overboard, skittering along the hollow-bridge and down to the dock with a quickness that made Emma squeal and left me light-headed.

Finally back on dry land, I herded the other hollows into a circle of protection around our two, and, in that formation, we took off running. The hollows were fast, and used their tongues almost exclusively to power themselves along, which acted like shocks and made the ride not unlike being on the back of a fast horse—only this was an animal I was psychically connected to, and my confidence level on hollow-back was much higher.

Finding the Acre wasn't hard: Caul had left us a block-wide trail of destruction to follow. All along the way he'd ripped up cars and shattered windows, had raked his deathly arms over anyone he saw, leaving dozens of normals lying sickened and gray amid the wreckage. Fires, smoke, bodies—it seemed cruel even for Caul, and bafflingly secondary to his real goal. A waste of time. But then I saw the way people screamed and ran from our monstrous troupe, as I'm sure they had run from Caul himself, and I realized he was terrorizing people for the same reason he'd made his new hollows visible: to make normals fear and hate us. He was sowing the seeds of an apocalyptic war, the kind the Revelator's prophecy foretold. One that would force us all to choose sides, and fight if only to defend ourselves.

But first things first.

We made quick progress across the city. Fortunately, we didn't have far to go; the ship had docked less than a mile from the Acre's loop entrance. I hoped Bronwyn and the light-eaters had made it to the safe house, but we wouldn't be meeting them there as we'd promised. There was no time.

As we got close to the Acre, the destruction grew worse. When we turned down the narrow tributary of the Thames that led to the loop entrance, it became total. The glass-walled office buildings and apartments that lined the river had sustained massive damage. There were bodies floating in the water and scattered along the concrete banks. Some of the dead were normals, just innocent bystanders. A few were ambro addicts, their eyes still glowing white even while their life drained away. Others I recognized as peculiars who'd been posted outside the Acre to defend its loop entrance.

Our first layer of defenders had fallen along with the ymbrynes' shield.

Noor squeezed me tight as our hollow raced along the banks, bucking and rolling beneath us. Emma and Horatio kept pace to our left, and all around us was a surging sea of hollowflesh, their heavy breaths leaving a fine mist of stinking black air in our wake. Ahead was the loop entrance, the same one we'd used to enter and leave Devil's Acre many times: a section of waterway capped by concrete to form a tunnel below. We were a block away when something massive emerged from the tunnel and unfolded itself: a giant man tall as a mature oak, his muscled body clothed in moss and leaves. It was another of Caul's lieutenants, one of the wights who had been monstrously enhanced in the Library of Souls.

He stood there blocking the loop entrance, water up to his waist and pounding his chest like a gorilla. Then he turned and picked up a small car parked on the overpass and launched it at us. My hollows scattered. It landed on its roof behind us and skidded into the water.

"Think you can kill him?" Noor shouted.

"Yeah," I shouted back, "but it's going to cost us time!"

Caul knew his wight wouldn't stop us. He was just trying to slow us down.

I stopped most of my hollows a half block away, made two leap from one side of the water to the opposite bank, then sent four of them at the giant—two from his left and two from his right. He swatted one away with a hand the size of a dumpster. The hollow flew into the concrete bankside and fell, broken, into the water. Another jumped onto his head and wrapped him with its tongues like an octopus. The giant roared, reached behind him, and tore it off, but while his hands were occupied, the other two wrapped their tongues around his neck and squeezed as hard as they could. The giant turned to face the overpass and smashed the hollow he was holding against it repeatedly, until I felt the life go out of it. But by then his face was turning red and he couldn't breathe, and he began to stumble around, swiping at the hollows and trying to pry their tongues from his throat without success. Finally, he blacked out and fell face-first into the water, unconscious, and the hollows fed upon his eyes.

"Good show, Jacob!" Emma shouted.

"Two hollows for one huge wight," Noor said. "Not bad!"

"That depends on how many more he's got," I said. "Now hang on and get ready to hold your breath, we're about to get wet!"

With a barely perceptible nod from me, my hollows took off running again. We raced down the banks to the overpass, then leapt in the water beside the unmoving giant. The two hollows who'd felled him rejoined us, and I could sense something in them that felt like happiness, or giddiness; the adrenaline spike of predators who'd just made a kill.

We swam through the tunnel, water soaking us to the neck. The hollows' tongues pulled us quickly along until the circle of light behind us equaled the size of the one ahead. And then the change-over gripped us, and in a moment we were flying out the other side, into the middle of a war.

◆　　◆　　◆

We emerged into the Acre to find a smoking ruin. A battle must have raged here not long ago but had since moved on, leaving craters and shattered buildings behind—and more bodies, Caul's addicts and our peculiars both.

My hollows swam to the bank and climbed out of the water—straight into a cloud of stinging bees. We were swatting the air like mad when I heard a familiar voice shout, "Jacob! Is that you?"

It was Hugh. He was stretched out on the ground with his back against a concrete bridge support, panting and sweating and dirty—but alive. "Hugh!" I called out to him. "You're back!" And as he leapt up and ran toward us, the cloud of bees around us dissipated.

"We never left—couldn't find a way out!" he shouted. "And never mind me, *you're* back! And Emma and Noor! Thank the birds you're okay—" He skidded to a stop at the outer ring of my hollows, turning a bit pale. "Say, you're controlling these, right? Like last time?"

"It's perfectly safe," I said, my hollow fording through the others to meet him.

"Hugh, you're a sight for sore eyes!" Emma cried. "What happened?"

"The shield's gone!" he said. "The minute it disappeared, lots of us started running for the loop entrance because we were expecting an attack. We thought it would be hollows, not these giant wights. The Americans sent a windstorm and lightning bolts at them and shot them loads of times, but it didn't stop them. And Caul . . ." His eyes cut to a peculiar lying nearby, gray as death and breathing in stutters.

"We know what he can do," Noor said darkly.

"Just have to figure out how to kill him," I added. "Climb on." I made a hollow kneel before him. He hesitated.

"Hugh, get on!" Emma shouted.

"You're sure you've got them well in hand?"

"Very sure."

Hugh gave a steely smile. "Then we've got a chance." He mounted the beast's shoulders. It wrapped a tongue around his waist and stood. Hugh opened his mouth and sucked the cloud of bees down his throat.

Hugh directed me toward the fighting, but I hardly needed directions; judging from the debris-darkened sky and roaring crashes in the distance, the battle was raging in the center of the Acre. I followed a trail of wreckage down crooked alleys, through the mazelike domain of looped normals, through a section of Acre that was burning so badly the smoke had turned day to night.

I kept Hugh's hollow close to mine and Noor's so I could hear him, and we shouted to each other as the hollows ran.

"Where are the ymbrynes?" I asked him.

"Fighting!" he replied, bear-hugging his hollow's neck to keep from being flung off. "Most have turned into birds and have been launching attacks from the sky."

Our shouts echoed off the close-set walls around us.

"And Fiona?" Emma said.

"Laying a trap for the giants! Near the ministries building!"

My stomach dropped as the hollows took a running leap over a flipped wagon, then skidded around a sharp corner.

"How many giant wights does Caul have with him?" Emma asked.

"Five, including one at the loop entrance! And they're tall as houses!"

"And how many ambro addicts?" I yelled.

"Could be dozens! We outnumber them, but they've all taken massive doses of ambrosia, and they're *powerful*."

"Did Bronwyn come back?" Noor said, and I could feel her tense. "Did she have a boy and two girls with her?"

But there was no time for him to reply, because I'd found our way out of the maze and into the middle of a skirmish. We sped out of the tenement zone into Louche Lane, where many of the shops were burning—more smoke, more bodies—and right away something collided with one of my hollows and I felt its leg shatter.

Down the street there was a towering mound of humanity that looked like a cross between a melting ice cream cone and Jabba the Hutt—and it was spitting something sharp from its mouth at deadly velocity, white chips that looked like fragments of bone. Blanketing the street in volleys of it. On the other side, a trio of Americans were taking shelter behind a low wall and firing at the flesh-mound with rifles. They saw our horde of hollows arrive and started shooting at us, too. A few bullets caromed harmlessly off my hollows' armor-plated chests.

Because I knew the Americans by sight—one of them was Wreck Donovan—I took an educated guess that the flesh-mound was an ambro addict and sent three hollows at him. One caught a burst of bone projectile in the face and died instantly, but the others leapt on the addict and chewed him to pieces in no time. When the

Americans realized what was happening, they stopped shooting at us. Wreck recognized me and stood up, alarmed.

Someone who didn't know me might've thought we'd been taken by these hollows and they were about to devour us, but Wreck grinned and pumped his fist in victory. "Thank you!" he shouted, leading his comrades out from their shelter. "Come on now, battle's this way!"

They sprinted alongside us toward the heart of the Acre. We skirted the fires of Smoking Street and cut through Attenuated Avenue, where my hollows killed an addict as he crouched in a doorway tipping back his head to fortify himself with a new dose of ambrosia. He was dead before he hit the ground, the contents of his vial splashing across the cobblestones in an arc of sparkling silver. They had a bigger stockpile of the stuff than anyone had realized and seemed intent on using every last drop of it today, either to dominate or exterminate us. And I wondered—inasmuch as I had time to wonder anything—how they had gotten so much, and whether it had anything to do with the Library of Souls. Was Caul distilling new batches from the souls there? A question, one of many, that would have to wait for an answer, if one ever came.

While Hugh hung on for his life, Emma pressed him for vital information: Where were our friends? Where could Miss Peregrine be found, and had Caul's forces spread all through the Acre or were they concentrated in one place? But Hugh was a famously bad explainer of things even when he wasn't juiced with adrenaline, and the fighting was moving so fast that minutes-old intelligence was next to useless, anyway.

We crossed through Old Pye Square, where a few ambro addicts were engaged in a running battle with a couple of outmatched home guards. I peeled two hollows away from my herd to help them while the rest of us charged onward. There wasn't time to stop and oversee the fight; the main battle was raging up ahead.

From a distance all I could see was a smoke-obscured chaos of rampaging giants and flying debris, the ambrosia addicts' powerful eye-beams piercing the haze like searchlights during a bombing raid. Caul's forces were sweeping down the wide avenue and leaving a tide of devastation behind them. I tightened my grip on our hollows and spurred them faster, and as we covered more ground, things came into focus. The tip of Caul's spear was dozens of ambro addicts, shock troops who swept ahead of the wights in a shield formation to attack anyone they saw, and they did so rabidly; the ambrosia had made them not just powerful, but fearless. Behind them marched Caul's four remaining enhanced wights, each toweringly large and a unique flavor of monstrous. Three of them thundered along tearing at the walls of buildings, hurling the pieces down the street like cannonballs. One of them was Murnau, returned to fight by his master's side. The fourth thrummed the air with huge leathery wings while spraying down streams of corrosive liquid. Hovering in the middle of it all was Caul, or rather his blue-glowing head, grinning like a madman and as big as a Thanksgiving Day parade balloon. A thinner contingent of ambro addicts ran behind them, a buffer against attacks from the rear. My hollows would chew through them soon enough.

I sent a single hollow racing ahead as a scout, and my view of things became clearer still. Our peculiars were mounting a brave defense. From doorways, windows, and rooftops, squads of defenders were firing guns and using whatever offensive abilities they had—telekinesis, bolts of electricity, the strength to launch heavy objects long distances—to slow the horde's progress. Some of our people had tried to face the onslaught head-on and been crushed. Their bodies lay crumpled in the streets.

My scout passed a giant wight who was howling with anger as reels of thorny vines pulled taut around his legs, which I guessed was Fiona's handiwork. A gang of walking corpses that could only have been Enoch's were hacking away at a group of addicts with hatchets, and more were on the way. A grimbear charged past them and knocked Murnau to the ground with a resounding crash, but a moment later the animal was flung away, the wight left with a gash across his face but still in fighting shape. Exploding eggs landed among Caul's horde, dropped by ymbrynes circling above. The leather-winged wight shot a stream of black acid at them and the ymbrynes banked quickly to avoid it, then dropped another pair of eggs that landed right in front of the wight tangled in Fiona's vines, knocking him violently backward.

None of it had been enough to stop Caul's army, or even to slow them down much. Not one of the four wights had been killed. They were making slow but steady progress toward the ministries building, where a phalanx of defenders stood waiting in the Ministry's courtyard behind a fortification of metal plates and sandbags. If things kept going the way they were going, they would get crushed.

Fortunately, I'd brought an army of my own.

"Jacob!" Noor was shaking me by the shoulders. *"Jacob!"* She pointed to an ambro addict running toward us with a spike-tipped club in his hands. I'd slowed our advance while my scout got the lay of the land, and somehow I'd allowed an enemy through our shield of hollows. Just before he reached us I made the hollow we were riding whip a tongue around his neck and slam him to the ground. He landed face-up, and I felt the beams from his bulging eyes singe my legs as they swung across me. He was aiming for my face and might've blinded me had Noor not reached out and snatched his light from the air. Then his head disappeared between my hollow's jaws, and I felt the crunch of his collapsing skull rattle through the hollow's body and my own.

"Sorry," I said, "I got distracted . . ."

"What are you waiting for?" Emma shouted. "Send in the hollows!"

"I'm about to!" I said, my cohort of monsters tensing like sprinters before the starting gun. "Right . . . *now.*"

Twenty-one hollowgast shot away from us, all I had save the

three we were riding. Within seconds they had scattered the rear line of ambrosia addicts and begun tearing into the wights. Killing them was my first priority, and I assigned four hollows to each one. I sicced four more on the ambro addicts with loose instructions to just, you know, *kill them.* My last two hollows, besides the three we were riding, I dedicated to Caul. Two weren't enough to do more than annoy him, and they probably wouldn't live long, but their sacrifice would keep Caul busy for a short time while my hollows picked off as many of his lieutenants and foot soldiers as they could.

Hugh shouted that he thought a lot of people, including more ymbrynes, were inside the ministries building. Through the smoke I could see people firing at the horde through its doors, home guards launching metal harpoon nets from its upper windows, and more ymbrynes circling the roof in bird form. It was the strongest and most solid building in the Acre, and probably the most defensible— but if my hollows couldn't stop Caul's forces from reaching it, they would take it apart and smash whoever was inside.

"We've got to try and reach it!" Emma shouted at me. "We need to get to the ymbrynes and make sure they know the hollows are under your control!"

We shot forward, hugging the buildings on the far side of the street as I tried to maneuver us around and ahead of the battle without being spotted. That took half my attention; the other half was immersed in the fray. My hollows had killed several addicts already, but lost a couple of their own. I had hoped they would make quick work of the wights, but they were significantly bigger and nastier than the one we'd faced at the Acre's loop entrance. I'd judged the smallest of them to be the most vulnerable, but only realized his touch made things burst into flame after he'd turned four of my hollows into Fourth of July sparklers. The hollows' direct-contact style of killing wasn't going to work on him. It did work on a gargantuan wight with the thousand-eyed face of a housefly: They pulled his limbs off one by one and left him writhing helplessly in the street, though not before he'd removed three of their heads with the terrifying pincers he had for arms.

That left thirteen, plus the three we were riding. We ran around the worst of the fighting in a wide arc, narrowly avoiding a blast of the winged wight's acid. Meanwhile, the two hollows I'd sent to fight Caul were having no luck: Their tongues and teeth passed right through him. His giant head was an empty projection, like the one he'd sent to frighten us at the all-Acre assembly. Which meant, worryingly, that the real Caul was somewhere else and had yet to reveal himself. His likeness was screaming and ranting like a carnival barker, though his words were barely audible over the din of the battle: "Look, children, how your ymbrynes have failed you! Look, and despair!"

We pulled ahead of the battle. Our three hollowgast steeds sprinted around the vanguard of ambro addicts, now scattered and fighting fiercely, too occupied with fending off attacks from my other hollows to pay us any notice. As we galloped up the steps to the ministries building's forecourt, Dogface recognized me and shouted for his cohort to hold their fire. I gave him a grateful nod and he returned a grin as we sped past them to the door, where Miss Peregrine and Bronwyn were waiting.

We dismounted and threw our arms around them.

"Oh, thank the bloody elders!" Bronwyn shouted, pulling me off my feet.

I saw Miss Peregrine staring at Horatio. "This is Horatio, H's ex-hollowgast," I said to Miss Peregrine. "You can trust him."

She nodded, then looked me over. "Are any of you hurt?"

"We're fine," Emma said, rushing forward to embrace her. "I'm so happy you're safe!"

"Are the other light-eaters with you?" I said to Bronwyn, suddenly frantic to know.

"They're inside," Miss Peregrine said, and a flood of relief shot through me. "When you called from the train station, and I heard Caul's voice, I feared that was the end of you. And when Miss Bruntley and your new friends snuck back from the safe house into the Acre and told me what you were attempting, I nearly lost all hope." She broke into a grin, her eyes darting to the hollows behind me. "But I see you've done it again."

"I thought you were going to kill all of them," Bronwyn said.

"This is better, don't you think?" I said, glancing back to watch a trio of hollows tear a spider-legged wight off the side of a building. The wall he'd been clinging to tore away with him, crushing them all.

"Manifestly," said Miss Peregrine. She was beaming with pride, but then something ricocheted off the arched doorway above our heads and her smile vanished. "Now get inside before all this celebrating gets one of you killed." She gestured to the hollows we'd ridden in on. "Not them. If they come in you'll spark a stampede for the exits."

I ordered the hollows to stay outside and help Dogface's squad defend the building, and then we were pulled through the doorway by Miss Peregrine and Bronwyn. Miss Peregrine drew me into a corner and said, "Tell me what you need. Help me help you."

"I need a window where I can see the fighting. And enough quiet to concentrate."

"You shall have it." She took me by the arm and led us from the hallway into the Ministry's lobby. It was crowded with peculiars, though not the officious functionaries in waistcoats who usually occupied this space. Instead, there were wounded being treated by bone-menders on the marble floor. There were people clustered to watch the battle from the room's large windows. Home guards were running up and down the staircase to the upper floors, where we could hear them firing volley after volley of bullets into the fray. A few anxious ymbrynes were rounding up the smallest and most vulnerable peculiar children and leading them toward the back of the room, ready to evacuate. Everyone else was preparing for battle however they could, improvising helmets from food bowls and strapping on welding goggles borrowed from the Acre's defunct tin smelting factory, a sight both touching and pathetic; though unafraid of war, we were profoundly ill-suited for it. We were not superheroes. We were not born fighters, but had been forced into the role. We were simply peculiar.

And here were our friends, thank God: Horace and Olive and Claire, running at us with open arms; Millard, circulating among a group of invisibles in modern clothes; Sebbie and Sophie hovering over Julius, who was slumped in a chair and looking not at all well. Enoch and Josep stood at one of the windows, and Fiona, who'd already been joined by Hugh, stood at another. They were all preoccupied with controlling their proxy armies of corpses and vines, and Francesca was hovering around them to make certain no one approached them and broke their concentration.

Miss Peregrine cleared a space for me at the window beside Fiona and Hugh. Fiona looked at me and smiled, then returned to her work. There wasn't time for a reunion. My head was mired in the battle, too, and Miss Peregrine shooed away all comers with a sweep of her arm, then stepped back and planted her feet.

The tide of the battle was starting to tilt in our favor. Caul's assault had been interrupted, his soldiers shocked by my hollows' blitz and fully engaged in a close-quarters defense of their jugular veins and soft bits—but it wasn't over. Caul's horde had been halved, but so had my hollows, and those who remained in the fight were hurt and losing steam.

It was coming to a stalemate. We needed an extra push or our enemies would break through my hollows and overrun the ministries building. I turned to Miss Peregrine and said, "I need everything you've got. Any firepower we have that won't cost us more lives."

Miss Peregrine gave a grim nod. "One final assault." She looked to Miss Cuckoo, who was standing at attention in a vivid blue jumpsuit. "Isabel, you heard the boy."

Miss Cuckoo put two fingers in her mouth and blew an

ear-splitting birdcall, which a moment later was echoed by every ymbryne in the room.

"Fiona's got a trick up her sleeve," said Hugh. "Time to use it?"

"Yes, Fiona, now," said Miss Peregrine.

Fiona grinned, then bowed her head in concentration.

Emma cupped her hands around her mouth and shouted, "ALL HANDS ON DECK!" And then she ran upstairs to lob fireballs from the roof.

"Let's go, Josep," Enoch said, hooking his American friend by the elbow. "We've got a tomb's worth of bodies waiting in the wings," he explained to me, "just got to slap a few hearts in 'em . . ."

"Don't go out there!" Miss Peregrine cried. "It's far too dangerous!"

Before Miss Peregrine could stop him, they had run out the door. Seconds later, Millard and his invisible friends had followed them, shedding their clothes so they could throw exploding eggs at the wights from close range without being seen. I was moved by their courage, but anxious that there were now friends among the foes on the battlefield. I worried it would be too easy to mix them up in my splintered state of mind.

I slowed my breathing and attempted to focus. The street outside was a maelstrom of bullets, explosions, and flying debris, which was hurting my hollows just as much as the wights and addicts. (Caul, still just a projection, floated amid it all, seemingly untouchable.) I decided to change strategy and sent all of my hollows at Murnau, one of only two remaining wights. While they descended on him, the other, winged wight and the addicts were kept busy with new attacks on several fronts: a swarm of Enoch's and Josep's dead from the right, a hail of exploding eggs from the invisibles on the left, a barrage of gunfire from the home guard and fireballs launched by Emma from the roof.

Our enemies were pinned from three sides and had nowhere to go but backward, which Caul would never allow them to do.

< THE DESOLATIONS OF DEVIL'S ACRE >

They began dying. The ambro addicts fell, one after another. My hollows tore Murnau limb from limb, but before they could kill him the winged one spewed a thick stream of acid at them, melting Murnau's head and several of my hollows in the bargain; each one sent a burst of pain through me before disappearing from my mind.

Murnau was dead. But the fight was far from over.

The shooting had stopped. Our defenders on the roof and in the courtyard had apparently run out of bullets and eggs, and the ambro addicts took the opportunity to rush the building. I heard Fiona cry out next to me and wrench her hands in the air, and the next moment all the addicts went sprawling as hidden cables of thorned vines pulled taut before them on the ground. Fiona turned her palms upward while her fingers danced like a pianist's. The vines writhed and wriggled over the addicts until they were fastened to the ground. And then the last of Enoch's and Josep's dead army descended on the addicts, hacking and chopping them to bits.

Cheers went up around us, but I was too fixed on my next target to celebrate. Out the window, something big, black, and rapidly approaching blotted out the sky. "Get away from the windows!" Bronwyn yelled, tackling me, Fiona, and Hugh to the ground just as the glass shattered and a mass of black acid splattered the floor beyond us, steaming and eating through the marble.

"Elders above, that was too bloody close," I heard Hugh say.

I'd hardly even noticed that I'd hit my head hard on the floor; in my mind I was outside, scaling the face of the building with my eight remaining hollows. The winged wight who'd nearly melted us was swooping around to make another attack. This time I'd be ready for him.

He was an ungainly bastard, a half man, half dragon almost too heavy for his lizard wings, so it was easy to anticipate his trajectory. I spread my hollows across the roof. They got a running start and leapt off the roof toward him just as he launched another

< 435 >

burst of acid—and this time he launched it at them. Two of my hollows were hit full in the chest and died instantly. Another hollow missed its target and fell several stories to the ground, impaling itself on one of the now-fully-dead undead's pikes. The rest used their tongues to grapple onto the winged wight like Spider-Man. He roared as their sudden added weight sent him spiraling. He crashed into the roof, narrowly missing Emma and a contingent of home guards.

A ferocious fight commenced, the wight and my hollows rolling and grappling, the hollows tearing at the wight while the wight tried to melt them with its corrosive spit, which sprayed across the roof and sent up torrents of steam. Although I needed every hollow I had, I forced one to peel away from the pack and sweep Emma and the home guards away from the fighting to safety.

A minute later, the four hollows were dead, the wight nearly so, its wings broken and face bloodied. The fifth hollow returned to finish it off with a savage twist of its tongues around the wight's neck. Before it died the wight shot one last blast of acid that melted the hollow's head into a concave puddle. And then I had only three left—the ones we'd ridden in on.

But Caul had no one. Now he was alone.

I returned fully to my own mind and peered through the shattered window. The street was empty.

"Have we won?" Hugh asked cautiously. "Are they all dead—even Caul?"

"He couldn't be," Miss Peregrine said, her eyes narrowing. "Unless he was somehow linked to his cohort . . ."

"And his life-force piggybacked theirs back into the world," said Miss Cuckoo, finishing her sentence.

"It's possible," said Miss Wren, combing pulverized plaster from her hair with her fingers. "Our understanding of the Library and its powers is woefully incomplete."

There was a thunder of footsteps as Josep and Millard rushed in from outside. "Someone help!" Josep cried. "Enoch's been hurt, I fear badly!"

We raced outside. Hugh, Noor, and Miss Peregrine were beside me. As we passed the line of addicts who'd been felled by Fiona's vines and Enoch's dead, a hand caught my ankle and I tripped. One of the addicts was still alive, though a hatchet was buried deep in his back. "It's all happening!" he said, blood spilling through his broken-toothed grin. "All according to Master's plan . . ."

Having no interest in the ravings of dying traitors, I kicked him in his ambrosia-melted face, shook loose, and ran on.

Enoch lay in the street with gashes raking his face and blood soaking his shirt. His brow was knit tight in pain, eyes squeezed shut.

"It's all right, old chap, we've got you now," Hugh was saying, and together the four of us picked him up as gently as we could.

Then a sound like an earthquake came from way down the street, and we turned to see a low bank of storm clouds moving toward us. The clouds were blood red.

Below them, gliding on a pedestal of whirling blue wind, was Caul. The real one, not his projection.

"Alma! Alma, I'm coming home!" he was crying, and his voice seemed to boom down from the heavens.

"Get inside!" Miss Peregrine shouted.

We ran, Josep and Bronwyn helping to shoulder Enoch. I looked back only once. The wind he rode funneled down into a black hole that moved with him along the street. His arms were spread and his wriggling fingers were ever-lengthening, their span wide enough to rake the buildings on both sides of the street. He brought with him a wave of desolation. Every wooden thing they touched turned black with rot, every piece of metal flaked to rust, every wounded body on the ground withered into a corpse.

Inside, Miss Peregrine and the ymbrynes quickly organized an evacuation through the building's rear door. "We are going to Bentham's house!" Miss Peregrine announced. "We have enough ymbrynes to make a diminutive version of the Quilt around it, and once it's established we'll evacuate via the Panloopticon."

"We can't give up now!" Horace groaned. "Not after defeating Caul's whole army!"

"We're not giving up," Miss Cuckoo said. "We're making a tactical retreat."

They were turning away when Noor ran up to them. "It's our time to fight," said Noor. "See his blue light? I think that's his soul—the one we light-eaters are supposed to eat. It used to just flash before but now it's constant, and I think—"

"Absolutely *out of the question*," Miss Peregrine said, flapping her arms to shoo Noor toward the exit with everyone else. "That's a guess at best, and we can't have you throwing yourselves at Caul based on a guess."

"It's more than that!" Noor shot back. "And this might be our only— Wait!" She looked suddenly concerned and snapped her head around. "Where'd Sebbie go? She was just here!"

We heard a scream from the window and turned to see one of the ymbrynes-in-training pointing outside. We ran back to the window to see Sebbie outside alone, running straight toward Caul. She was gathering light as she ran, leaving long stripes of undulating dark behind her, clearly readying for a fight.

"SEBBIE, WAIT!" Noor screamed, but all three ymbrynes grabbed her and wouldn't let her go.

"Elders help her," Miss Wren said, her face etched with pain. "But we cannot slow."

Noor struggled as they held her back, looked to me for help, but I was vacating myself, going inward to send my last three hollows to help Sebbie. They bounded across the courtyard, past the Americans' abandoned fortifications, then past Sebbie and into the street.

Caul saw them and cried out in glee. "Come to me, pets!" his voice sang down from the bloodred clouds.

One hollow wrapped its tongues around Caul's neck while the

other two grabbed Caul by his long arms. But then his even longer fingers curled around their two bodies and I felt them start to wither and die. Their sacrifice bought Sebbie a chance to get near Caul without being touched by him. She bravely ran toward him, slowed a little by the cyclonic wind that whipped around his lower half, but only briefly. She swept her hands through the wind, scraped up the blue light that glowed brightly from it, and when she had it all, she sucked it into her mouth. And then Sebbie was the one glowing blue, and Caul's tornado began to slow and shrink and he seemed to melt into the black hole below him. Sebbie was weaving and wobbling as if about to lose consciousness, and then she tipped forward and fell into the hole.

Screams from my friends. From Noor.

My hollows were dying. All of them.

"Look!" Miss Cuckoo shouted.

A hand had appeared at the hole's rim. Someone was pulling themselves up and out of it.

But it wasn't Sebbie. It was Caul. Noor's face fell into her hands.

He was glowing blue, bluer than ever, and the last thing my lone remaining hollow saw before it died was Caul grinning down at it.

"It's good to be home," he said. And then he laced his long fingers together and cracked his knuckles.

CHAPTER TWENTY-TWO

*N*inety-nine peculiar children, their allies, and their ymbrynes—all refugees in their own loop—fled across Devil's Acre. We were pursued by a drumming rain of blood, ash, and bone fragments, as well as the demon who'd summoned them. By the time we made it to Bentham's house, panting and spent, we were covered in a clinging paste that made us look ghostly. Noor and I and our trio of ymbrynes, Peregrine, Cuckoo, and Wren, were the last to arrive, and Sharon and Addison were waiting to slam and bolt Bentham's great entry doors the moment we raced across the threshold.

A lock on a door would hardly protect us from Caul, though, so the ymbrynes immediately got to work creating a new shield around the house. Miss Peregrine explained that they hadn't built one around the ministries building because it probably wouldn't have worked—there were certain enhancing elements in the Panloopticon itself that would help compensate for the lack of Miss Babax, their assassinated twelfth sister—and even if it had been possible, the ymbrynes would not want to have been trapped there, anyway. That would only have sentenced us to the slow starvation of a siege. The Panloopticon and its many doors were our ticket out.

So, while all their wards took shelter in the bunkerlike basement, the ymbrynes wove their Quilt, singing and circling in the wide foyer. The desolations were rapidly getting worse, blood seeping through cracks in the ceiling and bone fragments breaking windows. Even in the basement we could hear Caul's approach, his gloating, cackling laughter and the freight train roar of his personal tornado getting louder by the second. Then a tremendous quake rattled the floor, and despite it having felt like Caul had just torn the building from its foundations, Francesca assured everyone that it was the Quilt. Over her objections my friends and I ran upstairs to look through a window, and sure enough the Quilt's reassuring green glow was shining outside.

Caul was out there—we could hear him roaring, enraged—but for the time being, it seemed we were safe. We could think, plan our next move. And Rafael, the only bone-mender who'd survived the battle, could tend to the injured. Enoch was one of the worst hurt, and Rafael set to work right away easing his pain and patching him up.

We were all tired, hurting, rattled. My head was full of ghosts, the echoes of my dead hollows. Emma found the washroom and we each took a long turn inside, doing our best to wash the battle off our skin and our clothes, to scour the dried blood from our hands and rinse the ash-paste from our faces. Even after five minutes of effort it still coated my hair, making me look like I'd gone prematurely gray. It wasn't hard to believe; I felt a hundred years old. I imagined finally washing my hair to find that it really had turned the color of ash.

Ulysses Critchley was waiting for us. We'd been summoned to Bentham's library, and we followed him there to join Miss Peregrine in a grim-faced discussion with Miss Wren, Miss Avocet, and Perplexus Anomalous. They were huddled before a darkened hearth, discussing our escape, and they wanted our input. We sat on a long fur-covered couch and listened to our options.

There were many, none appealing. There were one hundred forty-three doors in the Panloopticon, eighty-six of which had survived the wight's rampage through the building earlier in the day. Eighty-six loop doors leading to eighty-six loops. But were any of them someplace Caul wouldn't be able to quickly find us?

"He and Bentham created these loop doors themselves and

know them intimately," Millard pointed out. "And once you choose one, we're trapped there. We won't be able to return to the Panloopticon."

"But if we can find an exit membrane in one of them, we can escape through it into the outer past," said Miss Wren.

"Or leapfrog somewhere even older and more *oscuro*," suggested Perplexus.

"Yes! We could find somewhere to hide in, say, medieval Spain," said Horace.

"Or Italia," Perplexus mumbled into his shirt collar.

Emma was shaking her head. "He found us in Miss Tern's old collapsed loop, and right quick. And there were only a handful of us there. I don't think ninety-nine peculiars would stay hidden long, no matter where we went."

There were nods of reluctant assent.

"Unless you created a new loop somewhere," said Olive. "One Caul knows nothing about."

"Too many of our wards are loop-trapped," Miss Wren said. "We have to find an existing loop to hide in, one at least a hundred years old, to keep everyone from aging forward."

"If only the damned reset was safe and we could scatter into the present," said Miss Cuckoo.

Perplexus's head sunk still lower. "I am sorry, *signore*. We truly tried our best."

"It isn't your fault, sir," said Millard, to which there were more nods of assent.

Fiona was whispering to Hugh. "She says to hell with safety," Hugh relayed. "These are desperate times."

"We'll never be that desperate," said Miss Peregrine. "If the reset reaction goes wrong, not only could our wards be killed, but the resulting loop collapse could flatten a square mile of present-day London. I'd say we've done enough to terrify the normals as it is."

Fiona scowled.

I imagined what Enoch would've said, if he'd been there and not recuperating in a dormitory bed. "Well then," I said, crossing my arms, "what?"

"You still have me." Noor rose from the couch where we'd been sitting and stepped toward the ymbrynes. "Has everyone forgotten about the prophecy?"

"No one has forgotten," said Miss Peregrine. "But you're the only light-eater left standing, Miss Pradesh, and we still don't know how best to use you."

"We can't let what happened to Julius and Sebbie happen to you," Bronwyn said.

"You're our ace in the hole," said Hugh. "Our one shot."

Noor's jaw clenched tight. I could see her biting back some bitter comment. Instead she just sighed and sat down.

"Then where does that leave us?" I said. "Running for our lives again, and giving up the Panlooticon to Caul."

"Just like we said we'd never do," said Emma.

"Caul's ruined us," Claire said, near tears. "And poisoned the world against us, too."

"It's a bitter pill to swallow," Miss Peregrine said quietly. "A bitter pill indeed."

"And now we're about to be exiled from the place we'd already been exiled *to*," moaned Horace. "Is there no home for us anywhere on the whole cursed earth?"

Miss Peregrine drew up her chin. "We will find one, Mr. Somnusson. One day we will find a real home. I promise you."

"For now," said Miss Cuckoo, turning to face a loop map they'd pinned to the wall, "we must find another temporary one."

"Excuse me," came a voice from the edge of the room. Horatio was standing politely in the open door. He was scrubbed clean and had changed into a new pair of pants and an oddly summery, wide-collared shirt from one of Bentham's closets, one sleeve of which hung empty. "I know a place you'll be safe."

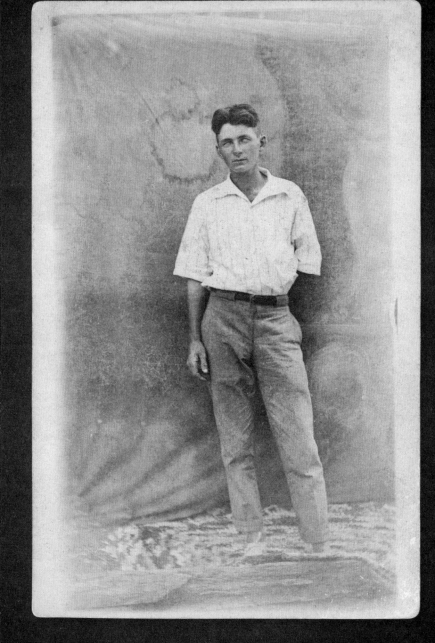

Miss Cuckoo planted her hands on her hips. "I am not taking advice from a wight on this matter."

"You can trust him," I said. "He worked for my grandfather's partner H, and he's saved our lives I don't know how many times."

Miss Cuckoo glanced skeptically at Miss Peregrine. Miss Peregrine was gazing out of the library's high window. Beyond the semi-translucent green shield, Caul's fingers were curling around the building. He seemed to be wrapping us in a giant hug, and as he did the sound of his wind rose ever higher. The air inside the house had begun to chill.

"My brother will not be content to wait," she said. "He will try and drive us out, if he can." She turned to Horatio. "Please, tell us what you know. And do close the door."

Horatio shut the door and crossed the room to stand before the ymbrynes. "My master, Harold Fraker King, spoke once of a special loop in the Everglades swamps of Florida. An old loop that few are aware of. It is a well-protected secret, a place where peculiars have sometimes gone to seek refuge in times of extraordinary persecution. The hollow-hunters had an emergency protocol which involved an evacuation to this loop, and Harold Fraker King told me the directions to it were in Abraham Portman's home, among his most guarded possessions."

"In the bunker," I said. "He's got all kinds of books down there."

"One's literally called *Emergency Protocols*," Noor said.

"And this swamp loop, it's quite old?" asked Miss Wren.

"Quite," replied Horatio.

Noor snapped her fingers. "We can take the pocket loop to Jacob's backyard."

"That's the one loop Caul isn't intimately familiar with," Miss Peregrine said. "Because I made it."

"And *we* connected it to the Panlooptican, not him," said Miss Wren, who I could tell was warming up to the idea.

At least it was a workable idea, something that was in short supply. And, I thought, if Caul did manage to follow us there, we could blow him to hell with my grandfather's home defense system . . . if anything was left of it. It might at least slow him down a little.

"I'll destroy the pocket loop as we shut it behind us," said Miss Peregrine. "So he cannot follow."

"He'll have other ways of reaching Florida," said Miss Cuckoo.

"Other ways will take time," said Miss Wren. "Enough time for us to disappear."

"And find ourselves right back where we were in 1908!" Miss Cuckoo shouted. "Refugees again, trembling inside a loop while Caul runs free, poisoning the world against us!"

"The fickle opinions of normals do not rank high among my worries," said Miss Peregrine, "when compared to the wrath of my resurrected brother."

"We will be refugees," said Miss Wren, "but we will be *alive*, Isabel." She tried to grasp Miss Cuckoo's arm, but the other ymbryne turned away.

"I say we stay and fight," said Miss Cuckoo. "Fleeing now will only postpone a war with Caul, and allow him the chance to grow a new army in the meanwhile."

"But it will also allow us the chance to learn how best to fight him," said Horace. "We've hardly had a moment to breathe since he came back, much less study his vulnerabilities."

"He'll never be more vulnerable than he is *right now*," Noor said, her eyes glinting. "If you just let me out there . . ."

"Does he *look* vulnerable to you?" Horace said, pointing to the window. Caul's arms and his fingers had now wrapped twice around the building; he was growing into a giant, and I wondered, if he got big enough, whether he might swallow the house whole.

"You're not going out there, and that's final," Miss Peregrine said, her eyes wide and angry. "Miss Pradesh, you may be our kind's last hope for salvation, and I cannot allow you to gamble your life away now because passions and fears are running hot—"

"Running hot indeed!" said Miss Avocet. We turned to see Bettina wheeling her chair through the door. She looked deathly pale, as if the exertion of speaking at full volume was draining her.

"Esmerelda!" said Miss Wren, surprised. "I thought you were resting!"

"I've been drinking Perplexus's coffee," she said. "You know I can't afford to sleep. None of us can, or even this meager shield we've raised may fall."

"I defer to you, mistress," said Miss Cuckoo, bowing at the waist. "What would you have us do?"

Bettina parked the elder ymbryne's chair by the darkened hearth. Miss Avocet pulled her shawl around her and straightened, painfully, as best she could. "If we run he may still find us. If we stay and fight and lose again, those who survive will be enslaved and forced to do Caul's evil work." She fixed each ymbryne with a grave stare. "Our mandate is to keep our wards alive—but not at any cost. Caul wants to make the world a graveyard, and we his executioners. That we cannot allow."

"*Please,*" Noor said. "I know what to do, I have to take his light. And *run* with it, this time. Sebbie didn't run, she just *stood* there . . ."

"Miss Pradesh, you must calm down," said Miss Avocet. "I do think Julius and Sebbie had the right idea. Caul's blue light is almost certainly the key to his resurrected soul. But they were striking at the branches of his power, not the root."

"And where's the root?"

"Inside the Library of Souls. I imagine that's where his blue light comes from, and where his cyclonic half-self originates."

"But getting there isn't—"

"I thought there was a door here," Noor said.

"It was destroyed," said Miss Peregrine.

"And there our discussion must end," said Miss Avocet. "We will go to Florida. As soon as the Panlopticon can be repaired and made stable. It sustained some damage earlier today."

"And how long will that take?" Emma asked.

"I've just been speaking with Sharon and Miss Blackbird. They tell me it could be several hours. So I suggest everyone who isn't an ymbryne get some sleep."

◆   ◆   ◆

Night stole over the Acre. Daylight dimmed from the windows but the green glow of the Quilt never did, casting a sickly pallor over everything. The gaslights had stopped working, no doubt thanks to Caul, so Emma circulated through the rooms and halls lighting candles. Sharon, Perplexus, and most of the ymbrynes were working in the basement to repair the Panloopticon, and we could hear the clanking of their tools through the floor. The wight that had gotten into the house when we'd gone to Miss Tern's loop had destroyed not only a large section of the lower Panloopticon hallway, reducing many of its doorways to splinters, it had also burst a crucial pipeline connecting the loop rooms to the machinery downstairs. Fixing it was straightforward enough, Sharon said, but the work was painstaking and slow.

Caul hadn't moved from outside the house. He was singing some old song in the ancient tongue, had been repeating it over and over again for an hour, his voice audible through the walls and so low in frequency it was almost subliminal. Was it an incantation? Psychological torture? Or had he finally and completely lost his mind? Meanwhile, his fingers had grown so long that he'd now wrapped the building with them ten times over, and the view out most every window was of those overlapping digits, squirming and flexing like a nest of snakes. It seemed that if he couldn't drive us out, he meant to suffocate us.

He couldn't, of course, at least not while the ymbrynes' miniature Quilt remained intact. It also prevented him from making physical desolations inside the house, but there was another, more insidious kind of desolation he had conjured to torment us with: one of mind. The air in the house grew stale and cold, the atmosphere oppressive. Had it been less intense, and not accompanied by a strange, skin-crawling itch, I would've chalked it up to exhaustion and the emotional aftermath of a lost battle. But this felt unnatural, and so palpable you could almost rake it from the air with your fingers. Caul was infecting the house with despair.

The ymbrynes had given all their wards orders to try and sleep, though in shifts, so there would be enough of us left awake to warn the others in case of sudden emergency. Few of us could do more than rest our eyes. We lay in a makeshift dormitory that had been set up in the small library, a room stuffed with overflow books from Bentham's main library. The sofas and study desks had been removed and replaced by military-issue cots.

There were ninety-nine of us in one large room. Some were talking quietly. A few did manage to sleep, or fake it. Others were being looked after by Rafael, who had recruited the American girl Angelica to be his assistant, a small dark cloud trailing them as they dragged a rolling table of poultices and remedies from bed to bed. In the corner, one of Miss Blackbird's wards picked gently at a banjo and sang, soft and mournful.

I lay on my back praying for sleep, but my eyes seemed propped open. I stared at rococo angels painted on the ceiling. My thoughts wandered, turned morbid. The angels blurred into an angry, torch-wielding mob. I was dreaming with my eyes open. I dreamed of men in suits with killer smiles and lists of names going door to door. Of camps ringed by razor wire and guard towers. Not the ones my great-grandparents had been condemned to, but new ones, built just for us—for peculiars.

At the edge of my mind I heard a voice, a voice of infinite calm and reason, saying over and over: *Come here. I want to tell you something.*

I bolted upright, gasping, and threw off my thin covers.

"You okay?" Noor asked from the next cot. "You've been tossing."

"Had a nightmare," I mumbled. "Or something."

"Did you hear a voice telling you to go outside?" Emma asked, sitting up suddenly in her own bed.

"I did!" Millard said before I could answer. "*Most* unsettling."

Emma hugged herself. "I thought I was dreaming."

"I'm fr-freezing," Claire said, wrapping herself in sheets and shivering.

"God, me too," Noor said, her breath pluming, though it hadn't been ten seconds earlier. "What the hell's going on?"

"Caul's desolating our brains," said Bronwyn. "Trying to make us give up hope."

"Or let him in," said Hugh. "I hope someone's guarding the door."

"Well, it isn't going to work," Olive said bravely.

Claire's teeth were chattering. "I hope not."

"We just have to hang on until morning," Olive said, sidling next to Claire and rubbing her arms for warmth. "Then we'll go to Florida, and no one's ever cold in Florida."

I smiled, something I hadn't done in what felt like a long time. I loved Olive and her irrepressible optimism. I loved them all.

"What do you think, Horace?" I turned to my well-dressed friend. He was sitting beside the bed where Julius lay unconscious. I hoped to turn his mind to something happier. "Ready for a beach day?"

"Somnusson could catch a sunburn in full shade," said Enoch, mumbling through split lips from his bed. It was the first I'd heard him speak since he'd been hurt, and my heart leapt. "I'd like to know if he's had any more useful dreams. That one you sleep-narrated to Sharon was a cracker."

Horace didn't say anything. He was staring at me. Or *through* me, to be more precise.

"Horace?" I creaked out of bed, every joint in my body complaining, and waved a hand in front of his face. "Did you fall asleep on us?"

Suddenly he went rigid in his chair. His legs shot out, his mouth opened and closed soundlessly, and then he pointed at me and shouted, "MONSTER!"

I stumbled back in surprise.

"CREATURE FROM HELL!"

Everyone looked shocked. "Horace, knock off that bellowing!" Olive said.

People were staring. Horace was still shouting. "Beast spat from the gullet of Abaton! Fashioned from a thousand dead souls! It shakes the dirt from its flanks and rises, monster of dust and carrion—"

Then someone slapped him, hard, and he went silent, eyes wide.

It was Miss Peregrine, flushed from running and standing above him with her hand ready to slap him again, if need be. "Everything is fine!" she shouted to the room at large. "Mind your business, please!"

Horace was blinking and rubbing his cheek.

"I'm sorry, Mr. Somnusson."

"Quite all right." He gave a tiny shake of his head. "Don't know what got hold of me." He glanced at me meekly. "I'm very sorry, Jacob."

"Maybe you were dreaming about Jacob's hollows," said Emma.

"Yes," he said quickly. "I'm sure that's what it was." But he looked shaken, as if that wasn't quite the truth.

Miss Peregrine crouched beside him and put a hand on his knee. "Are you sure, Horace?"

Horace met her eyes, then nodded.

"My brother's mental suggestions can't hurt you," Miss

Peregrine said. "He can make things unpleasant for us, but he can do nothing to cause us real harm. Remember that." Someone on the other side of the room woke up screaming—Wreck Donovan, I think it was. Miss Peregrine stood up. She had ninety-nine other peculiars to look after. "This will all be over soon," she said, and hurried off to see about Wreck.

Horace started apologizing to me again, but I was feeling strange and irritable and didn't want to talk about it.

"I'll see you guys in a little while."

"Where are you going?" Noor asked.

"For a wander," I said. "I need to clear my head."

She slid her legs out of the cot. "Want company?"

"No, thanks," I said, and though I knew I'd hurt her feelings, I needed very badly, in that moment, to be alone.

✦   ✦   ✦

I wandered halls lit by candles and crawling with shadows, jumping at shapes I mistook for human. There was an itch in my brain, the after-echo of a voice in my head. Not Caul's—someone else's.

Come here.

That wasn't the only thing bothering me. Horace's strange outburst had gotten under my skin. Sometimes his dreams meant nothing, but more often they were loaded with meaning that wasn't apparent right away. He had called me a monster, and I couldn't understand why. Maybe I had spent so much time inhabiting the minds of monsters that they had come to inhabit mine, as well. Or maybe I was a monster for bringing us so close to victory, only to fail. Despite all my efforts, despite all our successes in battle, Caul was closer than ever to destroying us. In time he would raise another army of hollows, and he'd make them even stronger, even harder to control, and he would never again make the mistake of bottling them up in a small space. And with us preparing to run,

THE DESOLATIONS OF DEVIL'S ACRE

and all his enemies gone, he was about to have all the time he needed.

This will all be over soon, Miss Peregrine had said. She wasn't in the habit of lying to us, but I knew that wasn't true. We were giving up. Fleeing the field of battle. We had been beaten. And Caul would never stop coming for us.

I found myself climbing the stairs. I'd been so lost in thought, I hadn't even realized what my legs were doing until they'd taken me to the landing of the lower Panloopticon hallway. The itch in my brain had become a pull, and it was pulling me upward.

I want to tell you something.

The voice was so familiar, and yet I couldn't place it.

I climbed another floor, and another. The air grew colder. By the time I reached the top and came out among Bentham's museum displays, my breath was crystallizing in ghostly plumes.

The pull was getting stronger, leading me down shadowy aisles of peculiar curiosities.

And then a figure stepped into my path, and I startled so badly I nearly attacked it.

The figure cowered and cried "It's only Nim!" He stepped into a shaft of green window light. It was Bentham's old manservant, his hair like a feather duster, eyes wide and haunted. "The master would like to speak to you."

I cocked my head suspiciously. Was he dreaming, too?

"Your master is dead."

"No, sir," he said, shaking his head vigorously. "He's in the washroom."

He led me in the very direction I'd been pulled toward—to the washroom. And there, pressed against the outside of a small window, was Bentham himself in ghostly blue outline. His neck was long and wriggling, like another of Caul's fingers. He seemed to be attached parasitically to his brother.

"You see?" said Nim.

Bentham's mouth moved, but I couldn't hear what he'd said.

"Ear to the glass," Nim instructed.

The glass was frosted with ice. I pressed my ear to it, and it was so cold it felt like it was burning.

"Leave us, Nim," Bentham rasped, and a bolt shot through me when I heard his voice. It was the voice I'd heard in my dream.

Nim slipped away, and Bentham continued. "I haven't long; my brother has fallen asleep." His face distorted as he spoke, lengthening and shortening grotesquely, and he sounded like a drowning man gasping for breath. "The door is behind a painting in the corridor. There's a lock in my ear and the key is in the farting-case."

"The *what*?"

"Sir John Soane's final flatulations. Which is simply a pretext to stop people from reaching inside and finding the invisible key."

"The key to what?"

"To the Library of Souls," he said, his voice nearly slipping away. The blue outline of his face faded for a moment before returning. His connection to our reality seemed tenuous. "Haven't you been looking for it?"

"I thought the only door got destroyed."

"Every loop door in the wights' fallen tower"—he paused to gasp for air—"had a copy in this house. *Except* that one?" He wagged his finger. "Of course not; that was the most important door of all. It's here, but not for *anyone* to find. No one, I should say, but you, my lad."

I pulled my face away from the freezing glass and looked at him. "Why me?"

"Because you are the librarian. And your power is even greater than you know."

Now my mind was reeling. "I can manipulate the soul jars. But what good does that do me?"

"Not just *manipulate*," he said. "To bring forth the totality of your power, you must *drink*."

< THE DESOLATIONS OF DEVIL'S ACRE >

I nearly choked. "Drink souls?" A cold shudder went through me. "Never—that would make me like them."

Horace's outburst replayed in my memory. *Monster. Beast from hell.*

"Not like them. Like yourself." His voice was almost inaudible. He seemed to be struggling to remain here, on this plane. I smashed my ear to the freezing glass and heard him say, "Did you never wonder why you could control the hollowgast? Why your mind could inhabit theirs?"

"Yes. I've wondered."

"Because, Jacob. There's a part of them inside you. An ancient remnant. The hollowgast of our era are soulless corruptions, but in the age of our elderfolk there were tri-tongued peculiars who were anything but soulless; feared and bloodthirsty, yes, but brilliant, even respected by some. You descend from them. You and your grandfather. Their remnant was inside him, too, but in you it's much stronger. Drink, and you'll become the most fearsome hollowgast the world has ever known."

A shard of ice seemed to pierce my heart. The idea was terrifying—but strangely exhilarating, too.

"Strong enough to kill your brother?"

"Strong enough to protect the ones who can."

"There's only Noor left," I said. "Julius can't even stand, and no one's been able to tell Noor what she's supposed to do!"

Bentham groaned. He was clinging to the window casement while some unseen force pulled him away.

"His light must be drained," he managed to say. "Drained to its lees!"

"But *how*? The others tried, and they all—"

And suddenly he was torn away. I pounded the window with my fist. "Come back!" I was babbling, desperate. "You have to tell me. I need to know."

Then, as suddenly as he'd disappeared, he came flying back, his

< 459 >

face smacking the glass. His eyes bulged as he spoke, each word a painful struggle. "The one . . . meant to kill him," he said, grimacing, "is the one . . . who will know."

"What's that supposed to mean?" I shouted.

Before he could answer, he was torn away again, and then his body, or the image of his body, disintegrated in a shower of blue sparks. And he was gone.

* * *

I stumbled out of the washroom and searched the hallway for Nim, afraid he had heard everything—but he was gone. There was no time to worry about him, anyway.

I tried to focus. My thoughts were a mess. First, I needed to get the key to the Library, if only to keep it from falling into anyone else's hands. Then I would find Noor and tell her what Bentham had said—about *her*, not me. I had no intention of drinking any soul jars, or of turning myself into . . . *anything*.

Unless I had no other choice, that is. But I couldn't think about that now.

I ran to the aisle where I'd last seen the glass box Bentham had mentioned. It was right where I remembered it. I kicked the flimsy lock open. A slight brown haze escaped the box with a hiss. I held my breath and felt around inside it until my hand nudged against something I could feel but not see. I knew what it was by touch: a large key.

I pocketed it, ran to the stairwell door, and started down the stairs. To my surprise it was filled with people. They were all going to the upper Panlopticon hallway.

Bronwyn grabbed me. She was out of breath. "Jacob—I was looking for you! The ymbrynes and Sharon got the Panlopticon working sooner than expected. We're leaving in ten minutes!"

I was about to ask what the hurry was when I saw the

ymbrynes-in-training carrying Miss Avocet up the stairs. Her eyes were glassy and she was struggling to keep her head up. If she passed out, fell asleep, or God forbid, died, the Quilt would evaporate.

"Wait, *what*?" I looked back at Bronwyn. She'd said something and I'd missed it.

"I said we're still looking for Noor. Was she upstairs with you?"

"No," I said, a tight knot forming in my chest.

"Anybody seen Noor?" called Emma, running up the steps behind her.

"Has anyone checked the kitchens?" said Enoch, limping up the stairs with Francesca's help. "Maybe she went scavenging for a midnight snack."

"I'll go check," I said quickly.

I raced downstairs, passing a quizzical Miss Peregrine in the stairwell. "Pocket loop door!" she shouted after me. "Nine minutes!"

"Looking for Noor!" I shouted back without slowing.

I raced down the ground floor hall toward the kitchens. There were only a handful of people around now, hurriedly gathering their things. One was Olive, and I skidded to a stop when I saw her. She was making up the sheets of her cot, even though we'd probably never come back.

"Olive, have you seen Noor?"

"You can't find her? That's funny."

"Funny? Why?"

She turned a bit red. "Well . . . I really shouldn't say—"

"Olive, you *have to* say. We're about to leave Devil's Acre and nobody knows where she is."

She sighed. "She told me not to give you this till after we'd reached Florida. I promise I didn't open it!"

She handed me a sealed envelope from her pocket. I tore it open. Inside was a note addressed to me.

Dear Jacob,

I write this as you've gone off to think. I've been thinking, too.

You've probably realized by now that I didn't go through the pocket loop with everyone else.

I'm still in Devil's Acre.

If the loop door hasn't closed yet, please don't come looking for me. You won't find me. As you know, I'm good at hiding.

My destiny is here. I can't run from it anymore.

I'll find you again, if it's meant to be.

I really hope it is.

Love,
Noor

A desperate sadness shot through me. I knew exactly what she was planning. She was waiting for us to leave, for the shield to fall, and then she was going face Caul. *By herself.*

The letter shook in my hands.

Noor knew as well as I what retreat would mean. Caul would build a new army. He would crush more loops, devastate cities, and make all humanity hate us, if they didn't already. And she was prepared to give her life to stop it.

But that wasn't a sacrifice I was willing to let her make. At least, not alone.

"What does it say?" Olive asked, her face screwed up with worry.

"Just sweet things," I lied, faking a smile as I folded the letter into my pocket. "She's going to meet us at the loop door in a few minutes."

"I don't believe you."

"I'll meet you upstairs," I said—another lie—and turned to go. "Hurry up now, okay?"

"Wait! Where are you going?"

I tried to sound calm as I said something about a last trip to the bathroom, and then I was running full out and didn't look back.

I couldn't let anyone know what Noor was planning.

They would try to find her. They wouldn't leave. And when the shield fell, Caul would kill them.

They couldn't do much to protect her from Caul, anyway.

Neither could I. Not as I was.

I had no hollows. No power. I was just a weak boy.

My hand closed around the key in my pocket.

But I could become something else.

I rounded the corner into the hall and bounded up the steps.

I heard the echo of Horace's voice:

Monster.

CHAPTER TWENTY-THREE

*E*verything Bentham had told me was true: The key fit a lock in the ear of his portrait, one of many portraits of Bentham that hung in his house but the only one mounted to the ceiling outside his office, and the only one in which he was, ever so slyly, smiling. To access it I had to roll a ladder on casters into the middle of the floor, climb it, and reach up with my key like Michelangelo painting the Sistine Chapel ceiling. When I turned the key, the painting swung downward on a hinge to reveal a passage. Above me was a duct, handholds built into the sides.

I climbed until I felt the disorienting rush of a changeover. I looked down to see only darkness, the vestibule below me gone. Now the light was coming from above. I climbed toward it, then out of the passage, up through a hole in a floor, and into a bare and primitive room of gray rock walls.

Before me was a door carved from stone, and through it shone the light of a cloudless orange sky.

I ran outside and into Abaton. The lost loop, an ancient city carved from rock whose inhabitants had once protected the Library of Souls from invaders.

Invaders like Caul.

The city had been crushed, reduced to a waste of ruined hills and guttering fires. Its rock spires lay humped across the land like kicked sandcastles. The few that still stood were scarred with the claw marks of giant beasts. Caul had trained them here before loosing them upon the world.

I began to run. The rocky path forked and split and split again, but I never slowed, never hesitated. The route had been burned into my memory.

A watched feeling stole over me. The watchers were many, and they were angry. I understood why. Their resting place had been violated.

At last I came to the entrance, a vine-choked patch of wall, a stone room open to the sky, a door and two windows arranged like a misshapen face.

The Library.

I walked through the door and came into a stone room, its walls honeycombed with empty coves. The air here was clammy, colder. At the back, several doors led away into darkness.

A sudden fear gripped me. What if he'd stolen them all? What if there were no jars left?

I chose a door at random and ran into the dark. This time, I didn't have Emma and her flame to help me navigate. But after a moment my eyes adjusted to the dark, and I saw, distantly, a beckoning blue glow.

I followed it into the dark. As I ran, my fear began to subside and a strange peace settled over me. I knew this place. I knew what to do.

I rounded a corner and found the source of the glow: a spill of bright blue suul on the floor. There were shards of broken jars all around it, and more jars, unbroken, in coves built into the walls.

Such a waste of good souls.

A voice reverberated in the dark.

No. In my *head.*

Bentham's voice.

He got greedy. Tried to take them all. But even in his resurrected state he could only handle one at a time—and even then, he could not tell one from another.

"What do I do?" I asked him. "Which one do I use?"

THE DESOLATIONS OF DEVIL'S ACRE

Not here. In the incubation room . . . gather as many as you can carry and take them to the spirit pool . . .

There was a trail of blue suul droplets leading out of the room and down the corridor. I started to follow them, then froze.

A voice was shouting my name.

"Jacob? Are you here?!"

It was Emma. A new wave of terror crashed over me.

"JACOB!"

Another voice—Bronwyn's. They'd found the ladder, the open door in the ceiling. I cursed myself for not shutting the painting behind me. For not *locking* it behind me.

"Jacob!"

That was Hugh. *Goddamn it.* My stomach knotted in anger. They were putting themselves in danger for no reason. I thought about answering, screaming at them to go back, to run while they could. But I knew they would only follow my voice and come faster.

"Jacob, come back!"

I couldn't stop now. I had to do this. This was the only way I could protect Noor, and if she was to have any hope of draining Caul's light, she would need all the help she could get. Even if it meant turning myself into a hollowgast, possibly forever.

I raced ahead, following the trail of luminous droplets past room after room stacked with jars. Enough souls for Caul to create an army to dominate the world, given enough time.

The trail led to a room filled with jars and dozens of deflated whitish sacs, each the size and shape of a sleeping bag.

The incubation room.

They were egg sacs, empty now, the birthplace of Caul's new hollows.

On the floor by the wall of jars was a bag woven from straw, left there as if for me to use.

"These jars?" I shouted into the air.

Yes, Bentham's voice came back.

I started grabbing jars from their coves in the wall and stuffing them into the bag. They were heavy, sloshing with liquid souls. I could hear the jars whispering to me as I dropped them into the bag.

I'd nearly filled it when my friends arrived. Bronwyn, Hugh, and Emma, lighting the way with her flames.

And Miss Peregrine.

"Jacob, stop," she cried. "Nim told us what you're trying to do—and you mustn't!"

"I have to," I shouted, slinging the bag over my shoulder and backing away. "It's the only way!"

"You'll lose your soul," Emma said. "You'll become some monstrous corruption of yourself!"

I looked at her face in the firelight, her features creased with pain. Miss Peregrine, deathly afraid. Bronwyn and Hugh, begging me. It killed me to see them like this. I knew that if I did this it might make the difference that saved us, but what would I become? Would I ever see them again? I remembered how Horatio described the state of being a hollowgast: agony forever.

Go, Bentham echoed in my brain, *hurry, lad . . .*

My heel knocked against something and I nearly tripped. I looked behind me to see a hollowgast, armless and half-formed, that had failed to emerge from its sac.

My friends were approaching. "Please, Jacob," Hugh was saying. "You don't have to do this."

"We love you," Bronwyn said. "We'll fight Caul together."

Their intentions were clear: They were going to tackle me and drag me out here.

I couldn't let that happen.

I unshouldered the bag, knelt down, and pressed my fingers into the embryonic hollow's still-soft skull.

Rise up.

"What are you doing?" Miss Peregrine cried. "Jacob, *no—*"

Bronwyn sprinted at me. The hollow's jaw sprung wide and its tongues splayed out and caught her.

"Jacob!" she screamed, writhing against them.

"I'm sorry!" I shouted, picking up the bag again. "I love you all. That's why I have to do this."

I turned and ran, leaving them stunned. I hoped they would understand. I hoped one day they would forgive me. I knew it now: I would never see them again. After I helped Noor destroy Caul, I would disappear. Find the farthest, backwater loop I could and exile myself to some forgotten corner of the past. I was about to make myself into something unrecognizable. Something dangerous.

I would not saddle them with a monster.

*　　◆　　*

The trail of droplets led me to the Library's central chamber: a huge cavern shaped like a beehive, wide at the bottom and tapering to a point at the top, several stories up. But the top had caved in, and so had part of the rear wall, the work of monstrous giants that had been born here. Beyond the missing wall was a vacancy of orange air and the sound of an angry, pounding surf. A cliff's edge.

The walls were festooned with glowing jars. Water poured from a tap shaped like a falcon's head into a channel that ran around the edge of the room, then flowed into a wide, shallow pool pulsing dimmer and brighter in a breathlike rhythm. It was all the same way I remembered it, but for one thing: a column of undulating light that rose from the pool and beamed upward through the caved ceiling.

Into the channel, lad. Pour them all in.

I overturned my bag of jars, then emptied them into the channel one after another. The water bubbled and churned violently as it mixed with the suul. As those souls flowed into the stone-rimmed pool, its water steamed with silver-white vapor. And as that vapor joined the column of blue light, the slowly turning column pulsed brighter and turned faster.

I was moving toward the pool now, half-hypnotized by its beauty but filled with dread at what stepping into the water would mean.

The end of me. The birth of something unrecognizable.

And yet I had to. To spare the friends I loved from being hunted the rest of their days, which would be few if Caul lived out the night, I stepped toward the pool. To spare the world another murderous tyrant who believed himself a god, I stepped toward the pool. To save the life of Noor Pradesh, who was even now prepared to die to save all of ours, I moved closer still.

For Noor.

I had to.

I stepped toward the pool.

But the pool was starting to push back. The column of light was turning faster, making a wind of blue-and-silver sparks that blew back my hair, and faster still, whistling and howling and growing so strong I had to set my shoulders against it.

On a lower plane of mind I felt the hollowgast in the incubation room being overpowered. I had to let it go.

The light and the wind were strengthening in tandem. And in the periphery of my vision I could see something lowering through the hole in the roof, blocking out the disc of smoky orange sky above.

Then a voice rang down from the open roof: "Trespasser! Thief! Get out of my library!"

The wind roared in tandem with the voice, knocking me onto my hands and knees.

Hurry, lad! Bentham's voice, in my head again. *He's found us out!*

Every instinct was screaming at me to turn and run, to let the wind blow me back through the door, but I forced myself onward, dragging myself across the floor by my hands as Caul descended from above. He was enormous now; it was a tight squeeze through the hole in the broken roof. His tail of racing wind came first, tapering down to end—or rather begin—in the blue beam at the center of the spirit pool. No; it had always been here, had been here since I entered, but only now that he was lowering down from the outer world was it racing and roaring. The spirit pool was his source, the spring that fed him, and he was tied to it umbilically by this cable of wind.

A deafening crack from above. Boulders came crashing down as more of the roof gave way. Caul's arms and fingers spidered down the walls.

I reached the edge of the pool and began to drag myself over the lip. I heard Bronwyn's voice from across the room, shouting my name. I couldn't stop to answer, or to think about what I was doing. I couldn't afford to entertain even a moment of doubt.

The suul flowed all around me in veins of bright pulsing blue. I cupped my hands, let the liquid flow into them, brought them to my lips. And I drank.

No feeling came over me. No transformation. Nothing at all.

Caul was fully in the room now, his giant body filling the top half of the cavern. Bronwyn was coming, too, walking backward against the gale with the others gathered in her arms, shielded from the wind by her great frame.

I plunged my hands into pool and drank again.

Caul roared. If he'd meant to form words—*Alma, what a delightful surprise!* would've been his style—they were indecipherable. I craned my neck to see him raise his hands and spread his awful fingers. And then one of them, thick as a python, slithered around my waist. I was ripped into the air and flung away.

The world swam and tumbled and spun. I slammed into the rough floor and slid all the way to the corner. Things went black for a breath.

I shouldn't have survived it. I was sure my bones were shattered. But after a moment I was able to pick up my head again. And there were my friends in Caul's grip, wrapped in the tendrils of his long fingers, suspended high in the air. Emma, Bronwyn, Hugh, and Miss Peregrine—

An intense cold seized me. A terrible weight pressed on my lungs, and my vision swam and started to go black again. I leaned forward to vomit.

When I was done, I raised my head and saw Caul leaning down to grin at me. He held my friends in one giant hand. They were going limp, their lives draining slowly away. His other hand was empty, and closed, and coming at me fast.

He backhanded me out of the room. I flew through the doorway, skidded down the connecting tunnel and back into the incubation chamber.

For a moment I lay stunned. When I raised my head again, there was someone else in the room with me, and a strange pale light.

It was a girl. She was navigating by a stream of scintillating light that she'd blown out through her lips.

Noor.

Get up, I told myself, willed myself, and somehow my body, which should have been shattered, complied. I felt no pain. Only cold, and a heavy weight pressing on my lungs, and a lurching in my stomach. My legs took the weight and I rose. I rose—and kept rising. I thought for a baffling moment that I was floating like Olive, disconnected from the ground, and then I glanced down at my legs and they seemed wrong, too long, someone else's . . .

Noor was staring at me, recoiling as her head tilted to take in my height. I tried to speak her name, but the word came out as a cry, a high keening wail.

And then I understood what I had become.

I felt no urge to kill her. No primal lizard-brain had overtaken my thoughts. In my head, at least, I was still myself.

I knelt down, my head touching the ground. An invitation.

She must have known on some level that it was me, because

she let the wind push her in my direction, then climbed onto my back.

And then I opened my mouth, whipped out a long tongue, and secured it around her waist.

❖   ❖   ❖

I ran into the chamber with Noor on my back, and when Caul saw us together he reared up in horror like an elephant who'd seen a mouse. He made the wind blow stronger, which slowed me a little, but I could feel new strength rippling through my limbs and my core. I bent my head, tightened my grip on Noor's waist, and plowed ahead.

I tried to shout to Noor, to tell her what Bentham had told me, but I couldn't form human sounds, and the words came out as a screech.

But then Bentham's voice echoed through the chamber, his real voice, not just in my head, but in the room—

"Drain his light! Drain it to the lees!"

I'd nearly reached the spirit pool when Caul brought his hand down again. I was knocked into the air, but before I could hit the ground and crush Noor under my weight, I shot out my other two tongues and whipped them around Caul's arm. We swung upward through the air toward him, and I clung to his giant forearm.

Noor took a swipe at him. A stripe of blue light vanished from Caul's torso. He bellowed in anger and tried to fling us away. My tongues were like elastic, and we snapped right back. Noor clawed at him again, tearing more of his light away and stuffing it into her mouth.

He dropped my friends to free up his other hand.

"You cannot kill a god!" he bellowed. "You are nothing, your prophecy means nothing!"

Yet he was wincing and howling at every swipe of Noor's hands like he was being burned. And as she stuffed his light into her mouth, he began to both dim and shrink.

Caul raised the arm we were clinging to and swung his other hand, big as a dinner table, toward us. He was giant and lumbering and slow, and before he could smash us to jelly, I let go. We dropped fifty flailing feet to the spirit pool. I unlashed Noor from my waist to break our fall with my tongues and she rolled safely into the water.

Here in the pool was the source of Caul's light, and Noor started vacuuming it into her mouth in great wide swaths. If Caul had had feet, he would have stomped her, but he had only his arms and his hands, and they were growing smaller by the second as Noor consumed his life-force. He was half the size he'd been when he first descended, though no less terrifying. He swung down both of his still-giant hands. With one he scooped up Noor. With the other he smacked me, hard, and I went flying, landing in a heap at the edge of the pool.

I heard her scream. I tried to intervene, but I could only raise my head. I saw Caul bringing her toward his mouth. Even as he drained her life, she was carving the light from his hand and from the column of blue around her.

"Give me back my sooouul!" he screamed, dangling Noor above his open mouth like a treat.

She had gone limp in his hand. I struggled up but couldn't summon the strength of my tongues.

Caul was about to drop her down his throat when Miss Peregrine dove at Caul in bird form, slicing him across the cheek with her talons. He turned away to scream at her.

"You're next, little sis—"

A thick cloud of bees flew into his mouth and down his throat. And Noor, who was not unconscious, who had been faking, reached out her hand and stole the light from Caul's eyes.

Choking and blinded, he dropped her. She was much higher now, nearly to the broken roof, and a fall into this shallow water would probably have killed her. I raced toward the spot, flinging out my tongues to make a flying catch in the air, and we crashed down into the water together.

Caul thrashed, still trying to kill Noor by slapping blindly at the pool, and she wasted no time clawing away more and greater helpings of his light. And after a few more swaths and a few more swallows, he had shrunk down to the size of a mere sideshow giant. He couldn't see, his throat was clogged with bees, his light was nearly gone; now it was inside Noor, shining so brightly from every pore that it was nearly impossible to look at her.

His wind had slowed to a breeze. With nothing left to support him, Caul's torso came to rest on the stone rim of the pool, and his long arms flopped across the floor, twitching like downed power lines.

My friends surrounded the pool. Noor approached Caul, ready to deal a deathblow. He tried to speak, to beg for mercy, but his throat was clogged, and the only sound he could make was a buzzing gurgle.

There was but one speck of blue light left in the center of his forehead.

Noor stumbled. I shot out a tongue to support her.

"Can't . . . hold it in . . ." She sucked in a pained breath.

She'd been weakened by Caul, and now she was so full of his light she was near to bursting. God only knew what it was doing to her.

"Just one more bite!" Bronwyn cried.

I helped her cross the pool to Caul. We'd nearly reached him when Noor put a hand on my tongue and pushed it off. "I've got to do this myself."

I let her go. She took a wobbling step on her own, then another, until she stood before Caul.

With great effort he raised his head, as if to meet his death with some shred of dignity.

With one finger Noor scooped the light from his forehead.

"Go to hell," she said, and then popped it into her cheek and swallowed.

Caul began to turn brittle, his skin to flake away. Holes opened in his chest, and Hugh's bees flew out in a puff of ash.

In a croaking voice, he uttered his last words. "If I must . . . I'm taking you with me."

He stretched out his arm toward Miss Peregrine. And with a single flap of her wings, she blew him to dust.

Caul was gone.

It seemed the cavern we were standing in would be soon, too. The ground was trembling beneath us, and more stones from the damaged ceiling were beginning to loosen and tumble down. One fell into the pool not far away, sending a wave of icy water over us.

Noor staggered into me, close to passing out. Bronwyn and I supported her arms and dragged her out of the spirit pool, and then Emma and Hugh ran with us toward the giant opening in the wall that led outside. Still in bird form, Miss Peregrine led the way.

We were running toward a cliff's edge. We had no choice; the Library was collapsing behind us. There was nothing beyond the precipice but a steep drop to wave-tossed rocks and a black sea. Miss Peregrine flew out over the emptiness, scanning for some other escape from Abaton.

Over the deafening sound of the Library's collapse, Noor was shouting, "Let me go! Get back!" Before I realized what was happening, she'd jerked out of our grasp and was running toward the edge of the cliff.

"NOOR!" the others screamed, but she'd stopped and fallen to her knees. With a great heave, she began to vomit a jet of silver-flaked blue into the void, so bright it knocked us back a few steps, so bright the others could only watch through split fingers.

It went on and on, racking Noor's body until I feared she would burst apart. When it was finally over, she rocked back onto her heels,

< THE DESOLATIONS OF DEVIL'S ACRE >

spent, the last gleams of Caul's soul dissipating in the wind and the black ocean current.

And then she slumped to the ground.

We ran to her. I slid my arms under her, scooped her up. Her eyes were glassy but open, and she looked at me. I tried to speak but could not. I was still a hollowgast.

She said to me, "You're glowing. It's inside you."

"My God," Emma said, near tears. "Oh, Jacob, what have you done?"

"He's saved us," Noor said weakly.

"*You* have," Hugh insisted.

"Put me down," Noor said, and carefully, I did. She turned to face me, wobbling on unsteady legs. "Open your mouth."

I hinged open my mouth as wide as I could, careful to keep my tongues back.

She reached her hand inside, past my rows of razor teeth, up to the elbow. When she pulled it out again, I felt the cold that had inhabited me ebb away. In her hand was a ball of glowing blue light. She put it into her mouth, closed her eyes, then turned and spat it over the cliff with the rest.

And then Miss Peregrine screamed as the cliff gave way beneath us.

< 479 >

CHAPTER TWENTY-FOUR

*F*or a long time there was only darkness, and the sound of distant thunder, and the hazy sensation of falling. That and the dark were all there was, for a long time, until another sound joined the thunder. Wind. Then rain, too. There was wind, and thunder, and rain, and falling.

And then, one sensation at a time, I came into being.

My eyes blinked open. Blurred shapes resolved into focus. Rough green fabric. A row of storm-blown plants tick-tocking from the rafters. A wall of insect screens shuddered and flapped.

I know this porch. I know this green floor.

How long had I been here? How many days? Time was playing tricks again.

"Jacob?"

I twisted where I lay and sat up, surprised that I could. My brain seemed to slosh from one side of my skull to the other, and the room swayed.

"Jacob!" Noor staggered into my field of view, then dropped down next to me, grasping for my arm.

I couldn't yet form words. Wet black hair framed her face like a cowl. Her eyes were wide and searching, her lips parted slightly as if to speak, though she didn't, her face raked with shallow cuts. I had a sudden, wild urge to kiss her.

She said: "It's you!"

And I said: "It's *you*."

This time, words came out. English words.

Noor said, "No—I mean, God, it's you! And you're . . . *you!*" She was touching me all over, patting my chest, my face, as if to make certain I was real. "I was praying that would work, taking your light, and wouldn't hurt you—and—wait, you're not hurt, are you?"

A crack of thunder startled us both. And then I looked down at myself. My legs were a normal size again, though my pants were shredded. I moved my tongue inside my mouth. Just one.

I was *me.*

I threw my arms around her, laughing, half crazed with relief. "We're alive! We're okay!"

She hugged me hard, and then I kissed her, and for a long sweet moment there was nothing else in the world but the two of us, and her lips against mine, and her face in my hands. But as we drew apart, questions flooded in.

She looked outside, where a storm was blowing, and said, "Did we dream it all?"

"We couldn't have," I said. "Because, look—"

The wight Noor had killed was gone. There was a wide, rust-colored stain where his body had been. The porch screen had a giant hole in it, and half the aluminum ribs that anchored it to the house lay broken in the yard.

"The hollowgast did that," I said.

"But what about everything *after* that?"

Something terrible occurred to me. What if the explosion we'd set off from the bunker had knocked us unconscious, and we were only now waking up from it?

What if we'd never left my grandfather's house, and it was all happening again, for the first time? The whole long nightmare cycling. *My God. Such horrors I could hardly name them.*

Then we heard something bang from inside the house and jumped again.

"Jesus," she said, "what if that's—"

"There," I hissed, pointing outside.

Someone was walking at the edge of the woods.

"Weapon!" I whispered. *"Grab something—anything."*

Both of us lurched in different directions, collided, and fell into a pile.

"Jacob! Noor!"

Emma came running out of the house onto the porch.

"Emma?" shouted the young man by the woods, and then he was running toward the porch, too.

"Hugh!" Emma shouted.

And then Bronwyn came through the door with Miss Peregrine, back in human form and wearing an old housecoat that had belonged to my grandmother, and a second later we were all hugging on the floor, delirious with gratitude to see one another again.

"What happened?!" Hugh said. "Did we just kill Caul or not?"

"This happened," Emma said, and she pulled a cracked and soot-blackened stopwatch from her pocket. The Expulsatator. "Millard handed it to me just before we went through the loop door into Abaton. He said the old man had lied about losing it, and got it working again. The second Caul appeared I hit the button, and five minutes later . . ."

V's watch had saved us again. We were alive. And we were in *Florida.*

"So . . . Caul's dead?" Bronwyn said. "We won?"

Miss Peregrine smiled. "Yes. We won." She wrapped us all in her arms, our heads clonking together in her embrace. "Oh, my children, my children, my children. I swear on our ancestors: From this day forward, I am never, *never* letting you out of my sight again."

"But there's something I don't understand," Emma said. "How did Caul follow us to the Library of Souls if he was outside your shield in the Acre?"

"My brother was forever anchored to the Library," said Miss Peregrine. "It seems when Murnau resurrected him, it merely lengthened his leash. A *lot*. Enough for him to go wherever he liked. But part of him was always there, and when Jacob arrived, the rest of him was able to return quickly enough." She turned to me. "That was very rash of you, racing in there like you did."

"Noor was going to face Caul by herself. I had to do something to help her."

"So *you* were going to face Caul by yourself instead?" said Emma.

"I didn't expect him to be waiting for me in there."

Bronwyn shuddered. "It was terrible, seeing you that way."

"I thought it was quite cool, if I'm being honest," said Hugh. "Though I'm glad you're not a hollowgast anymore." He looked at me sideways. "Are you?"

I laughed. "Apparently not."

"It seems Miss Pradesh was able to remove the suul you'd swallowed before it had fully set in," Miss Peregrine said. "Thank goodness for that."

"Thank goodness for *her*," I said. "That was not a future I was excited about."

Emma turned to Noor. "You were ready to sacrifice yourself to save all of us. Thank you."

"I'm sure you would've done the same," Noor said.

"I hope I would've. But I've known these people a whole lifetime longer than you."

Noor's shoulders went up and down. She didn't know what to say.

"Let's get you somewhere we can finally rest," said Miss Peregrine, rising to her feet. "Everyone else will be waiting at Jacob's house. They're more than anxious, I'm sure, for our arrival."

"Goodness, what must they think," said Bronwyn.

"That we're dead," said Hugh.

Miss Peregrine smiled. "Let's disabuse them of that notion, shall we?"

◆　　◆　　◆

We limped out into the rain, carrying each other, miles beyond caring about wet weather or the state of our clothes. Someone had tied a blue tarp over the hole we'd blown in my grandfather's bathroom, and it flapped in the wind. We ducked under a line of police tape and walked down the street knocking on doors until we found a neighbor who was at home. Miss Peregrine memory-wiped him while I found his car keys in a bowl in the hallway, and then we borrowed his car.

I drove us across town, over the bridge to Needle Key, back to my house. Along the way, the storm passed and the weather cleared up. There was a big crowd waiting in my yard. Ninety-five peculiars and ten ymbrynes, and God, were they glad to see us. I hadn't even parked the car and they were already running toward us, shouting, cheering for joy as they recognized us.

Everyone wanted to know what had happened, but the story was too long to tell, and I worried cops would start showing up any minute, and at this point I didn't have the energy to deal with any more trouble, however minor. For now, the peculiars were satisfied to learn that Caul was dead and we were safe. They didn't need to know that I had briefly been a hollowgast, and my friends who'd seen it happen understood without being told that it was best kept between us.

At that point I assumed everyone would immediately head back to the Acre, but instead the ymbrynes gathered everyone in the backyard and made an announcement.

"We have some very happy news to tell you," Miss Peregrine said. "After a great deal of painstaking work and study we have perfected the reset reaction, and anyone who'd like to have their internal clocks reset will be able to do so."

The crowd was stunned. Miss Peregrine was asked to repeat what she'd said. When everyone was sure they'd heard her correctly, whoops of excitement rang out. Hugh picked up Fiona and spun her around. Ulysses Critchley, not known for his exuberance, climbed halfway to the top of one of my parents' palm trees and started singing.

My friends and I rushed to Miss Peregrine.

Millard was breathless. "But how did you manage it?"

"My brother Bentham," said Miss Peregrine in a hushed voice. "Caul being so near the house last night allowed him to get close, too, and he appeared to Perplexus in the washroom and whispered the answer to him. A slightly revised incantation, requiring only ten ymbrynes, not twelve."

"And you're sure it's not some kind of trick?" said Hugh, one arm around Fiona.

"The other ymbrynes tested it just a short time ago—on Miss Babax's old loop, sadly now unneeded. And it *works*."

"And?" Dogface boomed, intruding on our conversation. "How soon can it be done?"

"How does right now suit you?" Miss Peregrine said loudly, and the whole yard exploded into cheers once more. Today, finally, they would be free. The only ones not here to enjoy the victory—or the reset—were the American clan leaders.

Then something alarming occurred to me. Miss Peregrine had turned away to speak with Miss Wren, but when I tapped her shoulder and she saw my agitated expression, she excused herself.

"You're collapsing *this* loop?" I said.

"Perhaps that was presumptuous of me. There aren't many left to spare."

"It's not going to blow up my neighborhood, is it?"

She smiled. "No. It's a nondestructive collapse. But removing this pocket loop will make it a great deal less convenient for you to return here. Perhaps I misjudged your . . . attachment to this place. If you'd rather preserve it, I could discuss alternatives with the other ymbrynes."

I looked around. My old house, my old town. My parents, sitting on the back porch, staring placidly at Lemon Bay as if their lawn weren't crowded with extremely odd strangers. One of the ymbrynes had memory-wiped them again.

"You didn't misjudge," I said. I nodded toward my parents. "I'd like a minute to say goodbye though."

"I can give you five. We're about to begin."

"That should be enough."

Miss Peregrine turned to rejoin Perplexus, and I walked through the grass to the porch. My parents sat a few feet apart on a padded bench. I perched on the porch rail beside them. I wasn't sure how to start.

"I need to tell you guys something."

They wouldn't look at me. I snapped my fingers. No reaction.

It was better this way. I could say what I wanted to say and leave, and they couldn't hurt me any more than they already had.

"I want you guys to know that I'm not angry at you anymore. I was, for a long time, but I'm over it now. You didn't understand what you were getting with me. And how could you? You're not peculiar. Pretty much zero percent of parents get it, from what I've heard. I think you could have tried harder, been more open-minded, but whatever. You didn't sign up for this. At least you didn't tie me down and try to sell me to the circus, like Emma's parents." I sighed. I felt like an idiot, talking to zombies who couldn't hear me.

Out on the lawn, all the peculiars had gathered in a pack near the glinting pocket loop entrance. All the ymbrynes had joined hands in a circle, even Miss Avocet, who had been helped out of her chair and was being supported by Francesca.

I felt a strong pull to join them but turned back to my parents instead. Even if they couldn't hear me, there was more I needed to say.

"I made a decision. I've gone back and forth on this a bunch of times, since Grandpa died and all this peculiar stuff started. I thought maybe I could live with you part-time, and have this life and my other one, too. But it didn't work out. Not for me, and definitely not for you guys. I mean, you're sitting here drooling, and you've been memory-wiped so many times you've probably forgotten your own birthdays. Or mine, anyway. So what I'm trying to say is: I'm going, and I won't be coming back anymore. This isn't my home."

My dad sighed, and I jolted. "That's okay, champ," he said woodenly. "We understand."

I almost fell off the porch rail. "You do?"

He was still staring out at the water. "We're buying a boat. Isn't that right, honey?"

My mother, with absolutely no expression on her face, started to cry.

A clench was tightening in my chest. "Mom. Don't."

She kept on, quietly, eyes fixed on nothing. I slid off the rail, sat beside her, and hugged her.

"My boy," she said quietly. "My little boy." Her arms stayed limp at her sides.

I stayed there hugging my mother for what felt like a long time. My friends kept glancing at me from the edge of the lawn. The ymbrynes were singing an eerie, lilting song, which grew louder with each verse. Eventually my mother stopped crying. She didn't speak again. When I finally let her go, her eyes were closed. She had fallen asleep on my shoulder.

I laid her down on the padded bench, a cushion beneath her head. Then I went to go see my father. At some point he had risen and walked out to the end of the dock, passing the crowd of peculiars without a glance. He lay on his back with his loafers in the water, gazing blankly at the clouds.

My shadow fell across him. "Goodbye, Dad. Thanks for trying, sometimes."

"Goodbye, Dad," he replied, his eyes rolling back in his head.

Was he making fun of me? Or had he thought, for a moment, he was talking to my grandfather?

I turned to leave.

"Good luck, Jake."

I stopped. Turned back. He was looking right at me.

It felt, in that moment, like we were a million miles apart and as close as we'd ever been.

My mouth opened, but my throat had gone dry. I nodded.

"Love you," he said.

"Love you, too."

It was time to go. He watched me walk away. The pocket loop's glimmer had widened and brightened to a hard, shining point like a mirror reflecting the sun, and it was shuddering in the air, unstable.

The ymbrynes sent their wards through in groups of three. I waited at the edge of the lawn with my friends; except for Fiona, none of us needed the reset.

Fiona was the last reset to pass through. My friends went next, and then all the ymbrynes but Miss Peregrine.

She walked over to where I stood. "I could always make another pocket loop for you here one day. If you like."

I looked at her. Smiled gratefully. Then shook my head.

"Thanks. But I don't think so."

She nodded. Then, sensing that I wanted to be the last to leave, she turned and went ahead without me.

I waited a few seconds in the silence. A humid breeze picked up. I felt no urge to stay. No pang of regret. When I reached the loop's mirrored glimmer, I paused to lift my hand in a last wave to my father. In return he lifted his, but his expression was so blank I wondered if it was automatic.

Choking back a swell of emotion, I stepped through the door.

CHAPTER TWENTY-FIVE

*M*iss Avocet died at dawn. She had fought hard for a long time, but she was weak and worn out and could fight no longer. She breathed her last in the arms of her sister ymbrynes, many of whom she had taught as girls, and her beloved Francesca. Her last words were a quote from Emerson: "Nothing is dead: men feign themselves dead, and endure mock funerals and mournful obituaries, and there they stand looking out of the window, sound and well, in some new and strange disguise."

None of us had witnessed an ymbryne funeral before. Three were held that day. There was no digging, no burying, and per explicit instruction, no crying. Miss Avocet, Miss Babax, and V were each wrapped in a thin white shroud. The whole Acre turned out to accompany their bodies in a procession that was more celebration than funeral, with chants and demonstrations of peculiar ability and songs in the old tongue. Some were shocked to learn that V had been an ymbryne, but as shocks went, it was a minor one weighed against those we'd endured the past few days. Our parade ended at a small stone roundhouse that had once been used to germinate barrenwort, an ingredient in a foul alcohol the maggot farmers of Devil's Acre had been infamous for making. That wasn't important—the only requirement for an ymbryne *bælstede* was that the building have doors that latched and a roof with holes in it, and this roof had many.

There were no speeches. When the last ymbryne was laid inside and the door had been sealed, the crowd was ushered so far back from the building I half expected it to explode. Instead, Miss

Peregrine made a loud birdcall and a massive flock of starlings circled down from the sky, then flooded through the holes in the roof. There was a great commotion inside.

"What are they doing?" I whispered to Enoch.

"Picking their bones clean," he replied, his eyes rimmed with tears. "They'll be powdered and made into medicines. Ymbryne bones have many uses and it's a crime to waste them."

It was fitting. An ymbryne's life was one of endless service. Even in death they had a job to do.

The birds began to filter out from the roof. A few ymbrynes and ymbrynes-in-training approached the door and peeked through the keyhole to make sure the bones were clean.

I turned to Noor, leaning against me. Her eyes were closed.

"You all right?" I asked her, as I always did.

She slipped her hand into mine. After a moment her eyes opened. "Just saying goodbye. Hopefully for the last time."

The cloud of starlings rose and disappeared into the yellow sky.

◆   ◆   ◆

There was a great deal still to be done in the Acre—more funerals to hold, much to be cleaned and repaired and discussed—but all that could wait a day, or at least a few hours. We had finally earned a rest. A real one, without the looming threat of annihilation hanging over our heads.

The crowd dispersed. Everyone headed back to their houses and dormitories. There was no rush to the loop exit and the present, as the ymbrynes had once feared there might be following a mass reset. Even without wights and hollows to harass us, or a ticking internal clock to worry about, the dangers of the outside world were more than anyone was ready to face right now.

My friends and I walked back toward Ditch House, heavy in heart but happy, too, enjoying one another's company. We had won.

After more than a century of struggle, Caul and his evil cohort had finally been vanquished. The threat peculiardom faced now was broader, duller, and much older: normalkind.

It was a threat our society had been designed from the start to guard against. Normals were the reason ymbrynes began making loops, millennia ago. Normals were the reason we hid our true natures, and why there were ymbryne code laws against the flagrant display of peculiar abilities in the outside world. The ymbrynes had long feared our being exposed and had worked diligently to prevent it. But now that it had happened, they were sanguine. Millard had overheard them discussing it in my parents' backyard: that with enough time and effort, perceptions of us could be changed. Not with memory-wipes—we would've had to wipe half the globe—but through a long and steady campaign of good works, we might one day engender some goodwill toward us in return.

That day would not be coming anytime soon. Until it did, we would need loops. There was some strange comfort in that, like we were returning to an older way of life, one whose limitations and dangers were at least well understood.

The world had never been an easy place for peculiars; that wasn't about to change. But it was enough. Even Devil's Acre was enough. I had my friends. I was falling in love. I could be happy here, working together to rebuild our society, making it into something that could never again be splintered. Something unbreakable.

In the end, our real home had always been one another. And a real home was all I'd ever wanted.

◆　　◆　　◆

My friends and I had only just gotten back to Ditch House and were tilting fast toward our beds when Miss Peregrine returned and called us into the kitchen. "Don't kick your shoes off just yet," she said. "I've got something to share with you. But not here."

She wouldn't tell us a thing until she had dragged us all the way across the Acre to Bentham's house, then upstairs to the lower Panloopticon hallway, still heavily damaged. "As you all know," she said, walking backward past boarded-up loop doors as she spoke, "the loss of Miss Avocet has created a vacancy which must be filled as soon as possible. She was a giantess—a lion. None of us alone could fill her shoes. That is why Miss Cuckoo and I will be sharing the role of Head Ymbryne together."

"What!" exclaimed Millard. "It's never been done."

"It's a complex new world," said Miss Peregrine, "and there are more young ymbrynes to teach than ever."

"Then you'll both run the Ymbryne Academy, too?" asked Emma.

"That's right," Miss Peregrine said.

"But will you still be our headmistress?" Claire asked, her little hands at her cheeks.

"Of course, dear! I'll be a bit busier than before, but you'll always be my wards."

Claire practically melted with relief.

"Does that mean you'll live with the ymbrynes-in-training somewhere else?" asked Olive. "*Please* don't leave, miss."

"No, no—they'll live with us, and we'll all be together. Oh, you children have the wrong idea completely."

"But we won't all live at Ditch House, will we?" Horace said in mild horror. "I mean, it's wonderful, but—"

"A bit cramped and dingy?" said Miss Peregrine, laughing. "No, we'll need some space to spread our wings. And I'm sure you'd all like to have bedrooms of your own again, wouldn't you?"

"Yes! Oh, a million times, yes," cried Horace, cutting his eyes at Enoch. "There are people no one should be forced to share a room with."

"What have you found for us?" asked Olive, peeking past Miss Peregrine for clues. "Another loop?"

< RANSOM RIGGS >

"I hope not somewhere *tropical*," Enoch grumbled. "That weather does not agree with me."

A lot of us were in foul moods. After so much upheaval, Miss Peregrine's wards had grown wary of change, and this was shaping up to be a big one.

Miss Peregrine wasn't letting their grumbles get to her. "I think the weather will suit you just fine, Enoch. Right this way."

We came to a section of hallway with newly built doors. There were ten altogether, and Miss Peregrine stopped at the last one. There was no plaque on it, no marking.

"Where does it go?" I asked her.

"If I told you, it wouldn't be a surprise."

Smiling, she pushed open the door. Beyond the usual bed, nightstand, wardrobe, and missing fourth wall, there was a leafy, summery forest. It could've been almost any place, almost any year. We walked through the room and into dappled sunlight. A pleasant breeze was blowing, and it rustled the branches around us in a calming *shh-shhhh*.

Miss Peregrine walked ahead of us. "There's a path just up here, though I haven't marked the way yet. I've had to make a few adjustments, you see . . ."

We followed her through the trees. My friends were looking around with eyes like plates, trading whispers in a state of nervous excitement. I felt it, too, though I wasn't sure why.

"Perplexus has been hard at work on a secret project," Miss Peregrine said, "one I didn't want to tell you about until he'd cracked it. For a few years now, we've been saving tiny, essential bits of loops, like a seed bank or a DNA archive, in the hopes that one day they might be used to regrow certain—"

"Miss?" interrupted Claire, her voice high and tremulous. "Why does this forest look so . . . familiar?"

Miss Peregrine held out her arm. "Go and see for yourself. The path's just through those trees."

< 500 >

Claire broke into a run, passed through a screen of leaves, and a moment later we heard a scream.

We all raced after her. I broke through the green and onto a familiar dirt path. Claire was in the middle of it, jumping up and down and squealing. Tingles shot down my spine.

Emma stopped dead beside me and gasped.

"It's Cairnholm!" Olive cried. "We're on Cairnholm!!"

This was the path that led from the old bog up to the house. *Miss Peregrine's house.* The tingles began to spread through my whole body.

"As I was saying, I made a few alterations," Miss Peregrine said, grinning from ear to ear. "The entrance doesn't go through the cairn any longer . . . far too mucky out there . . ."

But we'd all started running up the path, and her voice quickly trailed off behind us.

I was pulling Noor by the hand. "What's everyone freaking out about?" she said.

"We're back on the island!" I shouted.

It was still here—or rather, here *again.* The woods, the path. But what about . . .

Then, around a bend in the path, at the top of a gentle slope, there it was. Miss Peregrine's house. *Our* house. And it was glorious: not a stone out of place, not a window broken. Fresh paint, flower beds a riot of color, sun glinting off the roof. I stopped at the edge of the yard to admire it while our friends ran through the grass, shouting with glee and disbelief.

"It's even more beautiful than I imagined," Noor said, catching her breath.

I could only nod. A lump had formed in my throat.

"Our house, our lovely old house!" Horace was shouting. "It's perfect!"

Fiona and Hugh were dancing in the rose garden. Bronwyn was overcome and stood bawling by the old well, tears wetting her cheeks while Emma and Millard hugged her.

Miss Peregrine jogged up alongside Noor and me. "September 2, 1940. Another adjustment: I managed to wind the clock back just a bit, and now you've a whole new day to learn—one with no cursed bombs falling!"

She went to comfort Bronwyn, then gathered us all in the garden path. Nine other ymbrynes had also gotten their loops restored, she told us, and now all the peculiars marooned in Devil's Acre would be able to go home again, if they chose. "And of course, no one's stuck in their loops the way they used to be. The Panloopticon's just back through the woods, and from there you can go—"

"Anywhere, almost," Millard said.

"I don't want to go anywhere ever again," Claire declared. "From this day forward I'm never stepping foot off this island."

Miss Peregrine stroked her blond ringlets and smiled. "That's entirely up to you."

Claire let out a hitching sob and latched on to Miss Peregrine's leg, and Miss Peregrine limped along with Claire attached to her like a koala.

"That's all right, love, have a cry."

Cairnholm was no longer a golden prison. It wasn't a life sentence of postcard-perfect days you could never escape. We could leave anytime we liked. Or not at all.

We circled the house. The air smelled like ocean breeze and flowers. The sun shone off the windows. It looked absolutely new, but otherwise most things about it were just as I remembered them, down to the arrangement of the wicker chairs in the back garden. One thing had changed, though: Our famous topiary sculpture was no longer a replica of Michelangelo's Adam pointing to the sky, but a leafy memorial statue in the likeness of Miss Avocet, spreading her arms in welcome.

With Claire still clinging to her leg, Miss Peregrine climbed the steps to the front door, then turned to look at us. Tears glistened in her eyes. "I'm so very, *very* . . ." She sniffled, looked away, then drew a deep breath. "I'm so very proud to call you my children. It's been the honor of my life to care for you, and to have been cared for by you. You've made me a very happy ymbryne."

"Oh, miss, we love you so much!" Olive burst out, and having unstrapped her shoes she flung herself up the stairs and around Miss Peregrine's other leg.

The rest of us quickly followed, and one by one she gathered us into her open arms. "Welcome home," she said. "Welcome home, all of you."

We stood like that, all in a knot, some of us crying and some of us laughing, until Miss Peregrine finally extracted herself and clapped her hands for quiet. "Now, then! Supper's on the table. Everyone at your usual places, please. Horace, set a new one for Miss Pradesh."

Then she turned and opened the door, and the smell of something delicious wafted out, and together we went inside.

ABOUT THE PHOTOGRAPHY

The images that appear in this book are authentic, vintage found photographs, and with the exception of a handful that have undergone a bit of digital processing, they are unaltered. They were painstakingly collected over the course of several years: discovered at flea markets, vintage paper shows, and in the archives of photo collectors more accomplished than I, who were kind enough to part with some of their most peculiar treasures to help create this book.

The following photos were graciously lent for use by their owners:

PAGE	TITLE	FROM THE COLLECTION OF
68	Girl in front of pictures	Jack Mord / The Thanatos Archive
81	Bentham and pets	Jack Mord / The Thanatos Archive
294	Bear	John Van Noate
453	Banjo-playing boy	Jack Mord / The Thanatos Archive